HEART OF THE WORLDS
BOOK 3

FAERIES DON'T HIDE

TF BURKE

Sylvan Sword Press

SYLVAN SWORD PRESS

MILTON, PA

To sign up for TF Burke's Wyrd & the Wisp newsletter, visit https://BookHip.com/PMWQAPV

Or visit her website at https://tfburkeauthor.com/

To my sister, Rachel Cawley, for being a light in the darkness and an ear in the chaos.

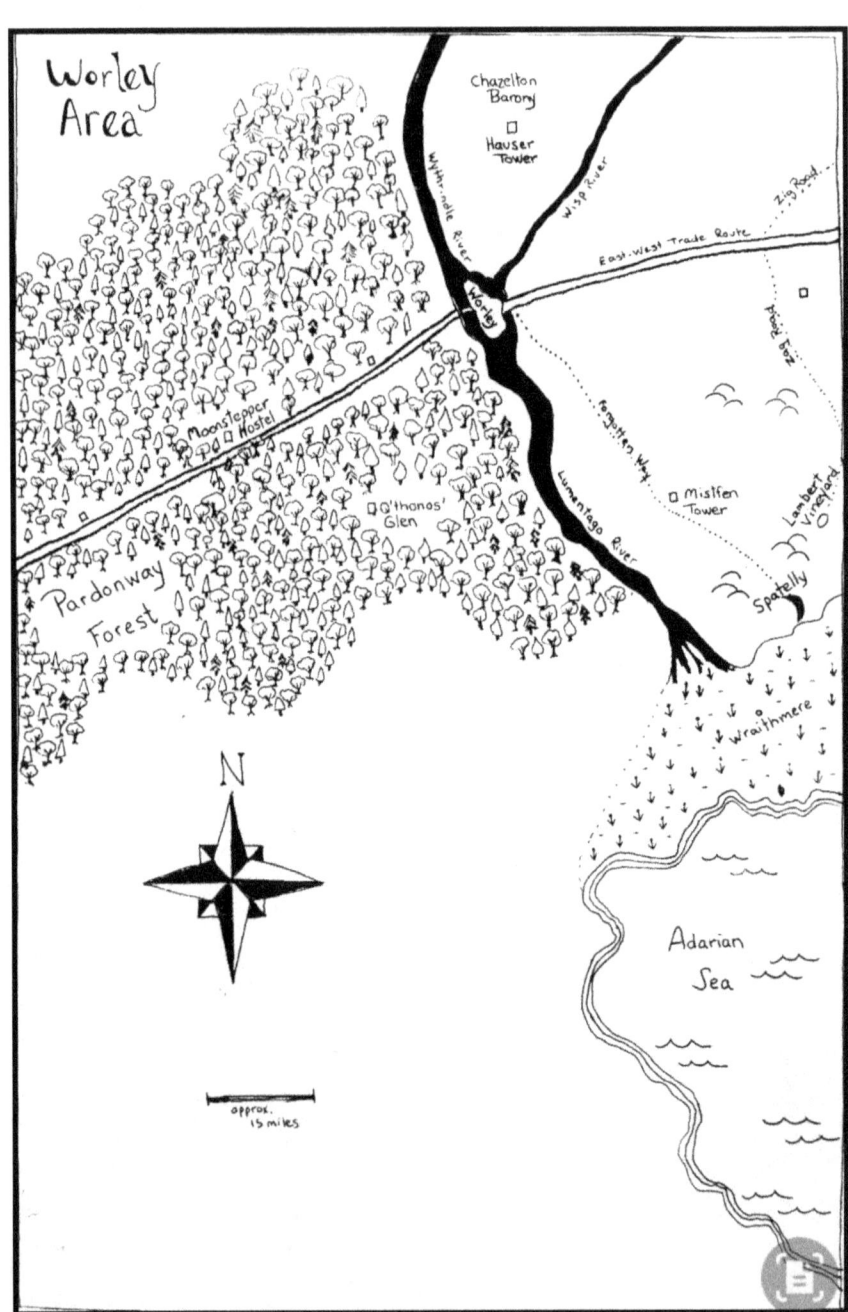

Worley
Area

Chazelton
Barony

☐ Hauser
Tower

Wisp River

Wythinville River

Zig Road

East-West Trade Route

Hood Road

☐

Worley

Moonstepper
Hostel ☐

Forgotten Way

Lumentago River

Pardonway
Forest

Q'thanos'
Glen

Mistfen
Tower ☐

Lambert
Vineyard ☐

Spatelly

Wraithmere

N

Adarian
Sea

approx.
15 miles

CONTENTS

Chapter One

The Broken Door

I stood for the longest time looking out my front door wondering how long, if I left, until I walked through the next one. —
Ferris Runoldi of Bellatine

How could a castle float atop a poofy cloud over tree-topped mountains? But then again, how could she, Aunia, be floating beside such an enormous construction while two constellations of stars wheeled around her? The Harp. The Hammer. She turned away to look through her periphery as Mathias had instructed. It was the only way to see the Dama star. It hovered close to the Harp constellation... a hair's breadth from entering. It meant the time of the choice was coming. It meant a world would die.

A pop jarred Aunia awake. She sprang up in bed, blinking back tears.

The augury... She'd been dreaming of the augury... Something both her father and Mathias had chased with ideas on how to fix it. She wanted to fix it too, but there were more pressing things. Like finding her missing father. Like being brought to the cloud castle. They were heading there next, whether they wanted it or not.

Her attention darted to her brutalized door, which separated her small bedroom from the common area in their suite at the Green Harpy. The door sagged crookedly in its frame, hinges twisted and useless. Well, one still clung half-heartedly to the splintered door frame. Mute affirmation of last night's violence.

Light wood smoke floated in the air. Fallo, the commander whom she hated, or Jovaryn, a wererat who she didn't really know, must be up. Or never went to sleep. The air temperature was mild for a late spring morning. Starting a fire in the communal gray-stone hearth wasn't necessary.

A light snore drew Aunia's attention to Mathias. He slept on the floor beside her bed. Mathias. Her heart and possibly her bane. Dark wavy hair, a sturdy jaw, tanned olive-tinged skin, and a medium muscular frame. Handsome. With a spring green aura that matched his flashing eyes. Those eyes were closed right now. It had taken him a long time to fall asleep; him holding her hand in the early morning while they both stared at the guttering candle perched atop a dresser. He had shoved his saddlebag under its broken leg to keep the light from toppling over. A broken leg carved to look like a harpy's limb. That candle was out now. It had melted to a stub with ridges of hardened wax puddled over the glass holder.

She had poured her worry and her sorrow into that flickering flame. Wanted to burn the worst of her emotions away so sleep could carry her off. Worry for her father. Anxiety over being arrested. Those feelings rose again, sloshing against her ribs.

Aunia escaped the blankets and set her feet onto the ash-dusty carpet with a shudder. Mathias had cleaned up much of the ash pile before they had retired, she in the bed and he on the floor.

If only there were a way to clean up the image of Mygul, her wayward magical globefire, melting her father's doppelgänger. The Boggleman, her nemesis... actually, the enemy of all ... took delight making her believe she had killed her father. But her dad had been very alive when they chased the Boggleman into his own domain. She had meant to rescue her dad. Bring him back to the mortal world. Only in the middle of battle, he'd disappeared.

She padded to the window, shoved aside the carved wainscot chair—the one the Boggleman had lounged in as he awaited her to enter her room the night previous—and yanked back the heavy red curtain. He was alive. And she needed to figure out where he was. But to do that, she needed to calm the storm whistling through her body. Do it before Mygul showed up, and destroyed everything that wasn't broken yet. Maybe even people.

Could Mathias help her? She turned toward his sleeping form. Without hesitation, he had joined her when she confronted the Boggleman. He had tried to free her dad while she attempted to destroy the Boggleman's faery-eating cloak. She did by severing its manifest spell. But she almost failed. Mathias. When he saw her in danger, he had manifested an entire army of himself.

Aunia squeezed her eyes shut. Those fake versions. Each time a Mockmen troll hacked into one ... The blood, the pain shining through spring-green eyes... She pressed her knuckles against her mouth against a new push of tears.

The real Mathias was here. Had escaped with her after the Boggleman had been defeated. But not her father. The figures captured in the Boggleman's Chand ice columns were also free. Edvaras and Naoma skipped away... teleported to somewhere else. But Olivia lay dead. The only other one to escape had been a captive wererat. Jovaryn. He had fought alongside Mathias, with her dad. He was one of the good wererats. Not all of them were good. Mathias was quick to tell her that.

Aunia dropped to her knees in front of the window. She ached to run outside and feel the grass under her feet. The wind against her skin. Nature brought comfort when everything else failed, but she wasn't allowed to leave the suite. None of them were. They had been put under arrest by the Hauser Tower flyers because Mathias and his unit had abandoned their post.

Stupid. People were not meant to be caged in towers or other buildings. But here she was, caged in a tiny room.

She gazed out into the azure morning sky... and stiffened. Men in bearskin cloaks, dozens, gathered yards away at the Green Harpy's gate. Several shook the iron bars. Their aura glows bled with angry crimson and smoky browns. Stars! Da Vennen soldiers.

The floorboards behind her creaked, and Aunia twisted around.

"The Hauser commander won't let them in." Mathias stood behind her, body tense.

Aunia tapped a forefinger on the glass. "They don't mean to stay put."

"Wants and actions aren't the same. And storming the gate—"

"You're not seeing their glows." Aunia scrambled to her feet.

He gripped her shoulders. "Storming an inn inside Lord Lyle's home city would destroy all the goodwill they gained from capturing that band of rovers."

"Capture?" Aunia's voice squeaked. She had heard of the caravan's fate when they had crossed into Worley. Knew the prejudice that many Tamorians held. "Like we're captured?"

"We can't save them. We're in too much trouble. We must—"

"Hide?"

"Bide our time." Mathias pressed his hand against the windowpane. "And as for the Da Vennen... If need be, our pegasi will sleep them before they arrive at the inn's front doors."

Aunia chewed on her lip. Casting a sleep spell on the Da Vennen would get Mathias and the others in more trouble, but what choice would they have?

A knock on the door in the other room sent Aunia scuttling to the foot of her bed. "When will we be forced to leave?"

Mathias shrugged. "The soonest after Revellie is better, I imagine."

Aunia scooped up her poppet. It was the doll her dad and her foster mom, Nehla, had made for her when she was six years old. She was supposed to carry it with her whenever she left the village. "And where will they take us? I need... I need to find out what happened to my dad."

"We might have to wait until—"

"We can't stay. Zevara's geis—"

"I think she meant that we have to stay together."

"No." Aunia rubbed at the poppet's bone eyes. "My dad would kill nothing. Even when it would keep someone else from dying."

"Aunia."

"Listen. Zevara said he had visited her court. I think that was his geis. Not to kill. But he did. I think he got pulled back into the faery world."

A shadow crossed over Mathias' jaw. He had to remember her father had saved him by killing a mockman troll. But her dad also had let Nehla, die.

Mathias' green glow tightened around his body. "You think he's in Pavari?"

Aunia shrugged. "I don't know. But we need to find out. Tatia has—"

The broken door groaned like an old bull struggling to rise from muddy ground, with popping joints and slipping hooves. Aunia jumped.

"Best to keep all that quiet." Jovaryn stuck his sandy-brown-haired head through the door frame, wrestled the door completely off its hinges and leaned it against the wall. He lifted on tiptoes, gasped and sprinted for the window. "That's not good."

"The Da Vennen?" Mathias said. "Yes, we're aware."

"That many?" Jovaryn said. "Bibb will make an appearance soon."

"You've heard something?" Mathias asked.

Jovaryn tapped at the center of his collarbone with a staccato beat. "Least it's not the Elderghast."

Mathias snapped, "For Yasendra's sake, don't call worse on us."

Jovaryn winced, and his pale skin turned paler. "Just letting you know that breakfast came. And well, Frehn and your tower commander should know about these Da Vennen."

The Da Vennen had attacked when she, Mathias, and Keston had been in Dalin. One had tried to impale Keston. Had almost succeeded. But then Mygul, her globefire, shot out. Stopped the man but... Aunia swallowed hard. "Do you know what they'll do?"

Jovaryn turned to face her. "The flyers?"

"The Da Vennen." Aunia stood from her bed. "Why are they here? Why are they chasing us?"

"Your magic. They're not going to stop, I can tell you that," Jovaryn said.

In the next room, Fallo's voice raised... something about wine.

A youthful voice said, "But they do use magic."

"Da Vennen didn't before Bibb," Jovaryn said. "That one won't stop gathering faebloods and magic-users until there's no more."

"Destroy?" Mathias' face drained of color. "How do you know that?"

Jovaryn moved to the dresser, frowned at the saddlebag stuffed under a broken leg. "I know because I escaped them nearly a year ago. Before then, I'd learned much of what was being planned."

Mathias crossed his arms. "And you said nothing before?"

"When would I have said?" Jovaryn tapped his collarbone again. "I escaped many times, but that witch compass keeps finding me."

Aunia hadn't seen Arch Vicar Bibb's witch compass but Mathias had described it to her. A palm-sized circular device with a moving arrow on its face and tiny red crystals lining its outer rim. Bibb had pulled it out in

Dalin and it had pointed directly at her. Because of that, he had ordered a horde of Da Vennen to attack her and Keston.

"You know what Bibb is planning?" Mathias asked. But it didn't sound like a question.

"He's training an army," Jovaryn said. "Wererat troops. Faebloods. He finds them and has them bitten."

Mathias dropped his arms to his sides. "He what?"

"He offers a home to the newly bitten. A place safe from persecution. Being a faeblood and a wererat? Generally, your life is forfeit."

The room tilted and Aunia swayed. "He wants to change me into a wererat?"

"He won't." Mathias stepped between her and Jovaryn. "And if he really has an army, we have exactly what we need to take him down."

"How?" Jovaryn asked. "You're under arrest because you left your tower."

"It's because—"

"I know. You sought wererats."

"Why we left is more complicated than that," Mathias protested. "They set Britchway ablaze. They bit a flyer. If Nyrissa learns why—"

"How do you know that your Dar-Elect hasn't already been told? Repeatedly?" Jovaryn asked.

"Repeatedly? By whom?" Mathias demanded.

"Does it matter? If something isn't believed, what can be done?" Jovaryn said.

Mathias raised a fist and Jovaryn scuttled back.

The wererat ran into the corner of the dresser, and almost in slow-motion the dresser toppled.

Mathias leaped forward, caught the furniture piece, and guided it to the floor. With a curse, he shook his fingers and pulled his thumb to his lips. Then, he straightened. "Where's my saddlebag? What did you do with it?"

Jovaryn blinked. "I did nothing."

"I don't see it." Aunia tightened her grip on her poppet. That saddle-bag had been one of the items manifested... created in the faery world... and then locked into permanent existence with a spell.

She and Mathias traded looks. She considered asking him what locking memory he used... and then, a boom shook the floor. The smell of burned roses filled the air.

CHAPTER TWO

EVIL WINE

Shall I repeat it again? The sweetest vice often turns rancid at desire's apex. — Nyrissa Rieson, Dar Elect and flyer of Lydinairre

M athias grabbed his sword and bolted through the empty doorway where blue smoke billowed. Wispy arms swept toward him. It tasted like ash and flowers and wine. He blinked. His head felt as if a damp blanket had been wedged behind his eyes.

"Cover your face," Jovaryn yelled with a muffled voice.

Gripping his sword, Mathias pulled the neck of his linen shirt over his nose and mouth. He walked through the haze to where Fallo stood before the stone hearth, his broad shoulders quavering. Thick smoke curled in slow, lazy spirals.

A boy stood transfixed between the fireplace and a low table. He was maybe ten years of age.

"Evil," Fallo croaked. "Evil wine."

A chink sounded from the low table. A toppled silver goblet rolled and clinked again on the tray's corner. Breakfast. It was laden with bread, cheese, fruit... And somehow red wine bled across the cherry-wood surface.

Mathias forced himself forward, the red carpet swallowing his footsteps. It brushed his bare toes like velvet moss. Better sensation than his head. He hadn't felt like this since... His heart hammered, and static pictures of memory surfaced. The morning his mentor had died. Died at the hands of wererats and a hooded figure stood by Zeller's body. Mathias ran. Shoved. The figure stumbled to the ground, hood flying back. Arch Vicar Bibb. The room spun, blurring past and present. It made no difference. Mathias was powerless.

Weight in your legs. Hooves on the earth, Tafiriel, his pegasus' voice, sounded inside his head. Taf was in the stable but he often overheard Mathias' thoughts. Something Mathias complained about but not now.

Mathias straightened. Concentrated on the table and the spilled wine. Bibb was at the Bellows when Mathias had been poisoned with Navenra...even if he couldn't prove it. And wererats had burned Navenra on the Grashbear Mountains. This smelled the same except there was also a blended acrid tang of burning leather and hair.

Fallo. Within the magical mural at the Pavari Court, he and Keston had witnessed Fallo sitting with the traitorous knight-sons at a campfire sharing a wineskin. A wineskin that easily could be laced with Navenra poison. Fallo had been poisoned. Had his free will been taken away?

The burning leather. Mathias hurried forward to the hearth. The remnants of a wineskin burned atop logs and ashes. How long had Fallo been compromised? And Paderro? Fallo's pegasus was still loyal. Or had been as of last night.

Mathias glanced over his shoulder. Aunia stood near the empty doorway, with the neckline of her white chemise covering her nose and mouth. It made her lace-loosened gown droop on her shoulders. Jovaryn, dirty beige shirt covering part of his face, stood nearby. Too near. He shouldn't be so near to Aunia.

He opened his mouth to say something, only the door to the hallway burst open, and two city guards and a Hauser Tower flyer barreled in.

"What's going on?" A female voice snapped. Young, trumpet-bright, and crisp.

"Poison smoke," Jovaryn muffled against his long, dark tunic. He hastened to one of the tall windows and ripped back the heavy drapes. "Breathe shallow."

Mathias shook his head, trying to force his mind to stay clear while Fallo, both hands braced over the hearth arch, muttered about evil wine.

The boy, sandy-haired, took a step toward the guards.

"Wait," Mathias called to the child. The boy had answers about what had happened. "We need you to wait on us."

"No window," one guard commanded.

"Need to clear the smoke." Jovaryn yanked the window open one-handed. "Teach me to toast bread, I guess. But we're fine. And three floors up? Too far a drop. Really, makes no sense you having to endure our smoky mishap, eh?"

Mathias blinked. Navenra stole free will. Was this wererat trying deliberately to control the guards through suggestion? Wouldn't work against the chestnut-haired flyer... Or would it? The boy remained fixed in place. Either way, they needed the guard to leave. The best chance Mathias could see was to play along.

He eased forward, set his sword against the green and gold couch, lunged, and grabbed the child by the upper arm.

The female flyer... Breen, that was her name. She stepped into the room. Mathias vaguely remembered her from his last days of training at the Silver Tower. She was younger than him. Probably the youngest in the Hauser unit. Curly chestnut brown hair and freckles, and a blue scarf around her neck. It was the only loose-fitting and non-leather thing she wore. The guards, dressed in simple pants and tunics, remained behind her, looking slack-jawed.

"Breen." Mathias kept his gaze on her face and his grip around the boy's arm. "Mine will vouch we're only looking to clear the air." Mine, meaning his pegasus. Too many non-flyers were nearby for him to be more plain.

Breen cocked her head with a frown and gave him a once over before she nodded.

"Take me with you," the boy yelped. He pulled away from Mathias.

"We need help with this cleanup," Mathias said. "And the girl in our company deserves to be served breakfast proper."

"Breakfast? You mean lunch," Breen called from over her shoulder as she exited the room with the guards.

The door closed and Mathias dragged the boy to the table.

"I... I didn't do nothing," the child protested. He pointed at Fallo. "He... He..."

"Mathias, wait," Jovaryn said. He rotated his hands as if he were mixing the air.

A breeze swept through the room, and the haze clinging to Mathias's mind thinned. It left his head aching, but the sensation of a woolen blanket stuck inside his head had reduced to the feel of a washcloth now. He could work around that. And they needed the truth. Who had burned the Navenra and why?

Another curl of sweet rot hissed on the coals and it jarred a thought. *You warned us not to drink anything at Dalin.*

Yes, Taf sent back.

You could have said... We bought apple cider—

Eavesdropper.

Mathias closed his eyes. He had forgotten completely that someone was magically eavesdropping on flyer-pegasus communication. And he hadn't discovered how yet. "Boy. You brought poisonous wine. For all of us. Why? Who are you working for?"

The boy stammered but the sounds made no words. Mathias dragged him toward the couch and the lad dropped like a sack of coal. The movement wrenched Mathias' arm but he didn't release his grip.

"Aunia." Jovaryn waved her over.

"Keep back," Mathias said.

But Aunia, being Aunia, walked over to the wererat. She kept the chemise fabric over her face.

Jovaryn leaned toward her. "May I?"

"Keep your hands off her." Mathias lifted the kicking boy to the ornate couch.

"You've Chand crystal or ice. I just need to touch it to contact Basil." Jovaryn reached for the chain lying bare against her neck. "Get rid of the rest of the smoke."

"Evil wine. Evil wine," Fallo continued to mutter.

Jovaryn pulled at the chain until her amulet appeared. A finger-knuckle orb of Chand ice clutched by a small silver-wrought hand.

Aunia shrank back but she nodded. She glanced at Mathias. "Basil will know what to do."

Basil? Mathias hated to admit that rover-Mystic had good sense.

Jovaryn pinched the orb between index finger and thumb and whispered a chant. After that, he released the orb and leaned against the wall next to the window.

Aunia stepped back.

Rescued by a rover-Mystic. What kind of flyer was he? Mathias frowned. The kind who had gotten them all arrested and in a room with lingering Navenra smoke.

The knight-sons betrayed us, Taf sent. *Even Paderro has to admit that.*

I almost had Keston drink from Garret's wineskin last night. Mathias forced the boy onto the couch.

Maybe Aunia was right to trust the wererat. Basil could probably get rid of the rest of the smoke. Make it easier to think.

"Be still," Mathias barked at the boy and the child turned docile.

Keep to clean air best you can, Taf sent. *We've some immunity—*

Immunity?

From the Cold Festival. When I ate those flowers last night it only made me sleepy. Not like Revellie.

Mathias clenched his fist. Taf and Rev had been fed Navenra flowers. Rev with colic. Keston probably sleep deprived caring for her. Mathias yanked the boy to his feet. "Who are you working for?"

The kid cried.

"Evil wine," Fallo said again, looking as if the hearth was the only thing holding him up.

"Da Vennen soldiers are gathering at the gate, and you've thrown poison on the fire for all of us to breathe," Mathias snapped. His pulse drummed in his ears and his attention centered on the commander. Fallo was bulkier... stronger than he was. "For the love of Yasendra. What side are you on? Be honorable. Stop hiding the truth."

"I was duped. Fighting the effects of..." Fallo turned, face ashen, and tottered to the couch. He sat down heavily. "The child. He brings more. I knew the taste as soon as it touched my lips. And the smell..."

"Burned roses," Aunia murmured from the window. She stood too close to Jovaryn.

The air cracked like an angry whip. And then, near the window, two new figures stood beside Aunia and Jovaryn. Basil and an older woman.

Silver hair threaded through the woman's raven-dark hair. Her tanned complexion was slightly lighter than Basil's olive. And her coal-bright eyes... They were the same color as... This was Basil's mother. Mollie Mae. A wererat.

Niall, a rover from Basil's caravan, had told Mathias days ago the story of the woman's fall from grace. Days? No. Weeks. He, Aunia and Keston had lost ten days in the Faery world. But Mollie Mae had been bitten years ago and had left the caravan.

Not only that...this was the same woman who had helped Aunia on the Grashbear Mountains when the marble giant had thrown the girl high into the sky. When Basil's magic had saved Aunia from a plummeting death.

"Steadied power burns brighter," Mollie Mae said, setting a hand on Basil's shoulder.

Basil frowned and raised his hand. "I don't have Jennium right now."

"If there're any potentials, borrow from them," she said.

Mathias narrowed his eyes, waiting for the wererat lady to stare at Aunia. She didn't.

Basil splayed his fingers wide and uttered a string of melodic yet nonsensical gibberish. What looked like haunted moonlight, poured from his outstretched hand. It filled the room, devouring the poisoned smoke. The haze thinned and dissolved.

Mathias sucked in a lungful of air to steady his quaking knees. The fire snapped, and he jumped at the plume of smoke. This time the smell was sweet and woodsy.

Basil lowered his hand. He took in Mathias, then Fallo, Aunia, and finally Jovaryn. "Jovaryn. Thank the Eaburrai Court you're safe. What is happening here?"

Jovaryn stepped forward. "This was unexpected and—"

"We've got a situation," Mathias interrupted.

"Yes." Jovaryn gave Mathias a long look. "Perhaps we should get the story from the boy first. Before the Da Vennen soldiers lining the gate decide to break in."

Fallo jerked his head up. "Da Vennen?"

Mollie Mae fastened her hand onto Basil's. "If there's a Da Vennen here, we have no time."

"I agree. Little time. Not only this, but we have to find out what Bibb is up to." Mathias gave the lad a shake. "Why'd you give us poisonous flowers?"

"I don't know nothing about poisonous flowers." The boy burst into another storm of tears. "It's the richeys and the lords. You think they do you favors? They don't. It just costs you more."

Basil stepped forward. "Who set you up to this?"

"Craymore." The child wiped his face on his patchwork sleeve. "He wanted them lights, so he traded my sister for 'em."

"The salamander lights?" Mathias asked.

There could still be glass in the carpet from where the glass tubes holding the fire faeries had smashed the night before. Anger boiled in Mathias' belly. The innkeeper was trading people for them? "Who'd he trade with?"

"Caravan." The boy turned wide eyes on Basil and then stammered. "Only... not rovers. I saw. They wore dark clothes, and a symbol stitched."

"What kind of symbol?" Mathias asked.

The child drew a figure-eight on its side in the air. Then, slashed the number's middle joining spot with a vertical line.

Mathias had seen that symbol. Saw it recently on a couple of Da Vennen soldiers when they were in Dalin. "Go on."

The boy wiped his eyes again. "We have to save her. My sister dumped chamber pots and cleaned rooms. Anything to keep us fed and not go to the... giggling rooms."

"Giggling rooms?" Aunia asked.

"Don't," Mathias said. "The answer is. . . repugnant."

"None of my people wear that design." Basil took a step forward.

"But the Da Vennen do. Keston and I saw it in Dalin." Mathias turned back to the boy. "And what were you supposed to do... afterwards?"

The boy hiccupped another sob. "I was... I was supposed to tell you to sit still and be happy."

Keston would have had a joke for that comment. But Keston was still tending his very sick pegasus. Mathias clenched his jaw. *Taf, how are Keston and Revellie?*

Revellie's trembling has eased. Her ears aren't pinned back anymore. Taf's voice sounded soft inside Mathias' mind. *Commander Frehn says Rev's almost ready to try a boiled mash. She is not up to flying from here.*

Another thought hit Mathias, and he glowered at the boy. "Are there more poisoned wineskin you've given out?"

The boy's eyes went wide and shook his head.

Taf, warn the Hausers, Mathias sent. *If any wine comes, tell them they must refuse it.*

"Those Da Vennen soldiers outside. They'll be coming in," Aunia whispered. She turned to Basil. "Take us with you."

"I can't with so many and certainly not far," Basil murmured. He crossed the room and squatted down in front of the boy. "Your sister. Is she faeblood?"

The boy paled, drew back even more. "I'll scream."

Taf, Mathias sent. *We can't have him...*

The boy's eyes glazed over, and he fell boneless onto the floor.

"The sleeping sickness," Mollie Mae said dryly.

"Probably passed out from the smoke." Mathias scooped the boy's slight form from the floor and walked him to the chaise lounge in the corner. He set him down gently and covered him with a crotchet throw.

Jovaryn said. "Bibb finds all sorts of ways to gather faebloods."

Mathias moved closer to Aunia. "We need to escape."

Chapter Three

Not Myself

What is a lie, but a truth shriveled and dried? — The Philosophical Ramblings of Lord Chance

Too many eyes painted over her skin with Jovaryn's pronouncement about Bibb and faebloods. Aunia fidgeted, curling her fingers in front of her face. Her mind had cleared of the burned rose smoke, but anxiety reared its head.

She wasn't really a faeblood. Was she? And she didn't have the power that Edvaras, a Chandarion, had. Basil had told her that her father was a Mystic when she had been at the caravan. She could be that. Or...did she have the signs of being a Chandarion potential? A possibility perhaps.

Aunia straightened to look at Mollie Mae, who had said, "if there are any potentials, borrow from them." Had Basil borrowed from her? How could she tell? Stars, she would've liked to talk to Olivia, Basil's multi-great aunt, but the woman had died in Nonderu. Had Aunia told Basil that yet? She couldn't remember.

Basil narrowed his eyes as if he suspected she was hiding something.

She shook her head. "Da Vennen are here for my magic."

"If you've strong magic, yes." Jovaryn faced her. He stood inches away. "They don't come out in numbers like that for a typical faeblood."

Aunia shuffled closer to Mathias, who now stood beside the couch. She hated not knowing things about herself. She'd been raised to believe a piece of Edvaras' magic had attached itself to her but that was a lie. It was her magical globefire, and while it was blue, like Edvaras', it was a much darker shade. She had seen his Nymer, his magical energy, over the Grashbear. It lay now imprisoned inside her mother's amulet, which the marble giant held in his keeping. Lies. Always fed lies... was she Mystic-born and faeblood? Or was she a potential like Olivia?

Jovaryn remained by the window. "They will seek to turn you. Leave you with no support but to them."

Turn her? Like into a wererat? Had they done that to the sleeping child's sister. The innkeep had bartered her life away for salamander lights. Salamander lights a fireling had made. A fireling who worked for the Boggleman. She had seen that for herself when she had dreamwalked

"Maybe Bibb makes the unfortunates believe they've no choice." Mollie Mae placed a hand on Jovaryn's shoulder. "But we've created a home on the side of good under Lord Chance."

"I won't let her be bitten," Mathias said. His outer glow had turned fiery red. "And what do you mean by Lord Chance?"

Mollie Mae's eyes hooded. "What is a lie, but a truth shriveled and dried? A prune perhaps, and sweet. But sink not your teeth there. Seek instead those banded for sight who rummage through shadow, the dim, and the light."

"I know all of Lord Chance's quotes," Mathias snapped. The red around his green glow thickened. "Jules would quote from those books every day."

Aunia bunched the silky skirting of her gown into clenched fists. She understood Mathias' ache to find his missing friend but quarreling would do no good. "Jovaryn. Do you think Jules would be at Spatelly?"

Fallo swiveled on the couch, fingertips pressed into the side of his skull as if pushing a headache away. "We can't go against the will of the Dar-Elect. Not in a frontal attack. Every flyer from Worley and beyond would be on us. We'd be stripped of rank and steeds."

I would never leave you. Tafiriel's silvery voice sounded in Aunia's head. He'd often allow her inside the telepathic space that he and Mathias shared.

Mathias turned to face his commander.

Fallo's gaze, however, fixed on Aunia, glow turning a sickly yellow-green, and he said:

> "Silver tongues. Willow eyes,
> Lure you in with their pretty lies.
> Whispers sweet as lover's breath,
> And every promise reeks of death."

"And I'm to watch what side of the cage *I'm* on?" Basil tugged a strand of his dark hair.

"What do you mean by that?" Aunia asked.

"Not myself." Fallo gripped his head, and his glow threaded with gray-blue.

"You've willow bark?" Basil nudged Mollie Mae.

"For the one spouting Da Vennen poetry?" Mollie Mae wrinkled her nose, but she reached into a skirt pocket and handed a small linen pouch to Basil.

"He drank wine laced with Navenra," Mathias folded his arms. "The knight-sons did too. We need to confirm that Bibb and his Da Vennen are behind these attacks."

"The Da Vennen work for the Boggleman," Aunia said.

Basil straightened. "How do you know that?"

Aunia pointed to the broken bits of salamander lights hooked to the ceiling. "If the boy's tale is true about Da Vennen taking people to trade for those... There's a fireling who makes them. She was tending the Boggleman after he fell from the Grashbear."

"Again, how would you know that?" Mollie Mae asked.

Basil said, "She dreamwalks."

Mollie Mae turned wide eyes on her. "That magic is—"

"Rare indeed," Basil finished. He and his mother shared a long look.

Aunia bit her lip. What had she told Basil after he rescued her from Dalin? She'd been hit on the head with a brick and part of the rescue remained fuzzy.

"Making salamander lights to trade for faebloods," Basil mused.

"Bibb is building an army." Mathias dropped his arms to his sides. "That means they either have or are looking for a place to attack."

"We've... we've an army to defend ourselves." Fallo pressed his fingers deeper against his head.

Holding a steaming cup, Basil crossed the room. Aunia had not seen the Mystic rover magick the cup from nowhere, but he had pulled food-stuff out of empty air before. Basil stopped in front of Fallo and handed him the cup.

"The Boggleman wants the human world to die," Aunia said. "And the time of the augury is coming, yes?"

"You've noticed the star move?" Mollie Mae said.

"The star moves at a snail's pace." Mathias stepped away from the couch.

"One would wish that," Mollie Mae said. "It's scary to consider which world will be picked when we're missing four Chandarions."

"Three." Basil remained in front of Fallo while the commander sipped at the cup. "A potential would count, and Olivia, like Edvaras, is free."

"No, Olivia..." Aunia studied her toes that stuck out from under her blue gown. Slowly, she faced Basil. "She's dead."

The olive tone of Basil's cheeks muted as if a frost had crept beneath his skin.

Behind her, Jovaryn's voice came out hollow. "Bibb and the Da Vennen would not be turning faebloods into wererats simply to be a standing army. And if the Boggleman is involved..."

"You know his plans?" Basil asked.

Jovaryn stepped beside Aunia. "There's much that villain didn't share, but..."

"He's cut off from his power," Aunia said. When she and Mathias entered Nonderu she had been able to destroy his faery-eating cloak... the one that allowed him to consume and reuse the magic of others.

"Injured in a way, aye," Jovaryn said. "And nothing is more fearsome than a beast left with nothing but will and fury."

"What do you mean, cut off from his power?" Mollie Mae asked.

"She unmade his cloak," Jovaryn said.

"The cloak of shadow? I'm impressed." But Mollie Mae's back bowed and deep lines etched her brow. She whispered, "My little girl often had nightmares about that."

"Forgive me," Jovaryn said. "But we need to wrap this up. We've got Da Vennen at the gate. They want her. Me as well."

"Flyers too," Aunia said.

Mathias stiffened. "We're safe from—"

"You said it yourself. Your knight-sons were corrupted. Jules taken." Aunia pointed at Fallo. "Who knows who we can trust."

Mathias frowned, turning his attention to Basil. "Can you skip us to—"

"No." Mollie Mae jerked her chin toward the window. "We've got our own mission."

Aunia blinked. Basil had rescued her at Dalin. Had stood by her when the dark fae had attacked Worley Square. And now he was abandoning her?

Basil frowned. "I can't skip so many—"

"You did last night," Mathias said.

"I had my faery familiar with me too. And it was only a few blocks distance." Basil looked at Aunia. "I could take *you*."

"It can't just be me." She swallowed hard. The price of being allowed back into the mortal world after being in Pavari was to agree that she and Mathias had to stay together until both their quests were complete—his to uncover what Bibb was up to, and hers to find her father. "Zevara's geis."

"We've a lore master and children who must be saved," Mollie Mae said.

Aunia lifted her chin. Rovers did need to be saved. It wasn't like she was going to be executed. Just changed into a wererat, and who knew what else.

Mathias stepped beside Aunia. "What do you mean by lore master?"

"Do you mean Gavryn?" Jovaryn asked Mollie Mae.

Basil's mom nodded. "He had a dream about the Wanderwright. Told others he was instructed to gather halite."

Aunia crossed her arms. "What exactly does that mean?"

"Wanderwright... the Tinker. And halite, as in large salt crystals." Jovaryn turned to Mollie Mae. "M'lady, will you need me too?"

"You can't go against a lord." Fallo stood, and Basil backed away.

"Those rovers aren't guilty," Mollie Mae snapped.

"We know." Aunia pointed to the sleeping child. "He told us all about the Da Vennen pretending to be rovers. But why would they do that? What are they hiding?"

"What we need to find out," Mathias said. Murky lavender, worry, threaded through his glow.

"Shall we?" Basil said to Jovaryn. He walked back to Mollie Mae, his olive skin still ashen.

"Wait," Aunia said. "Do you know where Jennium is?" If she had to be on her own with only Mathias and the other flyers, she wanted her garden faery friend. There were answers she needed and Jennium was good at spying them out.

Mollie Mae snapped her attention to Basil. "Jennium, is it? Another Mystic's familiar? What exactly are you playing at?"

"Whatever I must, to keep us all safe, mother." Basil readjusted his orange bandana. His glow swirled with shadowy gray and amber. He stopped at his mother's side and faced Aunia. "Hide your abilities. Best as you can."

Basil," Aunia insisted. "Where is Jennium?"

"Don't know. She left moments before I did when the Hauser flyers arrived." Basil waved Jovaryn closer. "Sensible as neither of us should've stayed. Seeing me wouldn't have done Keston or myself any good."

"But I need to ask her if my father is in Pavari." She crossed the space between them and stood inches from Basil.

Basil blinked. "He's not a firm friend of Zevara's."

"He vanished after he killed a Mockman troll in Nonderu," Aunia said. "I... I need to know where he is."

"He was a prisoner of the Boggleman's," Jovaryn murmured to Mollie Mae. "Like I was."

Mollie Mae frowned. "Aunia. Dear. For you, it isn't a garden faery or Zevara you should be asking. It's Kai-Marin."

Basil shot Mollie Mae a startled look. "Mother?"

Aunia stepped back. Kai-Marin as in the Boggleman's mother? An Eaburrai known as the Sea-Witch? But she had held Aunia firmly in the

Birchwoods' creek to prevent the Boggleman from taking her. And in the dim recesses of her head, she could hear a voice saying, "it was up to the ocean," and an image of the salt spring which appeared right after the Boar Hunt surfaced. That had been right after Nehla died. Aunia closed her eyes. She'd been thirteen. Limi fifteen. And no one would talk to her.

A heavy knock rang on the outer door.

Basil grasped Jovaryn by the arm and Mollie Mae by the hand, and they vanished. Skipped away.

CHAPTER FOUR
WHEN DUTY WOBBLES

What is duty, if not protecting those who cannot protect themselves? The queen herself might agree with that. — Jules Mayrell, flyer of Brinsaber

"Hold up a moment," Mathias called out to whoever was on the other side of the door. He crossed the room and pulled the door open.

Commander Frehn of Hauser Tower entered with Keston directly behind him. Breen followed next and closed the door.

Frehn scanned the room, his gaze lingering on the low table with the untouched food and the spilled wine. Then Aunia by the open window. And the sleeping child on the chaise. He stepped to the stone hearth, sniffed, and wrinkled his nose. "What an interesting smell. Burned wineskin and... flowers."

"It's Navenra," Aunia said. She turned her back on him to look outside at the inn's yard.

"Get away from there, my dear," Frehn said. "Breen. Shut that window."

Aunia frowned but complied—with Mathias' deep gratitude.

Keston swayed on his feet.

Mathias frowned at the dark circles under his friend's eyes and the tangles in his sandy brown hair. Rough. Keston looked incredibly rough, down to his brown pants and bleached white shirt coated in straw dust. "How's Revellie doing?"

"Better." Keston shot a glance at Frehn. "But not well enough to fly yet."

"And that's an issue." Frehn sat at the opposite end of the couch from Fallo. "We need to talk."

"About the Da Vennen at the gate?" Fallo asked.

Mathias felt his heart slip into a steadier beat. Was it possible? Fallo would be his reasonable, commanding self?

"Among other things? Yes. But..." Frehn glowered at Aunia. "Breen? Would you escort our young miss to one of the bedrooms? And keep an eye on our guests at the gate."

Taf, Mathias sent, *tell Aunia that Frehn doesn't know she hears pegasi. Tell her to please keep that secret. Ok?*

He waited to hear Taf's silvery voice. Instead, Aunia folded her arms with a frown and stamped toward her bedroom with the broken door. Breen followed.

"Lack of a door doesn't do much for privacy," Frehn muttered. "Keston, why don't you go lie down in the other room? Get some sleep."

Keston glowered, eyes darting to the sleeping child and then to Mathias' face. His shoulders slumped and his fingers curled over his heart, a gesture to be careful. He entered the other bedroom and did not close the door. Frehn's gaze lingered on the not-so-subtle rebellion. He said nothing as he turned his attention back to Mathias and motioned for him to sit.

Mathias pulled one of the wooden chairs near the hearth, set it down opposite the couch, and sat.

"I have been in communication with Nyrissa despite your pegasus demanding we stop," Frehn said. "He is old enough to have learned—"

"If Tafiriel gave warning, it's for cause. There is someone listening in to our conversations," Mathias said.

Frehn sat forward. "An eavesdropper? Who?"

"Ask your..." Mathias frowned. He didn't remember Frehn's pegasus' name.

Morganstee, Taf sent.

"...Morganstee to ask Taf directly if what he says is true."

"Mine says yours can't identify a person." Frehn looked over to Fallo. "Only it's not a flyer. Which is ridiculous."

"It's true," Mathias said.

Frehn weighed his words, his expression guarded, and the minutes spilled away.

"There are Da Vennen soldiers at the gate," Mathias said. "What do you plan to do?"

Frehn leaned back and settled the side of his boot upon the opposite knee. "There's a...sleeping sickness on the premises. No one in. No one out. And the first who were stricken were, of course, Da Vennen soldiers from last night. We aided them. Returned them to their own people, but alas, more are succumbing."

Mathias squirmed. He well remembered Paderro unexpectedly landing before them and magically sleeping an entire band of Da Vennen soldiers. It had been the only reason he, Aunia, Keston, and even Basil, had escaped their clutches. He should have known better and they should have stayed inside the inn. Instead, he took Aunia out to the pre-Kankari festival because he wanted her to forgive him.

"There had been no other choice." Fallo sipped at his mug of willow bark tea.

But Fallo hadn't been with them. He had been talking with Worley's lord instead. Was in league with the knight-sons. Wasn't he? But Paderro had come to save them.

"The girl," Frehn said. "That's why the Da Vennen are after you?"

"It's more than that," Mathias said. "They're collecting flyers now as well. Jules—"

"And my kin, Patrick. Garret," Fallo said.

"And Zeller," Mathias said.

"He was killed," Frehn hissed.

"By Bibb's hands."

"There is no proof of that." Frehn wrapped his thigh with his knuckles twice. "And I'll be directing the conversation. Let's start with... why did you go to Nonderu?"

"You went to Nonderu?" Fallo asked, eyes wide.

Mathias stiffened, wishing the window was still open, and the breeze made the room feel larger. "The Boggleman was waiting here for us. For Aunia. We fought him back, and he dove through a veil door.

"Veil door?" Fallo set his mug down. "It's said they allow you to manifest anything you want there."

Mathias clenched his teeth. It wasn't the doorway into Faery that allowed manifestation. It was being in Faery itself. And to manifest anything that would remain when you returned to the mortal world? That required a geis laid upon you by the faery court's ruler, along with a core memory to lock it into permanence. "Well, I was able to manifest an army of myself to help fight—"

Frehn sat up straight. "You expect me to believe—"

"Again. You can ask my pegasus for confirmation," Mathias said.

"The Boggleman has been after her. And the girl wants her father back," Fallo said.

Frehn shot Fallo a puzzled look.

"The Boggleman took her dad," Mathias said. "Abducted him."

Frehn stood. "And he isn't a peasant tale."

Mathias frowned. "I assure you he is not."

Frehn scratched the back of his hand. "You do have interesting tales. Please. Regale me. What happened in Dalin?"

Fallo and Mathias shared a look, and Fallo flipped his palm up, tacitly allowing Mathias to go first. So, Mathias told Frehn about Dalin. He started with the terse conversation with the guards directing them to leave and being shot at. He spoke about the arrival of Lord Emmet's healer. How Mathias and Keston had tried to find out what happened to Jules and the knight-sons but they were ignored after Fallo traveled to the lord's keep. He spoke about the variety of answers when people would talk to them. And then how everything turned violent with Bibb's arrival.

"Bibb told so many lies about us flyers. And he had the people chanting for the Da Vennen." Mathias leaned forward. "One merchant told us he'd been an eyewitness and saw the knight-sons kill their own pegasi."

Fallo jumped to his feet. "Flyers wouldna do that."

"What if they'd been Navenra-poisoned?" Mathias asked. He turned back to Frehn. All he could do was plea. "Do you not see? We have to find out what this Arch Vicar is doing. Our very security depends on it."

Frehn looked as if he held a mouthful of nails. "Flyers wouldn't—"

"I saw them last night," Mathias growled. "They felt off. And there is no presence when I ask Taf to reach out."

"The wine," Frehn murmured.

Mathias nodded.

"From those little lacy blue flowers?"

Mathias nodded again. "And one more thing. The Da Vennen... they were collecting portal tiles from the ruins of the guildhall."

Frehn frowned. Nearly rolled his eyes. "They avoid magic at all costs."

"Maybe it was true once but no longer," Fallo said. "They're using Navenra in wine to steal the will from others."

Mathias swallowed hard. Jules. He had recovered from a wererat bite. What had his fate been after?

"I know," Fallo continued. "They gave it to me."

Frehn glowered and pulled off his commander's pin, a seven-pointed silver star, from his nearly black jerkin. "Hold out your hand, Fallo."

"Do you think Paderro would allow me to ride him if I were turned?" When Fallo received no answer, he held out his hand.

Frehn pressed the pin against Fallo's hand. No sizzle. No black threading under the skin. Mathias blinked. Had he expected a reaction? Perhaps a bit. Fallo still hadn't explained why he had been using a whisperer.

Fallo met Frehn's gaze and smiled. It was a cold one.

Frehn refastened the pin to his jerkin. "If you're not a wererat, how do you know they are turning flyers—"

"Not just flyers," Mathias said. "Faebloods too."

"The question still stands," Frehn said. "How?"

"My kin were turned," Fallo erupted. "I don't know why they didn't turn me, but they got me drunk on Navenra-laced wine."

Frehn stiffened more. "Where's that scruffy lad you supposedly rescued?"

Jovaryn. Frehn had seen him when Mathias and Aunia had entered the stable that morning. Telling Frehn that Jovaryn had skipped away... It would not make any of them look good. "He was a prisoner of the Boggleman's," Mathias said. "We rescued him. No one should be left in the Boggleman's hands...but he..."

"He skipped away," Fallo said. "No fault of our own. Wasn't wearing any iron bracelets."

"Like the faebloods who escaped Dalin, eh? Interesting. You seem to be in a few places where faebloods escape," Frehn said. "And you're seen at attacks with wyverns and walking mouths."

"Commander Frehn." Mathias stiffened. "We will see increased attacks. Zeller said we are getting closer to the time of the choice."

"The choice," Frehn said softly. "Nyrissa is right to call you in. I'll tell her—"

"You can't. The eavesdropper." Mathias interrupted. "We have to—"

"We've an army heading for the border to shore up against attacks," Frehn murmured.

"The training grounds are in Spatelly," Mathias cried out. "They're going in the wrong direction."

"Speaking of wrong directions." Frehn pointed at the kid. "Which one of you slept him?"

Mathias frowned. "He brought Navenra-d wine, and he gave the Navenra flowers to the pegasi."

"We'll turn him over to Lord Lyle for sentencing," Frehn said.

"No," Mathias said. "He... he only did it because he was promised his sister back. She was exchanged for those lights." Mathias pointed to the shattered salamander lights hanging above.

"A faeblood then," Frehn said.

"He's a child." Mathias said. He wished he had Basil or Jovaryn taken the child with them. "Spatelly isn't far. A day's travel and a day's travel back. We're duty-bound to find out what the Da Vennen... what Bibb is up to. They're using magical devices and—"

"No," Frehn said. "We're leaving before Kankari starts, and we'll make our way to Tatia. You and the remaining Eddac Tower flyers will be brought before the Queen and our Dar-Elect for questioning. After Nyrissa can decide if she wants anyone scoping out that cursed ghost-city.

"But—"

"I'll be allowing Keston to sleep for a bit," Frehn barreled over Mathias. "Give the Da Vennen time to give up and then we'll take our leave."

CHAPTER FIVE

THROUGH A WINDOW

A child's faith calls heroes to them. Perhaps when we re-alize all we have is ourselves...that we must be savior and saved...only then can we really be adult. — Breen Haldrayne, flyer of Korthalee

"Get away from the doorframe," Breen said, tone short, from the window overlooking the Green Harpy's gate.

Breen sounded like Limi's when she was feeling bossy. A part of Aunia wanted to join the broad-cheeked girl. Wanted both to see and not see what the Da Vennen were doing. But she needed to know her fate.

The anxiety rattling her bones flared to anger, brought a pinching to Aunia's head, but she complied. She could easily listen in on the Hauser commander, Mathias, and Fallo by standing further away. She sat on her bed, breathing deep. It would make the situation only worse if she accidentally conjured her magical globefire, Mygul.

Basil had told her days ago—no, weeks, as they had lost time in the faery world—to hide her magic. Magic was only permissible if it came from tangible items. Ingredients Basil had called it. Magic spells stored in crystals. Potions. That sort of thing. She had no ingredients, save her father's amulet. She rubbed the orb under her chemise. She had lost her mother's amulet by exposing it to the marble giant. She could not lose her father's. The amulets were identical except that the tiny gems embedded in the silver hand's fingernails had changed. Instead of blue they were red.

"What did you do to anger them?" Breen held the curtain in her fist. Her glow, slate blue flecked with amber, turned steelier.

Aunia frowned. Breen had the glow of someone who controlled her emotions with a rigid structure. Like the chief in her village often did. Beneficial because he rarely made snap decisions. Terrible, because he rarely changed his mind.

Aunia rose and walked to the window. She needed Breen to see that she and Mathias were only people. People who needed help. "The Da Vennen attacked us in Dalin, but we did nothing. Keston and I only walked to..."

"Keep back," Breen barked under her breath. "We don't need them spotting you. Who knows if one of them has a far-viewer?"

Aunia stopped half a man's length from Breen. It was close enough that she could glimpse the growing number of bear-cloaked figures at the gate. She swallowed back the jagged cold. "They attacked us. We fought back. We had to. To live."

Breen's thick lips turned into a thin line. "That's not what they're saying."

"You could ask Tafiriel," Aunia shot. Another wash of cold filled her. Stupid. She curled her toes into the gritty carpet. "I... overhear things sometimes."

"Another reason Eddac faces punishment," Breen said. She turned her attention back to the window. "That's a serious gathering. They're not posturing. They're planning. I don't like it."

"I don't like it either." Aunia forced herself not to ball her fist. Not to stomp her foot. She needed to show calmness. Contriteness. Show that she could listen. All the things Limi once tried to ram into her head. "What happens when you're arrested?"

Breen leveled a scowl dripping with disbelief. "It means you're in custody. Held for questioning. Bound by law."

"I'd never heard 'arrested' before coming here." Aunia shivered. She knew exile. That was the sentence Limi had foisted on her. And that order had to be obeyed on pain of stoning. Aunia straightened, refusing to feel the blood from that bite.

"Never heard?" Breen dropped the curtain. "Where are you from? You're not a fireling that pushed past the border spell, are you?"

Aunia shook her head. Foolish. Perhaps it was better that Breen hadn't known but... Threading through faery-truths. That's what she needed to do. She sucked in a long breath. "I came from Edvaras' village."

Breen's eyes widened, and the amber specks in her glow pulsed. A sign there was more to her than just hardness. "It means you'll be questioned. Watched—"

"I'm being questioned and watched now."

"It means your actions will be judged by someone above us both."

Aunia bit her lip.

"But you won't be harmed in Hauser custody," Breen said, her words rushed. "Not if you don't try to escape."

All Aunia wanted at this moment was to get away from the Da Vennen and find where her father went. And she couldn't do either.

"We just stay here?" Aunia cringed at how her voice cracked.

"We can't." Breen tugged at her blue scarf hanging around her neck. "Our Dar-Elect wants to question each of you. Know how you, a civilian, got involved with these flyers. Why are you with them?"

Why was she with them? Because she needed Mathias' help to rebox Edvaras' light. To keep the Boggleman from using it to destroy the human world. Because she saw Mathias as a lifeline when her father refused to tell her anything of her mother. Because Mathias had stepped out of Tafiriel's pen to help her when Fallo had threatened her father harm. Mathias always stepped up when she was in danger. But she hesitated to tell Breen any of that. "I love him."

"Him? Mathias? He used to be honorable. He's in competition for—"

"I know," Aunia snapped and brushed her fingers against her hidden amulet. Stars, maybe she should call Basil back to skip her away. "Mathias is helping me find my father. He was taken, you see, by the Boggleman."

"Mathias was providing help?" One of Breen's eyebrows rose.

"Yes." Aunia had to paint Mathias in a better light. "They came over the Grashbear Mountains looking for the wererat who had bitten his friend, Jules, and found my village."

"Edvaras' village." Breen breathed again. "And are the starcharts there?"

"They'd been destroyed." Aunia glanced at her knapsack, which sat on the floor at the foot of the bed. She had spotted charts inside her father's leather-bound book with its embossed stars when she had been in Eddac Tower. Could be copies of star charts. She had meant to ask Mathias what he made of them, but they had argued.

Aunia closed her eyes, remembering the letter Mathias had written to the heir princess, Keira. When he was in the suitor games. Before he had met her. He had called her 'darling.'

She needed to get out of here. Run through damp grass, have the wind pull away her fears and regrets and hurts. She turned to the bed and her gaze fell on her poppet. Her poppet. Leiaphae flowers were stitched inside it. Leiaphae that they had planned to use. Shroud themselves magically and be invisible... like her village currently was to the outside world.

She pulled the thought of Tafiriel, but before Aunia cast any telepathic thought, something else crossed her mind. Her eyes flew open. "For questioning... Does that mean we'll be taken to Tatia?"

Taya, a rover girl in Basil's caravan, had told her about a magical window within Tamore's capital city. It lay inside a chamber that had vanished. Disappeared. Like a betwixting tunnel. If she could find it, that window would take her anywhere in the Faery world. She could go directly to Zevara and... Mollie Mae's words came thundering back: "For you, it isn't a garden faery or Zevara you should be asking. It's Kai-Marin."

"That's where Nyrissa is." Breen turned back to the window and cursed softly under her breath.

Aunia's heart thundered in her chest. "How do you find an Eaburrai?"

"You can't ask an Eaburrai to save you from arrest." Breen snorted, but the amber flecks in her glow softened. "If they saved from anything..."

"I just want to know more about..." Aunia swallowed. "Kai-Marin."

Breen's glow turned steely again. "Why? They don't intervene in a mortal's life. I'm born under Branimir the Hunter, and I'm a flyer for Yasendra's sake. Think he's ever helped? Even Keston knows enough not to..."

Keston. With a very sick Revellie. And Breen had been in the stable to watch over both. Aunia cringed. "How are they?"

Breen grazed the top of a knife's handle that rose from the sheath at her belt. "Uriah found them all, you know, Branimir and Kai-Marin at the Eaburrai Court centuries ago. He had gone to ask for their blessing."

A faint smile tugged at the corners of Aunia's mouth. Mathias had told her the story of Uriah, second son of a king, and Yasendra, an Eaburrai, who had fallen in love.

"It would have been better if he never had," Breen said.

A knock came from the hallway door.

Aunia turned, but Breen bustled to the doorframe and stood inside the opening. Aunia caught up. She peered around the girl, who stood a finger-length shorter than Aunia.

From the hallway doorway a young man stood. He wore boots that stretched over his knees. "You've refreshments. Good. Make yourself ready. Lord Lyle is granting you an audience."

Breen's glow expanded, and her body relaxed. "Thank Yasendra, yes. Lord Lyle should be able to disburse that Da Vennen crowd."

Chapter Six
WHEN TOWERS TILT

Why must we always do it this way? Because it's tradition?
That's a tired excuse, not a reason. — Lord Lyle Worley

B oots drummed on the hallway floorboards, and the common room shrank.

I am here, Taf sent.

I know. Only last night, Mathias wanted to talk with the lord. Ask a favor... of being able to plant some of the Jaia seeds in Worley's greenhouse. To smooth away some of the trouble he was in by offering a previously unknown faery repellent plant.

Mathias stood from his wooden chair, jaw clenched.

On the couch, Fallo rubbed a hand over his short-cropped auburn hair.

Frehn pulled off his worn leather gloves from his knobby-knuckled hands. He set them on the low table away from the wine spill. "Perhaps someone should mop that up?"

Aunia rushed forward, snatching a napkin off the tray.

Bespeak her to return to her room, Mathias sent to Taf.

She says hiding in plain sight is easier, Taf sent back at the same moment Aunia, holding a now-soiled napkin, threw Mathias a glare.

Mathias waved his fingers at the fireplace, and Aunia padded to the hearth. She threw the napkin on the coals, brought a thumb to her mouth, and dropped her hands to her sides.

"Fallo, rise," Frehn muttered a moment before the boy in the tall boots opened the door.

Cassian. Mathias stiffened, feeling heat touch his cheeks. Of all the people that had to be here, Lord Lyle's son was in attendance. But it made perfect sense he would be. Lord Lyle had to know that the Eddac Towers flyers had been arrested. He'd have heard the reason. Abandoning their posts. Yes, their motive had been sound, but ever since they had followed that wererat out of Tamore, everything had gone terribly wrong.

Fallo staggered to his feet, his ruddy complexion pale, while Cassian filed in with members of Lord Lyle's envoy. A thick-bodied man dressed in Worley's colors of willow-green and amber walked at Cassian's right, his glare cutting into any semblance of calm for Mathias. Four other men, dressed in clothing of the same colors but less rich, followed like a soft triangle.

Mathias knotted his hands. Would Frehn help them now? Demand that Da Vennen stand down? The biggest problem was Uriah's edict giving the order sovereignty in most situations. The soldier order had often been employed during times that the country needed strength, had fought for the Queen during Aeryk's rebellion, but they had their own agenda. And they had just gained the lord's favor. Surely, the Da Vennen wouldn't want to spend that coin just yet.

Another thought reared its head. Yasendra be blessed. His chair, positioned opposite the couch with Fallo and Frehn, would be the spot the lord would want to hold court. That was why Lyle's captain—who else could the thick-bodied man be—remained glaring.

With a hurried bow, Mathias lifted his wooden chair and moved it back along the wall. He hurried to the cushioned chair near the window.

One guard broke from formation and helped Mathias position the big chair in place... exactly where the other one had been. Mathias scurried behind the couch, waving discreetly to Aunia to move away from the hearth.

Lord Lyle filtered into the room. He was a tall man with high cheekbones and an aquiline nose. Silver-threaded hair streamed from his temples like an unfurled war banner. He wore the mantle of authority. Or maybe the mantle wore him.

He took in each of them, and his gray-eyed assessment sliced across Mathias. But not as much as Cassian's gaze hurt. The young man adjusted his green and amber herald livery and pointedly ignored Mathias, but what else did Mathias deserve?

Cassian had been fostered at Wolfe's Eye, Mathias' childhood home. They had grown up together until Cassian confessed he loathed being noble born. That nobles hurt everyday people who only wanted to swim in undercurrents of song and art. Cassian wanted to be an artist. Now, he was a herald to his father.

Lyle and his men took position across the low table, and a whiff of patchouli and orange mingled with the lingering burned rose scent. Mathias wrinkled his nose. That was Bibb's cologne. Which man was wearing it?

"Frehn. Without a smile again." Lyle sank heavily into his make-shift throne but he did not give permission for the rest of them to sit. "Do you need an edict from our Queen to present one?"

"You honor me too greatly, lord, but as I stated before, I am only a pegasi commander. My energy is directed toward results, not..." Frehn's gaze drifted to the guards who stood behind Lyle's chair. "...matters befitting a lord. May I ask the reason for this pleasure?"

Mathias startled. Frehn had not asked for the audience?

"I merely wished to reflect on the tides of fortune and with currents you swim." Lyle smoothed the front of his green and amber brocade doublet, then turned his attention to Fallo. "Strange days when Eddac's finest are behind doors instead of holding keys, hmm? But I suppose even towers tilt when the wind changes."

Mathias struggled to keep the frown off his face. Holding keys. What authority was Lyle referring to? Fallo's former closeness with her majesty? Or perhaps the reason Fallo had been communing with a whisperer... one of the shadow-wrapped faeries who thrived on gossip and rumor. Shame threatened to stain Mathias cheeks. He had followed Fallo into many a skirmish, and the commander had defended Mathias after Zeller's death. His involvement kept Mathias' banishment from being imprisonment, but Fallo had also betrayed them.

Fallo examined the thick carpet underfoot, his voice like brittle leather. "Winds may shift, but the tower still stands."

Towers. Sturdy. And made of rocks. And... Mathias straightened. "The marble."

"Marble?" Lyle's gaze flickered over to Cassian. "Didn't the other Eddac flyers mention that?"

"You have Patrick and Garrett?" Fallo asked.

Lyle smiled slightly. "It's a conversation I will have with her majesty."

Cassian lifted the leather haversack he wore cross-bodied over his head and dropped to his knees at the low table.

"You seek the marble giant?" Frehn pivoted toward Fallo. "That is a recipe for awakening all the dark things under the mountain."

Mathias flushed. Why he had brought that up... It was stupid.

"Fallo has been fascinated with that peasant tale for a long time," Lyle said. "But perhaps not peasant tales. I keep hearing reports of the giant exploding from the Grashbear and the peak of Ag-haggy has fallen."

Fallo continued his perusal of the carpet and Mathias, squaring his shoulders like armor, slid toward Frehn's side of the couch.

"Don't look so glum, dear friend, Fallo." Lyle waved his hands at the two commanders, tacit permission for them to sit. He did not include Mathias, nor Aunia nor Breen. "I've decided to agree to your last night's request."

"What request?" Frehn said, his voice was mild but flat.

"I'm adding my forces to the Queen's."

Lyle waved a meaty hand at Frehn's frown. "Oh please, you must have heard the call to increase our forces along the Grashbear border."

"Last night?" Mathias asked.

Lyle centered his gaze on Mathias' chest. "Yes, the commander and I were discussing this when you were occupied. Remember? Running from aiding my citizens with putting out fires?"

Hold your temper, Taf sent.

Mathias forced his shoulders down. *Fallo was under the influence of Navenra wine. He'd been working with the knight-sons. With the Da Vennen. And Lyle...*

"Strange," Lyle continued. "All the faery lights explode in your presence. Da Vennen guests crumple to sleep when you're nearby. It makes one consider the gossip that's prattled in corners. Could there be truth that flyers can no longer be trusted to be her majesty's light?"

Frehn stood to all of his six feet. "The poisoned breath of gossip does little to dim the Queen's light nor make her forces flicker."

Lyle steepled his fingers. "Oh, Commander, I should explain. Lights go out every day with an explosion or perhaps they simply fade. Quietly. Long before we pay it heed."

"I assure you," Frehn said. "It is still day in Tamore."

Still day. And flyers would always do what was necessary to protect Tamore. Protecting Tamore was a flyer's number one duty. Bibb was setting himself up to be a threat, and troops were filing toward the eastern border.

"That would leave our heartlands vulnerable," Mathias said.

Lyle rolled his eyes. "Other than rogue rovers, arrested flyers, and an odd criminal or three, what threat do you believe is here? It's at the border where we have faery incursions. In this moon alone we've had walking mouth attacks, wyvern attacks, wererat attacks."

Frehn bespeaks for you to shut up, Taf sent.

Mathias ignored him. "We have to protect ourselves, yes, but we've training camps operating from Spatelly."

"I know about the rover camps there," Lyle said.

"Rover camps?" Mathias blinked. "I think you are mistaken."

Lyle leaned forward in his chair. "My little girl was rescued from a caravan of those patchborns. Rescued by the Da Vennen, now standing guard at the gate. They've told me all about the caravan heading to Spatelly. Setting up enslavement camps. Selling our own people."

Chapter Seven

One Hour and a Kiss

The fire of love burns bright but will often do strange and stupid things. — Gaitha, Eldest Daughter of Noama Sacella

"That's a lie." Aunia moved past Mathias, but he caught her arm. She shook it off. "The Da Vennen are lying to you. They took your daughter and then gave her back to trick you."

"That's a serious accusation, lass," Commander Frehn clasped his hands together. "Do you have evidence to go with it?"

"She is quite mistaken." Lord Lyle's eyes, cool gray rimmed in amber, narrowed and slid over her as if she were an annoying bug.

Aunia curled her fists. He didn't care if rovers caged in his dungeon were innocent or not. Rovers like the ones who had welcomed her when she first arrived in Tamore. People who had fed her. Laughed with her. Answered her questions. Even with her lingering anger at Taya, a young rover girl from Basil's caravan, rovers were good people. It was Tamorians who saw them as less than. And that was wrong.

The low ache in her temples surged with intensity—like badgers trying to claw their way from the inside of her head.

"Da Vennen." Aunia pronounced each word like a hammer to an anvil. "Are trading salamander lights for people and—"

"Who's lying now? Da Vennen hold no dealings with magic." Lyle tapped a finger against his cheek while his glow—a river rock gray—threaded with oily dark green. They rippled around his heart... and lower. "But you are lovely for a patchborn. Probably taken when you were small, eh?"

Aunia recoiled, but her outrage flared like bellows to coals.

From her periphery, she noticed Breen appearing at her right side while Mathias sidled closer on her left. To pull her back? To silence her? Was she the only one brave enough to champion the innocent?

"Aunia," Mathias whispered in her ear. "What was it that Gaitha would say? Breathe?"

Aunia glowered at Mathias. Didn't he see this imbecile had to be shown the truth? His spring-green eyes pleaded with her... gripped her with an intensity like the gasp before the fall.

"You're angry," Mathias murmured, his voice barely audible. "I need you to breathe."

"Young rover." Lyle's voice thundered with an icy wind. "My daughter pointed out her abductors."

The boy in the tall boots rose from the floor near the low table. His haversack lay on its surface along with scroll paper, ink, and pen. "And after, hasn't spoken since."

Breen's chin lifted, her gaze latching onto a space above the lord's head.

Stars! Mygul, her blue globefire and about the size of a deer's heart, rotated in the air there. She should breathe like Mathias said. But he was going to execute innocent people.

The boy in the tall boots looked to Mathias, to Mygul and to Lyle, and then back to Mathias.

Mathias shook his head slightly and whispered, "Aunia, please. Make it go away."

But she didn't want to make it go away. Da Vennen in Dalin had learned. That brought a wash of horror tapping down her rage. Mygul's blue flames wavered. But she had to protect... and those rovers... they were innocent.

Cassian stepped in between Lord Lyle and Aunia, his gaze on Mathias, his left-hand flicking fingers.

"Mind your place, Cassian," Lyle growled. "Back up."

Cassian's brows rose... a question. Who was he to ask her anything?

Mathias gripped her shoulders, pulled her toward him, and his mouth swooped down on hers.

Shock coursed through her. Mathias' face so close. Shadow and light. The curve of his cheek. His closed eyes. His lips. Warm. Honest. Confidant. But here? Now? Shifting boots and murmurs receded to a dull thrum around her. She forgot how to breathe. His hands on her back. Heat from his chest soaking into her palms. The fiery storm transmuted, turned to something more grounding, more expansive... more. Her eyes closed. And then he yanked back.

"What in Yasendra's blue sky do you think you're doing?" Fallo's voice grated against Aunia's ear.

Her eyes flew open. Mathias stood unbalanced several feet from her. Fallo hit him with quick, tight shoves. Mathias kept his footing. Just.

Aunia touched her lips. His kiss had been urgent, but his expression as he swooped in had been of fear. The clawing pain at her temples had turned to cool puddles, and Mygul had vanished. But his kiss? Had it only been to distract her? Make her globefire disappear? Her heart squeezed, and she bit her lip. She wanted his kiss but... in front of all these people? And the why.

"Interesting way to still her tongue. But only of specific merit." Lyle chuckled. "My own daughter was a child who never met a silence that couldn't be filled."

Mathias' face reddened.

Aunia turned her back on him. Worley's lord needed to know the error of his ways.

But, Basil, Mollie Mae, and Jovaryn had gone to rescue the prisoners. She pointed to the sleeping child in the corner. "It was not rovers who took your daughter any more than it was rovers who took his sister as a barter for salamander lights."

"Salamander lights? Yes. I had thought them useful things, but last night... seeing them as a weapon." Lyle snapped his fingers. "Cassian. Jot down the need for an edict. Those things are struck as illegal in my lands. And note that a forewarning needs to be sent to the rest of the parliamentary council.

Cassian returned to the low table, inked his pen and scrawled.

Lyle narrowed his eyes. "And perhaps a warning for them as well about Eddac Tower."

"Your Grace." Frehn stood, his back to Aunia. "That would be within Nyrissa's purview."

"Dar-elect," Lyle snorted. "Who knows how the vote will go when parliament reconvenes. "The nobles have a right to know about flyers running from aid when there's danger in a lord's city. And these are the same flyers who fled Britchway during a Besmarion Festival."

Mathias stood a few feet away, with Fallo glowering at his side. "That attack was because of wererats, not—"

"Says the flyer who loves a rover," Lyle snapped. "Yes, you put her in Tamorian clothes, but a rover is a rover is a rover. Your father will be so pleased."

Cassian paused in his scribblings; his gaze focused on Mathias.

Mathias' glow shrunk against his skin, and his complexion paled.

Anxiety pierced Aunia's heart. Mathias' parents wanted him to win the suitor games for marriage, or in the words of her former village, to be beaded. And he wanted to make his parents proud. She swallowed. But he had found her. Would he keep choosing her?

"Cassian. My words. Jot them down." Lyle rubbed a finger against his cheek. "Whether or not our resident tower likes it, I am a faithful servant to her majesty. I am also quite cognizant of the importance of keeping my sibling nobles apprised as well."

"You might not like the lad," Fallo said, pivoting his stance to face Lyle, "but Mathias was not the one who—"

Lyle interrupted, his voice thunderous. "I'm sure the nobles will understand the coincidental nature of one particular flyer being at two separate burnings."

His guards shifted, putting hands on the hilts of their swords.

"Frehn?" Lyle continued. "Would you consider gagging the prisoners?"

Aunia blinked, surprised that Fallo had tried to shield Mathias, but now they were being threatened with being gagged?

"Any decisions on this matter are mine to make," Frehn said in a soft voice.

A chorus of different voices and footfalls pulled Aunia's attention. They were coming up the hallway on the other side of the door. More people. More danger.

Aunia again pointed to the sleeping boy. "That child has proof that Da Vennen are using Navenra flowers—"

Cassian looked up from his scribblings. "Navenra flowers?"

"Enough," Lyle said. "I'm not asking for additional—"

"They're flowers from Edvaras that strip away free will," Aunia interrupted.

Lyle sat up in his chair. "What would a rover know about the rogue Chandarion?"

The noise outside the door grew louder. A dull drone of too many voices punctuated with boot scuffles. And then, sharp knocks shook the door.

Lyle pivoted in the plushy chair, and half his men moved as one to the door, blades sliding from their sheaths.

Cassian set the quill on the parchment and stood, hand on a dagger hilt under his tabard. Frehn crossed the room, his sword at the ready as well, and Breen crossed to the corner and stood in front of the sleeping child.

Mathias stepped in front of her. Aunia could barely breathe. Had the Da Vennen entered the inn? Part of her wanted to run to her room. Hide. She touched her temple wondering. . . but she had never had Mygul appear twice in one day.

More knocks came. And one of Lyle's men unbolted the door.

Over a dozen richly dressed men and women stood in the hallway. Two of them pressed in until the closest guard lifted his sword. The people halted, but their complaints rose.

"Is this how city lords treat their guests?" yelled one man, who had tried to push his way in. He was a stout fellow in a maroon brocade doublet that strained at the seams.

"Oh yes, it would have to be Baron Chazelle banging on doors like field hands denied his ale," Lyle muttered.

"Lady Ysabel Ferente is thirsty, too," said an older woman with gray hair coiled with tiny bells atop her head. She thumped a cane with a dragon's head on the floor and stepped forward. "We would speak to you about our release."

The guards stepped in the woman's way.

"A moment of your time, your grace," Baron Chazelle said. "To address our unlawful confinement."

Aunia sidled closer to Mathias.

"There's a festival soon to start," said another voice from the hallway.

"Let the first two in," Lyle said.

More complaints rose.

"Enough," yelled the guard.

Lyle's voice also bellowed over the crowd. "The door remains open only if they can behave."

The crowd settled, and the baron and the lady entered. More faces appeared in the doorway, but the guard stood firm before the door. Or did, until Keston stepped out of the other bedroom.

Keston's hair was rumpled and his complexion pale but at the guard's glare, he shoved the hem of his linen shirt into his britches and walked to Mathias. A handful of flat crystals stitched onto his leather belt sparkled from the sunlight coming in from the closed window.

Lyle frowned at Keston, then turned his attention to the baron and lady who delivered a bow and curtsy.

"What's going on?" Keston whispered to Mathias. "I'm assuming he's not granting you audience to grow those Jaia seeds."

"No," Mathias whispered back. "And those Jaia seeds weren't really with us. Copy, remember Pavari and the manifestation?

Keston groaned. "Why didn't we remember that?"

Mathias shrugged stiffly. "Too much going on."

"Or a faery glamor comes to mind," Keston replied.

Aunia startled. "Why would Zevara make us forget?"

"Why do faeries do what they do?" Mathias said. "How's Rev?"

Keston rolled his palm up, a sign for so-so.

"Justice?" Lyle's voice rang out. He then sat back, fingers steepled. His gaze landed on Aunia. "What about my justice against the villains who stole my daughter?"

"My lord, we would never suggest you not do what you must," the Lady Ferente said.

Coldness hammered against Aunia's heart.

"Justice?" Keston whispered to Mathias.

"He means to kill the rovers," Aunia murmured. Stars, she hoped Basil had already freed them.

"All we are saying, Your Grace, is we traveled a long way for the festival," the Baron said. "How long before we are allowed departure?"

"And of course, may justice be done," the Lady said, bowing her head.

"The inn's gate will open long before dark," Lyle said. "Go now."

"The invitation," a voice from the hallway shouted out, "Is that for all of us?"

"Indeed," Lyle said. "All of you may watch from my table."

The baron and lady bowed again and walked backwards until they were halfway across the room. It was only then that they turned and departed outside the door.

Lyle snapped his fingers and pointed at the sleeping child. "I want that one taken."

"No!" Aunia shouted. She pushed off to run to Breen but Mathias caught her wrist.

His whisper came out hoarse. "Have a care. We're in danger."

Breen, her slender form rigid, remained at the child's side, but she looked to Frehn.

The Hauser commander cleared his throat. "May we ask his fate?"

"You believe I make the innocent suffer?" Lyle asked. "I want him for questioning. And if his sister can be retrieved, that we will do."

Frehn's stare was long and searching.

Mathias' fingertips pulsed on Aunia's wrist. "The boy should be fine."

"Lyle threatened him earlier," Aunia hissed. She wished she hadn't pointed out the child.

"Give him berth," Breen said. "I believe he fell to the "sleeping sickness" as well."

The guard drifted back.

"Pick the child up or you'll be suffering from a lack of a head sickness," Lyle snapped and then, he singled Mathias out with a glare. "I once supposed that, despite your father's faults, his lectures on duty would've had purchase on my son. How naïve. The seed resembles its sire in every shameful respect."

Mathias flushed.

"Steady," Keston whispered.

Lyle rose to his feet. "But to get to the ultimate reason for my visit. The girl is accused of murder, theft, resisting arrest, and fleeing. Seeing that these are guilty actions, I will grant the Da Vennen's claim on the girl."

"She stays with us," Fallo said, propelling himself toward the lord. He halted as sword tips from Lyle's guards targeted him.

Aunia shrank beside Mathias, and he angled her again behind him.

A fair amount of people to sleep, Tafiriel sent. *Even with Paderro's help. And the Hauser pegasi will fight us on it.*

"Your Grace," Frehn said. He was pulling Breen off to the side. "Might we discuss this?"

Lyle folded his arms. "I am lord here. And before you cry jurisdiction from the Dar-Elect, I am obligated to answer to her majesty only. I am, after all, a loyal subject of this realm. I've kept my traveling room, and I have all the access to the voices that you must obey."

"Father," Cassian murmured in a low voice. "Perhaps it's better to allow her to stay—"

"Because your friend loves a rover?" Lyle snapped. "Call thy wits home from wandering."

"Lord Lyle," Fallo remained still though he sneered at the guards' swords. "The Queen has need of her. The girl knows how to make a faery repellent."

CHAPTER EIGHT
DOODLE-THOUGHTS

Your doodle-thoughts might fill the air, but they'll never fill a belly. — Wallace Habrett, Lord of Wolfe's Eye

"Faery repellent?" Lyle waved a hand dismissively. "I'd hoped for a better story."

"It is the truth." Mathias moved forward, blood churning through his limbs. He stopped when his knees touched the back of the couch. On the Harp, he so wanted to haul Lyle up and throw him on the coals of the hearth. Let any lingering Navenra poison invade the man's mind and make the lord let them go free.

Go free. Mathias almost snorted. He, Aunia, Keston, and Fallo would still be under arrest. He balled his fists. "That repellent is the reason we came into your city. I was seeking you last night for permission to plant the seeds needed in your greenhouses. Seeds that have been newly discovered."

Taf sent, *Your saddlebag went missing.*

I know. And it was a copy besides, Mathias replied. *We'll chase that storm when it breaks.*

Lyle tapped a finger against his chin and exchanged a look with his captain. "You would say anything, wouldn't you, to keep your giggle-girl."

Another surge of heat jolted into Mathias' fists, and the room grew red-tinged. "She is not—"

"Oh. It is a pleasure to allow one's guard down. To say and act as we please." Lyle sat, leaning forward with his legs spread wide. "We all saw the kiss. A perfect lady she obviously is not."

Mathias' insides pulled tight, then emptied. If he hadn't kissed Aunia, who knows what her globefire would've done? He'd seen it take off a man's head in Dalin. She was right to do so. If she hadn't acted as she did, Keston would have died. The problem was he doubted Aunia had conscious control over her globefire. It reacted based on her feelings. Her anger. And that was a problem.

Mathias straightened, willing calmness and reason to envelop him. "Lord Lyle—"

"Enough." Lyle cocked his head and gave Aunia a little wave. "One hour. Gracious of me. And it should be more than adequate time to do what you want, then say goodbye."

"We are in her majesty's custody," Mathias said at the same time Aunia, voice tight, snarled, "I am not yours to trade."

Lyle stood. "You want it to be now?"

Fallo, standing diagonally from Frehn, locked gaze with the Hauser commander, and slid a fist across his chest. A hand gesture used among flyers to signal 'Danger. Watch leadership.'

Frehn's jaw tightened, and he shifted, weight redistributing evenly on his feet.

"You there." Lyle snapped his fingers at a guardsman. "Go tell Craymore to dress up his best giggleroom. I've an hour to pass."

Shock tinged the thudding in Mathias' throat. Lyle, who over the years had spat fire at Mathias' father for straying from his wedding vows, was sauntering off to spend coin on flesh? *Taf, has Lyle been poisoned with Navenra?*

"On my return. I will collect her." Lyle headed for the door, his guards filing both ahead and behind him. The one guard, sleeping child in his arms, moved to join the column, and Breen sprinted in front of him.

"The child is under Lord Lyle's jurisdiction," Frehn rumbled, his voice low in warning.

"Well-done," Lyle said, voice rich with amusement. "A good commander defends his lord. You'd be well to remember that child."

The guard shifted the boy's weight in his arms and stepped around Breen. And Lyle and his men, except for Cassian, departed. The guardsmen barked orders to disperse at the guests still lingering in the hallway. Questions rose and fell out there. Including questions about whether flyers could ever be trusted.

Fire prickled at the base of Mathias' neck, and something colder beneath it. Everything was slipping away, and he needed to stop the free fall. A breath, too fast and shallow behind him made him turn. Aunia.

Mathias took her hands. "Look at me."

Her red-rimmed eyes met his, and despair gripped his belly. They had to escape.

Keston slipped beside them, his voice barely a whisper. "We need to leave."

"I know," Mathias mouthed. "How?"

"Never thought I'd see the day Mathias Habrett turned into a hypocrite," Cassian said.

Mathias squeezed Aunia's hands, released them, and Keston stepped in, pulling Aunia to the window.

Mathias turned. "Cassian."

"Do one's duty—it's the armor we wear." Cassian's words bit like cold metal. "The spine to stand tall despite all else. Isn't that what you'd tell me all those days bleeding into one another?"

Mathias' skin prickled, his linen shirt and doublet feeling much too warm to wear. He counted the small loops of lace atop Cassian's tabard.

"Tell me," Cassian said. "Why is your want more important than duty now?"

Near the bedroom where Keston had exited earlier and the empty chaise chair, Fallo and Frehn gathered, voices low. Breen hovered behind Frehn.

"Answer me," Cassian said.

Mathias ran a hand through his hair. "It's—"

"The girl?"

Mathias sucked in a breath. No way out except through. "The girl is from Edvaras' missing village."

Cassian blinked. "How?"

"Forget the how. She knows more about the augury than any of us do. You never wanted to see—"

"A world die. I didn't. Don't. But my father—"

"Doesn't care about the faery world. I get that. But he doesn't know which world will fall, and neither do we." Mathias straightened his jerkin hem, fingers curling into the fabric.

Cassian frowned, shadows gathering under his cheekbones. "Father says she's a rover lass."

"She's not. We rested at a caravan after I flew her over the Grashbear Mountains. They gave her clothes. Hers had been bloodied during battle. Wyverns. Wererats."

Cassian took a half step back.

"We journeyed then to Dalin. To find out what happened to the rest of our unit. We learned the Da Vennen meant to betray her majesty. They're gathering an army. An army close to your borders."

"Oh, no." Cassian raised his hands. "I am not helping you escape arrest. You can keep your far-fetched doodle-thoughts."

Mathias cringed. Doodle-thoughts was his father, Lord Habrett's term. And Mathias had been stupid enough to use it at times. He tried to turn away from the memory, but there he was, ten years old on the training grounds. Sweaty tunic clinging to his back. Wooden swords clattering. Boots grinding in the gravel.

He'd been sparring with an arms-man. Hand and foot agreement. Rhythm. Flow. Discipline. Everything expected of him as Lord Habrett's heir. He looked to see how Cassian fared. His father's ward. Mathias' responsibility. They both did well, and supper would be plentiful. A chance to make his father proud. But Cassian was gone. Again.

The arms-man left the field for water, and Mathias ran. He had to get Cassian. Then, explain away the absence.

He found Cassian behind the stable, fingers smudged with charcoal, and kneeling in the dirt over a scrap of parchment.

"What are you doing?" Mathias demanded.

Cassian startled. "Just need to get his hind legs in right."

An outline of a pegasus with its wings caught mid-motion. "We're supposed to be training."

"I'm almost done."

"You can't do this." Mathias snatched the parchment. Tore it in two. "They'll think we're soft. That I'm soft. Unfit to... just go get your sword. We have to be on the training grounds."

Cassian stood, pain shimmering in his hazel-flecked brown eyes. "I don't want to be a soldier."

"We're lord sons." Mathias' voice echoed his father's. "We wear duty like armor. Get up."

The memory faded, and Mathias straightened. He'd been wrong to rip up Cassian's drawing. Wrong not to listen to what his friend had tried to tell him. But what choice did he have then? They would've both received a lashing. "Cassian. This is more than doodle-thoughts. We need to get Aunia out."

The storm in Cassian's expression eased, and his eyebrow lifted. He pointed at Aunia and Keston as they headed into her bedroom. "Almost believed you. But don't both rovers and giggle-girls run off to the next dance?"

A pang of jealousy and uncertainty squeezed Mathias' gut.

They are seeking the Leaiphae, Taf sent.

Leiaphae, the shrouding flower. But their timing...he'd been so close to convincing Cassian to help.

Breen shadowed Keston and Aunia into the room. Mathias' breath loosened. "Aunia is under our unit's protection. But I would suppose since your father is now visiting for those endeavors, your vision is compromised."

Cassian reddened. "I do not approve, but it isn't my mother he dishonors."

"No," Mathias said slowly. "But it is your sister's mother. How long has your father—"

"Since the Da Vennen came to town," Cassian snapped.

"Is he drinking with them?"

Cassian glanced back at the low table. "The sticky surface. And the lingering smell. What poison are you suggesting?"

"Navenra," Mathias said. "A lacy blue flower. It's in wine sometimes. And if it is, others can make you do things you wouldn't do."

Cassian's eyes grew wide. "And how do you escape the effects?"

"Cassian, I believe your father will be looking for you." Frehn appeared at their side, his expression dark. "And I do have jurisdiction in this room."

Cassian raised his ink-stained hands, palms out. "If you're looking to escape with her, I can help. But you must help my father escape this Navenra wine."

CHAPTER NINE

HIDDEN FLOWERS

Capturing memories means locking ourselves in time without change or prescription — Jules Mayrell, flyer of Brinsaber

"But our locking spells would keep all magical qualities... like in the Leiaphae, wouldn't it?" Keston asked from inside Aunia's bedroom.

Aunia snagged her poppet from the bed. She and Keston had formed half a plan at the window while Mathias had argued with Cassian, and Fallo with Frehn and Breen had their quiet and intense talk. Heads close together and fingers flicking. "I hope."

It had been jarring when Mathias' saddlebag had disappeared, and with it a sharp realization that their belongings were copies, or like her gown, freshly manifested from scratch. And things manifested in Endynia, the faery world, typically disappeared when brought into Ahnu, the mortal one...unless the conjurer locked their manifestations with a core memory. It was the way to make any items 'real.' Like the Boggleman had locked his awful carnivorous cloak.

She rubbed a thumb over the poppet's button eyes. This was a copy of what her dad and Nehla had fashioned...a doll they had said would keep her safe. The real one though was at Eddac Tower. They had abandoned all their belongings when they had escaped from the hordes of whisperers.

"Did you know faeries could wipe out memory?" Keston asked. "I mean, you forgot these were copies too, didn't you?"

She was going to say no but she paused as a ghost of a thought reared up. Aunia braced herself for something horrible. But... whatever the thought was, it vanished before it crested into her conscious mind. Her fingers trembled from the cold weight pressing against her heart.

"What core memory did you use?" Keston asked.

She looked up, startled. "Better maybe not to delve."

Keston placed a hand over his heart. "The day Revellie chose to be mine changed my life."

Aunia bit her lip and whispered, "Nehla teaching me to create animals from clay..."

It was one of her memories that had lodged itself in her ribcage. Like the feel of Mathias' kiss tingling on her lips. But would he only kiss her when he feared for her life or safety? Her gaze went back to the fallen dresser. "Maybe Mathias didn't pick a strong one."

Keston's gaze followed hers. "Get the flower. Glamor ourselves—"

"Shroud." Aunia wriggled her fingers against the poppet's seams and a waft of rich pepper rose. "Glamor is what faeries do. Get to the window."

"Right."

Their plan, if someone barged in, was to say they were keeping an eye on the Da Vennen. Keston could distract, if needed, as Aunia pulled Leiaphae from the doll. And he'd let her know if the flower worked—she became invisible— by tapping his forehead.

Keston crossed the room and looked out the window. "There's more of them out there. Maybe three dozen."

Aunia's fingers slid from the doll's stitching. "Is... Revellie well enough to fly?"

"If I need to stay behind to get you out, so be it," Keston said.

"Maybe Revellie can fly." Breen entered the room, pausing long enough to fluff out her chestnut hair.

He crossed his arms. "Unless you're here to order us out, I don't see that this is any concern of yours."

"Is that what we're doing now?" Her voice cracked whip-like. "Flirting with another lass when in less than an hour the Da Vennen dogs will be dragging her out?"

"Distraction from doom can be a mercy." Keston shot Aunia a glance with his 'keep-doing-what-you're-doing' nod.

Mathias and Keston often shared that look. Aunia glanced at Breen, wriggling her pinkie inside the seam to widen the hole.

Breen crossed the room to the window. "And you'll sigh a breath of relief when they cart her off?"

Aunia stiffened. The idea of being taken by Da Vennen soldiers sent glass shards down her throat. This copy Leiaphae had to work. For the second time since she re-entered this room, she mentally called out to Jennium, but there was no reply.

"I will impose my body in front of her," Keston said.

"You'll... you have to be kidding," Breen said. "You?"

"We've taken an oath to protect her," Keston spat.

The amber flecks flashed inside Breen's steel-blue glow. "An oath from the flirtatious son of Jayden Pendar, sculptor extraordinaire? You've not a care of the hearts you break. A girl awaits you in every village and—"

"I play bold but not sly," Keston interrupted. "I flirt. I do. But neither I nor my words cloak themselves with false promises. Ever. I speak with true intent, and I hold in my heart every kindred spirit I've enjoyed a dance beside."

"Hold in your heart?" Breen scoffed. "Each and every girl on your long, long list?"

"Each and every. How can you discount even one ray of sunshine? I would rather lie to the sun."

"You are a flyer," Breen said. "That means you are held to a higher standard."

Aunia pulled out one stem of Leiaphae from the poppet. It bore three small clinging buds. Not enough by far. She pulled at the seam. Another inch came with a faint snap-rip, and she dropped the doll onto her lap, but neither Keston nor Breen took notice.

"Breen. I'm common-born. My time is rarely my own. And I'm young to boot. I am no prize." Keston gave the brown-haired flyer a shallow bow. "I offer simply a dalliance, a happy memory, a laugh. Nothing more."

Breen set her hands on her hips. "And the hearts you break?"

Keston gave her a startled look. "I give a wide berth to those who look for marriage or commitment. I'd never take advantage of someone else's dream."

Breen leaned to look out the window, and she tugged at her blue scarf. "I do not like the Da Vennen. They... helped Aeryk during the rebellion."

Keston's attention went to Breen's scarf, and he paled. "You're... Thalric Haldrayne's daughter, aren't you?"

"Loyal unto the leaves." Breen turned from the window.

Keston whistled, low and soft. "Then you hate them even more than I do."

Another finger's width of seam gave with a dry, stuttering hiss. Aunia wriggled her fingers through dried leaves, stalks and flowers until a thicker stem poked her. Leiaphae. She pulled it out, bumping some of the flower clusters onto her lap. This one still held more bumpy yellow flowers. Maybe enough for one person to disappear if Aunia could remember the spell that Gaitha and Limi used to shroud.

"What are you digging for in that doll?" Breen's sharp voice caught Aunia's attention. "Explain."

"I don't think Breen's our enemy." Keston moved to the bed and sat at the foot.

Trust? That was a dangerous venture. Aunia pulled out another piece of Leiaphae, dropped it beside her, and shifted to cover it with her knee.

Breen padded to the side of the bed.

"It's okay," Keston whispered.

Aunia bit her lip and returned to widening the hole in the stitching. ""Edvaras created magic flowers. This one helps with shrouding."

"Shrouding?" Breen said.

"Make invisible," Keston said.

Breen whistled low. "How?"

Aunia frowned. This was part of the plan that was shaky. In her village, Leiaphae would be placed in pots along the village periphery, and Gaitha... now Limi would activate the magic with power words. There certainly was not enough Leiaphae to encircle a room, but that shouldn't matter because she wouldn't be staying stationary either. "I think if I hold the flower and speak certain words, it should work."

"Should?" Breen asked sharply. "Will it mute your footsteps?"

Another wave of tightness gripped Aunia's midsection. "I don't know, but... I can't go with the Da Vennen."

"Aunia," Keston glanced at Breen. "We're not going to let you go with the Da Vennen."

"Indeed," Breen huffed. "She's our prisoner. Not theirs. And she... she has the means to help the Queen. I don't think Frehn will allow—"

"Frehn won't." The Hauser commander stood inside the doorframe, and his dark eyes measuring Aunia.

Aunia set the poppet down. "Then you believe me?"

"You are too erratic. An unknown. But I believe them." Frehn glanced over his shoulder, presumably at Mathias and Fallo, who remained in the common room. "Breen, go back to the stable. Get all the pegasi saddled."

Breen straightened and glanced at Keston. "And Revellie?"

"She has a mighty spirit." Frehn turned his attention to Keston. "I think she's the strength to fly out of the city at least. Yes?"

Keston winced, and his yellowish glow grayed. "She can do that much."

"They'll be after us just as soon as they see us leave," Mathias' voice sounded behind Frehn.

"We'll be safe in the tower," Frehn said. "And Revellie can recover more before—"

"Da Vennen attacked Eddac Tower." Mathias appeared behind Frehn, and sidestepped into Aunia's bedroom. "They were waiting for us when we escaped Dalin."

"They said you attacked them," Frehn said. "With no provocation..."

"Wererats were waiting at Eddac," Keston said. "Some of them Da Vennen too."

Frehn's dark eyes went wide. "What?"

"Wererats in bear cloaks fighting beside their human counterparts," Keston said. "We buried enough of them to know—"

"There's more than one band of wererats," Mathias said.

"And dark fae," Keston said. "Didn't you say kobolds? And then there was the horde of whisperers."

Frehn's jaw clenched as if he were weighing his words.

"Ask Taf if you don't believe." Mathias waved his hand at Frehn's pinched brows. "And Aunia knows pegasi talk. She hears them on her own."

Aunia blinked. Both Mathias and Keston had warned her several times that she had to keep her abilities hidden. Mathias had blurted one of those things out.

"She could be a future flyer," Breen said.

Keston leaned forward. "I've said the same thing."

Frehn's expression turned distant. It was the same expression Mathias or Keston used when they were conversing with their pegasi. But she couldn't hear Frehn's pegasus.

"We'll head for the Pardonway," Frehn said. "Breen. Go. And prepare your Korthalee for two. The girl will ride with you."

"Aunia has a flower that might make her invisible," Breen said. "Might make it easier to sneak off."

"It's a flower Edvaras made," Mathias quickly said.

"And she's from Edvaras' village," Fallo said.

Aunia frowned, half surprised that Fallo wanted her to escape as well.

"Edvaras' village exists," Frehn whispered. "Would you be able to find it again?"

The tiny branches from the Leiaphae stalk jabbed at Aunia's knee. She hid the discomfort. Better they didn't know how much Leiaphae she dug out. Enough for one. Maybe two. That is... if she could make it work at all.

"I don't know," Mathias said. "They used this shrouding flower to make their entire village invisible."

"How does it work?" Frehn asked. "Breen, go."

Breen nodded and left the room.

"There isn't much here. I'm hoping it's enough." Aunia tried to ignore the nausea rising in her stomach. "But if I hold it. Say the spell words. This is... ingredient magic, isn't it?"

Frehn tilted his head. "How much other magic do you use?"

"She's not been raised in Tamore." Mathias said. "And she was apprenticed with their Dar there."

"*Their* Dar?" Frehn said.

"They've a Chand crystal wall surrounding their village," Mathias said. "Just like Zeller's stories. Edvaras' descendants have access to that power."

Aunia frowned. The power that the Eldest Daughter wielded came more from the Naoma and Edvaras stones—two fist-sized Chand ice stones embedded with Edvaras' three magical flowers—than the blue wall. And Fallo had stolen one. Aunia rocked forward. She wanted to confront him, demand where it was. Mathias had talked her out of it when they were at the caravan. But now...

Mathias stepped beside the bed and mouthed, "Wait until we're free of here."

More time for Fallo to keep ahold of a piece of her village. She *would* get it back. And she'd also figure out how to find Kai-Marin, but first things were first. Like getting out of here.

CHAPTER TEN

LEAVING YESTERDAY BEHIND

Yesterday's memories can be a sweet and painful path to tread. But I've been told all my life that if you remain there too long, life will surely pass you by. — Wendalin Mensani, Dar apprentice to Dar Syrick

Frehn is bespeaking Nyrissa, Tafiriel sent to Mathias.

A familiar pain, like a bruise pushed against from the center of his chest, made Mathias slow. Nyrissa—his mentor's daughter and Dar-elect, in charge of all pegasi commanders and towers—blamed him for her father's death.

She had been like a big sister to him once, and he missed that. However, that cold, shuttered look she had given him the last time when she commanded his banishment... When he returned to Tatia, he'd have to face her. Face her again with the disgrace of arrest. On the Harp, what would his own father think?

Mathias shuddered and stepped back into the common room.

But if he could show her proof...show all of them ... that Arch Vicar Bibb had been on the Bellow grounds when Dar Zeller died... How else could Bibb's witchcompass be so powerful? He'd have to have pocketed Dar Zeller's Chand ice amulet. Bibb was using it now. Mathias just had to prove it.

Warn, Frehn. Tafiriel's voice broke into Mathias' thoughts. *The eavesdropper.*

Ice slid down Mathias' back. Another thing wrong. Mathias had tried to apologize to Aunia for the kiss and she had rebuffed him. Told him it didn't matter. Mathias refrained from touching his mouth where that kiss yet lingered.

Now this. He had told Frehn about the danger, and the commander obviously didn't believe him. But Frehn's action endangered all of them. Mathias hurried to the window. "Commander Frehn. We can't bespeak across the miles."

Frehn turned from the tall window that Jovaryn had opened earlier and threw Mathias a venomous glare. "Faery repellant and a flower to turn one invisible. Nyrissa wants proof of these magic flowers."

Mathias stiffened. He wanted to talk Frehn into going to Spatelly... but he needed to show Frehn Jaia seeds? His pulse raced. Copies of Jaia seeds that had disappeared?

Spatelly later, Taf sent back. *Leave Worley first.*

Aunia stepped by Mathias's side and gripped his wrist. Imploring him to be careful or seeking comfort? Mathias wasn't sure. He covered her hand with his own, grateful she wasn't shying away from him.

Frehn's lips tightened into a thin line. "I must see proof before we gather at Moonstepper."

Mathias blinked. Moonstepper was the hostel on the Pardonway where spelled trees—ones that could rend the disloyal apart—hadn't been cut back. But if the eavesdropper knew where they were going... It could be the safest place they could go.

Keston coughed. "Will Breen be alright with—"

"She'll see the wisdom of it," Frehn said.

Aunia tightened her grip on his arm. She had to be scared. And that thought alone made Mathias wish it were possible to leave Frehn and his Hauser flyers behind. It would be to Tamore's benefit. But he couldn't. The oath of a flyer meant following the chain of command. If he didn't... Mathias shuddered.

Maybe he could convince Frehn after they were safely at Moonstepper.

Mathias shifted on his feet while Frehn opened the window, stuck his head out, and examined the inn's exterior.

Revellie would still need rest. Reasonably safe space. Going back and forth to Spatelly would take maybe two days. And saving Tatia and Tamore grief... That certainly was a small price to pay.

"I'm still waiting, Mathias." Frehn pulled his head back inside.

"You'll be able to walk all of us to the stable?" Mathias patted Aunia's hand, noting she also held a Leiaphae stalk.

"No," Frehn said. "I'll take Keston and our soon to be shrouded guest. Aunia, isn't it?"

She nodded.

"You will stay right beside me, will you not?" Frehn said. "I don't know what oath holds you, but—"

"I need to stay near Mathias," she said.

Frehn raked Mathias with a gaze that took him soles to cap. "My unit, me, and Aunia will fly out. Revellie will go with us riderless. With your word. No escapes. Otherwise, we keep a gold pegasus and a young girl."

"I'm a flyer," Mathias said.

"We all are," Fallo rumbled. "We serve the Queen."

Keston also nodded his agreement.

"I'll have your Tafiriel and Paderro land on the roof," Frehn continued. "It's a bit flatter on this wing. You can manage getting up there. No?"

Mathias swallowed. He well remembered all the aerial drills, particularly the falling ones, performed around the Silver Tower when he was dorming in the capital city. The plummet to earth was far greater there, but the chance to remount was also better. He tightened his jaw. "Of course."

"This Leiaphae," Frehn said. "How long will this spell last?"

Aunia released Mathias' wrist. "I don't know."

You worry about spell words, Taf sent to Aunia. *Become the wind and breathe. Yesterday is there if you allow it to form behind your eyes.*

"And this plant... from Edvaras himself?" Frehn reached for the flower in Aunia's hand. "There's certainly a part of me screaming not to trust anything that rogue created."

Aunia wasn't relinquishing the plant.

Frehn's gaze centered on Mathias' face. "But I remember Zeller and his desire to find Edvaras' village."

"And we found it." Fallo stepped beside the hearth and leaned against it.

"We did." Mathias' voice came out thick. "Starcharts were there but destroyed. But we came away with some souvenirs. The Jaia seeds and this."

Mathias plucked the Leiaphae from Aunia's hand, the bumps of its stalk digging into his thumb, and held it out to Frehn. The commander reached for it. And the Leiaphae vanished. It was simply gone.

Aunia's quiet intake of breath beside him cut like a knife.

No. No. No. Mathias stared at where the flower had been.

Frehn dropped his hand. "Was that supposed to happen?"

The plan. Their way out. There wasn't even the tiniest flake of the dried flower.

"I take it no." Frehn paced. "I don't want to sleep everyone. Nyrissa certainly won't like that."

Mathias closed his eyes. There was much that Nyrissa wasn't going to like. "You can't tell her. Not here. The eavesdropper."

"Eavesdropper. A magical one. Exactly how far is the range of this so-called eavesdropper?" Frehn demanded.

"Taf believes we're fine if we don't go beyond the distance between where we are and the stable. Closer is better. The greater the distance, the more chance we're overheard."

Morganstee bespeaks me, Taf sent. *To confirm what you've said.*

Frehn tapped again at his chin. "It'll draw the truth from every cloak and shadow should we bring so many falling to a "sleeping sickness.""

"Plague comes with a contagion," Keston said. "Why not this as well?"

Frehn leveled a glare at Keston.

Keston raised both hands, palms out. "I know. Zeller warned me about sleeping. But one that's light and quickly over? We just need to..."

Frehn's glare halted Keston's words.

"What does it matter?" Aunia asked.

"It matters because we take away free will," Breen said. "For people to choose to do right or wrong."

"Yes, and most of us want the mundanes to believe the pegasi are simply horses with wings," Mathias murmured. He turned to Aunia. "It keeps them safer. It's why we lie."

Keston wrinkled his nose. "Lie is such a strong term. We let them believe what they wish."

Frehn shook his head. "Maybe we could get her into different clothes. Mathias?"

Mathias balled his fists, wishing he could squeeze all his failures away. "My saddlebag has disappeared."

"Mine's still in the stable," Keston said.

Frehn's eyes turned distant for a moment. "Mathias, why is your saddle missing?"

"We..." Mathias ran a hand through his hair. Things he had manifested in the Court of Pavari were being unmade. He was afraid to look at his sword, which should be near the couch.

"Saddlebag and saddle missing. And the flower." Frehn took a menacing step forward. "You don't even have this faery repellent, do you? You expect me to risk my office as commander of Hauser Tower. Throw away the goodwill of all nobles perhaps for all flyers on—"

BAM. BAM. BAM.

Someone was at the door.

Mathias' limbs went cold as if his blood had forgotten how to move. "It's too early."

Aunia huddled against his back. And Frehn, his mouth tightened into a thin line, strode to the door.

Taf, get ready to sleep everyone here except Aunia, myself and Keston, Mathias sent.

You want me to sleep flyers? Taf's voice sounded startled in Mathias' head.

To save Aunia? Yes.

The door swung open. Mathias braced.

Cassian and a servant woman a little older than Aunia stood on the other side of the door.

Frowning, Frehn waved them in and shut the door. "Lord-son. The purpose of your visit?"

"Doing a favor for my friend... even though he's a terrible friend." Cassian crossed the room to Mathias while the dark-haired servant in her unbleached linen chemise and a rough-spun brown kirtle, remained still near the door.

Mathias shifted uneasily. Taking on Cassian wouldn't be too difficult. He had no advantage in height or weight, but Mathias also remembered Cassian playing dirty in the exercise yard at Wolfe's Eye. "Are you here for your father?"

Cassian rolled his eyes. "You never did see clear, have you? Nor listened to my words."

"Cassian," Frehn said. "Your purpose?"

Cassian pointed to Aunia. "And all for a girl. Though I can't imagine you'll continue with the...um...politics when you return to Tatia."

Aunia stepped beside Mathias, fire in her eyes.

Mathias widened his stance.

Cassian raised his hands, palms out. "I'm figuring you'd want to get her out. I brought a maid to swap clothes with your pretty companion. Darla, of course, will expect to keep her frock."

The maid stepped forward, eyeing Aunia's blue gown.

Aunia clasped Mathias' hand.

Fallo pushed off from the hearth. "And the guarantee she or you won't betray us?"

"The three pieces of silver you'll be giving her," Cassian said. "Oh, and she'll show you the crawl space up to the attic."

Mathias frowned. "Why would we—"

"There's an opening leading straight to the roof from there," Darla, the maid, said.

CHAPTER ELEVEN

BENEATH THE DISGUISE

You can wrap yourself in a hundred guises, but that will never change the rhythm of your heart. — Keston Pendar, flyer of Revellie

Aunia allowed the servant to help her with the sleeveless kirtle dress, pulling it over her head and settling the wool yardage over her hips. The fabric prickled through the thin linen chemise, but it smelled of lavender soap and ash.

"Lift your hair," Darla said.

Aunia complied, and Darla, with practiced fingers, tightened the back laces.

"You almost done?" Mathias asked through the boys' bedroom door. He, Keston, Cassian, Fallo, and Frehn all awaited her. "There's barely fifteen minutes left."

"You may enter, young master." Darla yanked a final tug on the laces and tied a bow near Aunia's mid-back.

The door swung open, and Mathias entered. He gave Aunia a once-over, his jaw tightening. "We'll find you better before we get to Tatia."

Darla stepped in between the two twin beds where a small mirror hung on the wall. The maid twisted her dark hair into a braid, then coiled that at her nape. After that, she tucked her midnight hair under a linen cloth. Linen made from the bottom inches from Aunia's chemise. Aunia stiffened. The chemise that Darla now wore, along with Aunia's blue gown.

The gown, manifested from the faery world in the court of Pavari, hugged Darla's curvy figure. It did nothing, however, to soften the shadows clinging to the woman's cheekbones. It was something, though Aunia didn't want to admit that. She also didn't want to admit how much she wanted her dress back.

"How far is the entry to the crawlspace?" Mathias' gaze was only on Darla.

The maid turned, hands gliding over the gown's smoothness. "Down the hallway just a bit."

Cassian appeared in the doorframe. "The guards my father came with are guarding the steps. You'll have to go by them. Maybe with Frehn and our servant girl... Darla, didn't you bring something to tuck her blonde hair in?"

Darla frowned and shook her head.

Cassian rolled his eyes. He reached into his satchel, which hung cross-bodied, and pulled out an ink-stained rag about the width of the serving platter but longer. He snapped it first, then handed it to Aunia.

She took it with a grimace. And then Darla was there, pulling the cloth from her fingers and tying it onto Aunia's head. She bunched Aunia's hair into a ponytail and wedged it up under. The cloth smelled of ink, metallic and sour blood left out too long in the sun. It prickled on her scalp. For a moment, Aunia felt drawn back to Gaitha's apothecary house with fingers stained black at the cuticles... her back stiff from hours bent over a parchment page. A favorite punishment of Gaitha's… making Aunia copy old histories about Dagel Demons.

"You didn't mention guards before," Frehn said from out in the common area.

"I'm saying now," Cassian said. "I'll cause a disturbance right after you and Aunia get to the bottom of the stairs. Get their eyes on me so they won't notice Darla, Mathias, and the others hurrying down the hall."

Mathias shot Aunia an encouraging smile, then his gaze returned to Darla.

Aunia kept her arms tight at her sides, but she flexed her fingers. She wanted to cross the space between herself and Mathias. Lean into him so she could ignore the scratchy, smelly clothes. But he looked so distant. Like he didn't even want to see her. But they had to stay together. Did he not remember Zevara's geis while they were in Pavari? They stay together or they were transported back to the faery world.

Zevara's distance is more mindset than physical, Tafiriel sent.

You know that for certain? Aunia shot back.

"One more thing," Cassian continued. "Darla's been told she gets to leave Worley as well. Ride on a pegasi."

Mathias spun. "We're already needing to—"

"Pegasi on the roof is safer than jumping out the window and hoping you'll catch the saddle," Frehn interrupted. "We agree."

"Keston goes with us," Fallo said.

Frehn narrowed his eyes, then shrugged. "We still have Revellie."

Aunia stiffened. Would Mathias be flying with Keston? Or Darla?

"Aunia, let's go," Frehn said.

She bit her lip and walked to the Hauser commander.

"Wait," Mathias stepped in Aunia's way. He wrinkled his nose at her, then cupped her cheek. Kissed her on the forehead. "Be careful."

She bit her lip. Nodded. And brushed past him. She didn't want him to notice her eyes had gone wet.

She crossed into the common room, where Keston sidled up to her. "Keep your head down and remember this is Kankari night. The sun will be down soon. Most are thinking about their own enjoyment, not if you belong. Just behave naturally in the role that you're playing."

Cassian opened the door and gave a brief nod to Darla, who stood by the chaise...now devoid of the sleeping child.

Aunia glanced back at Mathias. He stood near Keston with his dark hair, slightly damp with sweat, curling around his face and neck. He nodded at her, and her shoulders folded around the pang in her chest. And then she, Frehn, and Cassian exited the room.

Their footfalls creaked against the dark wood planks covering the long and narrow hallway. They passed heavy oak doors; each fitted with iron latches and bearing a metal room number. Periodically, candles flickered from newly hung iron wall sconces. The salamander lights—glass tubes with imprisoned fire salamander faeries—were gone.

They approached a waist-high long railing where a stairwell ran parallel to the hallway. And almost immediately Aunia counted Lord Lyle's five guards standing watch. Or rather, they were leaning and talking amongst themselves.

Aunia kept close to Cassian and Frehn.

"Oy," one guard said. "That's not the same one who came up with you."

"How many tankards of ale have you had, Bran?" Cassian said.

Another guard straightened, hand going for his dagger hilt. He barely touched it before all five of them blinked in unison and toppled over boneless. They hit the floor, snoring.

Cassian turned to Frehn, blinked a few times, and traced a seven-pointed star over his heart. "Thanks be to the Eaburrai Court. I have been spared from the sleeping sickness."

"Yes, thanks be to the Eaburrai Court," Frehn murmured.

The three of them maneuvered past the sleeping bodies while Darla, Mathias, Keston, and Fallo hurried along the hallway past the stairwell to the west side of the inn. Wherever Darla was taking them so they could get to the attic crawlspace. Darla, head held high, walked too close to Mathias.

"Aunia," Frehn hissed. "Come on."

Aunia tried to make eye contact with Mathias, but he kept going.

A hand caught her wrist. Cassian. "We need to keep moving."

Aunia kept her fingers curled around the wooden railing as they descended. Footsteps echoed on the stairwell, but the third-floor faded behind them. Passed the second-floor landing. Turned. Descended. Here, the yellowing walls were camouflaged with dozens of ornately framed paintings. Faded landscapes with flaking paint. Portraits of dour men and women who seemed to glare as Aunia passed by. It felt like Aunia was stepping through someone else's memory.

She paused at the painting of Olivia and the Boggleman. The Boggleman with no scar across his face. Both eyes were intact. He was now trapped within Nonderu without his faery-eating cloak. And Olivia was no longer trapped within the Chand ice column. She'd been freed...by death. Aunia hurried down the stairs to the first floor.

"You could hold her hand as you pass the giggle hallway." Cassian stepped off the stairs and turned. "She's dressed like a low ender."

"I'll say she is escorting me to speak to Craymore. I don't like the quality of the feed for our pegasi." Frehn stepped off the stairs.

"That'll get you to the dining room at least." Cassian gave Aunia a quick bow. "I can't be seen by my father, but I wish you luck."

He then disappeared around a corner.

Aunia glanced at the ceiling above. The metal poles and salamander lights were gone here as well. Frehn waved her to him, and she complied.

They entered the dining room, where several groups ate meat pies, stuffed trout, and poached pears. Or they simply talked while holding prettily painted cups.

Her stomach quivered. She hadn't eaten since the night before... except for the accidental taste of wine that she had licked from her finger.

Baron Chazelle sat in the center of the dining hall with the older lady with bells in her hair and two others. He was oblivious that other diners had lowered utensils and stared. "It'll be fine. We're promised front-row seats for the execution and—"

The baron swiveled to face Aunia. She quickly bowed her head and matched pace with Frehn. If they were caught... Stars. All she wanted was to stay hidden at Mathias' side, only Darla had taken her place.

A watering hole can be a dangerous place, but to avoid danger means dying of thirst, Taf sent.

Several more steps and they exited through double doors into the broad alcove, and into a narrow hallway with raised paneled walls.

More candle lights flickered on the wall sconces. Yesterday's fire salamander lights were gone but the giggling, female and male voices, were not.

Frehn quickened their pace. "I apologize for the necessity of traveling through here."

Aunia shrugged, her voice low. "Velli would find out-of-the-way places to wile away hours with boys from the village."

Frehn raised an eyebrow.

"I never. I was always waiting for... well, Edvaras and Naoma... They knew true love." Aunia grimaced, remembering when she found the village's founder and his mate locked inside Chand ice in the Boggle-man's underground grotto.

Finding Edvaras and Naoma should have been marked by awe, but surviving had been the focus. And now Edvaras and Naoma had escaped and disappeared. Maybe they were now back at the village they'd abandoned centuries before. Maybe her foster-sister Limi had been relieved of leadership as Eldest Daughter. "I never thought I'd find a beading."

They passed by several doors, most shut tightly. A few slightly ajar.

"Beading?" Frehn asked.

"I think you call it marriage."

Frehn's brows furrowed. Like he didn't know what to say. Why was she telling him this? She sucked in a breath. When she was talking, she wasn't hearing the giggling.

"Not to anyone specific," she offered. She and Mathias. Tenderness, calm, joy, and fear reared through her body. She loved him, but after she found her father... then what? "Edvaras and Naoma exchanged beads because they knew. You pick wisely, or you suffer. You're alone. Or worse, with the wrong one."

Shushing her, Frehn slowed the pace. A side door opened with a groan, and a short, furry man exited. Craymore, the innkeep. The one who exchanged his people for salamander lights. A strangled whine lodged inside Aunia's throat. And behind one of these doors was Lord Lyle.

Frehn yanked Aunia against the wall, covering her body with his own. Too close. The leather and feather dust smell was familiar, but not his scent. She recoiled tighter against the wall. He was not Mathias.

"Oy," Craymore called. "That's for the gigglerooms."

Frehn grunted, sliding Aunia toward the nearest door while keeping her covered with his body.

Hurried footsteps sounded behind them, and another voice pierced the hallway. "Master! Lord Lyle's guards are sleeping at the top of the stairs."

"Oh, for pity's sake." Craymore hurried toward the new voice. "Get pepper leaf tea a-brewing. I don't want the lord disturbed because his lads imbibed a few too many."

Frehn tugged her toward the hall's exit. They'd gone a few steps when another sound rose. Aunia hesitated. That wasn't giggling. It was crying and it came from the nearest closed door. A large pebble-stone lodged into Aunia's throat.

"Need to keep going," Frehn breathed. He pulled her firmly.

"What's in these rooms?" Aunia demanded.

"Regret." Frehn's expression was filled with disgust and pity. Not directed at her but at the door. "Move."

A large heart is desirable, Tafiriel sent. *But there are times you can only look after your own herd.*

Aunia bit her lip. She wanted to insist they help whoever was on the other side of the door.

"Think of Mathias," Frehn muttered. "Come on."

Mathias. She allowed Frehn to pull her along but she kept her fists curled and her jaw tight.

They exited the inn's side door. Across the large yard, dozens of Da Vennen sang violent songs. Some rattled the bars to the gate. A fair distance from the bear-cloaked men and inside the Green Harpy's property, stood some of the folk who had complained to Lord Lyle.

She and Frehn hurried to the brown-stoned stable, which stood beside and slightly behind the inn. They were halfway there when a glimmer, a jeweled circle set mere feet from the stable, caught Aunia's eye. Its oddness sent icy prickles up her spine.

She ran, forcing Frehn to stretch his legs. They entered the stable with its hay-lined stalls, each neatly partitioned with dark timber slats. Dry hay, leather, and a body-warm richness filled her nose. How many times had she hidden in a stable? It felt both comforting, and it made her feel alone. She wished Jennium were nearby.

Breen tossed a saddle blanket over a dark blue pegasus with streaks of starlight silver across his upper wing bones.

"But it's Kankari Eve. And a perfect night. You have to stay," said a wiry and dust-smudged stableboy. He was talking to Breen's back.

"Forget it, chap," said a flyer with a dark brown braid. It hung to the center of his back. Murtagh. One of the flyers who had escorted Aunia and Mathias into their suite earlier in the day. "She is the fire in the high hall, and you aren't equipped to strike flint."

"Found a loaner." A second stable boy emerged from the back room, which was nestled near a ladder and a loft. "But I'm not sure Craymore will—"

"Trust his tower flyers to bring it back?" Breen exited the stall and stepped into the corridor. "Commander, best option is to put a horse saddle on Mathias' pegasus."

The second stableboy walked the horse saddle over. Breen took it and strode to Tafiriel.

The first stableboy shuffled to a knot of other flyers. "Hey, can I have my wineskin back now?"

A flyer with coppery brown hair held the wineskin up over his head. "I will if you cluck like a chicken."

The boy clucked and Frehn yelled. "Rowan."

"Commander?" Rowan's eyes went wide and he quickly handed the skin back. "Didn't mean any harm."

"You didn't drink any of that, did you?"

Rowan flushed. "No. Of course we didn't."

"Move. We need to be ready to go," Frehn said.

"Commander," Breen called from Tafiriel's pen. "You want to saddle up the prisoner's pegasus?"

CHAPTER TWELVE
SMUGGLED WORDS

Every variable is accounted for...nearly. There is always risk, but risk is just another problem to solve — Darla Valesco, servant girl at the Green Harpy

No room number marked the unadorned door at the end of the hallway. Darla opened it, waving them inside. Mathias, followed by Keston, and Fallo entered a small storeroom. The raised paneling running chest-high along the room declared that it had not always been for storage, but it was small for a single bedroom.

A multitude of shelves lined the walls. Some held fresh linens, thick green blankets, and fat pillows. Others carried candles, spare lanterns, and, presumably, lamp oil housed in gallon-sized glazed ceramic pots. One set slightly apart from the others held garlands, banners, paper mache harpy wings, and long ribbons in a variety of colors.

Darla hurried to a waist-high stack of clean chamber pots and pressed the wooden panel beside it. It gave with a snick, and the panel swung open, revealing a constricted space and a set of narrow stairs. The boy that Lord Lyle insisted on taking could have easily gone up these stairs. Mathias wasn't sure he could.

Darla's dark eyes flicked over each of them. "Shall I go first?"

Mathias swallowed down the claustrophobic weight crushing his midsection. Better to climb this minuscule space with no bodies ahead of him. "I will."

"I'll go next." Keston flashed Mathias a gentle smile.

Mathias set his hands on the dusty stairs and set his foot on the first step. One. Two. His back scraped along the panel frame, and he was inside the walls. Three. Four. Thuroes, Eaburrai I was born under, help me. This space was barely wide enough for his hunched-in shoulders. The walls pressed in. Threatened to crush his arms, his back, his skull into a pancake.

No, he could do this. Five. Six. His heartbeat thundered in his ears. Seven. He reached for the next step, and his hand shook.

Better to think about Aunia. Please watch over her, Thuroes. He hoped no one exited the giggle rooms as she and Frehn passed by them. On the harp, if Lord Lyle exited at the wrong time... He shouldn't have touched the Leiaphae. He made it disappear. Yasendra be blessed, why had it disappeared? He refrained from touching the hilt of his sword even as the sheath's tip scraped over the wooden stairs.

Behind Mathias, Keston mounted the stairs. His friend had granted him extra space despite Darla urging them to hurry.

Panic clawed at Mathias' chest.

You're almost there, Taf sent. *Almost in open sky.*

What number was he on? Twelve? How many stairs could there be? Yasendra, please let the attic be bigger.

Mathias sucked in dusty hot air. His body screamed to go back. But he'd have to get past Keston and the others on the stairs. And he'd be endangering Aunia. He had to keep moving forward. There was no choice. Fifteen. Sixteen.

The scraping wall finally receded, and he hauled himself into the attic crawlspace on his hands and knees. The dusty beams overhead, along with rough planks remaining inches above his head, forced him to keep his head down. However, compared to the narrow stairs behind him, this was like stepping into open sky. Almost. Sort of. No, not at all.

Mathias scuttled ahead. Thankfully, early evening daylight filtered through the window slats at the corridor's end. It would be worse if it were dark.

"The opening is about three-fourths of the way back," Darla called, presumably behind Keston.

Mathias reached the crawlspace's halfway point and slowed. Crates, burlap-wrapped bundles, and narrow chests lashed shut with cords, sat on either side of him. "What's stored here?"

"Supplies," Darla said. "Mostly things that Craymore doesn't want other eyes to see."

Smuggling? Mathias shifted on his elbows, rough boards scraping his sleeves. He twisted back to glance at Darla, who crawled behind Keston. He could just make out her linen-wrapped head and the dark-hair peeking out. If Craymore was smuggling, flyers had a duty to stop it. His left shoulder hit something hard. Falling items crashed around him. A stack of dusty ledgers glanced off of his left arm. Dust rose. Mathias coughed. The taste was sharp and stale, like cobwebs and chalk.

Another box hit the floor. Split open. Folded letters spilled out. So, did a steel stylus wrapped in silver cord, along with packets of blue dust.

Mathias shuffled some papers back, pausing when his hands touched a small painting. This one was of a mermaid dancing atop the stormy waves, like how Kai-Marin was depicted on older murals. But this figure held a silver-painted vanity mirror. It was unusually glittery. He set the painting on the ledgers.

"Just push that all aside," Darla said. "We can't linger."

Mathias frowned, holding his hands out to scoop... then stopped. He picked up a folded letter and stared at the spidery script. It read, 'Thread must be bound to ice before the Dama star rises.'

When the Dama star rises? What augury script was this? A shiver ran through him as he remembered Mollie Mae's words, 'You've noticed the star move?'

He flipped over the vellum sheet and read, '...shatters if the ice isn't anchored by a counterweight of living magic.'

A crude diagram—an upward curve dotted with marsh symbols—rose over these new words.

"Matty," Keston called. "You okay up there?"

"Um...yeah," Mathias said.

"You...um... conjured a light."

Mathias turned his head. His egg-shaped white light glowed there but he hadn't asked Taf to conjure it. Yes, he wanted to rummage through more of the vellum sheets, but they had to go. Clenching his jaw, he shoved the paper he held and two more, along with the stylus, inside his jerkin. He pushed the rest aside.

Taf, he growled.

The light vanished, leaving the space in greater darkness.

Sunlight leaked through the ceiling up ahead. Mathias picked up his crawling pace until he was directly under the hatch, which lay flush against the ceiling. He rose, banging his knee against a long iron pole lying nearby. He cursed softly, unhooked a simple iron latch, and pushed the hatch open. The wood creaked, and cooler air mixed with chimney smoke, breathed in. Mathias hastened onto the rooftop.

Keston was next up, and then Darla. Mathias pulled her out child-fashion. Last came Fallo. He shut the wooden hatch and grinned wryly at a bolted fastener jutting from the middle of the hatch. Two inches in diameter, it was... like the iron pole below.

"Smuggler lantern rig?" Fallo said, turning to Darla.

Keston half-stood, balancing on the low pitch of the roof. He peered westerly toward the river. "Light the way for guests in the middle of the night and signal all clear?"

Mathias lifted higher on his knees. The inn's height, three stories plus, gave an adequate view of the island city's western side. A few buildings stood between the Green Harpy and the water, including several stone-block warehouses that pressed themselves against the city's wall. Past that lay the wide Wythrindle River and the western dock. Two large cargo ships, and twenty-some river skiffs and fishing boats were moored. Lanterns were being lit preparing for evening to surrender to night.

And the broken western bridge...its stone piers jutted up like broken off snake teeth. Lord Lyle had never repaired the bridge after the king-consort's rebellion, though it made sense why Lyle had originally ordered it destroyed. Today, travelers crossed a makeshift wooden bridge... one that needed replacing with every flood.

"Simple way to signal, yes," Darla said and eyed Mathias. "There are those who don't want information about the augury to come to light. And Craymore is a student of—"

"He's interested in prophecy?" Mathias interrupted. The desire washed over him to go back for more spilled contents below.

"All in Worley are." Darla's melodious voice honeyed. "After all, what would you expect from a city that stood beside the Queen?"

"Mathias," Keston called. He had moved to the roof's low rise.

Mathias frowned, torn. Who knew what treasure trove lay among the boxes below.

Keston waved a circular 'come here' signal.

Mathias climbed the gentle incline to Keston's side. Beyond, stood dozens of Da Vennen soldiers by the gate, and they were howling at the small crowd of the city's wealthier folk, who awaited the gate being opened. Mathias stiffened. Lyle would be coming up for Aunia in moments if it hadn't happened yet. And the lord would probably call a search party or let the Da Vennen in. Mathias glanced back in the direction of the stable. Frehn had to get flying with Aunia now.

"Hope they all sweat through their heavy bear fur," Keston muttered.

Mathias rapped his thigh with a fist and glared at the enemy. "How's Revellie faring?"

"Well enough for a short solo flight." Keston swept his hand back toward the stable. "Look."

Mathias turned and his heart rose. Flying beside Frehn and his mint-green pegasus with its snow-white wings was Revellie. And past the golden pegasus flew Breen and Aunia on Breen's indigo pegasus. Trailing behind came the other five Hauser flyers. They were all riding the wind toward the western docks.

Aunia was safe. Not snatched at the giggle rooms. Not discovered by Lyle. A roar erupted below. The Da Vennen, fists shaking, had spotted them too.

"Come on," Mathias muttered and slid back toward the hatch. The last thing they needed was to be spotted. *Taf? Where are you?*

A pang hit Mathias, and he scanned the closed stable doors. Surely Frehn hadn't left them to their fate. *Taf?*

A pulsing flash caught Mathias' attention. Left side of the stable. He blinked. A tall man with black hair streaked with white had appeared on the left of the stable, dressed in his beige colored robes. Bibb. And laying in the grass all around him were iridescent portal tiles. Stolen portal tiles. And Bibb had transported in using them. Da Vennen not using magic... that was an outright lie.

Bibb raised his face to the inn's roof, met Mathias' eyes, and smiled. Mathias jolted. And then, Bibb sauntered to the stable with long strides.

"Oh dear. Whatever will we do?" Darla hid her nose and mouth behind cupped hands. Her nervousness sounded like a snicker.

Tafiriel and Paderro burst from the stable. They clattered by Bibb, who was forced to jump aside, and they flew to the roof. Relief washed over Mathias. And then frustration. Instead of a bucket-seated pegasi saddle, Taf wore a horse one. Their hooves clattered on the weathered timber-shingled roof.

"Keston with me," Fallo said.

Mathias blinked. He had assumed Keston would fly with him and Darla with Fallo. There was no time to consider. Bibb was running for the inn.

Keston clambered up behind the commander, and Darla, not looking pleased, turned her attention to Mathias.

Mathias clenched his jaw. He wasn't happy with it either. The last civilian he gave a ride to, other than Aunia, had beat on his heeble-bitten shoulder. A shoulder mostly healed now. Two weeks in mortal time... less than in reality, but flyers healed fast.

Mathias pulled himself onto the horse's saddle. This flight would be more perched than seated. If any projectiles or spells were cast... He held an arm out to help Darla up. "Make sure you hold tight with your thighs. You can hang onto my middle."

It wasn't until Fallo and Keston launched up that her expression softened, and she took his hand. "I'm sure I'll be fine."

She settled behind him; arms wrapped around him. Taf ran across the expanse of the roof, spreading his wings wide.

Bibb's shouts, or maybe it was Da Vennen soldiers, rose from below. Taf's wing strokes muffled any individual words, and they left the Da Vennen and its Arch Vicar behind. Mathias wanted to crow. Instead, he sucked in a deep breath and quietly enjoyed the Green Harpy, the broken bridge, and the river being left behind.

They flew toward the Pardonway Forest with its beach and sycamore trees. It was easily half a duchy or better in size. Surprisingly, little of it had been cut down before Dar Syrick spelled the place to defend against Aeryk's rebellion. He remembered his father saying the forest had always been rumored to be haunted, and it was one of the few times his mother had agreed. Spell only or haunted besides, the Pardonway was perilous unless you stuck by the road. And then there was Moonstepper.

I see them up ahead, Taf sent after they had flown several miles over the leafy canopy.

At first, Mathias could barely make them out. He spotted Breen with Aunia flying near Frehn, and the other flyers flew in a ring formation around Revellie. Were they slowing the pace?

They were. But not to be nice. Revellie was struggling. Her wingbeat grew shallow. Her rhythm staggering. Oh, dear Thuroes, don't let her fall.

Mathias leaned forward, a nonverbal request for more speed. Fallo and Keston on Paderro raced by his side. They grew closer. Revellie's head dipped lower. Ears pinned to her mane. Sweat darkened her gold coat. She dropped several feet.

Keston's anguished cry released adrenaline into Mathias' throat and fists. Paderro dove for Keston's mare. Mathias followed.

Rev fell several more feet. The Hauser unit dove to her, stayed close, but not so close to foul her wings.

Another drop. They were almost there... and then a tiny flash of yellow appeared by Rev's head. Inside that ball of light was... Jennium. Aunia's faery friend. He had seen this tiny figure before when heeble poison ran through his veins. Aunia must have called her. But what could a faery do?

Jennium landed on Revellie's head, the faery's yellow light washing over Rev's gold.

Revellie shuddered. Her wings stuttered... and then, she straightened. Wing strokes growing sure. She dove toward the road below.

Mathias sucked in a long, steadying breath. Had Revellie only been winded? Or... *Is there something more to Aunia's little faery friend? Something I don't know about?*

Faeries can be mysterious things, Taf sent back.

Mysterious? That's all you're going to say. What if I order you to... Mathias paused, instincts prickling. A ringing grew in his ears like someone or something was listening.

Chapter Thirteen
A Road to Battle

There is a look in a man's eyes when riding out to battle. A clear window to his uttermost soul, save for a few. Beware those men who hide behind murk. Or worse. Window dressing. — Frehn Bracae, commander of Hauser Tower and Flyer of Morganstee

Pegasi hooves struck the stone-laid road with sharp, ringing clacks. They echoed into the trees, which stood a few yards back, save for fresh growth and a sea of tree stumps. Aunia frowned. Why had all these trees been cut back?

Frehn's pale green pegasus pranced nervously and the Hauser commander patted his neck and murmured calmly. Keston vaulted off Paderro's back and rushed to Revellie, clasping his arms around his pegasus' neck.

Revellie had almost fallen from the sky. If it hadn't been for Jennium. Golden light from the faery's hand, brighter than the pegasus' gold, surged into Revellie. Steadied her. Though the landing certainly wasn't graceful, Revellie was alright. More than alright. Aunia hadn't known faeries could do that.

Breen's Korthalee remained stoically still, closer to Frehn than the others.

Aunia shifted, working leather buckles to free herself from Korthalee's passenger wind straps, but Breen twisted in the saddle and leaned her weight against Aunia's thigh.

"Stay," Breen said. "We've got troops who'll reach us in an hour."

"But Keston—"

"We'll travel by road. An easy pace," Frehn said from beside Korthalee. "For Revellie."

Mathias guided Tafiriel over to Aunia. *Jennium saved her.*

She... Aunia frowned. Darla sat behind Mathias with her arms wrapped around his waist. Chin against his shoulder.

"Keston," Frehn barked. "Remount. Not Revellie. Back where you were."

Aunia waited for Mathias to protest. To insist that Darla ride with someone else. He didn't.

She clenched her jaw, turned her face to the severed trees, their memorial stumps covering the ground, and the forest beyond. Troops. As they had dove for a landing, Aunia wondered what the long ribbon of grays, browns, and blues passing over the pale, gleaming road was. She did not like the sound of that word 'troops.' "We should hide in the trees. Let them pass us."

"The trees?" Breen choked. "Don't you—"

"She doesn't," Mathias interrupted.

Darla tightened her embrace around Mathias' middle. Heat flared through Aunia's chest.

"She's never seen or heard of the Pardonway," Keston offered as he remounted behind Fallo.

"Never heard of..." Breen frowned. "Edvaras' village. Right."

"Does something live in the trees?" Aunia snapped. Why couldn't they just say instead of treating her like she was stupid? Explain why there was a gap yawning from road to tree line with only tree stumps there.

"We move," Frehn commanded.

"Those trees are spelled to rend apart anyone disloyal to the Queen." Breen rocked her hips forward with practiced ease. Korthalee ambled behind Frehn and Morganstee. "Best you and all of Eddac Tower stay out of them."

Tafiriel took pace beside them, on the right. Aunia forced her glare away from Darla. "But why would trees be spelled?"

"Aeryk's rebellion," Mathias offered. "King-consort. He tried to depose the Queen, and he had, to our great disgust, some nobles who followed him. During the last battle... here on the Pardonway, his troops were intercepted, and Dar Syrick cast a spell on the forest for the trees to rise. It was... well, bloody. After that, no one wanted to go through here, even with a strengthening spell on the road for safety. It disrupted commerce for a while. This is a major thoroughfare."

"What do you mean, a strengthening spell on the road?" Aunia asked.

"First spell conjured on this road was before Queen Didianne's time," Breen said. "There have always been strange things rumored to live here but with Dar Syrick's spell, many thought the road's protection would falter."

"Queen Didianne's time was centuries before." Mathias leaned forward toward Aunia, green eyes soft. "Aeryk's forces thought they were safe marching up to Heavenfeet to attack whatever target they had planned. The road protects."

"I'd wager it would've been the Court of Nobles," Keston said.

"Parliament?" Breen asked.

"Aye," Keston said. "Then up to the travel chambers to Tatia herself. That's what I'd do."

"Then we should all be grateful you are on our side." Breen looked over her shoulder to Keston, who peeked a head out from behind Fallo. "You'll tell us when that changes?"

"I'm a flyer, Breen," Keston said. "I serve Tatia and Tamore."

Aunia closed her eyes. To Tatia. That was where they were going. If she knew where her father was, she could find that magical window that Taya had told her about. She could cross. Rescue him. But the question was where? Mollie Mae said she needed to ask Kai-Marin.

Aunia pulled at her chemise's scratchy neckline while Darla wore *her* gown. She had spent at least an hour imagining that dress before conjuring it from thin air. But gown and her place on Tafiriel? Limi would have told her to be grateful for the help she had received. But it was hard to feel grateful when she'd been robbed. She reached up, untied the dirty cloth wrapped about her head and allowed it to fall onto the road.

If she were riding with Mathias, she'd be asking him what they would do when the troops approached. Darla lifted her eyes to Aunia, smiled, and waved. A bracelet at her wrist jingled.

Aunia's posture sank. Stars, she hated Tamore. How was she going to find Kai-Marin when she couldn't even make any choices on her own? She bit her lip, tears forming behind her eyes. This place was nothing like the stories Caedmon had woven when she visited him in the smithy. And Caedmon was now dead. Heebles had killed him, and she had been exiled.

And Tamore's guiding light? Its beauty and wonder? This place was where guards arrested children because of who their parents were. Where people cried behind closed doors. Where good people were taken for execution because they lived in wagons. Yes, her mother may have been from this place, but Tamore was awful.

And in the distance, boots, hundreds of them, hammered against the stone highway like an uneven heartbeat. Voices, closer and closer, floated on the air.

There is good here too, Tafiriel sent. *This is only one time, one place. Night gives to daylight and winter to spring.*

Aunia sniffled, wanting to slide off Korthalee. Escape into the woods past the eerie tree stumps. Nothing moved in the forest, save a light breeze, but there was a sense of watching. Waiting. Jennium would have told her if the forest was truly dangerous. But the faery had disappeared again. She had called once for the faery, but she didn't return.

"Sit still, will you?" Breen snapped.

Sit still? She needed to find Kai-Marin and save her dad and... knock Darla off Tafiriel's back and... How did she know these soldiers would not bring them harm?

I will protect you, Tafiriel sent.

We all will, sent a deeper silvery voice. Paderro.

Fallo's pegasus had saved them from Da Vennen soldiers the evening before. The problem was she didn't trust his flyer.

"The Queen has ordered troops to secure the Grashbear border," Fallo rumbled. "It's probably nothing more than that."

"I don't trust it," Mathias said. Tafiriel slowed his pace, exiting Aunia's peripheral vision. "Moving forces in mass. This will leave the heartland vulnerable."

"It's what happened during Aeryk's Rebellion," Keston said.

"Shut it, you two," Fallo said.

"Didn't you advise Lyle to send his troops?" Breen asked.

"Breen," Frehn warned. "If we can hear some of their talk, they can hear ours. Keep quiet. File in twos. I'll be the one talking."

"Of course," Breen replied at the same moment the other Hausers gave their assent.

Breen took a position beside Frehn. Tafiriel, Mathias, and Darla stood behind Frehn with Murtagh, the flyer with the long skinny braid. Paderro and his passengers came behind Murtagh and beside the copper-headed flyer who demanded a stableboy to cluck like a chicken. After that came Revellie and three other Hauser flyers.

Aunia chewed on her lip. Lord Lyle had mentioned troops being sent to the Grashbear Mountains. Sent because of heeble and wererat attacks. But not all wererats were evil. Jovaryn wasn't. Neither had been Ryven, whom they left behind in Pavari. She wondered briefly how Basil, with Jovaryn and Mollie Mae, were faring. If they had rescued the captured rovers.

She closed her eyes and forced her breathing to stay even. Please let the soldiers mean no harm.

Dust lifted with the column's synchronized steps, a column that seemed to go on forever. The leaders appeared to be the ones on horseback in the front. One horse, a bay, restless and proud, shook its head, and its tack cut through the air like a snapped chain.

Frehn raised his hand, and all the pegasi halted.

"Shouldn't be in bow range," Mathias muttered from behind her.

Frehn snapped his fingers.

A few more steps and the column halted about six wagon lengths away. Three of the men walked their horses closer. One, a tall man with a dark steel breastplate pocked with tiny dings, rode a dark thick-necked bay. A second with angular features and armor etched in decorative lines rode on a gray gelding. The third, riding an iron-gray mare, was a bulky, broad-chested man. He wore full plate and a fur-lined gorget. They all looked so different, unlike the flyers, who wore similar leather jerkins and britches, even if they each favored different colors. The only thing that these three shared besides riding a horse was the wary confusion glinting in their eyes. The men halted two men's heights away.

"Commander Frehn," the tall man on the thick-necked bay said. "We did not expect a Tower presence on the Pardonway."

"Colonel Varren," Frehn replied with the briefest of nods. "Your orders have never extended to monitoring our movements."

"Of course, of course," Varren said with a hand wave. "Still, ten pegasi on a border road is not a routine patrol."

"Not everything is a routine patrol," Frehn said.

Varren frowned. His eyes flickered to Aunia, and then behind her. "Transporting civilians? I don't recall flyers ever doing such a thing."

"A flyer issue. Not yours," Breen said flatly.

The man in the decorative armor lifted in the saddle. "A response those holding secrets would utter. We will not—"

"Peace, Serel," Varren interrupted.

The third man rubbed his chin. "Talk rears its head. Whispers cry out, and people wonder how trustworthy flyers are. Wonder if they serve the Queen or themselves."

Morganstee and Korthalee flattened their ears. Frehn, however, remained still. "We have no problem with your passing. All of us do our part to protect our fair kingdom."

The third man tipped his head, his gaze going toward Tafiriel. "Lady, wherefore are thee going?"

Lady? Aunia bristled. He was addressing Darla. Darla, who wore *her* gown.

"We had issues on the road." Darla's melodious voice pitched forward. "And these flyers were kind enough to come to the rescue of my servant and me."

"Servant?" Aunia snapped.

"Shut up," Breen hissed. "An insolent thing like you—"

"Should be whipped," said Seren. He brushed his dark hair from his high cheekbones; his gaze like ice.

The hundreds of faces behind the horseman glared at her.

Remain still, Tafiriel sent.

Remain still? Aunia wanted to rip her dress off Darla. Darla was the servant. Not her.

"Was this servant responsible for your lack of horses?" Varren asked Darla.

"Brigands, I'm afraid," Darla laughed airily. "But this tower of flyers frightened them off."

Varren frowned again. "I don't remember Hauser Tower being so large."

"Colonel," Frehn said. "Our business is our own. Do make off. We—"

"Are going where?" Varren asked.

Some of the soldiers shifted. Metal clinked. Varren raised a casual hand, and the soldiers settled into place.

"To Moonstepper, if you must know," Fallo said. "A place to rest before we continue on."

"To?" Varren asked.

Frehn sighed, loud and long. "To report to the Dar-Elect, if you truly must know. Now, do me the courtesy to tell me all your orders."

Varren chewed on Frehn's answer. He nodded. "Good travels then. But have a care. There's an encampment on the Tatian side of Moonstepper. They look motley. Moonstepper will know though, eh?"

"Moonstepper will only know if they are loyal to the Queen," Seren said. "They could still be criminals."

Frehn nodded. He and the other pegasi flyers moved to the side of the road, and the soldiers passed by, a long column of faces with dark expressions. Some angry. Some fearful. Some resigned. It seemed like forever, and then the leaders proceeded behind the column.

Seren, before he passed them, gave Aunia a once-over. "See that you learn how to remain silent when your betters are speaking."

CHAPTER FOURTEEN

MOONSTEPPER

Place looks like the forest tried to eat it and gave up halfway. Can't say I blame it—what happened here left a stink that even the trees remember — Breen Haldrayne of Hauser Tower, flyer of Korthalee

The rest of the way to Moonstepper was uneventful... if counting Aunia's cool anger as that.

Mathias lay on his back atop a pinewood framed bunk, its wool-stuffed mattress flattened with age. It was probably slightly more comfortable than the ground itself. But it had a less musty smell than most of the other thirty mattresses inside the bunkroom. And, more importantly, it was near Aunia.

He rolled onto his side facing Aunia's bunk. She had taken a top one against the wall, and the aisle between them was wide enough for a man to wriggle through sideways. If he slid to the edge of his bed and stretched, he could touch her. Not that he would. She'd likely scream given the mood she was in. And she had to be exhausted. That had to be part of her angry demeanor. It was a relief to see the curve of her face relaxed in slumber. The tenseness gone. Well, except for her fists curled around the scratchy wool blanket and her perfect bow mouth drawn in a disapproving line. She looked... small. Not weak. Never that. But vulnerable. The ache in his chest twisted.

He knew she hadn't been happy when she had seen Darla riding behind him on Tafiriel. Not that he had a choice. Fallo had insisted on flying with Keston. But after they landed on the Pardonway? He should have insisted that Breen exchange passengers and if it was to hold Aunia hostage, to let one of the Hausers give Darla a ride. But he hadn't done any of that. Didn't because he couldn't kick the hive before he talked with Frehn about going back to Spatelly.

I don't like the servant girl either, Taf sent. *Her knees dug in and she leaned into you like you were hers.*

Mathias rolled onto his back and tapped at his small, caged necklace under his linen shirt. A flyer's amulet with a crumb of Chand crystal inside.

Yes, Darla had pressed herself on him and more closely than Aunia ever had. Well, except for when they had left her village for good. Aunia had been crying. *I'll make sure Darla rides with someone else tomorrow.*

Tomorrow. They would probably see more soldiers on the road and in a handful of days, they'd be before Nyrissa and the Queen. Who knew what Bibb could get done during that time. The delay could be too late, particularly knowing that Nyrissa would put it to the council. Even if they said yes to investigating Spatelly, official channels could take weeks.

He cushioned his head with his hand and counted cricket chirps. One unlucky bug had trapped itself inside the timbered wattle and daubed outer wall. Or maybe it was hiding to keep away from the trees.

Mathias shivered. The forest had pulled so close when they drew near to this hostel, branches twitching. And he couldn't tell if the feel of branches against his legs had been coincidental or if a tree had reached out to brush against him, taking his measure. At least no one had been yanked from their saddle. But no one looked comfortable. Except Aunia.

She merely raised her face to the canopy, eyes wide as if a chorus of faeries danced for only her.

She wasn't so wonder-eyed about the hostel's box-shaped construction with a wraparound porch. Everything was weathered and overgrown. The porch itself leaned under the weight of creeping ivy. And the tenting yards on the building's sides had surrendered to wilderness. The growth was only twelve years old. The vegetation said thirty. At least.

But the inside of the hostel and the stable were habitable. Barely.

Mathias sucked in a long slow breath. The stable. Breen had turned waspish, clutching her blue scarf, when they opened the stable to house their pegasi. She even snapped at Aunia as they were forced to walk over a ten-foot-wide spot of blackened earth. But... she had hissed that was where her father had died. The great Thalric Haldrayne who had kept Aeyrk's forces busy until the forest picked them apart. He always thought the man had stood on the Pardonway road when he succumbed.

Mathias sat up. He couldn't sleep. A part of him wanted to leaf through the folded papers he had shoved in his pouch. It and his belt lay at the foot of his bed. The lighting was poor, and thinking about the Dama star... The Dama Star. Mollie Mae had said the star had moved. How close was it tonight to the Harp constellation?

He slid out of his bed, bare feet touching the thin grass mats covering the floor. He tiptoed past three sleeping Hauser flyers, and out into the main hall. Mismatched wooden chairs formed a half circle around a large fireplace.

"But I've heard of you." Darla sat beside Fallo near the hearth and leaned forward to gobble some of his territory. "You're the brave flyer who seeks Edvaras' marble giant. You're looking to fix the augury, aren't you?"

The firelight caught the hard planes on Fallo's face. He leaned further away as if to escape Darla's breath. Murtagh, on the other side of the half-circle of chairs, smirked.

"We've heard about the giant bursting from the Grashbear," Darla continued. "You stood against it. Forced it back under the mountains. You must tell us the story."

Fallo straightened. He scanned Darla from face to toes, and then back again. "We're away from Worley now. How many coins will it cost for you to give the girl back her gown?"

Mathias startled. Darla's curves were more pronounced in the blue gown's formfitting bodice, but Aunia in that dress was the epitome of innocent sweetness. And Fallo was looking out for Aunia. Was that so strange? Fallo had raised his voice on Aunia's behalf before. Despite his threatening to behead Aunia's dad in front of her.

But Fallo had threatened Rune because of Rune's deeds that cost Aunia's mom her life. And while Fallo never admitted it, he'd been in love with that woman. He had to have been. Maybe that was why the commander was sometimes protective of the daughter. It was the only thing that made sense.

"Sacrificing noble goodwill to keep the girl out of Da Vennen's hands," Darla mused. "Who and what is she?"

A creak snapped from the other side of the fire. Murtagh, readjusting himself in the chair. "I'd like to hear that one meself."

Fallo frowned. "She's someone who has knowledge the Queen will..."

Mathias hadn't made a noise, but Fallo swiveled to face him, his expression tight. Then it mutated into relief. "What are you doing up, lad? Come. Join us at the fire."

Mathias shook his head. "I need to go outside."

"For why?" Murtagh asked.

Fallo's eyebrows raised slightly in question, then he shrugged. "Breen and Keston are out there as well."

Paderro asked what you are up to, Tafiriel sent.

Mathias hesitated. He didn't trust Fallo. Not completely. He had put the entire unit in danger because of the want of magic marble. Marble that was revealed to be a living entity. And Fallo had been using a whisperer. Whoever Fallo had been contacting wasn't a flyer.

To stretch my legs, Mathias sent.

A moment went by, and Fallo frowned, but he flicked his fingers ever so slightly... the signal to go.

Taf's silvery voice sounded again. *Paderro bespeaks if you're looking for Frehn, he's in the barn.*

Mathias bowed slightly and pivoted to the dining hall portion of the room. It took only a moment to walk past several long tables and benches, pocked with divots and scratches. He put his hand on the handle to a thick wooden door. Voices murmured on the other side. Breen and Keston.

Leave it to Keston to discover inroads with Breen. That blue-scarfed flyer was a brash solitude with a chip on her shoulder the size of a boulder. It surprised Mathias that she had been deemed ready to join a Tower. It doubly surprised him when Breen did everything in her power to shield Aunia from looking or thinking about Darla as they traveled along the Pardonway.

"Yes, I know people think my father died on the Pardonway battling Aeryk's army," Breen snapped.

"But it wasn't on the road. It was here at Moonstepper," Keston said.

"I don't want to talk about it."

"Breen. Secrets fester. Always. I promise. Anything you say to me, I'll keep. On the head and my pegasus, I promise. And if it isn't me you talk to, that's okay, but you should talk to someone."

Breen's voice dropped to a murmur.

Mathias leaned in. He knew the story about Breen's father, the great Thalric Haldrayne. He had stood on the Pardonway facing an entire regiment of Aeryk's men. Thalric's order... to prevent the regiment from getting through while Dar Syrick finished the guardian spell over the Pardonway trees. And he did. Thalric held ground until he was completely overwhelmed. He had been torn apart, but Dar Syrick had been given the time. The spell was cast. And all of Aeryk's forces had been destroyed.

Keston's voice murmured next.

"No, it didn't happen like that. Bronaque had reached exhaustion. He had slept every single one that approached, but it wasn't enough. My father reached in and—"

"Are you going to use the door?" Murtagh's voice came from the fireplace.

Mathias startled, and Breen and Keston went silent. Mathias opened the door and exited. Both Keston and Breen sat on the porch floor and stared at him.

"Sorry," Mathias murmured. "I... I wanted to look at the Dama star."

Breen pursed her lips and then shot to her feet. "I'll go too."

Keston tilted his head. "Well, I suppose I'll go as well."

Mathias stepped off the creaking porch into what used to be a yard. It was still relatively safe from the beach and sycamore trees, but their branches obscured most of the night sky. However, at this time of night, the Harp should be rising high.

The three of them walked through the damp tall grass, past brambly vines bearing tiny green berries, toward the yard's center. Scanning the portion of sky above, Mathias kicked three flagstones underfoot, evidence that a walkway once existed.

He slowed his pace. Moonstepper's tree line pressed too close. Its tall, heavy-limbed branches framed the clearing like a dome. A window of stars twinkled overhead, but what he sought was not there. "I need to see Harp and star."

His words thrummed around him like an echo. And then, several of the tree branches groaned. Shifted. Just a bit. Making the gap wider.

Breen gaped. Rubbed at her arms. Took a step backwards toward the porch. "I think I'm ready for bed."

Mathias watched her go, glanced toward Keston, who hadn't moved.

Keston's voice was a hush, almost low enough to be missed. "Maybe..." He shifted his weight, jaw tight. "Maybe instead of starwatching, talking to Frehn would be the better idea."

Mathias frowned. He could see a corner of the Harp. And that was because the trees had moved. A few crickets chirped and he finally nodded. "Maybe you're right."

Clenching fists and jaw, Mathias strode toward the stable on the other side of the yard. Closer to the trees. But Tafiriel was in there. And so was Frehn.

Keston did not join him, and Mathias walked at a steady pace to the stable despite his fluttering heart begging for him to run. The trees would not attack. He was loyal to the Queen. But he was never so happy as when he stepped inside the weathered building and Taf nickered at him from one of the open stalls.

Frehn stood two pens down, sleeves rolled up and brushing his pegasus' pale green hide while Morganstee fluttered his white wings approvingly. Both were calm. Focused. No barked orders. No clipped sarcasm. Morganstee dipped his head and pressed his green-tinged muzzle to Frehn's chest. Familiar comfort.

Mathias glanced again at Taf. Nearly everything had gone wrong since he, Aunia, and Keston exited the faery court of Pavari and appeared near

Worley on Kankari Eve. Kankari. Tonight was Kankari. But that didn't matter.

"Commander?" Mathias said.

Frehn looked. "Mathias. What can I help you with?"

He thought about telling Frehn about the moving trees. He didn't. Instead, he took a step closer. "You must have seen how the soldiers treated us. Treated flyers."

"Doesn't help that people like you run off when a fire breaks out in the square. During a festival you attended to boot."

Mathias flushed. Frehn didn't realize they had been protecting Aunia. That the knight-sons and Da Vennen had tried to take her. "We didn't have a choice in that, but I'm talking even before that. The people in Dalin—"

"The people who'd been attacked by Walking Mouths when you and your unit weren't manning your tower?" Frehn asked.

Mathias closed his eyes. "Da Vennen were actively talking against us. They are inflaming the desire for Rhugante's return."

Frehn halted his brushing and frowned. "I don't trust Da Vennen either, and I certainly don't give them fuel to burn me with. Or didn't until Worley."

Mathias opened his mouth but then closed it.

Frehn turned to face him. "You know anything about Fallo calling a commander meeting for all the towers watching border towns?"

Mathias had heard of it but not the why. Fallo had taken Keston, along with the Naoma Stone, and forced a way through the be-twixting tunnel back to the Grashbear Mountains. But the meeting hadn't happened because of Heebles attacking Glevis. And then Dalin. "I... I don't. Fallo left me behind in Aunia's village."

"The mythical Edvaras village," Frehn mused. "Nyrissa has many questions about this. She has questions about why Fallo is working with Dar Heyden."

"Working with Dar Heyden?" Mathias took an involuntary step backward. Dar Heyden was the mage supposedly attached to Edvaras' powers. But he had no tethered Chand ice amulet to connect him to Edvaras' magic. Like Nyrissa did not have the connection for Illysa's power because Zeller's amulet had gone missing. The former queen had given Dar Heyden the position, but it was just an empty seat with a fancy title.

"You know nothing about this?" Frehn asked.

"I don't." Mathias balled his fists. "Whatever Fallo is or isn't doing. But I didn't come here to talk about him. I came because our country is in danger."

"So, you say."

"Bibb has Zeller's amulet." Mathias blurted. "He's using it to power a witch compass."

Frehn visibly startled. "You have proof of that."

"Circumstantial but compelling." Mathias' heart thudded against his sternum. "Bibb is using magic."

Frehn stepped forward, mouth open surely to protest, but Mathias shouted out. "A witch compass. I've seen it. A powerful one. And I tell you... He *was* on the Bellow sands when Zeller died. Tafiriel and I had been Navenra'd. It's why I had gaps in my memories. You yourself smelled that poison at the Green Harpy. You can vouch for that."

Frehn dropped the brush onto a lopsided stool and crossed his arms. "And Bibb's broken nose?"

"How hard would it be to fix a broken nose with magic?" Mathias snapped.

Temper, Taf sent. *Stallions who are challenged, fight.*

Mathias shook his head. "The Da Vennen are gathering portal tiles. Bibb is using them. He portaled onto the Green Harpy grounds while we were escaping. I saw him. Commander Frehn. Please. They are up to something. We have little time. We have to find out."

Frehn eased his hand to his pegasus' neck. It was a long moment before he turned. "I'll give you an answer in the morning."

CHAPTER FIFTEEN
WHERE SECRETS SWIM

The place you seek is not in waters or mountains, but it travels with you, whether you flee or fight. It is already under your feet. — Queen Didianne in the year 556

"Breen said that a bunch of those trees moved last night."

Aunia tiptoed past Murtagh and the copper-haired flyer who stood at the edge of the porch. They gawked at the trees standing nearest to the stable. They didn't turn. Aunia didn't slow. She had no desire to turn her face toward that enormous scorch mark, which stood near the stable's entrance. A mark that turned Breen's slate-blue glow gray and made Aunia think of the hollow where her mother's memorial stone stood.

"Her face was completely white," Murtagh continued.

"Did you go out to see them?" the copper-haired flyer asked.

"I did, but there wasn't anything moving," Murtagh said. "And I had to make sure all of Eddac Tower was inside."

"What do you think Nyrissa will do to them?"

Aunia slowed for a moment, wondering what the answer would be, but a sharp snap sent her rounding to the back of the hostel. They weren't pursuing. They probably didn't notice her. Aunia breathed in deeply.

Too long she had been cooped up with too many people. If she didn't get a moment to herself, feel her toes run through the grass, she'd scream.

The back of the building was bare of windows. A good thing, particularly with the branches from the trees nearly touching the roof. The flyers' conversation droned with no individual words, and birdsong warbled overtop besides. She had escaped. For a moment. She couldn't go far without Mathias. Her entire life she wouldn't be able to go far... Was that a good thing? He loved her. She loved him, but where would they go? How would they live? She wasn't even sure he understood how much she needed him to be at her side to find her father.

She walked toward the woods. The spell on these trees—polished beech limbs branching wide, sycamores curling their branching fingers like a hand paused in mid-grip, and even the wide-armed maples—they would only harm those disloyal to the Tamorian queen. But how could she be judged if she didn't even know the Tamorian queen? She sucked in a breath. Logically, she should be safe here.

And besides, she'd been warned before. Don't talk to faeries. Don't go near the sheep cave. Don't leave the village without the poppet. Aunia pressed her knuckles against her top lip.

A warbler, gold-throated and dusky green, cocked its head at her from its beech tree perch and then flitted to a lower branch beside a deer path. She blinked. It was almost like the bird had brought the narrow trail to her attention.

She stepped forward, shoving aside a branch, and stepped onto the deer path. A very narrow one. Blackberry brambles crowded the path's edge, their thorned vines knotted low, snagging against her rough-spun overdress. She picked up her pace. She might only get a few moments before others came looking for her...but a few moments to collect her thoughts? Calm the incessant worry chattering in her head.

She stepped on a thorn. She winced. Pulled her foot up. Nothing lodged in her barefoot heel. She should've grabbed her sandals. Would have, but she needed to escape before Mathias woke up. He had grabbed the bunk closest to her after an evening of barely talking to her. After hours of riding with Darla.

Her chest ached. Maybe two complete sentences he had strung for her after escaping Worley, and Darla clung to him as if she belonged there.

Morning sunlight dappled through the leafy canopy, and more birds sprang into song. Uplifting and questioning at the same time. She clenched her fists. Nothing needed to be that happy. She wiped at her eyes and clenched her jaw. She was not going to cry. She wasn't sad. She was angry. Angry that she was under arrest. Angry that she did not know how to find her father. Angry that no one could or would tell her how to find Kai-Marin. Mollie Mae said she had to ask her. The sea-witch. Her father used to pray to the ocean.

She continued with no sense of time until the trees parted wider. Up ahead stood a small clearing, and at its center was a pond. It was neither large nor small, but it had a cluster of pale pink lily pads floating near the far edge. And beyond the pond, day lilies raised their opening heads. Aunia stepped into the clearing where birdsong gave way to frogs chirping in short bursts.

She dropped her hands to her sides. It was beautiful here. The trees had pulled back less than a child's stone-throw, except for one tree, an oak. It almost looked as if it had walked itself from the forest and fastened itself by the water's edge. It didn't look old, but it had a presence. Not evil. More like a memory that couldn't be trusted.

Aunia settled near the pond's edge, feet curling against the soft grass as she breathed in the damp morning air. The air was rich with new life, and a coppery undertone of decay.

Movement had her turning her head from the lilies, past the oak's reflection, and then to the western side of the pond. Tiny figures, no bigger than her thumb, zipped over the pond water. Slender, almost translucent bodies pulling threads of thin mist behind them like ribbon trails. These were water fae. Water fae that once had stuffed Sigmus' boots with tadpoles. Water fae that, according to Gaitha, would dance atop Aunia's bathwater when she was a baby.

One darted to the eastern side of the pond, chased by a second. They both dove under a lily pad and burst from the other side. The second one tagged the first one.

Aunia smiled. It had been too long since she'd watched faeries play.

And then realization lanced through Aunia's chest. Water fae were kin to the sea-witch. They had to be. Yes, Ka-Marin was an Eaburrai from the Court of the Eaburrai, but these faeries would know where Kai-Marin could be found.

Capricious faeries who loved mischief. But they love beauty in words as well. Aunia just needed the right poem. She bit her lip, thought of what she wanted to say, and then lilted in a sing-song voice:

O water fae who skip and glide,
Who wake the pond where secrets hide,
With feet like light and wings like mist,
I ask for your enlightenment.

The faeries halted their game of tag and skated on the pond's surface to Aunia. She sucked in a breath. This was only the first step. They agreed to come over, but she needed more. She nipped at her lip and continued:

> You know the ripples, every wave,
> The fish that stir beneath the lily's sway
> You hear the frog, the frog hears you,
> You know what's false, and what is true.

> Where is the one the sea calls kin?
> With salt-bright eyes and tide-bound skin.
> I seek where Kai-Marin can be found,
> With coral crown and foam for gown.

"No. No. No," said one of the fae.

Another giggled with a squeaky voice. "She's a *when,* not a 'where.' Stir your shadow and try again."

A third jumped into the air while a fourth skated in a figure-eight pattern. "Kai-Marin? Brine-wine, tide-ray. She rides a jellyfish into yesterday."

Aunia frowned. Riding a jellyfish? She didn't know what that was. And it made no sense... a when not a where, but while faeries could deceive, they could not lie.

Their giggling ended mid-burst, and they scattered. Aunia rose to her knees but paused as slow bubbles rose in the darkening water.

And then something surfaced. Skin pale gray and glistening in a layer of slime. Hair long and tangled, the color of pondweed. Its eyes, completely black, gleamed with a hungry light.

Aunia scuttled back, the heel of her bare foot ripping up the grassy moss. This was Jenny Greenteeth. A water demon. Faery, yes, and very malevolent. They grabbed anyone they could reach, and they'd drown them.

Jenny Greenteeth's smile was filled with pointed sharp teeth. "I can show you."

Aunia swallowed, trying to remember... did Jennys have to remain in the water? Some memory told her they'd sometimes roosted in trees.

Jenny moved to the water's edge. Waist-deep, knee-deep. Aunia staggered to her feet. And the water rippled again. The blackness beneath Jenny dissipated and became crystal clear water. Jenny yelped. Dove under the water. Vanished.

Aunia sucked her breath through her teeth, felt her knees wobble beneath her. But what she saw at the water's edge... Light bent through great swaths of blue, and fish she had never seen swam in bunched schools.

A young woman's reflection warped on the water surface. She was blue-haired and slight. Her skin, radiant pale blues and greens. She looked up at Aunia with unnaturally large silver eyes. She looked familiar. But Aunia had seen it before. The likeness on the ceiling mural at the ruins of Edvaras' observatory.

Aunia's mouth turned dry, and her mind turned blank. She shook herself. An Eaburrai would not tarry long. "Kai-Marin."

The Eaburrai tipped her head, eyes brightening.

"I remember my father calling on you. Many times. I don't know if he was born under your...constellation, but he disappeared when we were in Nonderu."

Kai-Marin's reflection enlarged, and her hair swam on the current. "Nonderu? He went to free the energy needed? I feared that destiny was already lost."

"Edvaras was released, yes, but Olivia...she..." Aunia shook her head. "I need to find my father. The Boggleman took him, imprisoned him, and Zevara or another faery put a geis on him. Not to kill but... Mathias and I went to Nonderu. I had to destroy the Boggleman's cloak. And Dad. He killed a mockman troll to save Mathias. He disappeared...maybe somewhere else in Faery world...and Mollie Mae said—"

"Instead of bringing light, Ferris Runoldi was swallowed in shadow?" Kai-Marin's reflection covered the entire pond. "How disappointing."

Aunia cleared her throat. "Rune. His name is Rune."

"What the boys from the harbor would call him." Kai-Marin's image shimmered, and she again took on a more mortal size. "I understand."

"Can you help me find—?"

Kai-Marin raised her palm. Her fingers extended out of the water.

Aunia's voice vanished.

"Explain. How missing?" Kai-Marin demanded.

Aunia swallowed and then launched into how she and Mathias had entered Nonderu. How they had battled the Boggleman. How her father had vanished.

"And the Boggleman's cloak?"

"Destroyed," Aunia said.

"I had thought you merely a thread the sea has touched. A weft in the weave. One that would break."

"Kai-Marin?"

"I know not where he is. His task was to bring the doomed together. He has failed me." Kai-Marin looked Aunia over. "But perhaps not completely."

"I don't understand."

"Mortals and their limitations." Kai-Marin rolled her silver eyes. "Do you perhaps have your father's star book?"

Aunia startled. Kai-Marin knew about the book?

"Wisdom unfollowed means nothing," the Eaburrai said.

"What should I be looking for?" Aunia took a step closer.

"Take the time to read." And then, Kai-Marin disappeared, and the clear water returned to murky green.

"You should know that the sea will sacrifice children when it suits," a voice from behind Aunia said.

Aunia whirled around.

Darla stood in the clearing.

Chapter Sixteen

MISSING AND REVEALED

*In utter darkness, strange things lurk, perhaps unseen
but felt. But what can we do but wait for the striking of
daylight, when evil scurries for the shadows, and we see?*
— Dar Syrick, advisor and mage to her royal majesty

The bunk groaned as Mathias shifted onto his back, his wool
cloak rough against his neck. He exhaled long and slow, his
breath turning to mist. It was colder than usual. Several voices bled
in from the other room. He stretched, glanced over at Aunia's bunk,
and frowned. Her cloak was there, bunched around a pillow, so at
first glance it looked like she was still abed. But she was already gone.
So much for talking to her before everyone else was about.

His gaze trickled over a guttering lamp hanging from one of the
ceiling beams and over some knotholes. A coal-black eye winked at
him. Mathias startled up. No, just a shadow. He leaned forward. Yes,
just shadow. He rolled out of bed, yanked on his boots and reached
for his sword and sheath to buckle them onto his belt. They weren't
there. Mathias frowned.

Frehn told the others to take it. Same with Fallo and Keston, Taf
sent.

And you didn't wake me up to tell me? An iciness crawled along Mathias' back, and he glanced back at the knothole in the beam. Better to deal with this later. It was morning. Frehn would have an answer. Mathias headed out to face the others.

Frehn had to believe what he told him. If Da Vennen were skipping with the help of portal tiles... they could do almost anything. Go almost anywhere. Who knew where Bibb and his minions would show up next. But not Moonstepper. It had to be too dangerous for Bibb here.

That meant it would be reasonably safe to leave most of their party here. Aunia would be safer here too... but the distance between them would probably be too great for Zevara's geis. She might need to go as well. Flying with her and not Darla... that just might sweeten Aunia's mood. She was jealous. He could see it on her face. But how could he have any interest in any other girl? There was no one like Aunia.

He sucked in a breath. Hoped she'd forgive him for getting them arrested. His fault. He shouldn't have trusted that they could attend a pre-Kankari celebration. They should have stayed at the Green Harpy. Or better, never have set foot inside Worley at all. He'd still have his sword. Well, a copy of his sword.

Three of the Hausers were inside, Murtagh and two of the youngest flyers. They sat near the door at the table munching on seedcakes and jerky.

"Saved you one." Murtagh pushed a hand-sized cloth bundle toward Mathias.

Mathias frowned, wondering if it was Murtagh who had snuck in and taken his sword. Better to deal with that later. Mathias nodded his thanks and scooped up breakfast. He paused, considering asking if they knew where Aunia had gone. Didn't. Instead, he opened the door and found Frehn and Fallo sitting on the porch steps.

"You know she'll never recover." Fallo looked over his shoulder at Mathias and frowned. He then waved to Mathias to close the door. "But with this marble we could."

Mathias shut it. He was well-aware of Fallo's fascination with Hebsolum's marble. And he remembered Fallo said it had properties to heal wererats... if that were even possible. But if that were true why was there a contingency of wererats following the marble giant. And who was this 'she?'

"Marble." Frehn chewed on that word. "You know about this how?"

"Does it matter?" Fallo said. "Someone she trusts. Mathias, don't you have something to do?"

"No, he's come for an answer." Frehn stood. "I'll give one to you both. And mark this. I stand loyal to the Queen. We'll do nothing without her consent. And yes, Mathias. That goes for you as well."

"But sir." Mathias took a step forward, holding the seed pack package to his chest. This couldn't be Frehn's decision.

"No buts about it," Frehn said. "I've Breen and Leon saddling the pegasi. Soon as you finish breakfast, we're off. And time to wake the girls."

"Wake the..." Mathias stepped to the porch rails, looking out where Keston and the copper-haired Rowan stood. His mouth turned dry. "Aunia is already up."

"She's inside?" Frehn asked slowly.

Mathias turned. As much as he didn't want to, he shook his head.

"And Darla?" Frehn asked.

Mathias shrugged. He had avoided looking at the servant girl from the moment she had selected a bunk and crawled in.

"Go look," Frehn barked. Then he called across the yard to Rowan.

Mathias hurried back into the hostel. Not that he wanted to see Darla. That seemed ungrateful. She had helped them to escape. Still, something about her didn't set right. But if Darla were inside it meant, at least, she wasn't around Aunia.

"We can't find Aunia," Mathias said as he passed Murtagh and the others.

The two younger flyers bolted out of the door.

Murtagh stood. "And the other lass?"

"Looking," Mathias called over his shoulder.

Darla was not in the bunk room either. Mathias headed outside, where Frehn berated his men.

"Not one but two," Frehn bellowed. "How could you let two girls past you?"

Murtagh and Rowan's shoulders slumped.

Oh Thuroes. Mathias glanced up at the rising light. Not yet crested over the trees, but dawn had made its showing at least two hours before. He stepped off the porch. Could Aunia be with Breen?

The two had quarreled almost as soon as they reached the stable. Aunia had only asked a simple question about the scorch mark in front of the stable doors. Breen told her to shut-up about it.

She's not here, Taf sent, almost at the same time that Breen, chestnut hair flying behind her, and Leon with his skinny frame, raced to Frehn's side.

Can you sense her? Mathias walked to the side of the hostel.

She's close, Taf sent.

Close where? Mathias stilled. Aunia liked to run away into the wild when she needed to nurse hurt feelings. Dread flooded his chest. On the Eaburrai. How deep into the Pardonway Forest could she have gone? He cursed.

Mathias hurried back, almost to the corner of the hostel, and nearly collided with Breen.

The girl rocked back on her booted heels. "I shouldn't have yelled at her. Do you know where she went?"

Mathias shook his head. "She's upset. Yes. It's more about..." Another thought crossed Mathias' mind. Cassian wouldn't have set them up with an assassin in their midst, would he?"

"We'll find her," Breen said. "We're getting into a search pattern. In pairs. I doubt the rabble that the soldiers warned us about made it into Moonstepper. But the loophole. Loyal to the Queen doesn't mean you can't be a criminal. Come on."

Mathias followed Breen back to Frehn, but he slowed at Frehn's words to the youngest two flyers.

"You two stay here and guard." Frehn turned toward Fallo and Keston, who both sat on the porch steps. Fallo looked surly. Keston, resigned.

"And Fallo?" Frehn said.

Fallo rose.

"Your word you won't escape," Frehn said.

Fallo pulled himself up to all his inches. "Of course."

Keston remained seated.

"I can take ground," Mathias said.

"No, "Eddac Tower stays here," Frehn commanded. "That's an order."

"I'm sorry, Mathias." Breen set a hand on his shoulder. "We'll find her."

"We'll go inside," said the taller of the two youngest flyers. "Habrett, come on. An order's an order."

Mathias fumed. He caught Keston's slight headshake with his fingers wriggling to come here. Mathias crossed the yard to the porch. He stepped up onto the creaky porch steps, and the two Hauser flyers took position at the bottom of the stairs.

Keston leaned toward Mathias. "If you remember Zevara's words."

Mathias glared at Keston, but his friend's words filtered in. Aunia wouldn't risk being too far away. But how far was too far? They'd been separated by a few miles during the escape from the Green Harpy.

Together is not always a matter of physical distance, Taf sent.

Frehn, Breen, and Leon took to the sky. Rowan strode toward the southeastern part of the grounds, toward the trees. Murtagh padded toward the road and the northwestern section.

"She has to be near," Mathias whispered.

They also still needed to get to Spatelly. After Aunia was found. Finding her took all precedence, but afterward... If he didn't go to Spatelly, he'd have to resign himself to disgrace when they returned to Tatia. And if Bibb attacked Tamore and more people died? Mathias would bear that guilt as well.

A cold sickness filled Mathias' body. It meant someone else from the inside had scattered portal tile to Bibb had materialize onto the grounds of the Green Harpy. All the bear cloaked Da Vennen had been on the outside of the gate. A hand gripped Mathias' shoulder. He turned.

"They'll find her, Matty. And after..." Keston leaned in closer and lowered his voice. "We listen, or we disobey. The choice is simple."

Simple? In a way perhaps and in another way... no.

An odor reached sticky fingers into Mathias' nostrils. It made him shift and wrinkle his nose. Citrus and patchouli... mixed with wet dog... no, something more pungent than that.

Movement turned Mathias' attention toward the barn. He scanned past blackberry brambles and wild roses, past ferns and tall grass. He straightened.

Lurching forward on four paws...or was it hands and knees... came man-sized shapes.

Bristly fur wrapped in leather armor. Beady eyes. Claws. Teeth.

Wererats.

Chapter Seventeen

PROBLEMATIC GIFTS

Sometimes wishes will be brought before you, but their packaging isn't very nice. It makes you think... well, this isn't what I want. — Nyrissa Dar-Elect, flyer of Lydinairre

"Go away!" Aunia curled her fists into her rough-spun skirt. Darla's rough-spun skirt with its stupid bodice digging into her ribs. It smelled like hearth smoke, old ale, and the sharp scent of the woman standing before her.

"I may go where I wish." Darla wriggled her fingers at the oak tree across the pond and sauntered past Aunia. "But you do seem to gather protectors, don't you?"

Aunia turned. A dryad with rich polished wood skin stood beneath the oak's broad, low-sweeping limbs. Her dark hair, tangled with acorn caps, shimmered in the morning sun and fluttered over her short bark and oak-leaf dress.

The dryad didn't wave back at Darla. Instead, it looked at Aunia with glowing brown-green eyes, and its earthy voice breathed through Aunia's mind. *Beware of treading near waters that hide secrets.*

Beware of Kai-Marin? Her reflection had just left the pond. Or was the dryad talking about the Jenny Greenteeth? Aunia chewed on her lip. All she had gotten from Kai-Marin was for her to read her father's book. A strange thing to request. But since she had it in her possession, she had barely touched it. Despite hunting through her father's room repeatedly to leaf through its pages. But it wasn't really her father's book... the thing that she had. It was a copy because she had to manifest what she left behind at Eddac Tower.

"I was here first," Aunia said. She needed Darla to leave. Maybe she could get Kai-Marin to come back then.

"You wouldn't be here at all if I hadn't helped you." Darla's eyes slid from the dryad to Aunia.

"You helped. Yes. And you took my dress. I think we're even." Aunia said. And Darla tried to turn Mathias' head. It was something that the promiscuous Velli would have done.

Darla trailed her fingers along the front of the blue fitted gown. "Never had anything faery made before. But perhaps you do deserve something finer."

The dark-haired serving maid snapped her fingers, and the itchiness of wool vanished, leaving Aunia cold but only for a moment. Warm mist coated her skin, and then fabric bloomed inch by inch. Wool again but a lighter, softer weave. The dress, deep mulberry, wove itself onto her body. Down her legs.

Aunia stood at the water's edge, tugging at the fitted gown's square neckline. Fingers sliding over the raised edge of embroidery. Golden vines. She dropped her hands, and the sleeves brushed her knuckles. Magic. "Who are you?"

"A friend. But I must admit, for someone Gabryella wanted to spy on, you're a sad disappointment. Only a bit of faery sight and maybe a touch of summoning." Darla shook her wrist, and her bracelet, a narrow band of copper braided with thinner strands of blackened bronze, chimed against her wrist. "But you're good at slipping away."

Aunia's insides went cold at Gabryella's name. She had dreamwalked to the fireling's domain and had seen her nursing the Boggleman back to health. Had watched her shove salamander faeries into glass tubes.

"You're the one who brought the salamander lights to Worley," Aunia said flatly.

"Not I." Darla's smile widened. "Or rather, not directly. Clandestine Da Vennen make wonderful chumps."

Aunia shuffled back a step. Considered if she should run.

"Oh, please." Darla shook her wrist again, and a small gray sack appeared in her hand. "I mean you no harm whatsoever. I made you a pretty gown after all. I made sure your sweetheart knocked over the best box in the attic. I'm looking to help you. Allow me to show."

But Darla's glow wasn't with greens or blues or even bright yellows. It was black and gray.

Aunia took another step back, her foot pressing into the pond's damp mud.

Darla shook the gray bag, and shimmering tiles poured onto her hand. She walked in a circle, dropping portal tiles onto the ground. "Handy things to skip miles. And I do believe I have enough for it to be miles. I'll take you with me. There's so much you can learn."

Aunia bunched her knees, ready to sprint past her.

Darla shook the bracelet a third time, and the gray woven bag disappeared. Instead, Darla held Aunia's canvas knapsack with its metal buckle. "Look familiar? Almost identical to the one inside the hostel. I assume you want it."

Identical to the one in the hostel? Aunia stepped forward. She couldn't help it. "How'd you get it?"

"My whisperer didn't attack like the Boggleman's. That wasn't its mission. I wanted to know what items you carried, and then you left them all behind."

"Give me my knapsack."

Darla tossed the knapsack inside the circle. "Step inside and take it."

The portal tiles flickered in the short grass. Aunia hesitated. In Dalin, Keston had told her about portal tiles being formed like mosaics. That they could transport people over vast distances. Like skipping. But tiles sprinkled in a circle? Was that even safe? And if she stepped in the circle and was transported elsewhere? How would she get back?

She considered how she could fetch it. A long stick. Or maybe she could run through and out before it worked. But Darla would be there to stop her. Maybe she could shove Darla into the pond.

The dryad stepped to the water's edge. *That one before you wears fire—not to warm but to consume.*

I'd have guessed as much, Aunia thought back to the dryad. But she wrinkled her brow. There had to be another reason the dryad appeared, besides warning her about Darla. "I'm not leaving."

"Wrong, you want to go to Ignivar." Darla held out a hand. "It's our oldest university. We seek knowledge, you and me. It's what firelings do. It's what you've been trying to do. Impressive that you called Kai-Marin. We can teach you techniques to call on her anytime you wish."

Aunia wavered. A chance to find answers? Like maybe where her father was?

The morning sun vanished behind a cloud, and the wind picked up.

Darla shook her outstretched hand. "I'm a friend. If I weren't, I would have stashed Etos' astrolabe right in my pocket."

Etos? Aunia curled her fists and glared at Darla.

"You need my help." Darla said. "I need yours."

A crack of lightning flared. The portal tiles took on a reddish hue. And Darla's glow turned darker. "You need to hurry. He's coming."

"How are you at Moonstepper?" Aunia hissed. The buzzing in Aunia's ears grew into a high-pitched whine. She winced, grinding her teeth. Answers. Darla promised answers. And she couldn't leave Mathias behind. The problem was... her knapsack was inside the glowing circle.

"How am I..." Darla laughed. "I have no intention of doing anything against your Queen."

On Aunia's periphery, she caught the dryad hustling to her tree. *Brace yourself,* it said, then vanished.

Another rumble of thunder and branches cracked. But it was a growl... low and feral... that sent Aunia's heart to racing.

"Not now," Darla muttered. She scooted around the circle in two bounds and grabbed Aunia's wrist.

Wererats. They approached not in ratman form like on the Grashbear Mountains but as great beasts with ravenous eyes and wet teeth.

The first one, broad across the shoulders with mottled gray fur and yellow eyes, scrambled forward. It was followed by a second that was more bone than muscle. Both leaped forward while a third lurched into view.

More followed. One with dark patchy fur and an ear torn at its base. One with mismatched eyes. And a ratman with a spear in its hand.

"Stand down," Darla yelled.

The broad-shouldered one glared at Darla. "Fireling. He's angry with you."

Darla yanked Aunia toward the tile circle. Aunia dug in her heels.

A high-pitched squeal ripped through the clearing, powdering the air like when the Boggleman ripped his way into the mortal world. It felt like metal on bone and glass breaking.

Aunia cringed, and the portal tiles on the ground shook. Then shattered. Aunia flung her arms up to protect her face. Sharp flecks of burning magic hit her forearms as she was flung back.

The wererats had been tossed yards away as well. Darla had kept to her feet, though she was folded in half, fingers grazing the grass. Her bracelet glowed red. And Aunia's knapsack, in the center of the circle, fell over.

The high-pitched squeal faded, and the ratman leader regained his feet. He snarled to his pack. "Bite only."

Chapter Eighteen

Mist and Limbs

You said the first wererat came into being because a Ty faery bit both a human and a faery. That explains the human, yes, but what did the bitten faery turn into? — Wendalin Mensani at age eight

The wererats had drifted back into the brambles and trees, and then a scream came from Rowan's location at the front of the hostel and away from the road.

Mathias sprinting toward Rowan, sent to Taf. *Sleep them!*

There's a spell wrapped about them, Taf sent back.

"Come back," Fallo yelled. "You've no sword."

Mathias slowed. Yanked his dagger from its sheath. His heart hammered against his sternum. What good would a dagger do against several wererats? This weapon was effective in close quarters. Inside the range of claws and teeth. One on one. But certainly, more effective with a shield. All he had was an open hand.

A sharp crack split the air, and Mathias glanced over his shoulder. Keston stood over a chunk of broken off porch railing and yanked hardwood spindles from the broken mess. It would do little to cause hurt to a wererat, but it would deflect... blade. Claws. Teeth.

"Matty, wait up!" Keston jumped from the porch. He held two porch spindles in his left hand, and his dagger was drawn.

Mathias slowed. Three wererats, the size of large hounds, slunk in the grass. Closing in from twenty paces. Better odds having Keston at his side. Mathias gripped his dagger. The wererats rose on rat legs... bones cracking... becoming more animalistic.

But the dark mist that swirled around them... it sucked all hope and lightness into a never-ending void. The trees rustled. Branches swayed. Deep groans and limbs striking mist. Striking nothing.

Other wererats came. Humanoids but with rat faces and claws.

Two could have been shorter than Mathias. Starved-looking creatures dressed in patchwork clothing. The third, a barrel-chested powerhouse with reddish fur, swaggered forward in mismatched, dented armor. It swung a double-edged ax. Two more scurried behind him.

Three on two. Not great odds. Why weren't the trees attacking? Where were the two Hauser flyers left to guard them? And Fallo?

Mathias sent, *Taf bespeak Frehn. We're under attack.*

He knows, Taf sent back.

Snapping brush pulled Mathias' attention. Yet more wererats entered the Moonstepper clearing. Blood stained cloth and leather armor. Oh Yasendra. Was the copper-haired Rowan still alive?

Mathias glanced back at the hostel. Fallo stood on the porch with the two Hauser flyers pulling their swords from their sheaths. They looked scared. What should they do? Hole up in the hostel? On the defensive? What about the others? And Aunia? *Taf, you and Rev need to fly.*

From the east, twilight-indigo Korthalee with Breen on his back swept over the trees. She held a notched bow. An arrow flew, and it struck a wererat who was bounding out of the trees.

Frehn appeared from the north-northeast on Morganstee. And Leon on his dark brown pegasus sailed overhead from the west. More arrows flew. More squeals erupted. The dark mist thickened. Made the wererats difficult to see. Yasendra be blessed, how many wererats were there?

A fist grabbed Mathias' shoulder. He spun, dagger raised.

"Woah!" Keston yelped. He shoved a spindle into Mathias' hand.

Exiting from the dark mist sauntered the barrel-chested brute. He deflected arrows with his axe head as if they were nothing more annoying than mosquitoes. That brute and the other wererats stood between Mathias and the stable.

Frehn drew an arrow and flew toward Mathias' flank. Mathias staggered back, flicking the spindle up to deflect as Frehn released. Frehn's arrow caught a skinny wererat in the neck. The thing had broken formation and was sliding under the mist along Mathias' right flank.

Mathias cursed at himself as the wererat fell into the tall grass. He should have caught the movement.

Frehn released another arrow, again at the barrel-chested wererat. It again deflected.

"Mat. Kest," Fallo yelled from the hostel porch. "Fall back."

Frehn says hole up in the hostel, Taf sent.

A fresh wave of wererats exploded from the underbrush. Ran for them.

Fallo appeared. Shoved Mathias aside. Mathias toppled, hitting an elbow on a stone on the ground. One wererat leaped. Struck Fallo, claws and teeth. Keston plunged a dagger into its back. Mathias scrambled to his feet.

Another arrow sang. Caught a chink in barrel-chest's side. The barrel chest was almost upon them, and all that arrow did was make it grunt.

Overhead, Breen notched another arrow.

"Retreat!" Fallo roared. His ruddy complexion was pale. Blood at his throat. And a dark pool growing at the front of his jerkin.

More wererats ran toward them.

Mathias, Keston, and Fallo bolted for the hostel. Aunia. All the Eaburrai. Aunia was still out there.

The two Hauser flyers stood by the open hostel door. Waited for them to race inside. Mathias and Keston sailed through the door. Then Fallo. The Hausers slammed the door shut. Braced it with their bodies.

Wererats thudded against the wood.

"Hold the door," one of the Hausers cried.

Mathias and Keston took the door. Braced their legs and backs against the wood. This hostel was not the best place to hole up. Why hadn't the Pardonway trees protected them? Fallo joined them. Back against the door. Breath labored. On the Eaburrai, Fallo had been bitten.

Swords drawn, the Hausers took position at the shuttered window. Thank Yasendra there was only one window.

More slams rattled the oak door. Threatened to shake Mathias' teeth from his gums. He leaned harder into the wood. Twice, the door opened a gap. And twice he, Keston, and Fallo pushed it back.

A sharp crack sounded on his right. Brittle. Crashing. The window. Pieces of translucent cattle-horn, shattered against the inner shutters. Pieces tinged onto the floor through a narrow gap. And then, claws wrapped the edges of the shutters.

The shorter of the Hauser flyers stabbed at the claw knuckles. The other flyer pushed at the shutters to keep them closed.

The claws drew back with a howl. Then more claws appeared. The shutters cracked. Wood pulled from inside to outside.

Dark mist poured into the open frame. And with it, seeped in imagery of destruction and death. Of Aunia pale. Her lifeless form... A low gasp escaped Mathias.

Whistles and thwacks filled the air. Thumps and groans shook the porch. Then silence.

Mathias and Keston shared a look.

"They're running," one of the Hausers said, his voice shaking.

"Good." Fallo pulled his hand from his neck. It came away bloody. Fallo had been bitten. He'd need to be treated with no-turn if he had any chance of not becoming a wererat himself. But they had no potion healer with them.

There was nothing for it. Mathias flung open the door. "Aunia!"

The taller of the Hausers grabbed Mathias' shoulder. "You have to stay."

Mathias shrugged him off, and clocked the Hauser flyer in the head with the spindle. The boy dropped to his knees and Mathias raced out. Still bodies lay around. And a glimpse of fur disappearing around the corner.

"Crap," Keston's voice sounded behind him. Scuffling. A blow. And then, Keston ran by his side.

Mathias picked up more speed. Keston yelled. Mathias turned.

From the barn and saddled with that inferior seat, Taf galloped toward Mathias. *I come to you.*

Behind Taf came Rev and Paderro, also saddled.

Mathias ran for Taf. *What took you? Why didn't you fly?*

Hiding sometimes is the best option, Taf sent. *The others are following the wererats. They broke toward the west.*

Keston ran at his heels.

Ran west? Back to that encampment? And why had they attacked?

Near the middle of the yard, Mathias grasped the saddle horn and flung himself onto Taf's back. Keston ran beside Revellie, leaped up, foot in a stirrup. Both pegasi launched into the sky.

Aunia is at a pond. She bespoke, Taf sent. *She's in danger.*

"Oy," a voice called. Murtagh. The dark-haired flyer with the braid ran along the back of the hostel waving his arms at them.

Mathias didn't acknowledge him. Yes, he was glad another ground flyer survived the attack, but his focus was on finding Aunia. Saving her.

They flew west over the thick canopy. Heart in his throat. Twenty breaths. Thirty. The trees rushed beneath them for an eternity, and finally they thinned. Ahead stood a grassy clearing, and at its center, maybe a half-acre across, lay a pond. Water lilies decorated one end, and a tall oak tree sat near the water's edge.

Aunia. Blonde hair gleaming in the sun. And in a different dress? She was screaming. Darla had her arm. Was pulling Aunia toward the wererats. Pulling her toward a portal tile circle. Like the one that Bibb had emerged from.

Taf. Come on!

One of the wererats, thick-bodied and crouching, sauntered to the circle edge. Darla yelled at him. The wererat stopped. Mathias blinked. Darla was working with wererats?

"You will not!" Aunia's voice rang through the sky, and she smacked Darla across the side of the head. Forced the woman to release her arm.

The dark-haired woman raised her arm and shook her wrist. A burst of fire erupted from her hand. Danced off her palm. Engulfed the air above the tile circle. Brilliant reds, oranges, and greens.

Yasendra be blessed, Darla was a fireling.

Mathias stretched out his hand, desperate to reach Aunia. Still yards away. But then, a groan creaked beneath him. A silver-gray beech limb lurched. A second. And a third. These weren't breaking branches. These were living, moving arms. The Pardonway trees attacked.

One caught Darla across her stomach. She flew into the pond. The second and third struck the wererats. Sent them flying in an arc out of the clearing.

The remaining wererats turned and ran. Paderro flew after them.

Tafiriel flew to Aunia, and Mathias leaned as far as he could. He grabbed her under an arm. Wrapped his second arm around her middle.

Aunia clamored up in front of him. "Knapsack!"

Revellie dove low over the portal tile circle. Keston leaned heavily to one side. Nearly inverted and snagged the fabric near the flap. He hoisted the knapsack up.

Aunia leaned against Mathias. She shook, but she was alive. And not bleeding.

We can't go back, Aunia bespoke through Taf.

Mathias blinked. He had planned nothing beyond saving Aunia. But she was right.

Keston and Rev approached on Mathias' right side, Rev's golden hide gleaming in the sun.

Taf sent, *Keston bespeaks... Ready for Spatelly?*

Chapter Nineteen

TIME-TURN SPELL AND THE EAVESDROPPER

Are you sure that magic is different? It seems that both faery and ingredient magic, their origin, come from the same place. — Dar Syrick, age fifteen

Aunia didn't mind leaving Fallo behind, and she said as much through Tafiriel. Mathias did not bespeak back, and she regretted her harsh tone. She shivered, more from the recent danger than the chill wind. Mathias wrapped his arms around her.

Keston bespeaks that Fallo brawled with the other flyers to give us time to escape, Tafiriel sent. *And Paderro came for you too.*

She glanced over at Keston, who flipped his palms over as if to say, "it is what it is."

She huffed out a breath. If Fallo was the reason that Mathias came... She frowned. Would he have not otherwise?

The three of them, on Tafiriel and Revellie, flew south enough for the morning sun not to blind them and high enough according to Mathias that the Hauser flyers wouldn't be able to spot them... provided Tafiriel could block Revellie's gold, which was why Keston and Revellie remained on their left. But being up so high... she wriggled her bare, icy toes... it made the Pardonway Forest look like a large woven mat.

We might want to bespeak Paderro, Mathias finally sent. *Tell him what we're—*

Tafiriel interrupted. *Paderro bespeaks do not say. He and Fallo can guess and they're drawing the Hausers away.*

Mathias squeezed her middle. *And his bite?*

"Bite?" Aunia said out loud.

Mathias intertwined his fingers between hers. *A wererat bit him when he was defending me.*

He was... Aunia frowned again. She didn't want to be grateful to the Eddac Tower commander but saving Mathias... she guessed he couldn't be all bad.

Paderro bespeaks they're going back for the item, Tafiriel sent.

"Marble?" Mathias barked the word. *On Thuroes' Harp, why?*

Tafiriel's wing-stroke staggered, and he dropped half a foot.

Aunia gripped hard with her thighs, one hand hard around the saddle pommel, the other digging into Mathias' arm. Stars! Why did Mathias' saddle have to disappear as well! What core memory had he used to lock them into reality?

There's someone listening. Tafiriel's silvery voice sounded like a whisper wrapped within a buzzing bee. He dove again before he angled up... like he was trying to outrun a presence.

If he could outfly... she wished he'd out distance the high-pitched whine in her ears. She'd been hearing it off and on since the portal tiles shattered. She squeezed her eyes shut and a moment later, it receded.

Tafiriel? Mathias sent.

It's faded... or gone. The pegasus again flew straight and steady. *Fallo says it's a needed ingredient for a time-turn spell. Turn back what was. Save the Queen from madness.*

Save the Queen from... Mathias hugged her tighter.

"I need to breathe." She patted his hands.

Mathias loosened his grip. *Sorry.*

It's a dangerous thing the commander tries, Tafiriel sent.

"Indeed," Mathias said. *Taf, bespeak Keston all of this.*

Keston bespoke a few choice things. Mostly about events that Aunia knew nothing about.

Aunia hunched her shoulders. It felt like cold fingers tapped at the base of her skull. Probably just the cold. She wished she'd have grabbed her cloak and shoes. But there was nothing to be done about that. She turned her mind back to what she was learning... time turning.

That thought pulled her belly to her knees. She might never have met Mathias. Never learned answers about her parents. But she wouldn't have made a mess releasing Edvaras' magical Nymer for Hebsolum. And the marble giant wouldn't have stolen it.

She shook her head. If Fallo tried to get marble from Hebsolum, the giant would squash him flat.

Her father's face fluttered in her mind's eye. If time were reversed her father wouldn't have been taken by the Boggleman. But then the Boggleman's cape wouldn't be destroyed, and that monster would still be eating faeries.

Olivia would be alive. Maybe the augury would be in a better state.

Moments passed as Aunia turned inwards and considered if her intentions would ever outweigh the damage that followed her.

Aunia, Mathias sent. *Why was Darla after you?*

That'll have to wait, Tafiriel sent. *Hausers have spotted us.*

Aunia swiveled in Mathias' arms for a look behind. Several specks of muted colors dotted the sky. Twilight indigo, a pale green, dark brown....
Red gold...

They must've given up the chase for Fallo, Mathias sent. *Lucky us.*

Do they see us? Aunia sent.

I doubt they've seen Taf, Mathias sent, *but...*

What do we do?

Another voice threaded through Aunia's mind. It sounded muffled. Unfamiliar. *Respect isn't given nor kept by running.*

Frehn bespeaks, Taf sent. *He says to come back.*

Frehn? No, that was Morganstee. She didn't know how she knew, but she did. And it wasn't exactly what Frehn said. She shifted, trying to ease where the ghost fingers, at her nape, tied knots.

Mathias' green glow, barely visible along his arms, grayed. *It won't help answering him.*

You've given your word, Morganstee sent.

Tafiriel broadened his wing strokes and did not repeat Frehn's words. For that, Aunia was grateful. Mathias didn't need to feel more guilt. But it made her want to shout back to Morganstee and tell him to leave them alone. To go do something useful.

The dots were coming closer.

You hear Morganstee? Tafiriel sent, mental voice barely audible.

Yes. Aunia's skin went damp under her gown's fitted bodice, and she shivered against the cold rattling against her skull. *You can outfly them, can't you?*

I do not know. I can fly, but not endless, Tafiriel sent. *Keston bespeaks that we should hunker down. Let them pass overhead.*

Mathias sent, *Not much cloud cover. They'll see where we put down unless we get more lead, and we don't have a good where.*

Another voice sounded in Aunia's head. Old. Cobwebby but semi-familiar. It sent ice sleeting along her veins. *You have power. Manifest what you desire.*

Tafiriel looked back at her, wind whipping his mane across his eyes. *Whatever that is, fight it.*

Mathias' body turned rigid. *What are you bespeaking about?*

Something, Tafiriel sent, *is in her mind.*

Darla, Mathias sent. *Firelings use all sorts of dark magics.*

Aunia startled. Darla? But it made sense. The woman brought portal tiles to capture her. Threw her knapsack in its center to force Aunia in. And when wererats attacked, they had listened to her. Could Darla be invading her mind?

But the voice didn't sound like Darla. It sounded older. It reminded her of the woods and terror and a wild pig snuffling. That thought tore at her heart. She pressed a hand to the back of her head. But the woman held fire in her hands. Had a bracelet for magic. Ingredient magic, Aunia supposed.

She glanced behind them again. The Hauser flyer dots now had little lines for legs. They were catching up. *Can't you just explain to Frehn? Tell him what we know about Bibb and the wererats? Tell him we'll take whatever punishment when we're done.*

They just had to discover what Bibb was up to and then find where her father was. Tatia after that would be a blessing.

Interesting, murmured the cobbwebby voice.

I did try, Mathias sent. *He said no.*

Keston sends it's a shame we can't reach out to Nyrissa, Taf sent.

Aunia turned to watch Mathias. His lips were pressed hard together.

She won't help, Mathias sent. *Thuroes, help us. They're less than a mile away. Taf! We can't maneuver. Not on this saddle.*

"What do we do?" Aunia yelled.

Keston bespeaks, Tafiriel sent. *The mad wizard.*

The mad wizard? The cobwebby voice mused. *I wouldn't have thought of him.*

Mathias hissed through his teeth. *"Do you know where he is?*

Power. The voice had said earlier that she had power. And she did. But Mygul never showed when she wanted it to. She felt a whisper touch at her shoulder as if her little garden faery were perched there. Then her blood heated. An image filled her mind like she was sailing on the arms of a storm... like she was dreaming. *Turn right.*

Mathias straightened. *Angle for the morning sun? Well, we won't be the only ones sunblinded. We fly and dive when they can't see us. We just need any semblance of a clearing.*

The vision lingered in her mind's eye and she could see further than she could physically. A mile. Three. Seven. Ahead and below sat a stone house. It was surrounded by a garden with a press of trees edging the grounds. Trees that would move.

Five miles away. Mathias. Five miles. Aunia winced against another wave of pain and dark whisperings. It pulled at her consciousness. Threatened to pull her under.

She reached under her burgundy dress and gripped her father's amulet. The voices softened. They did not disappear. The voice whirled around her. Pinched at her. Her fingers loosened. They slipped off. She was falling.

CHAPTER TWENTY

THE MAD WIZARD'S HOUSE

Halite salt is one of the most precious minerals. It will hold the echo of every spell cast in its presence, like frost holding the shape of breath. Treat it mundanely, and it will crumble. Honor it, and it will reveal what even stone has forgotten. — Q'thonos the Mad Wizard

M athias caught Aunia tight against his chest as Tafiriel dove for the clearing below. Five miles, as Aunia had said. She had fainted at two.

Tafiriel brushed against a few tree limbs, sending a cluster of leaves a fluttering, and they touched down inside a glade. A stone house—cut granite and river rock—squatted at the clearing center. Its upper floors gave way to weathered beams holding pattern for a patchwork of soot-gray plaster. It looked like whoever constructed the house didn't know what they wanted. Or someone spelled three different buildings into merging. The roof jutted at odd corners. Three gables. Bent iron chimney. Small, uneven windows.

Mathias rubbed his knuckles against Aunia's cheek and shook her gently. Nothing.

Keston looked over with concerned eyes.

"She's breathing," Mathias said.

"Why did she faint?"

Mathias shrugged. "Taf said something was attacking her mind."

"She... she didn't drink any of that Navenra wine, did she?"

Mathias shook his head. Sucked in a breath. Straightened as much as he could with Aunia in his arms.

The place felt wrong. Not menacing exactly. Watchful. With the Pardonway trees—elm, sycamore, and beech—creaking and leaning in.

"We should get away from the T-R-E-E-S." Keston pointed to the house. "And we should find the owner."

Keston took the lead with Rev clip-clopping over the grassy yard and onto a loopy dirt path, which led past the back of the house where they were to the front.

Mathias followed, Aunia's head cradled on his shoulder. Smoke and fear clung to her, but underneath it, it was still the sweet summery scent of her. He would have done her better by leaving her in her village.

You saved her from isolation and probable death, Taf sent.

He had... but the reason for her exile was that he had talked her into going to the ruins. That choice had led to the attack on her village.

They rounded to the front, and the air turned metallic and sweet. A tangled garden stretched before them. Thick purple-veined leaves grew beside pink and purple bell-shaped flowers. He wasn't sure of their names, but he identified belladonna, yarrow, and valerian with its delicate white flowers. One plant, a squat yellowish weed, reeked of spoiled food. Mathias wrinkled his nose as they went past.

Keston tossed a look over his shoulder and pointed ahead. "There."

Near the center of the garden, an old man hunched over a patch of inky black berries. He moved with the stiffness of age and muttered to himself as he pinched berries off and dropped them inside a tin cup.

The mad wizard of the Pardonway. They passed another flower bed. This one with plants with curling blue leaves. Another bed overflowed with slender stalks and with purple flowers.

I should take the lead, Mathias sent and tapped Tafiriel's sides.

He had just passed Keston and Rev when the old man straightened and turned to face them. The man was narrow-shouldered and draped in a patchy cloak. Wiry gray beard. Strange spectacles. One lens was made of circular glass...spider-cracked near the rim. The other "lens," if it could even be called that, was a hag stone. Mathias' mother had a few. Flat riverbed pebbles, gray with a hole bore through by time and water. In the glasses, the man's hazel gray eyes looked mismatched in size.

Mathias stiffened. It would have to be a madman to make such a ridiculous contraption. It made him wonder if his other contraptions were true. Q'thonos was rumored to bottle wind and unleash storms for anyone who tried to fly over the Pardonway when the moon was full. He caught shadows from mud pits and made them do his bidding. He turned unwanted visitors into trees.

A shiver ran through Mathias. The broad yard seemed to have shrunk with the trees leaning toward them. A mist rose from the ground, and the trees leaned in even closer. Sunlight faded.

The Hausers are flying overhead, Taf sent, his voice a bare whisper.

"Relax, flyer," the mad wizard said with a querulous voice. "I've glamored you almost as well as your little... um... faery friend here."

Jennium popped her head out of the tin cup. Mathias turned to see if Keston could see Aunia's faery friend. Faeries could be seen or unseen if they wished. Unless you have the faery sight, like Aunia. Keston seemed oblivious.

Q'thonos walked to a water barrel that stood near the house's front door. "Thirsty? Or might do for rousing someone who's fainted. She's not sick, is she?"

Mathias glanced at Aunia. "I think just..."

Aunia roused slightly, fluttering her eyes. "Where are...we?"

"We're at the mad..." Mathias glanced at the old man. "...at Q'thonos."

The wizard sucked water noisily from the ladle and let it clatter back into the barrel. He shut the lid. "So, running from your own. Story there, I'd wager. You are real flyers, are you not?"

Mathias dismounted and helped Aunia do the same. She leaned against him, shoulders hunched. The creak of a saddle behind him told Mathias that Keston had dismounted from Revellie. "Of course we're real flyers."

Aunia scrubbed at her knuckles, and her eyes turned wide. For Yasendra's sake, what spell had Darla cast on her? His heart started to race.

"You don't behave like a typical flyer," Q'thonos said.

"You want a story," Mathias snapped. "It ends with me walking into a madman's glen because everyone else who was trusted—"

"Forgive him." Keston butted in front of Mathias. "It's not every day we meet the legendary wizard who bends problems with answers."

"Problems into answers?" Q'thonos pursed his wrinkled, thin-jawed mouth, and his gaze focused on Aunia. "Strange glow on that one."

Keston bespeaks not to anger the wizard, Taf sent.

"You see glows?" Aunia said softly.

And a waist-high streak with dirty blonde hair tore from beneath the trees and pelted for Aunia.

"All the Eaburrai," Mathias hissed. He pushed Aunia back, squeezing her between himself and Taf as Reina tackled him. "You'll knock her over."

"Nonsense." Aunia wobbled but she sank to her haunches to better hug the little rover girl. "Basil said he was bringing you here."

"You know the Mystic Rover," Q'thonos said. "And he thinks highly of you, does he not?"

"Basil rescued me from the Da Vennen soldiers when I was in Dalin." Aunia rose, staggering a bit, but kept her arm around Reina. "He took me...took me to where I needed answers."

Mathias reached out and ruffled the little girl's hair. "Sorry for snapping."

Reina pulled away.

"You seek answers?" the old man said. "Many think they do, but only if the answers match what they want."

"Can you just change already?" Reina blew the wizard a raspberry. "You look silly all old."

"All old?" Keston asked.

"Anything you'd like, Sunray." Q'thonos' features melted, like clay in a too-warm room, and a much younger man stood before them. Still lean but sharp-featured with pale skin, high cheekbones, and angular brows. His hair had darkened to near black and had turned uneven instead of grizzled. And his eyes had shifted to the color of thunderclouds. "I don't usually invite guests into my home, but the little girl knows you. Likes you. You drink tea, don't you?"

Taf, you couldn't tell me he was in disguise.

He's a wizard. Taf nickered. *What do you expect?*

Q'thonos led the way into his house.

Mathias hesitated at the doorway until Reina grabbed his hand and dragged him forward. He didn't like putting trust in a wizard, but Q'thonos might be the only one who could help them figure a way to get to Spatelly without being seen.

He entered, eyes adjusting to the dim, amber-hued interior and his nose filling with sage's sharp-sweet scent. Bundles of dried herbs hung off the low ceiling beams, which were etched with carved runes. Shelves, some sagging under the weight of mostly books but also loaded with glass jars, and urns stuffed with scrolls. A table with mismatched chairs sat in a corner. Sliced bread and a crock of butter sat on its surface. Nearby stood a large stone hearth. Combination kitchen and workspace?

Aunia remained at his side, leaning against him.

"Are you alright?" Mathias asked her.

"She looks really pale," Keston murmured from behind them.

Mathias whispered back, "Do you have any coin on you?"

"Coin isn't necessary." Q'thonos stretched for the mantle, reaching past a jar of old teeth and a small brass clock frozen at 3:17. "But a good turn would be plum pudding."

He grabbed a teakettle—the largest item in the menagerie of strange oddities—from the mantle and fastened it onto the hearth hook.

Wizards like knowledge better than coins, Taf sent.

Mathias frowned. Pulling plum pudding out of his pocket wasn't going to happen.

"Sunray, fetch a crock of jam to go with our bread," Q'thonos called.

"I want pie," Reina said.

"Then do the charm I showed you." Q'thonos moseyed to the cupboards that lined the darker northern wall.

Mathias guided Aunia to the table, shoved aside a stack of books, and pulled out a chair. A tea tray sat by the bread. He must have missed that before. The cups loaded onto it were mismatched but clean. He grabbed one for Aunia and one for himself. Keston took a seat on Aunia's left, set her knapsack down at her feet, and helped himself to a cup.

Aunia's gaze went to the floor and her hands trembled.

"Hey," Mathias took her hand. So cold. He wished he still had his cloak. He'd wrap it around her.

Reina joined them at the table, set down two large crocks, and then held up a tarnished brass pendant, the size of a walnut. The curious thing was shaped like a fork with its tines curled up. "You want pie?"

Keston gave the young girl a smile. "Who doesn't like pie? Aunia?"

Aunia nodded, and Reina, dangling the pendant from its thin chain, pinched the brass fork. "Sweetsnap. Crustaboom."

Sixes slices of pie... blueberry, blackberry, and sweet custard appeared on small wooden plates.

Mathias startled.

"I should make us more room, don't you think?" Q'thonos, at the hearth and tea kettle in hand, snapped his fingers. The stacks of books and a map, which had lain across one of the chairs, floated up and into the back cupboards.

Reina reached for the pendant again. "I wanted apple."

"Stabilized conjuration loop with appetite attunement. Might explode if misused. Mustn't overuse it, don't you think, Sunray?"

"Fine." Reina crinkled her face and crossed her arms. A second later, she grabbed a slice of blueberry pie and took a big bite. "It only made potato pie once."

The last book floated into a cupboard, and the door closed on its own.

Aunia pulled over a slice of custard pie, but instead of taking a bite, she tapped on the plate.

Keston grabbed two slices of bread from the loaf and slathered them with dark purple jelly. "Looks like there's strawberry here, Matty."

"Not hungry," Mathias said. Under Keston's frown, Mathias took a seat on Aunia's left. How was he supposed to eat when he hadn't figured out how to get Q'thonos to help them?

Q'thonos stopped by the table, no kettle in his hand, and stooped for Aunia's knapsack.

Aunia grabbed it by the straps and hauled it to the table.

"Strange glow." Q'thonos tapped the knapsack. "You should drink your tea."

Mathias leaned closer to Aunia. "You haven't poured yet."

"Look again."

Steam rose from the cups, and an earthy-sweet scent filled the air... A bit of cinnamon swirling in the undercurrents.

Mathias swirled the dark liquid in his cup. "Most people serve tea without magic."

"May I?" Q'thonos tapped the knapsack. "There feels to be a bunch of tampering here, but for how long ago... I don't know."

At Aunia's nod, the wizard unbuckled the flap. He pulled out Aunia's blue leather-bound book, and the astrolabe. His eyes went wide, and he rotated the instrument in his hands. "You've never opened this up? Correct, yes?"

"My foster-sister and I brought it to the sheep cave." Aunia tapped on the astrolabe's rim. "And this started to turn on its own. There are funny grooves there too along the sides."

"That's called the rete," Mathias pointed to the overlaying plate.

"No," Aunia frowned. "The rim."

"The mater? That's impossible. It's there for coordinates only. Measurements," Mathias said. "I used Nyrissa's all the time when we watched the stars."

"I tell you it moved," Aunia said. "Soon as we got to the cave with its broken door. It spun around and opened a betwixting tunnel to—"

"Stop." Q'thonos set a hand on the top of Aunia's head.

Mathias rose. "What are you doing?"

"Matty," Keston warned in a low voice.

"Aurimite. A psychic bug," Q'thonos announced. "Recent. I think. Not well attached."

"Get your hands off her."

"I don't hurt, don't you think?" Q'thonos threw Mathias a dark look. "Unless you give me a good reason, my 'yes-I-am-a-real-flyer.' She has a spell on her. A listening bug. And one that has been whispering bad things as well, I'd wager. Would you say this is true?"

"Not all bad things." Aunia pulled her head back from Q'thonos' fingers. "There's somebody in my head?"

Q'thonos nodded.

"Who? How?"

"That is an excellent question." Q'thonos took Aunia's hand and dropped the astrolabe into it. "Good thing you had this. Even without the salt. Blocked some of the effects."

"Salt?" Keston dropped his half-eaten bread on the plate.

"You know something of salt, boy?" Q'thonos asked.

Keston swallowed. "In Adar, they use it for grounding and protection. Poorer households refuse to use their lot for seasoning."

"Then they are wise," Q'thonos said.

Mathias lowered himself back in the chair. He'd been an idiot to pop off. "A fireling did this. How do you get rid of it?"

"Fireling?" Q'thonos raised an eyebrow. "I thought flyers refused to have dealings with them."

"We didn't know Darla was one," Mathias said. "But the green in the fire she created sure spelled it out. The question remains. How do we get rid of it? And how much is it going to cost?"

"He's really good at magic." Reina paused in licking her plate. "And he's more polite than you."

"More polite?" Mathias gawked at the child.

"I'd suggest rerouting it. You've got the tool here and I've salt," Q'thonos said. "But perhaps we should do what Basil's faery familiar is asking."

Mathias frowned. "Faery familiar?"

"Jennium," Aunia said. "He's talking about Jennium."

CHAPTER TWENTY-ONE

VIRELIN'S THIRD REFLECTION

A heart split between banners feeds none well. It's a slow bleed that makes you hate mirrors. — Wendalin Mensani, apprentice to Dar Syrick

Q'thonos shifted closer to Aunia. He tapped a finger against the astrolabe's bronze mater rim, and a shimmer spidered over its blue-green patina, tracing out what looked like star patterns. "I thought so, don't you know."

"Thought what?" Aunia pressed her fingers against the back of her head to ease the ache, the sensation of something crawling through her head.

Where are you? The cobwebby voice said.

"I think I'll answer that later, don't you know," Q'thonos murmured. He tugged Aunia's hand, the one holding the astrolabe, a few inches up.

The cobwebbed voice disappeared.

"Confirmed," Q'thonos said. "Positive response upraised. Marked shift in the baseline."

"How... how did Darla do this to me?" Aunia whispered.

"Firelings possess a great deal of magic," Mathias muttered. He stood behind her, gripping the back of her chair.

Jennium clung to the underside of Aunia's disheveled braid. She'd been there since they'd arrived at the wizard's property, but the faery refused to send mind pictures. Even when Aunia had asked where she'd been. Except for helping Revellie the day before, she had seen Jennium last when the Boggleman attacked. That had been only two days ago. She shivered.

"Did that hurt?" Q'thonos wrapped forefinger and thumb over his hagstone lens to peer at her.

"She's talking to you, isn't she?" Aunia asked.

"She?" Mathias said.

"Jennium," Aunia said. "You see her sometimes."

"Does not matter, he can or not," Q'thonos said. "Tell your little friend to fetch her master. Don't say his name."

"She communicates in pictures," Aunia said.

"Then make the picture as nondescript as possible."

So, the eavesdropper wouldn't see. Aunia placed her hand on her shoulder, close to Jennium, and closed her eyes. She considered visualizing Basil as a shadow between curved-roofed wagons. But that identified rovers and those people were already in danger. Some had been scheduled for execution. But what visual could she use? And then it hit her. Scorched Earth clearing where Basil had taken her after rescuing her from Dalin. Jennium had been there. Aunia's throat tightened with the memory of her mother's stone there.

Jennium's weight disappeared from her shoulder.

"Sunray, the salt wrap. Would you?" Q'thonos said.

"Magic salt?" Reina said, a bit of blueberry syrup on her chin. "Because if it's moving, I'm not touching it."

Q'thonos snapped fingers at Keston. "You there. Go fetch. Top shelf. Left of the glowroot scrolls. If it hisses, pay it no heed. It likes to bluff."

Keston slowly got to his feet, his expression bewildered. "Likes to bluff?"

Q'thonos exhaled loudly. "Darkwood box. Now. Please."

Keston crossed the room and pulled out a stepstool hidden in shadow. He climbed up. Moments later, he walked over a wooden box so dark it looked black. Silver letters wrapped around its side. Lettering that looked like the ones on the cloth covering her father's cage when they were in Nonderu.

Aunia wrapped her hands around the astrolabe as Q'thonos tapped at the table.

Keston set the box down and wiped his hands on his trousers. "The thing blinked at me."

"Can't help the guardian can be flirty." Q'thonos pressed a crescent moon with a forefinger, and the box sprung open. He removed several stackable trays until he got to a recess at the bottom of the box. A gray silken bundle wrapped with a red ribbon lay there. And it glowed the same thundercloud color.

Q'thonos lifted the wrapped bundle, exposing clusters of tiny crystals. It looked as if part of it had been frozen.

Aunia pulled away, and the back of her head bumped against Mathias' fingers which gripped the back of her chair.

"Dabbles just a hint on the dark magic side, don't you know." Q'thonos unwound the bright ribbon. "But then, any magic can be used for good or evil."

"Smells like cold stone left out under the stars. And maybe just a bit of the sea." Keston retook his seat.

"How else would salt smell?" Q'thonos asked. "And how many times have you been at sea?"

Keston rotated his teacup in a circle with its handle. "Father's a sculptor. He'd travel for commissions at Adarian villas sometimes."

The cloth gave way, and Q'thonos held a small, delicate net that almost looked like lace. Fastened through the weave was crystalline salt. "Hold still now."

The mesh from the salt-woven thing prickled over her scalp like tiny needles. And it was cold. She shivered, and the astrolabe in her hands grew heavier.

"Relax," Q'thonos said. "Just think of... goats?"

Aunia froze. There were goat pens in the stables at her home village. Four-legged friends who helped her get back at Velli after Nehla had died. Velli had used the woman's pottery area as a trysting place but after goats had invaded a probable romantic encounter... well, Velli never forgave her but she stayed away from Nehla's space.

Aunia cringed at the feel of a mouse wriggling deeper into her head. Her stomach roiled, and she whimpered.

"Why's it hurting her?" Mathias snapped.

"Not supposed to. It should keep the little parasite from squirming about so I can draw it out." Q'thonos' voice sounded aggrieved but he pulled the salt cloth off Aunia's head and set it on the gray cloth. "Unless... Aunia, the astrolabe, please."

A sharp rap thudded against the cottage's warped wooden door, and without delay the latch creaked, and the door swung wide.

"What exactly are you doing?" Basil stepped within, orange bandana missing from his dark hair and with Jennium circling over his head.

Jovaryn followed, pale, and his hand at his throat.

"Brother," Reina squealed from the other side of the room. She thundered over and flung herself at Jovaryn. He caught her in his arms.

"Reina, love," Basil said. "Why don't you take your brother out to the garden? Your family gathering is long overdue."

"He's not taking her anywhere." Q'thonos still had his hand out to take the astrolabe.

"They won't go far." Basil pivoted so he could give Aunia a once over. "What happened?"

"She has an aurimite, a psychic bug, in her head," Mathias said. "Courtesy of one fireling who hides herself at the Green Harpy."

"So that was what Jennium was trying to tell me," Basil said.

"I tried a salt wrap. Overwhelmingly inefficient. We can rule out an ordinary spellcaster."

Basil stepped in closer. "Salt's a—"

"Negator of energy," Q'thonos said. "Aunia?"

Aunia passed him the astrolabe.

"I'm assuming it's a hard no for assistance from the Mystic Court?" Q'thonos asked.

Basil frowned. "They'd want to come get her immediately."

"Then it's Virelin's Third Reflection," Q'thonos said.

Basil's olive-skinned face blanched. "That's a soul-bending spell. You don't use it unless—"

"Do you see what she's holding?" Q'thonos removed his glasses and set them atop his head. "We've at least one part of the Tinker God's legacy in play."

Keston stepped forward. "Etos?"

"Do not say that name here," Q'thonos said, his voice deadpanned. "You should have said something, Basil."

"I...wasn't sure. Who do you think is in there?"

Q'thonos, glasses still on his head, gave Basil a steady stare. "Not sure? I think we both know you play on too many courts, and loyalty pulls you too many ways. And as to who? Does it matter?"

Aunia agreed. It didn't matter who. It just needed to come out. Adrenaline thrummed over her chest, and she picked at her cuticles. "What do you mean? Etos? Tinker God's legacy?"

"After, don't you think?" Q'thonos touched the corner of his eye and then scooped a bit of salt crystals from the bottom of the box. He sprinkled it along the rim of the astrolabe. The larger cluster stuck, turning the astrolabe's patina sides a glimmering. He handed the instrument back to Aunia. "Hold it loosely in your hands, please."

Q'thonos then shifted the trays and pulled out a round disc of obsidian. He held it up where the fire from the hearth glimmered on its surface. He nodded approvingly to himself. He set it on the table and then placed the salt mesh back atop her head. "You can close your eyes or keep them open. But you might not like what you see."

"What will I see?" Aunia asked.

"Not sure really," the wizard said in a low voice. "Reflections can't lie... any more than faerykind can. But they can reveal truths too dangerous to look at directly."

"How can truths be too dangerous?"

"You would ask that," Basil asked softly.

Aunia flushed. Her mother's memorial stone. Her father and the crimes others believed he did.

"One more thing." Q'thonos went through the trays again. He pulled out two silver rods, and Mathias gasped.

"Not going to hurt her, real flyer," Q'thonos said.

"It's not..." Mathias squeezed Aunia's shoulders gently. "Sorry."

Q'thonos fixed Mathias with a steady look, and then he plucked out a small glass jar. The wizard unstoppered its wide mouth, dipped a bony forefinger into a silvery-green goo, and smeared the surface of the obsidian glass. "I'll need to get your eyelids as well. It'll create a tether between your inner perception and the mirror."

"I got the candle," Basil said.

Q'thonos looked past Aunia to Mathias and then glanced at the astrolabe. "Wouldn't hurt for you to cover her hands with your own."

Mathias kneeled by the side of her chair. Aunia gripped the astrolabe tighter, the salt crystals lodged at its rim, dug into her palms. Mathias laid his hands over hers. They were warm.

Beside the obsidian mirror, a white burning candle appeared. Basil, so good at plucking things from thin air, must have conjured it.

The cobwebby voice laughed inside Aunia's head.

She took a deep breath and Basil began his chant:

"By root and wax and shadow's bend,
Let false light scatter, true form ascend.
Where mirror drinks but soul withholds,
Let silent truth be now foretold."

The obsidian on the table beside her rippled, almost like water. She clutched the astrolabe tighter.

Q'thonos waved the silver rod in her face. "Focus on a memory. Make it real. Make it safe."

Mathias' face loomed large beside her. Only inches away. Mathias. If she were going to end up broken into pieces because of this voice inside her head, she was going to remember how it felt to be kissed. And the last time had been standing inside the Green Harpy.

"Good," Q'thonos murmured.

Aunia closed her eyes. Remembered herself leaning into Mathias. Of his arms wrapped tight around her. His warmth. His lips firm, soft, insistent. Liquid fire coursed through her body. Stained her cheeks.

CHAPTER TWENTY-TWO
STRANGE CONTRAPTION

Yasendra blossomed among her kin as spring incarnate. She was radiance, renewal, and the gentleness of good. Though Etos fled jealousy on roads unnumbered, his heart broke, when the Dama cursed the favored one to suffer the insufferable. — From the story of Etos' Trinity

"Thought from thought. Separating thread from thread. That which does not belong... A reflection be made," Q'thonos crooned in a monotone while he rotated one of the silver rods a fingernail's width from Aunia's temple. He hovered the other rod over the obsidian mirror.

Ripples lapped over its surface making Aunia's smirking reflection swim... though the angle was all wrong. It should be the ceiling it caught. And if the reflection was truly hers... it should mimic Aunia with her eyes closed and a still expression.

The rippling halted, and the reflection's eyes snapped onto Mathias. He skated back. That was not Aunia behind the eyes.

"It cannot hurt you," Basil whispered from Q'thonos' left. His olive-tinged skin looked rather gray.

Mathias squared his shoulders. This was ingredient magic. The mirror. The salve on the eyes. The silver rods... like the stylus he had found in the Green Harpy's attic. He was beginning to wonder if it was a magical tool as well. Maybe one of Darla's. She had behaved as if the items in the attic weren't hers and maybe he could've forgiven the lie. Attacking Aunia, however... He'd strangle Darla if he ever found her.

Aunia jerked, her face pointed at the ceiling. Mathias barely kept the salt cloth from slipping off her head. He glanced back in the mirror, and his knees buckled. Two Aunia stared out at him. One seemed to undulate. The other, staring at him with open-mouth anguish, seemed to unravel like a knit blanket with a thread being pulled.

Aunia, his Aunia dropped her chin and her closed-eyed expression tightened with pain.

"You may hear it scream," Q'thonos said calmly. "Hear it demand things of you. Do not answer it. It is not of you. It is a cry separate from you."

The first Aunia in the mirror had dwindled into a dark shadow... taller... hooded. It thrashed. And the hood fell. Too dark. Mathias leaned forward, waiting to see Darla's features. The figure turned semi in profile, showing the curve of its face... not Darla.

Q'thonos touched Aunia's temple with the end of the silver rod. And the apparition screamed. It must have. No noise but Mathias' bones had vibrated from skull to toes. Keston leaned forward in his chair. His complexion had gone a bit green.

Basil wriggled between Q'thonos and Keston and held up a plum-sized stone, shimmery and milky white. Q'thonos nodded, and Basil pressed the stone to the mirror's surface. Glyphs blazed along the stone. The shadow caught in the mirror shuddered.

"Reflected. Anchored. Bound," Q'thonos said, his voice clipped on each syllable.

Basil yanked his fingers back as the shadow curled into the milky-white stone... saturating it with inky blackness. The stone jerked in Basil's fingers as if it were swallowing the darkness. The stone returned to milky-white. The burning glyphs faded. Went out.

And Aunia's remaining reflection? It turned its back on Mathias and grew smaller as if it walked away. A moment later, the circle of obsidian was dark and empty.

Q'thonos set one rod down and popped the moonstone into a small white pouch. "Return, little one. There is much to see and do."

The mirror remained empty, and Aunia, sitting in the chair, didn't move.

"The first reflection was her?" Mathias asked, his voice tight.

"The possibility of her," Q'thonos said.

Mathias gently tugged Aunia's cold fingers from the astrolabe but before her pinkie slid off the bronze, she straightened. Grabbed at the instrument. Her dark blue eyes looked almost black. "It's the where."

"Aunia," Mathias stroked her hair with one hand while the other touched the astrolabe's bronze. "Come back to me."

The astrolabe's outer ring slid counterclockwise, tugging Mathias' hand closer to Aunia. And the alidade... the center pointer... shifted. It pointed at the Eye symbol. It represented the sky's zenith where the Dama star spun between Harp and Hammer for centuries. Only shortly after Mathias' birth the star had been creeping closer to the Harp.

"We must find the where," Aunia said, and then she slumped. Mathias caught her before she could fall out of the chair.

Q'thonos lifted the astrolabe from her lap and pulled the salt cloth from her head. "Through the door near the hearth. Second door on the right. There's an empty bed. She'll need sleep for a bit."

Mathias pulled Aunia into his arms. Her head lolled against his shoulder. Too light. She felt too light, as if something integral had gone. But that was silly. Wasn't it? He crossed the kitchen workshop and moved into the bowels of the cottage.

Keston jumped up and opened doors as Mathias proceeded to the directed bedroom.

He wasn't sure what he expected from a guest room in a wizard's house, but walking into something cave-like hadn't entered his mind. It was a narrow space—rough-hewn stone for walls and shadows clinging to the beams overhead.

He walked past a wall of shelves cluttered with jars and boxes to a narrow bed and set her down. The bed creaked. She remained still. Too still. But her breathing remained even. And there was color on her cheeks.

A crochet blanket lay at the foot of the bed. Mathias retrieved it and tucked Aunia in. He also pulled the ribbon from the end of her tangled braid and gently pulled the braid apart. Disheveled, mud-splattered, and road weariness did nothing to distract from her beautiful heart-shaped face. Sweet innocence still clung to her, making his chest ache. Mathias cupped her cheek, bent down, and kissed her forehead.

He straightened. Stepped into a ray of pale light slanting from a single, narrow window, and took in the rest of the room. Keston stood beside a grated stone basin, which was sunk into the floor and rimmed with runes.

"Hear that?" Keston asked.

"The clicking?" Mathias pointed to a double oval mass of brass gears mounted over the door.

Keston took a step toward the door and frowned. "Looks familiar."

"Familiar, how? You've seen something like that before?"

"The shape," Keston said. "It's like an hourglass on its side except for..."

A double ring of metal pierced the center of the clicking. One of the rings, slightly bigger than hand-sized, swung out. Rotated slowly. And as quickly as the clicking had started, it stopped. The gears went still, as did the ring.

"Strange contraption," Mathias muttered, grateful for a moment to turn his worry elsewhere.

"Our king-consort was fascinated by stuff like that. Automatons. Making witch compasses." Keston turned to face Mathias. "You do know that witch compasses were created to imitate Etos' compass, yes?"

Mathias ran a hand through his hair. "I don't have time for silly stories."

"I don't think they're silly. That astrolabe of hers...and salt sticking to it? I think that's one of Etos' Trinity as well...and I don't think we'd be seeing them in the world if..."

Mollie Mae's words echoed in Mathias' head: 'You've noticed the star move?' Coldness trailed up over his shoulder blades, and he slipped a finger inside his jerkin to the folded letter stored in an inside pocket. 'Thread must be bound to ice before the Dama star rises. It seemed almost technical. "What are Q'thonos' allegiances to the augury?"

"Not sure anyone has said," Keston said. "But Basil trusted a rover kid—"

Mathias whirled. "What do we know of Basil except that he's a Mystic and a rover?"

"We know he's helped us. A few times now. And Q'thonos has too." Keston jutted his jaw out at Aunia. "How long do you think she'll be asleep?"

"I don't know." Mathias closed his eyes, then reopened. "I need answers, but..."

"I can stay with her if you'd like," Keston said.

Mathias frowned. Leaving Aunia alone with Keston... His friend would make sure Aunia stayed safe. He straightened his leather jerkin. "Thank you."

"Just... Matty?"

Mathias paused at the door.

"Don't anger the wizard."

Mathias re-entered the workshop kitchen where Q'thonos was repacking his magical devices. He had finished wiping the silver rods down with an ordinary but stained hand towel and was rolling the rods into a silk wrapper.

Basil stood by the wizard, asking something in a low tone.

Q'thonos raised a finger—a gesture to wait—and folded the salt mesh wrap three times. He then returned it to the dark wood box and loaded the trays back in.

Mathias strode to the center of the room. "How long until she's better?"

The wizard looked at him through his odd spectacles. "An hour. A day. A week. I don't know."

A week? We can't stay a week," Mathias said. "Bibb is... He's planning on attacking or something. We have to get to Spatelly."

"How?" Basil turned to face him. "Flyers dominate the sky."

Mathias crossed his arms. He wished Frehn would've listened to him. Agreed to go to Spatelly. And while Taf blended into the sky, Aunia wasn't capable of flying. And with Zevara's geis, he couldn't go without her. "Wererats attacked Moonstepper. The forest that should've raised up and squashed them, didn't. Our forces are heading to the border. We're vulnerable to attack."

"I understand." Basil flicked a hand at the table where the astrolabe... and Jennium stood. "She's filled me in on all that's happened. But we still have—"

"Portal tiles," Mathias snapped. "You can skip. Skip to Eddac Tower and bring me back my saddlebags."

Basil stiffened. "You know how many you have?"

"A pouchful. Why?"

"Because it's dangerous," Basil said. "Traveling rooms have an entire platform covered in portal tiles. Do you understand why?"

Basil didn't wait for him to answer. "For safety. The closer each tile is to its mate... the better focused the magic is. They touch in travel rooms so you actually get to your destination. That you don't reappear into nothingness."

Mathias swallowed hard. "Bibb risks himself—"

"The shorter the skip, the less dangerous it is," Basil said. "But any portal tile circle comes with danger."

"Basil is correct," Q'thonos said as he crossed the room with boxes and jars in his arms.

"We also have another worry beyond your Arch Vicar Bibb."

Chapter Twenty-Three
KAI-MARIN'S KIN

You missed the performance after you escaped the Green Harpy. Bibb threatened Lord Lyle during the start of the Kankari festival and wagged his Witch Compass like a badge from the Eaburrai. — Basil Mensani of the Mensani caravan and Mystic

Aunia's skull hummed. Not with pain exactly. More like a phantom echo of something that had been there. Only now, it wasn't. She glanced about the room, taking in her surroundings, and tried to piece all that had happened.

They had been racing to escape the Hauser flyers. She remembered that. Keston had suggested a place...Q'thonos'... a mad wizard. She rested her hand on her amulet. Yes, still under the burgundy gown Darla had conjured for her. Ugh...if she could rip this dress from her bones. Mathias had been afraid but agreed with Keston. If they could find the place.

She blinked. Had she spirit-walked as Gaitha had done? She had dreamwalked before. The only difference between the two—both meant having your spirit wander without your body—was if you were awake or not. And dreamwalking was more dangerous.

They had got to Q'thonos'. An old man... No. An almost hand-some man with angular features, unruly dark hair, and odd glasses with a hagstone for one of the lenses. Probably the most striking feature of him was his moon-silver glow.

They had found him. She had given directions, but... Jennium. Jennium had appeared to her when her head grew cold and fuzzy. Jennium had pulled aside the glamor that Q'thonos had over his land. Without her... they would have flown over, never seeing.

Q'thonos had fastened a salt cloth around her head. Voice com-manding and cool. His words had kept her heart from tearing out of her chest when he pulled that aurimite out of her head. She shuddered at the memory of being cloth sliding out of her own skin.

Aunia blinked again. The aurimite, the eavesdropper... It knew... Darla knew...where they were. Darla... who had commanded the attacking wererats to stand down and stay alert.

She had been by a pond. Aunia sat up. Kai-Marin had appeared on its surface. She had spoken to her.

The bed shook, and Mathias's face appeared at her side, his hair tangled with sleep.

Aunia leaned forward. "You were sleeping on the floor?"

"How are you feeling?" Mathias asked.

Feeling? Like a stiff cloth laying too long in the sun to dry. "Hun-gry, I think."

His glow spread out, and the stiffness in his jaw loosened. "That's a good sign."

An amber beam spilled in from a small window set high in the wall. "About when in the day?"

"Long past lunch." Mathias inhaled deeply. "And almost supper."

The warm smell of roast chicken, garlic and pepper reached her. Warm bread with herbs. Something with warm honey too. Aunia slid, setting her feet on the floor. Eating sounded amazing.

Mathias offered a hand up, and she accepted. Her head felt a little light, but her footing was firm.

They moved through the short hallway and into the kitchen workshop.

"Plates are atop the books on the stool by the hearth." Q'thonos pivoted from a chair at the table. He, Basil, and Keston sat on the closest side of the table before many platters of food. And something that looked like a tarnished brass horn. The thing shuddered, and out popped a pot and ladle too wide for the horn's mouth.

"We'll need more than plates." Basil plucked several bowls into existence from the air.

Keston grabbed one of the bowls and scooped up some of the pot's content. He smiled widely. "Lamb and barley stew."

"Have a seat." Q'thonos tapped on the horn's side. "We've plenty."

Aunia stepped forward, took in the words scrawled in chalk on the horn's slate tray. "Caution: Temporal Loop Risk—No Peeking Before Six."

Mathias handed her a plate, and they both took seats at the other end of the table. Reina with Jovaryn... her brother... Aunia remembered, sat on the far side of the table near the room's only window.

"Reina, you want some too?" Jovaryn asked.

"Not stew." The girl shook her head. "Dessert."

"Dessert is for after, dear girl," Jovaryn muttered. "Eat."

Reina scowled, and Q'thonos called her by her nickname. "Sunray." It seemed a strange nickname for a stormy child, but Reina flashed the wizard a grin, and dug into her food.

Aunia also loaded and attended to her plate until the emptiness in her belly lessened. Conversation went on around her. She barely listened until...

"Were you able to save the rovers at Worley?" Keston asked Basil.

Aunia wiped her hands on a snowy-white napkin.

"We did. It was close." Jovaryn's blue glow retracted and shrank even more under Basil's grimaced stare.

"Well, rescued is rescued." Aunia frowned. "Right? I am glad they're free."

"We are glad as well, but it's dangerous to be a rover right now," Basil said. "All the caravans will need to vanish for a bit."

"Helping us get to Spatelly might help your people as well," Mathias said.

Basil looked to Jovaryn, who took to studying his plate.

A silence fell, and after several minutes of utensils scraping along plates, Keston snorted. "Almost wish for Etos' hourglass. Speed past the discomfort."

Aunia looked up. "Etos?"

"I do not wish to tell that tale," Q'thonos' slate-colored eyes turned silvery. He pushed away from the table and wandered across the room to a standing table near the cupboards.

Keston rose. "But you said that the astrolabe is part of the Trinity."

An open book sat on the standing table, and Q'thonos brushed through its pages.

"Is it a secret?" Keston asked.

"Don't anger the wizard," Mathias muttered.

Jennium zipped by Aunia's head, buzzing loudly. She landed beside the book, stamped her tiny foot, and pointed at it.

Aunia rose. Mathias caught her hand, but she pulled away and walked to where Q'thonos stood. She got closer and stiffened when she saw her father's writing. "That's my book."

Q'thonos pivoted to face her, a pleasant surprise crossing his features. "You can read this."

"Of course I can read."

"I mean the book allows you."

Aunia stiffened. Allowed? She shifted on her feet. There had been plenty of times she had wanted to go through its pages. Show Mathias the starcharts she had found there. Read more about the augury. Something always seemed to distract her. Or she couldn't find the page she was looking for. Or the blank pages inside seemed to change, which of course, was foolish.

She frowned. The last time she had looked at it had been at Eddac Tower. Since then, or rather shortly after until only a few hours ago, she had a copy. A copy she had manifested. A copy that was still at the Moonstepper hostel. "Are you saying the book is spelled?"

Q'thonos turned another page to an illustration she had never seen before. It took up half of one page and read 'astrolabe.' It looked different from hers. Not rounded and flat but globular with concentric rings. The marking though... they were the same as her astrolabe that set beside the book. Some of the faded black ink mutated... shimmered gold and tiny lines spidered out in a dizzying pattern. And then more lettering blazed across the page. 'Halite Salt from Wraithmere.'

The wizard flipped the page and another one

"Wait. Turn back," Aunia said. "There's something about salt there."

Q'thonos froze. "You saw that?"

"Course I did. Turn back."

The wizard tightened his jaw, flipped back to the illustration, and read. "Salt crystals from the Wraithmere to act as a purifier. That salt is the most potent you'll find."

Aunia drew closer to the table, tapped at the edge of the astrolabe where a thin layer of salt clung to half its rim.

Mathias joined her. "I don't see anything."

"You can," Aunia said, then frowned. "Look at it like you would the sky."

Q'thonos flickered a gaze from her to Mathias, and back again.

Mathias frowned, reached out, and tapped the astrolabe. "I know after the salt fastened on the rim here, it moved. Spun to the Eye."

"Yes," Q'thonos said. "To the place where the observer watches the Dama star."

Iciness ran along Aunia's spine. "Kai-Marin wanted me to read this book."

"Wait." Mathias tapped a finger on the page. "I think I see something faint there. Like old, old ink."

"You spoke to her?" Q'thonos straightened. "When?"

Aunia frowned. It surprised her she hadn't thought about her meeting with the Eaburrai earlier. In fact, the entire interaction felt like a half-forgotten dream. "This morning. Before we got here. She appeared as a reflection. A Jenny Greenteeth and a dryad showed before then."

"And what did Kai-Marin say?" the wizard asked.

"She asked if I had my father's starbook," Aunia tapped at the amulet under her dress. "And that wisdom unfollowed means nothing. I should take time to read."

Q'thonos nodded to himself, and softly murmured:

The tale of Etos, silver-haired,
Wanderer of the Eaburrai,

Did mourn his sister's plight and dared
To save her from her destiny.

"What is the Wraithmere?" Aunia asked. "And what do you mean by Etos' Trinity?"

"Things obviously you need to know," the wizard said. "Particularly since you have one of the instruments and at least one other walks in the world."

He tapped on a page, written in her father's hand, "The place is not stone nor star, but heart and hand. Where the bearer stands, the worlds turn."

"I want the story," Reina said.

Q'thonos sighed. "Etos was an Eaburrai, who walked freely between the worlds. He was the youngest of the court, save for Yasendra, who everyone loved."

He continued spinning the story of Yasendra being the Eaburrai of spring, light, and laughter and how Etos' siblings whispered that he was often away because he was jealous of the attention his youngest sister got. Perhaps that was true.

But everything changed when Yasendra's love of a mortal caused the Dama's Heart to shatter, bringing an end to the free flow of magic between the worlds. At first, Etos believed Yasendra's punishment of accepting a yoke of sacrifice for her lover and their future offspring was just. That changed when he saw Yasendra's firstborn saddled with the power of being a Chandarion, and how the Elderghast destroyed him.

"Wait," Aunia said. "I've heard of the Elderghast before."

"I told you it," Mathias said. "When we traveled to the Grashbear. Yasendra meant to hand the heart to Uriah, but she mistakenly handed it to his brother—"

"Who was jealous," Aunia finished.

Mathias nodded. "The Dama's Heart stripped him of all humanity as it shattered."

"And the Elderghast swore to destroy Yasendra and her line," Q'thonos said.

"Hence the War between the Worlds," Keston said.

"Yes, but before that war, Etos decided to save his sister. But what he did made it worse." Q'thonos walked away, passed the table, ruffled Reina's hair, and stared out the window.

Aunia followed him. "Made it worse how?"

"If the fate-threads moving the Dama star were knotted tight, it's possible they'd never let the star slip into Harp or Hammer. A choice perhaps would never need to be made."

"Fate-threads?" Mathias stuttered.

Q'thonos turned from the window. "They are all around us, shifting and changing as we make decisions. They are free-flowing. Untethered. Free. Etos saw those threads as a way to control the augury. The compass to discover what threads needed to be tied and where they were. The hourglass to freeze time so he could get to the right spot before they shifted again. And the astrolabe... to reach into the heavens."

"An astrolabe can also tell time and location," Mathias said.

Q'thonos nodded. "It would seem your Arch-Vicar Bibb holds Etos' Compass."

"It's a witch compass," Mathias said. "There are others."

"Instruments copied from Etos' compass," the wizard said. "Yes, but none of those could channel through fate-threads to plant an aurimite. They're not powerful enough. However, the compass from the trinity... it offers power depending on who wields it and what it becomes tethered to."

Mathias stood perfectly still. "Zeller's Chand ice amulet."

"So, it wasn't Darla," Aunia said.

"No," Mathias said. "It was Bibb. And he's been looking for Aunia."

"The fate-threads would be pulled if he was looking for her. And he could travel along any threads that found her."

The food in Aunia's belly plunged to the pit of her stomach. "What would happen if I had been in the faery world?"

The wizard blinked. "You were in the faery world?"

She nodded.

"Maybe." Q'thonos paced back and forth in front of the window. After a long moment, he stopped. Looked up. "The trinity has caused other unexpected rifts—"

"Like breaking the timing when Chandarions appeared?" Basil asked.

Q'thonos snapped, "Etos didn't want Yasendra to suffer more."

"What do you mean by breaking the timing?" Aunia asked.

"Ilyssa came nearly seventy years later after Yasendra's son. The next one didn't come until Edvaras."

"It wasn't Edvaras who broke the augury." Keston turned in his chair at the table.

"Edvaras?" Q'thonos said. "Oh, blessed Dama, no."

"I wish my father were here." Aunia closed her eyes. "He was supposed to take care of augury things. Said the ocean told him to."

The wizard's voice turned stony. "The ocean told your father?"

"Yes." Aunia opened her eyes. "Mathias and I went to rescue him in Nonderu. He disappeared there. I don't know where. Wait. Could the astrolabe help me find him?"

"Disappeared likely into the faery world," Q'thonos muttered, shook his head, then pointed at Aunia. "You spoke to Kai-Marin. And you can read her book."

Aunia frowned. "That's my father's book."

"Who is your father?" Q'thonos' expression turned stormy, and he whirled to face Basil. "If you twirl another distract charm under the table, I will break your fingers."

Basil grimaced and set his hands on the table.

"His name is Rune," Aunia said.

"Rune?" Q'thonos walked past the table to the large open hearth. He leaned his head against the stone, and more minutes crept by.

"I'd like cloud-berry pudding, please." Reina's voice pierced the quiet.

Ignoring Reina, Q'thonos turned. "You're Ferris Runoldi's daughter?"

From the reading desk and the book, Mathias' voice sounded. "Your father is the Mystic who killed the royal family?"

His words struck hard. Aunia stiffened. "That was a lie. Your Fallo even said so."

Mathias blanched. "When Fallo first saw your father. He wanted to—"

"Behead him," Aunia snapped. A sharp pinching sensation formed at her temples. "I know."

"Aunia," Q'thonos said softly. "Daughter of Ferris Runoldi, son of Kai-Marin."

"Son of Kai-Marin?" Aunia's heart staggered. "No."

"Yes," Q'thonos said.

She hugged her belly to keep from vomiting. "The Boggleman was born of Kai-Marin."

Keston rose from the table. "The Boggleman's your uncle?"

Aunia couldn't breathe. Couldn't move. Couldn't look at Mathias. Basil's face appeared large in front of her. She pushed him back. And with that, her muscles unlocked. She ran out the front door.

CHAPTER TWENTY-FOUR

THE YEW TREE

And at the conclusion of the War of the Worlds, Uriah and Illysa bound the Elderghast within a yew, and around it they planted the sacred grove—not for beauty, but for vigilance. For even chained in living wood, all creatures remember the shape of freedom. — History of the Chandarions, from the Temple of the Eye

How long have you known who she was, Basil?" Q'thonos demanded.

Mathias stared at the open-door frame where Aunia had pelted through, wishing his feet would move. But he couldn't. A wizard spell. Q'thonos must have cast a spell.

There's no wizard magic upon you, Taf sent.

"I thought you knew everything," Basil said. "And yes, Keston. Ferris Runoldi and the Boggleman are brothers, though centuries separate them.

"You could have told me when you dropped off Sunray," Q'thonos snapped.

"Would you have taken her in?"

A low whimper sounded from the table.

"Tap on the cornucopia, Sunray. Ask for whatever dessert you want." Q'thonos faced Basil, who had taken several steps toward the door. "I promised Sunray I'd protect her. Always."

"I think your attention would have been too divided then," Basil said. "And I wasn't sure of Aunia until... She is the best hope we have."

Hope? That word fell like a rock. Mathias tried to swallow. Tried to loosen the sand on his tongue. In his throat. Aunia's father had murdered the royal family—save for the current queen—sixteen years ago. An episode that had a hand in driving the monarch mad. And Fallo knew who Rune was. He knew and he threatened Rune with a beheading. Looked for marble for the last ingredient for a time-turn spell. To save the queen? Or to keep the woman he loved, Aunia's mom, from dying. Or both?

On the Harp, Mathias had fought beside that traitor in Nonderu. No, not a traitor. Rune was not Tamorian. But he had been an ally. Trusted. Mathias' mother had told him stories about the regicide. And Aunia said that story was a lie.

Mathias opened his mouth but nothing came out. He tried again. His voice crackled like torn paper. "What is she? Faeblood? Mystic? Chandarion?"

"Does it matter?" Basil moved to the door.

"Oh, no, you will not be skipping away now, Mystic," Q'thonos said. "There are things we must discuss."

"You won't be turning him into a rug, are you? Reina asked. The horn had spat out several bowls of something with a fluffy top, and she had her spoon dug deep in her bowl.

"Reina," Jovaryn said. "Let those two argue among themselves."

"She's perfectly safe." Q'thonos stepped toward Basil. "And you're going to give me answers."

Basil and Q'thonos' voices merged with fast-paced sentences, most of it unintelligible. Mathias tapped a fist against his thigh. The two men stood nose-to-nose near the door. Jovaryn hovered over Reina. And Keston... Keston padded over to him with an expression of resigned determination.

Keston stopped at Mathias' side. "I'll go to make sure she's okay."

Keston to go console the girl? No, he'd go. Yasendra be blessed, it was still Aunia.

Don't let her fly headfirst into the gale alone, Taf sent.

"I won't." Mathias ran past the two men and out into the garden.

Rev looked up from nosing through heart-shaped and furry-stemmed lemon balm. Taf stood facing west where guttural croaks from ravens split the air.

She's opened a path beyond, Taf sent. *You better hurry.*

Mathias' heart dropped. The last time he had heard insistent raven calls was when he and Taf had entered the birchwoods. *What do you mean, opened a path?*

In the betwixt. Into the fringes of the Sacred Grove. Hurry!

Mathias ran for Taf. To climb onto his back and...

Taf shied away. *"Better on your own.*

Why?

I will wake what shouldn't be woken.

Wake what? But Mathias didn't have time to wait for the answer. He raced toward the trees where ravens had settled. A wide deer path appeared below and between the tree limbs where their black feathered bodies perched.

Adrenaline thrummed through Mathias' veins. There was nothing for it except enter the tree-lined tunnel.

He stepped inside and the trees pressed in closer. Branches arched low, blocking the evening sun from filtering down through the canopy. It grew dark. Too dark to see his feet. The air filled with the smell of wet bark and copper. He paused, tightened his fist. *The light, Taf.*

He and Taf's egg-shaped white light flared before him, illuminating branches that were closing in. But they withdrew. A trick of the light or an attack? Mathias swallowed. Continued on, twigs snapping under his boots. He counted.

Twenty-two steps. Twenty-three.

He was chasing after a murderer's daughter. And Kai-Marin's granddaughter. That meant she was part Eaburrai. Something snarled near Mathias' left. He gripped his dagger hilt. Wished he still had his sword. Another snapping twig. Twenty-six. Twenty-seven. Aunia with her fierce hope and the way she held her own ground. The care and the love that she showed to others. Thirty. Thirty-one.

Part Eaburrai. The royal Tamorian line was descended from Yasendra but Aunia's connection was more immediate. Granddaughter. Not multi-great, which spanned through centuries of generations. Her lineage could make her abilities more potent. It also would explain why the Boggleman went after both Rune and Aunia. But was it for conquest or potential alliance?

Mathias had fretted that Aunia was a potential... if not a true Chandarion. And he had been shoving that thought, and the fear that accompanied it, away. Chandarions and potentials awaited a horrible doom. They would save the worlds, yes, but they became the material to form the Dama's new heart. Zeller had spun out their fate explicitly several times when he and Nyrissa helped Zeller map the stars.

Aunia was the Boggleman's niece. Stop it, he told himself. She was still Aunia. Just Aunia. Nobody got to choose who they were related to. Would he have chosen his own parents if he had had a choice? Thirty-eight. Thirty-nine. Find Aunia and comfort her. And after, figure out how to get to Spatelly.

And go after the compass, Taf sent.

Mathias rubbed his eyes. The compass. The astrolabe. There was too much to worry about without an Eaburrai's magical devices. Keston knew about these objects. Why hadn't he?

Sounds of moving water reached his ears, and the tree tunnel expanded, letting light... noonday light in. They weren't in the mortal world. But all he had to do was walk back out, right? He set his shoulders back and stepped forward into a clearing.

The clearing was wide, with a black-stone bottom creek, like the one within the Birchwoods, running along its left side. Mathias smoothed away the shivers at the back of his neck.

Weeping willows marched along its bank with tendril fingers floating within the current. And Aunia was there. Standing in front of a willow, fingers unknotting a...wish knot.

This was a Wishing Willow Grove... like the one near the Augurite temple at Heavenfeet. But didn't she know? You weren't supposed to untie other people's wishes. There had to be hundreds of wishes here. Maybe tens of thousands. Who had tied them all? Faery creatures? They weren't in the mortal realm.

"My mother told me she must have tied a thousand wishes into the willow," Mathias said as he approached her. "Though she always warned you needed to watch how you worded them."

Aunia turned, her eyes red-rimmed.

He stopped in front of her. Tapped the knot in her hand. "People tie wishes on the willow tendrils and hope they are heard by Eaburrai and the Dama. You could...tie your own."

Aunia let go of the tendril and brushed a tear from her cheek. "Your mother had a wish go astray?"

"She wished for a life as a lady of her own estate," Mathias said. "What she got was my father."

"Your mother doesn't like your father." Aunia's voice sounded flat.

Astute of her. Had he told her? Or had she riddled that out on her own? "I would agree."

Aunia turned to the next tree. "Then why did they take a bead?"

"Marriage," Mathias corrected. He exhaled and followed her. "There are tales of them being wildly in love once. And I've heard girls my mother's age used to sigh themselves to sleep over the tale. My father, you see, walked away from...well, a very prestigious engagement. In favor of her."

Aunia turned to face him.

Mathias stopped inches away from her. "Scandalous at the time. The stories still circulate during court balls and festivals. A reminder, I suppose, that sort of love is doomed to fail. Eventually."

Aunia's beautiful dark blue eyes dimmed. It was like curtains drawn for the night. And her expression tightened.

You've hurt her, Taf sent. *Why?*

I didn't mean to... I offered nothing but... truth.

Aunia turned away from him, and his chest cracked.

"Apologies. Aunia, I'm sorry. My... father has been unfaithful to my mother for a long time now. And I... I've never wanted to be anything like him."

"Then don't be him." She shuffled to another willow. Brushed another wish-knot with her fingertips.

He followed her. Set a hand on her shoulder.

She shrugged it off.

Nausea wriggled in his gut. This was not going the way he had planned. He needed to fix this. But how?

She moved further off from him.

A shadow lengthened in the clearing. Tree-shaped.

Mathias pivoted... automatically putting himself between Aunia and a yew tree. One with crooked limbs, barely any leaves, and with its bark split like wounds that would never heal.

"It's time to go back," said another voice. Q'thonos stood near the tree tunnel entrance. He had changed into buckskin trousers and a loose shirt, both in the colors of healthy leaves. He carried a staff with him. "Things are in play that cannot be halted."

Mathias reached for Aunia's hand. She jerked away.

"Mathias," Q'thonos said. "Go back. I will bring her along shortly."

CHAPTER TWENTY-FIVE

THE STAR BEFORE THE HARP

The turning of the astrolabe, when starlight calls the night, awakens threads of ancient fate, still burning, fierce, and bright. — From the Summoning of Uriah

Aunia shivered. She stepped back from Mathias despite his brow creased with pain. She needed time to think. About what he had said. About what she had learned. And about the tree that had appeared and hovered nearby with a dark oily glow about it.

"Mathias." Q'thonos stepped between them. "She's safe with me. Go."

Mathias frowned, turned and walked back to the trail.

He did not look happy to go, but relief surged through Aunia when he went. He didn't want to love her. Or maybe it was just he didn't trust to love her. Her body thrummed as if pieces had shaken loose, and part of her wanted to collapse on the ground... except for that tree. It watched her. Not with eyes, but with a kind of hunger that marched imaginary ants over her arms and back. Every instinct said if she fell, its thick roots would jut out, grab her, and squeeze.

"We need to go as well," Q'thonos said softly.

Aunia turned to face the towering thing with its split trunk and monstrous limbed spirals. Every ridge puckered as if the wood had once writhed and screamed. She should step back, but she felt defiant.

Q'thonos moved in front of her. Not blocking her view of the yew, but forcing her to look at him.

"It's better to ignore it."

Aunia crossed her arms. "It's something more than a tree. Isn't it?"

"The Elderbind," he said in a bare whisper.

"What does that mean?"

"Best to discuss elsewhere."

"Why?"

"It contains something from a long, long time ago and for reason."

"Dangerous?"

"It can be if it's noticed." Q'thonos tapped his staff on the ground and it made a meaty thunk. The tree seemed to shrink a bit... maybe pull further away. Either was silly.

"Q'th—"

"Don't say my name," the wizard snapped. "It remembers names. Even if it's forgotten its own."

That sent a shiver along Aunia's spine. She whispered, "What's inside?"

"The Elderghast." The wizard mouthed.

Mathias had said that name once when he told her the story about Yasendra and Uriah. Aunia had wanted to hear about their great love. He had wanted to talk about how love doomed two worlds. Perhaps, in a way, Mathias was right. Uriah and Yasendra had fallen in love but Yasendra had done something she wasn't supposed to... and it caused the Elderghast to be created. It also created the need for Chandarions who were destined to remake the Dama's heart.

"We shouldn't stay." Q'thonos butted into her thoughts. "Walk with me, child... back to the mortal realm. There is much to do and we have another sign that the choice is coming."

She followed him onto the heavily shadowed path and while she didn't want to voice it, she was grateful that his staff conjured a bit of light. She felt more secure for a few steps before her mind swirled again on who she was and Mathias' pain-soaked words. She needed to distract herself. "What do you mean by signs?"

"The Elderbind appearing here for one," Q'thonos said. "It's worse than the ghouls arising near Idenweigh—"

"Ghouls?"

"The dead walking. When the choice is near, they appear where past carnage scars the land."

"Idenweigh is where?"

"The southern part of the Grashbear Mountains."

The Grashbear was far away. Her fear drained from her shoulder blades. "The Queen is sending soldiers to the border. Do you think Bibb is—"

"I do not know what that creature is up to—"

"Creature?"

"How to put this. That man changed completely from a dozen years ago." By the light from his staff, Q'thonos looked...sad. Everything was sad. But evening was coming. She was tired. Down to her bones tired. But she was not looking forward to sleep.

Q'thonos paused inside the tree tunnel... a mere step from his gardens and the purpling sky. "You need to retrieve the compass."

Aunia pivoted, surprised. "You'd save the faebloods?"

"I'd save all of us. Get the compass and get the halite salt."

"Why?"

"May I?" Q'thonos held out his hand.

Aunia frowned, but she took it.

The world slid through her, and she gasped, clutching Q'thonos' hand and grasping his arm. They hovered over the trees.

"You're quite safe," he said. "Can you identify the Harp constellation?"

She twitched her toes and swayed her dangling feet back and forth. Low on the horizon, seven stars stretched. They curved forming a harp. It wasn't difficult at all imagining invisible strings meant for plucking. "Up ahead."

"Good. And do you know how to see the Dama star?"

Aunia turned her head away to look on her periphery, like Mathias had shown her.

She spotted the house...scanned the grounds to see if Mathias' stood outside and gave herself a little shake. She scanned the heaven... and cried out. "It's almost in the constellation."

"Yes," Q'thonos said. "In less than a week, the Dama star has raced across the heavens. There it now rests. I do not know for how long."

Aunia squeezed Q'thonos' hand tighter not knowing what to say. If she wasn't afraid, she'd be holding her face in her hand. But she was... And then, they were descending to the ground. They landed by a planter with half-grown sunflowers. Tafiriel stood beside it.

"Your young flyer wants to go to Spatelly," Q'thonos said. "He wants to know what Bibb is doing. I say go there. Get that compass. Get the salt. Come back here."

"Come back—"

"I can help draw the Dama star away from the Harp. Knot up the fate lines. Put the star back in the middle."

"You can do that?"

"Somebody has to," Q'thonos said. "The astrolabe will allow me to but I need that compass."

"Why?"

"To find where I need to stand. And which fate-thread I must knot."

"But can't you go?" Aunia did not want to confront Mathias. She didn't want to go near him... but Zevara's geis.

"I think Kai-Marin's granddaughter will have an easier time in the Wraithmere. You'll find it in the salt marshes. It's Kai-Marin's home when she visits the mortal world."

Aunia's heart skittered over her ribs. Her grandmother. But what did that even mean? Aunia bit her lip. Nodded. And released Q'thonos' hand. She walked to the house. She had to work with Mathias. If he didn't want to love her... well, she wasn't going to force it.

The heart knows what it wants, Tafiriel sent. *It's only time. The moon hasn't even gone through a whole cycle since you met.*

Aunia kept walking.

We'll face the darkness together.

Aunia blinked back tears. *You don't know darkness.*

Basil held the door open for her. She stepped inside with Q'thonos behind her. She didn't look at Basil. She didn't want to look at anyone. It was a relief that only a few candles, not oil lamps, threw a minimal amount of light. The supper dishes had been cleared. Reina sat at the table with Jovaryn at her side. Keston stood at the cold hearth with Mathias at his side. Aunia slid her gaze away from him. They had let the fire go out.

"Jovaryn does have training from Heb," Basil said as Q'thonos moved back to the starbook.

"But we'll need a rock heap," Keston said.

Aunia blinked. "Rock heap?"

"To call up a betwixting tunnel." Jovaryn tapped a knuckle against the table. "But I don't think it's a good idea. I couldn't call one when we tried to free your kin, Basil. And even if I can call one up now... I don't know if I can keep it steady."

"Like Ryver called a betwixting tunnel." Aunia stepped closer to the table.

Jovaryn nodded, and Reina lay a head on his shoulder.

"You can do this," Basil said.

"And what happens if it crumbles—"

"Jovaryn," Basil said, "I can't skip this many from such a distance."

Jovaryn rose from the table. "But your faery familiar."

"You see her? She's blinked out."

"The Dama star is before the Harp," Aunia said softly. "If we don't go..."

Jovaryn turned deathly pale.

"The Dama star *is* before the Harp?" Mathias said. "You saw it?

Aunia sat down beside Reina. "We need to get the compass—"

"And find out what Bibb is doing," Mathias interrupted.

Keston bumped Mathias with his elbow.

Aunia closed her eyes. She needed to shut down her heart. At least for the moment, she had to. "And get halite salt."

"Seems the wanderwright did have a prophetic dream," Jovaryn muttered.

Q'thonos stiffened. "What do you mean?"

"Gavryn from the Loravi caravan said Etos approached him in a dream. Said to gather halite," Jovaryn said.

"And did he?" Q'thonos closed the starbook and returned it to Aunia's knapsack.

Jovaryn looked at the table. "He was one of the rovers we rescued from Worley."

"We could see about flying," Keston said. "Forces will be out looking for Fallo too. Maybe we can slip through."

"You'll be caught before you go five leagues," Reina said. "And they'll put you in irons. But I don't think it'll matter much cause we'll all be gone."

"You're seeing that, Sunray?" Q'thonos asked.

"Seeing that?" Jovaryn looked at the wizard. "Not all of Reina's fortunes come true."

"Enough do." Q'thonos repacked the astrolabe into Aunia's knapsack as well. "She has a gift. And I'm quite content to keep her safe here."

"Jovaryn," Basil crossed to stand in front of the table. "Hebsolum gave you and Ryver this ability. Trust it."

"Yes, do, big brother." Reina wrapped her hands around Jovaryn's arm. "I trust mine. Sometimes I get to yell 'yippee' and sometimes it's 'oops' but we don't know nothing unless we try."

Jovaryn clenched his jaw for a moment and then patted Reina's hands. "Fine. I'll try, but I haven't seen any rock heaps about."

"Ryver used a stone wall," Aunia said. "When we were at Eddac Tower. What about the hearth?"

Jovaryn exhaled slowly. "Natural stone is easier."

"All natural," Q'thonos said. "And why the fire is out."

Jovaryn walked to the hearth. "Not sure the pegasi will fit here either."

"That I can help with." Q'thonos strode over, scooped up the glass jar with the teeth, and unstopped the lid. "Wishes. The reason why the ghille dhu collects them."

The wizard threw a molar onto the cold ashes, and almost immediately the hearth expanded. Even mounted on a pegasus, they'd be able to walk into the cavernous space without ducking their heads.

"So, without any sleep we go." Jovaryn padded to the hearth and grumbled under his breath. "I hope this works."

"Aunia?" Q'thonos held out her packed knapsack.

She went over and collected it.

He also handed her a new pair of sandals. "You could use these."

She nodded her thanks, slipped them on, and laced them.

"Wait." Reina ran to her brother and squeezed him around his middle.

Jovaryn squeezed her back while Mathias and Keston went outside to get Tafiriel and Revellie.

"Be careful. You're the only family I have. That I'm actually related to." Reina gave Basil a cross look. "And hasn't given me away."

"I'll be careful," Jovaryn said. He freed himself from Reina's grasp and held out a portal tile. "Basil, you want to walk beside me?"

Basil conjured a new orange bandana from the air and tied it on his head. "I'm not going."

"What do you mean, you're not going?" Aunia stepped toward him. Yes, she was angry at him for keeping a secret about her connection to Kai-Marin...and the Boggleman... She didn't want to think about that piece. But he needed to go. He should go. It would be another buffer between her and Mathias. Otherwise...

Her gaze went to Mathias, who reentered the kitchen workshop with Tafiriel. She looked away.

"I've a few places I need to skip to," Basil said. "I have to find Cody—"

"Cody?" Aunia turned to face Basil. The name sounded familiar.

"My sister's friend," the rover said. "A contact to help us find out what happened to the... um, to our missing people."

"There are more important things in play," Mathias growled. "But you go run off as you need."

Basil blanched. "That isn't all. And if the Queen is going to get those Jaia seeds, someone needs to go to Eddac."

CHAPTER TWENTY-SIX

WHEN A BETWIXTING TUNNEL WAVERS

There's a storm in your skull, and you're pretending it's a breeze. — Mistress Madriel, healer to Queen Didianne

Mathias pushed past Keston to stand before Basil. "You would skip my things to the Queen. Cull the favor for yourself."

Basil blinked, stepped back, and laughed. "You think I'm stealing from you?"

Pulse thudding in his throat, Mathias lifted his chin. "Do not laugh at me. You charm everyone you meet. You act the martyr. But when it matters, you vanish. You always vanish."

"And you," Basil shot back, stepping close, "trust only your own dang guilt. Tell me, Mathias, when a world falls, will your duty save anyone?"

"I'm noble-born," he said.

"Does that mean you love our country more? I love our country too. I'd like to see this growing disease healed. I want it as much for my people as for yours. But I'd ask for one thing more."

"Do tell."

"That everyone receives basic respect."

"And that's why you are going to Eddac?" Mathias demanded.

"Matty," Keston said. "Come on. It's not like we can go to Eddac right now anyway."

"Q'thonos should turn *you* into a rug," Reina muttered.

Tafiriel butted his head against Mathias' side.

Mathias curled his hand around Taf's neck. Warm. Grounding. Mathias swallowed. He was behaving like a jerk. He turned his attention to the little girl and he gave her a small smile. "Perhaps he should."

"It doesn't matter who gives the Queen the ingredients for faery repellant," Keston said. "Only Aunia can make it."

The room grew uncomfortably quiet.

"Well, let's hope this works," Jovaryn said. With his Adam's Apple bobbing, he stepped inside the cavernous hearth with a portal tile extended in his hand.

Aunia followed the wererat with a hand on his back. "You can do this."

And the wererat who had turned Aunia's father into a wererat, smiled at her. Mathias clenched his fists.

Jovaryn touched a corner of the tile to one of the hearth stones. The back wall cracked and stone blocks shattered into pulverized sand around Jovaryn's feet. A hole, big enough for the pegasi, stood before them with darkness looming on the other side.

"Well-done!" Basil crowed.

Jovaryn smiled sheepishly. "So far, so good."

"I will meet up with you at Spatelly or here when you return," Basil said. "Aunia. Reina. Take care."

The rover vanished and Mathias exhaled slowly. He tried to stow his anger away but it really wasn't anger. It was shame. Guilt. Feeling unworthy. He shouldn't have said what he had to Aunia. She'd been reeling from learning... From learning who she was... learning something that would affect her whole sense of being. And what did he do? He pressed his fingers into his forehead. He had made it worse.

Do not worry about that now, Tafiriel sent. *Step forward and lead.*

No, Mathias sent. *We'll guard the rear. Keston can take the front with Jovaryn.*

He didn't want to get into another argument with Aunia. She shouldn't trust that wererat, but Keston would be nearby. Near with his pegasi saddle that hadn't vanished like Mathias' had. Why had his items vanished? He'd pick a strong memory... a core memory. His had been of his father the afternoon he had disowned Mathias, and then the promise he forced Mathias to make. It couldn't get more core than that.

Reina flapped her little hand at her brother, who hesitated a bare moment to wave back, and stepped through the hole. The girl waved at everyone before they stepped through, except Mathias. Mathias received a glower from her. He probably deserved it.

Mathias and Taf stepped into the near darkness. But then, a bit of light from a lit torch appeared in Jovaryn's hand. A conjuring, Mathias thought. Like Tafiriel's egg-shaped light only more mundane. But it showed a damp, cave-like tunnel that seemed to go on forever.

They walked for an hour. At first, being in motion was soothing. He could count footsteps, but after a while Mathias wondered when they'd exit for Spatelly. A betwixting tunnel should shorten distance. But Jovaryn said he wasn't very good at these types of tunnels. It was possible the wererat had them heading in the wrong direction.

He walked with his teeth clenched.

Aunia's footfalls ahead grew slower. She was getting tired too. Thuroes' Harp, they should have gotten sleep before this jaunt. A short nap while Aunia slept was all he got. He doubted the others got any.

But how restful could Aunia's sleep be? She slept because of that psychic extraction. Maybe Q'thonos should have withheld the awful truth of who Aunia was related to. Until at least later. She'd been through so much. And she'd be going through more. She shouldn't have to go through more.

The Dama star is almost in the Harp, Taf sent.

Mathias' ribs contracted against his heart. They had to go on this venture. He'd been looking to see the star himself, but the Pardonway Forrest blocked his view. And then, he'd been distracted. But Aunia said she'd seen it. Taf said too.

Taf, your light please, Mathias squeezed his hand tight and released, spreading his palm wide.

An egg-shaped white light popped above Taf's head. While it bobbed and weaved from the back of the line to the front, Mathias counted. He fell behind. A sad familiarity. Everyone eventually left him or pushed him away. His parents. Cassian. Nyrissa. Jules. Zeller.

Death and capture don't count, Taf sent.

I don't need you listening in.

Just apologize to her.

Mathias counted more steps. *You think we might find Jules in Spatelly?*

"But we have to get the compass." Aunia's voice trickled back to him. The words sounded worn. Like weights carried too long.

Mathias looked up.

"Well, faebloods everywhere will celebrate the Arch Vicar losing that thing," Jovaryn said.

"You a faeblood?" Keston asked.

"Maybe," Jovaryn said. "My mother was a quarter. Grandfather was a Sylvan from Varandu."

"Many faebloods count ancestors there," Keston said.

Jovaryn barked a short laugh. "Trade route shouldn't go through it."

"My Da says it's a matter of staying clear near festival moons."

Yes, Keston with his sculptor father had traveled all over Tamore and Adar. Mathias shook his head.

"And Bibb caught you with the compass?" Aunia asked.

"Don't know," Jovaryn said. "Maybe. I was laying out traps for rabbits when I was run down by a pair of wererats. Thought I'd die. What they did was worse. When I regained my senses, I was in Spatelly."

"Made into a wererat," Mathias said under his breath.

Jovaryn grunted. "Yes, they turned me."

Mathias grimaced. It only made sense that they'd have improved hearing.

"And since bitten faebloods have nowhere to go..." Jovaryn continued.

"What do you mean?" Aunia asked.

"Faebloods are hated. People already hate you and then you get cursed on top of it. You have nowhere to go. Then Bibb steps in. Offers you a home. Sure, it's with the Da Vennen but it's a home. And you get told you're special. That you can make a difference."

The tunnel walls wavered.

"I think your abilities are linked with how you feel," Aunia said.

"Yeah," Keston said, "Maybe we should talk about...happy things?"

"Happy? That's a tall order," Jovaryn said. "I left my family to protect them and all I have left is Reina. Thank the Eaburrai for her."

The tunnel walls flared with light.

Aunia said, "Gaitha always told me...just breathe."

They walked for another fifteen minutes at least.

"You're stronger than you think, Jov," Keston said. "Escaped Bibb... and the Boggleman too. Sorry Aunia."

"I'm glad most of us escaped the Boggleman," she said, her voice low.

"The Boggleman," Jovaryn chewed on that title. "Bibb, I think is worse."

"Why do you say that?" Keston asked.

Mathias leaned forward to listen, but something inside him wanted the wererat to shut up.

Jovaryn paused for a moment before he answered. "The Boggleman does what he does for the faery world to survive. He's not kind, but he's looking out for most of his people. Bibb, on the other hand, pretends to be nice. Gets you to trust him. And that trust betrays you. Forces you to betray yourself."

"How long did Bibb have you?" Aunia asked.

"Nearly a year in Worley's sister city," Jovaryn said.

"Sister city my trousers backside," Keston said.

Revellie snorted in Keston's hair.

He reached back to scratch her ear. "Yep. Spatelly looks like a sleeping dog with patchy fur. Houses stacked too close. Leaning chimneys and—"

"When have you seen Spatelly?" Mathias asked.

Keston looked over his shoulder and gave Revellie a final pat on her shoulder. "With my Da. We swung to the Forgotten Way as we were traveling east. He thought it be fun to look for ghosts. Didn't see any. No one in sight. But last I looked, we won't have to scale walls."

"They've shored up the walls," Jovaryn said.

Mathias rolled his eyes. "Exactly how long are we going to be walking until we're there?"

"I'm looking to have our tunnel drop us inside near the barracks," Jovaryn said. "But I haven't seen the walls change yet."

"Walls?" Mathias barked. The back of his head was aching.

"Ye...yes. The wall will recede. Be a lighter color. If I push somewhere else...well, I don't know where we'll end up."

"So, we can walk through this forever?"

"Matty?" Keston stopped walking and turned around. "You okay?"

Mathias swatted at his egg-shaped light. It was too close to his face. Everything was too close to his face. "I feel fantastic."

They walked for a few minutes in awkward silence.

"What did you mean about shoring the walls?" Aunia asked.

"The Queen punished Spatelly for siding with Aeryk during the rebellion," Mathias said. He couldn't let Jovaryn and Keston do all the talking. He tugged at the front of his jerkin. Warm. It was too warm here. "She had Dar Syrick bring down huge swaths of their walls."

"Because of the king-consort, Aeryk?" Aunia asked.

"Yes."

"Same reason why the Pardonway Forest was spelled?"

"Yes."

Aunia didn't ask Mathias anything more. Instead, she addressed Jovaryn, and that choice stung.

"What happened with the rovers at Worley?"

"Hopefully they're on their way to safety," Jovaryn replied. "No thanks to me."

No thanks, indeed. And then a cobwebby voice glided through Mathias' mind. *Why do you allow this wererat to steal your girl?*

"What do you mean?" Aunia asked Jovaryn.

"Opening and keeping a blade-cave open without a mountain around you... it's hard." Jovaryn said. "It took me everything to open one, and then, Basil and Mollie were fighting, and...well, doesn't matter the why... I got distracted. The tunnel collapsed. We barely got out. If it weren't for Basil's quick wit and Mollie Mae's talent of disguise, we'd have been caught. It helped too that luck decided to shine on us. Bibb came rumbling into the festivities demanding Lord Lyle's attention. And that gave us time to sneak everyone away."

"You had that because of us," Mathias snapped. "We drew Da Vennen eyes away when we escaped the Green Harpy."

On the Harp, his head needed to stop hurting. Mathias pressed his fingers against the pain.

Taf, geared in a horse saddle, edged closer to him. Horse saddle. Mathias wanted his own saddle.

The egg-shaped light over Tafiriel's eyes flared. Mathias winced...and when the light dimmed down... Taf wore his pegasi saddle. All Mathias could do was stare.

"Matty! How did you—"

"I don't know," Mathias said. And he didn't. It hurt to consider how. "Let's just...keep walking. We need to get out of here."

They continued walking.

Your sky has gone storm-wild, Taf sent. His silvery voice sounded bewildered at first, then stony. *You're being ridden. Cast it out.*

We're in a cave, Mathias shot back. The wall beside him seemed to waver. *There is no flying.*

"Say, didn't blade-cavers have songs they'd sing to shorten the way?" Keston asked.

Mathias clenched his jaw. Keston only knew that because he had told him.

"Ryver would hum while going through tunnels," Jovaryn mused. "Okay. How about Uriah's Summoning."

Aunia tripped and caught herself. "Uriah has a song?"

"Indeed. It's a song for if and when the Elderghast walks upon our world again." Jovaryn broke into song.

"O heart remade, O burning son,
The first to bear as chosen one.
Your soul divided, scattered thin,
That life might pulse through worlds again."

A wererat sings about Chandarions to your love. And you allow it? The cobwebby voice said. *He is delaying your journey to spend time with her.*

"Call Uriah where the stars belong,
Lest Elderghast's will grow strong.
When light is torn and night is long.
Rise, and right what has gone wrong."

Rage and fear broiled through Mathias. Jovaryn had no intention of helping them. If anything, he was leading them into a trap. Mathias strode forward, grasping Jovaryn by the neck.

"Mathias stop," Aunia gasped. She sounded tinny. Far away. Underwater.

"You're walking beside the man who turned your father into a wererat," Mathias snarled.

Aunia staggered back and Keston yanked on Mathias' fingers to free Jovaryn.

You have been invaded, Taf sent. *Fight it.*

On the Harp, what was he doing? Mathias dropped his hands from the wererat.

Jovaryn hunched down and moved away from Aunia... palms out... Squeezing the portal tile between thumb and forefinger. "I did, but I had no choice. Rune insisted. It was the only way to save you."

Aunia stepped backwards. Again. And again.

"Aunia, I'm sorry. Please," Mathias said. Panic shoved aside the anger and hate that had filled his heart. How could he make this right? There was no way to make this right.

"Aunia," Keston called. "Revellie bespeaks that he has an aurimite."

Aunia turned bewildered eyes on Keston, took another step, and lost her balance.

Mathias lunged. Desperate to catch her. Steady her.

Her back hit the tunnel's wall. And went right through.

CHAPTER TWENTY-SEVEN

CHAINS AND A MIRROR

You'd never suspect a pack of playing cards could speak across miles. But dust them with Chand crystal, and they'll listen, and answer. — Wendalin Mensani, apprentice to Dar Syrick

Aunia landed hard on her backside. And not in the tunnel. Not with grimy straw under her hands and nighttime pressing in from narrow windows. An orange glow threw dim light along the corridor. Salamander lights? Her stomach squeezed. Stars. Had she fallen into a fireling's keep?

She scrambled to her feet, pushing off from a timber floor that lay underneath the crackling hay. She brushed her hands off. No hanging glass tubes up ahead that she could see.

She stepped closer to the windows. Colored glass panes. Some broken. She couldn't make out what was outside. Grimacing, she wiped her hands off a second time... along peeling plaster.

Well, this place looked nothing like Gabryella's well-kept and breezy bedroom study. Aunia had accidentally dreamwalked herself there twice. Both times to see Gabryella stuffing fire salamander faeries into glass tubes and providing care for the Boggleman. But the fireling didn't have things dangling from long chains from the ceiling.

Aunia bit her lip. Here though...strange mechanical things swung overhead. Some looked like torso sized cages, maybe turned inside-out and slick with oil and shadow. There were also wire-made people with carved bone faces dangling upside down. Their little jaws fluttered as if trying to catch breath.

Aunia clenched her teeth to keep fear from making a noise.

Faded mural images with figures in robes, like the kind Bibb wore in Dalin, stood along the inner wall. More peeling plaster.

Keston said Spatelly was like a patch-furred dog. Was that where she was? Spatelly? Jovaryn had mentioned barracks. Was this a barrack?

She closed her eyes. Jovaryn. He had bitten her father. She thought he was a friend. Or starting to be.

She walked toward the orange glow up ahead.

Had her dad insisted on being bitten like Jovaryn said? The wererat hadn't denied it, and Dad had killed someone that day. To protect Mathias. But he had never killed before. Not even to save Nehla's life. Maybe that person in the cell wasn't even her father. The Boggleman had fooled her before with a doppelgänger in her bedroom at the Green Harpy. She had been fooled, and Mygul had incinerated her father's copy.

She blinked several times. Willed her eyes not to burn. The knapsack slid and she hefted it. Walked toward the light. Brittle straw dug into her sandaled feet. She walked past bubbled and blackened plaster with painted figures with no heads. Wiry tubing secured with metal bolts hung where the heads would have been.

Her heart thrashed against her sternum. This did not look like a safe place.

Where was everyone else? She wasn't back at Pavari. That meant she wasn't too far away from Mathias.

Mathias. She was so angry with him. But... what if he had been influenced with an aurimite? She rubbed a hand over the back of her head. That cobwebby voice told her to think things. To feel things. Aunia paused in her step. If he had one...

Stars, they needed to get him back to Q'thonos... But the Dama star. They needed to get the compass. Q'thonos needed it so he knew which fate-thread to knot. She wondered how the astrolabe knotted fate-threads. And Q'thonos also needed halite salt. She didn't understand why but...

Save Mathias. Save the worlds. She hunched in on herself. Stars, could she even save herself? She had no idea where she was.

An iron door appeared on her right, and shivers prickled along her spine. A whole door made of iron? It would make a prison for faeries. Faeries... Jennium could keep her glamoured. Invisible. Aunia fidgeted with her amulet and filled her mind with images. Images of her surroundings and an image of herself looking lost. *Jennium? You anywhere around?*

Seconds. Minutes spun out. Nothing. She squared her shoulders. What could she do but explore? Trust that the betwixting had dropped her in a place she needed to be.

Ahead, three salamander lights hung before an archway. Faeries to help her. Or set the timber floor ablaze. She bit her lip. And another door, wooden, to her right.

A low sound scraped beyond that archway. Into the darkness. Footfalls. Definitely more than one.

Her heart pattered. Mathias? Keston? She stepped forward, but a wet snuffling sent a chill through her. She backed up. That was not Mathias.

She flung herself at the nearest door, panic grating against her bones. Locked. She retreated. Ran back the way she had come. But to go where? Whoever...whatever was beyond that arch would soon appear. The iron door. She reached for the door handle. Pulled. It opened with a creak, and she winced, sliding herself through a narrow crack, and letting the door ease shut. It was dark except for a faint orange glow from a corner. And it was full of stacked boxes.

Outside in the corridor, doors squeaked open and slammed, and then raspy shuffles came near.

She slipped behind a pile of wooden boxes, and hunkered down, wrinkling her nose against the stink of something chemical and greasy.

"Keep looking," said a voice

"Maybe one of the rib braces fell," said a second voice.

"Shut up. Or should I have the master put you in one?"

Something squeaked.

Aunia froze. Wererats.

"Ain't no rib brace missing," said a third voice.

Footfalls passed by. Long minutes dragged and then the door handle to the room rattled.

"Locked," said the second voice. "Same as the master's room. Maybe the master has another experiment going in there."

"Better hope that's the case," said the first voice. "Come on."

Scuffling moved away from the door. Then silence.

The door was locked? Aunia closed her eyes. It hadn't been locked when she went in. She stood. Afraid to try the door. Locked in was better than found, right? No, no, it wasn't. But she was separated from wererats. And if there were wererats here... there was probably Bibb.

Aunia stepped away from the stacks of boxes and moved toward metal shelves that lined the far walls of the room. A reek hung in the air. Something like torched stone and old blood.

Glass jars in all shapes and sizes covered the shelves. Some filled with liquid. Some empty. More things were stowed here. Metal tools. Small boxes with lids. She opened some of these. Metal shavings in one.

Blue-colored salt or sand. One held sparkly silvery dust. She swallowed hard when she opened one that held dried Navenra petals.

It was possible that Bibb stored the compass here. She just had to look. She shuffled through everything on several shelves. No compass.

She turned to three empty long tables that stood off to the side. Iron legs. Stone tabletops and dark stains. She shivered at a long metal rod laying on the floor.

The compass had to be with Bibb. The only thing she accomplished by looking here was scaring herself. She looked at the lone salamander light that sat in the middle of the last table. She wondered if she could risk freeing it. She sidestepped toward it and spotted several loose pages beside it.

She lifted one, and the page crinkled in her hand. There were symbols on it she didn't understand and a red line that curved through the page. Beneath that line read, "Thread unstable without faeblood counter-weight. Must draw from living tether."

Aunia flipped the page over, set it down, and scooped a second page. This one had the Harp and Hammer constellations drawn out and between them stood a spindly yew tree with four spirals dividing its short, thick trunk. It looked like the tree from outside Q'thonos' gardens only a lot less scary.

Something moved between two stacks of boxes. Her breath caught. Well, better to find out what she was dealing with. She grabbed the metal rod, and with heart skating over her ribs, she padded over.

Between stacks of boxes, a painting in a dark ornate frame leaned crookedly like someone had knocked it over. Maybe it fell? She stepped closer.

The salamander light behind her flared, helping her to take in more of the details of the painted mermaid sitting atop a storm-tossed sea. The being's hair whipped around her, tail shimmering with pearlescent blues and greens. But it was the mirror in the mermaid's hands that caught Aunia's breath.

It was painted silver, like Taya's card. Like Basil's card. She imagined if she reached out to touch it, it would feel rough... like sand was mixed in with the paint. Basil had used his card to talk to his sister across miles when they had been at Scorched Earth... before Aunia had found her mother's memorial stone.

Maybe she could call Basil with this. The mirror turned dark. Rippled—not like water but like glass being breathed on. Aunia bit her lip. She extended her hand—both curious to touch and also scared to. The mirror enlarged instantly to take over the entire canvas.

A face emerged in the mirror.

Aunia staggered back.

"Hello Aunia," said Gabryella, the fireling. The fireling who had cared for the Boggleman. Who had spelled the fire salamanders into the tubes. "It's been a while since you visited me."

Chapter Twenty-Eight
The Hollow

I remember the day Gabryella warned the others on Ignivar University steps not to touch the veil. To allow the heavens to do so. But it unravels so easily. And I am only shaping what desires shape. — Darla Valesco, former fireling

The wind roared, ripping at Mathias' hair, his clothes. He flailed, windmilling his arms, and plummeted through the night sky. Toward a sprawling crescent pressed between two ridges. The city approached fast. Turrets rising up to skewer him.

And then, the thunderous, glorious flutter. Light blue wings. And... Tafiriel!

The pegasus shot beneath him, bucket saddle lifting.

Mathias twisted. Forced his body to align. His fingers grazed the lip of the saddle. Slipped. He tipped his body headfirst. Tightened his belly. Reached. Grabbed the saddle's front lip. His fingers screamed as they bit into the leather and the force of it nearly yanked his shoulder from its socket. He hissed. Gritted his teeth. His boots skimmed the saddle's side. And he landed hard, in the saddle, ribs jolting.

Tafiriel leveled them out, glided over the mostly dark city. And Keston? Already seated on Revellie.

A thin scream pierced the air from below. Jovaryn.

Tafiriel tucked in his wings, and dove. The city... a festering wound, raced toward them. Ashen. Oil-black.

Jovaryn curved with freefall. But too fast. Limbs flailing. Cloak snapping.

Mathias tightened his knees against Taf's sides.

The city's fractured skyline drew closer. Jagged chimneys. Cracked roofs. Creeping vines and black moss.

Taf soared under the falling wererat. He banked hard, wings snapping with a thunderous *whumph*.

Mathias locked his legs around Tafiriel. Reached out and caught Jovaryn by an arm and a handful of cloak. His weight nearly dragged Mathias out of the saddle.

Taf grunted, wings flaring wide. He steadily glided in descent.

Jovaryn grabbed ahold of Mathias' arm. Got his hand. With fingers locked tight, Mathias hauled Jovaryn toward him with everything he had. The wererat slipped. Caught the stirrup strap. Mathias still clung to Jovaryn's cloak.

The wererat scrambled up behind Mathias, breath ragged. "I thought... I thought that was it." Jovaryn panted.

"It nearly was."

And that's all that they said. What Mathias had done. He had deliberately attacked Jovaryn when the wererat was struggling to keep the betwixting tunnel open.

He still bit Rune, the cobwebby voice crooned.

Begone, Taf snapped.

Mathias mind quieted. He rocked in the saddle, catching his breath. And a sickening thought smashed against him.

I didn't see her fall, Taf sent.

Didn't see? A dark laughter burbled through Mathias' mind, and a wave of nausea rose.

I said begone. Taf's voice reverberated through Mathias' head. The dark laugh strangled but not the sick weight. *Mathias. You are not in Pavari. She is among the living.*

Mathias clamped his teeth together. Nodded. Alive. Alive. But where? He blinked back a stinging heat in his eyes that the chill wind couldn't erase.

Up ahead, Keston and Rev flew back and forth over the city.

Can you sense her? Mathias sent.

She's here somewhere, Taf sent. *But there's something blocking me from sensing where except down.*

Here. Alive. Mathias rapped knuckles against his chest, and murmured, "Thuroes, please, see her safe."

Mathias looked over his shoulder at Jovaryn, and yelled, "We need to land. Complete our mission. Where?"

Even in the bare sliver of moonlight, Jovaryn's wide eyes gleamed white. "The... the girl."

"Alive. Flyers always know. Where should we land?"

Jovaryn shook. Sucked in a breath. He then jutted his arm, finger jabbing at the southwestern part of the dark crescent shaped-city. "Peasant section."

Bespeak Keston where we're landing.

Taf veered from a jutting spire with a weathered bell tower. A temple. It stood alone. Every other building near it had tumbled. Part of Dar Syrick's spell when the Queen ordered Spatelly demolished.

They drew toward the end of the city where old roads glistened like polluted streams. More houses remained upright here but they sagged. Crooked chimneys. Fallen roofs. And a pungent rot. And laced throughout it was...salt. The sea marsh is close but not close enough to smell.

Obviously, it is, Taf sent back.

But the maps show Syrick's spell had shoved it back.

Maps can sometimes fail and true bearings walk in flesh.

Mathias frowned. With the city being cursed, perhaps Tafiriel was right. Best to see what was right in front of them. Up ahead the southernmost part of the city gleamed like midnight glass and ink.

"Torchlight," Jovaryn barked as he tapped Mathias shoulder.

Mathias counted seven torches. He then glanced to find the Harp. It had sunk low in the sky but not low enough for a typical guard shift. He turned away to look again with his periphery. To mark the Dama star. His stomach sank. The Dama star hung too close to the Harp. He had hoped that Aunia had exaggerated. She hadn't. If anything, she'd been too optimistic.

The torches. They were heading out of the peasant quarter and toward that temple they had passed.

Keston and Revellie glided beside them. Below, squat, lopsided buildings leaned against their neighbors like drunken merchants after a successful sales day. And they surrounded a stretch of bare land marred by the pieces of house foundations.

"The yard," Jovaryn said. "And the houses have been turned into soldier barracks."

Keston bespeaks there should be a place to land past the training yard near the slaughterhouse.

Mathias shifted in the saddle. *How does he—*

Keston bespoke he's been here at Spatelly as a boy.

At age three? Mathias shook his head. Spatelly had fallen over a dozen years ago.

But Keston was right. They flew over a lopsided but long brick building. It had a yard. And it was filled with refuse. Revellie overshot the mark and clattered down on cobblestone past the building and garbage.

Tafiriel landed a moment later. Mathias held a hand under his nose to filter the stench. Old rot and the new tones of burnt straw, blood, and wet fur. Jovaryn slid down. Mathias followed.

Keston patted Revellie's neck. "We should send our pegasi off."

"Agreed." Mathias leaned into Taf's side. *Keep trying to sense Aunia. And let me know.*

Of course. Be careful. And no word communication after. The eavesdropper, I think, is near.

Mathias frowned. *Then how do I tell you to come back?*

Think in pictures.

Taf and Rev flew off, and Jovaryn moved to the nearest wall. He motioned Mathias and Keston over.

You will fail here, the cobwebby voice whispered. *Nyrissa will see you rot in jail.*

Mathias hissed against the feel of a hand squeezing the back of his brain. He would not allow anything to control him. "Okay, Jovaryn. We need the compass. We need Bibb's plans. Where in this Dama-forsaken cesspit do we find them?"

"Plans? I don't know. But the command chain stays about two blocks past the slaughterhouse. And the compass? That would be with *him*, which is..." Jovaryn turned toward the north. "Toward the temple."

Where the torchbearers had gone.

"Matty, what are you proposing?"

"Bibb's command would know what his plan is," Mathias said. "We're right here. We should find out."

"We'd have to keep quiet," Jovaryn said. "Stay in the shadows."

"It's bloody night." Mathias snapped.

"Matt," Keston said, his voice very soft. "You have a hitchhiker in there."

"I'm fine," Mathias growled. He sucked in a breath. "I have help keeping it at bay."

"Help?' Jovaryn said. "By what? When Bibb barges into your head, he makes you betray yourself. Have you had the blue flowers?"

Cold seeped into Mathias' blood. He had been Navenra'd half a year ago. Poisoned by blade-cavers at the Iron Onion, the night that Zeller died. Tafiriel had been poisoned too. And Fallo. The knight-sons, and now Revellie.

Jovaryn huffed a breath. "We'll have to keep to shadows because wer-erats have keener sight than you. There's a bit of open space between here and where command lives. Still, best option. We cross at the next intersection to the block of buildings."

They got a half-dozen steps in when the scuffling of soft footfalls approached. Mathias, Keston, and Jovaryn pressed against the grimy wall.

"Saw them fly this way," one gravelly voice said.

"Should rouse the others," the second said.

"And if we don't find them?" said the first. "Ain't giving Wound-binder a chance to slice me to heal me."

"Stay here," Jovaryn breathed. He stepped from the wall, stripped off his trousers, and his face and body shifted. Melted. Shoulders broadened. Body thickened and filled against his dark, knee-length tunic. His wayward light hair darkened... lengthened... sprouted along his face. A face with a pronounced snout and curved rat-like teeth. A ratman stood before them.

Jovaryn shot them a wink and strolled forward. A minute later his voice sounded gravellier and his diction slurred. "I saw them. They flew toward the Stay."

"The Quayhold?" the first voice said. "What would they be doing there for?"

"Same as us," said the second.

"Well, bog iron has its uses," Jovaryn said.

"Too hard to find," said the first. "Glasswort would be easier. Heard the crown's commissioned another telescope."

"Now we rouse the others," the second said.

"And share the bigger rations that comes for heroics?" Jovaryn asked. "The three of us can get them."

"Us three?" the first voice laughed. "Sambo and I are perfectly able to handle this. We don't need your help."

"And you could blab if there's problems," said Sambo, his voice sounding further away.

Jovaryn's voice sounded further away as well. He was drawing the other wererats from them. "Just hand me something. You decide. Portions are meager here."

"Ain't that the truth," said the first voice. "Swear you'll keep your yap shut."

"I swear on the family I left behind," Jovaryn said.

It was a long moment after that with Mathias straining his ears, waiting for Jovaryn to come back.

Keston slid closer to Mathias until their elbows touched. "He hates Bibb as much as you do. Maybe more."

"Doubt that."

"Yeah, well, Bibb's the reason he and Reina lost their family," Keston said.

The sky lightened ever so slightly, and a few of the stars disappeared.

"He better hurry," Mathias whispered.

Keston drummed his palms silently against his thighs. "Matty, aren't you worried about Aunia?"

"Course I'm worried. Everything I think about comes back to her."

"Then why so much tension between you two? I mean, you were off to comfort her and you came back without her. Didn't want to talk. And even after, neither of you are speaking to the other."

"You're exaggerating."

"Am I?"

That presence in the back of his head went still. Mathias clenched his teeth. It was listening. Whatever it was. It was listening. "I don't need to be lectured by somebody who has a girl in every single town."

"I never mislead any of them."

"You cause heartaches."

"By being honest... from the start? I might. But Matty, what do I have to offer? I'm common-born. Just above patch-born. Yes, I fly a pegasus, but I've no assets. All I have is my good looks and witty personality."

"You two talk too loud," a gravelly whisper said and Jovaryn, still in ratman form, stepped in front of them. "This way. Follow."

They crossed the dirt-paved street, quick and quiet, and pressed into more shadows against small houses. These houses were in less disrepair. The best on the block only had its limewash peeling in curls from its upper half-timbered part. That one stood only three houses away.

"Lord Phrast and Ranth Tell live here. Or did before I escaped," Jovaryn said.

"Ranth Tell?" Mathias sputtered. "The missing Spatelly noble?"

"Same. He don't much like flyers."

"What about the Woundbinder?" Keston asked.

"That one? Probably up at the keep with the master. Keep quiet. Follow my lead. If we're spotted, we walk as if we mean to be here."

Mathias balled his fists. He wished night would keep them covered longer, but Jovaryn was right. And they needed to hurry. *Taf...if anyone needs their... rest...*

Don't need blankets, but I would wish anyone pleasant dreams.

Mathias smiled grimly. If they needed to sleep anyone, all he need-ed to say was 'pleasant dreams.' They strolled toward the house, Jovaryn in the lead. Mathias' heart thundered in his chest and he forced himself not to clutch his dagger hilt.

Jovaryn veered toward the second house and melted into shadow. Mathias and Keston followed just before the door to their target opened. Three wererat boys stepped out.

Or Mathias assumed them to be wererats. They looked like boys slightly younger than Keston. And they were arguing quietly among themselves. One of them was holding a plate of pancakes.

"Yeah, but Moonstepper ain't that hard to skip over," said the meatier of the three boys. "They've portal circles. Supposed to make your skin feel weird...like there's butterflies dancing on it."

The three walked toward a shed behind the third house.

"I ain't afraid," said the shortest. "I'd rather stay here and break the prisoner."

"Yeah, but sometimes... they say it don't work," the meaty boy said. "That soldiers never pop back out and they're lost in the Void."

"They come out somewhere," the shortest one said.

Jovaryn looked at his feet and shook his head.

"Well, I'm with Micoh," said the third wererat lad, and the one holding the food. "Rather stay here. Feed these Navenra pancakes to those louts and make 'em do stuff."

"Yeah," said Micoh, "Specially the new one."

"Ranth doesn't like you playing with his prisoners," said the meaty one. "Likes to do it himself."

Mathias' heart slammed into his ribs as the wererat boys walked by. On the Harp! They had Aunia. *Taf, pleasant dreams. The three walking away from us.*

The three wererat boys fell boneless in the yard, less than a man's pace from the shed.

Jovaryn hissed. "Flyers and their sleeping sickness. We need to hide these."

Mathias rushed forward, with the other two at his heels. They stopped before the sleeping lads and pulled them into the shed. Keston ran back and scooped the spilled pancakes back onto a wooden plate.

Jovaryn said, "How long will they be out?"

"Don't know," Mathias said. "A few hours?"

"And why?" Jovaryn said.

"They've Aunia."

"Don't see how they have prisoners here," Keston said.

The place was small, dark, and empty, except for a pallet-like wall with a doorframe hole.

Mathias squeezed his fingers, and Taf's egg-shaped light appeared.

The air between the sections hung like a dark curtain and strange iridescent glyphs hung in the air. Jovaryn said tightly, "A hollow."

"A what?"

"A pocket between our world and the other."

CHAPTER TWENTY-NINE

THE CHOICE BETWEEN EVILS

Evil or not, it is lazy to bind a mind. Influence is art. Control is desperation. — Gabryella, First Flamekeeper of the Fireling Order

Aunia scuttled away from the mirror painting. Gabryella was a fireling. A fireling who served the Boggleman. Someone who imprisoned faeries in glass tubes. She was an enemy.

She had to flee. Who knew if the fireling could step out of the frame or not. She turned, ready to fling the door open—if it wasn't locked—but her feet latched onto the wooden floor. Aunia windmilled her arms, but her stopped momentum toppled her over. She fell, palms smacking the wood. The metal rod in her hand rolled away.

"If you are genuflecting, you are pointed the wrong way," Gabryella said.

Aunia pushed off the floor, stood, and glared.

Gabryella flashed a wolfish grin, leaning forward as if she'd come out of the frame. Her words invaded Aunia's mind. *I've decided to take Bibb on his offer but only if he brings me, you at the appointed place.*

"Stay out of my head," Aunia hissed. She struggled to move backwards but her feet again were locked in place.

Do you prefer staying with Bibb? He kills faebloods. Or potential if that's what you are. And he'll do it just as soon as you're not useful to him.

"You imprison faeries."

Gabryella toyed with mahogany-brown curls and her gaze moved toward the orange light in the room. "Where is Bibb hiding?"

"Release me."

'Don't tell me you invaded Bibb's domain in a physical form. You were smart enough to dreamwalk into mine. Why be stupid now?"

"I don't answer to you."

"You don't need to be rude," Gabryella said.

"I want nothing to do with you."

Gabryella frowned. "Because of faeries? Silly girl, I didn't harm them. I only gave them purpose. Like this painting. Old magic. All one needs is ground Chand crystal. A clever girl rediscovered it."

Aunia curled her fists. This woman was trying to goad her into talking. To gather information. "I don't talk with monsters."

"That was hurtful." Gabryella patted her upper chest above her green dress' plunging neckline. "Does this look monstrous to you?"

"Monstrous is what you do."

"Yes. I'm offering you aid. Monstrous indeed." Gabryella's hand slid up from chest to chin. "You're looking for something. What is it?'

Aunia didn't answer.

The fireling frowned. "It's ill-advised to slap away my help. Bibb can be useful, I'll admit that myself. But you... You're so much more intriguing. And definitely more worthy of assistance. Tell me. What do you seek?"

"You work with the Boggleman."

"He founded our order. I'm obligated. But he's not here right now."

"Because he's in Nonderu," Aunia snarled. "But he's lost that awful cloak."

Gabryella's eyebrows rose. "You've taken his cloak? Impressive."

Aunia glared.

"Oh please. You can be upset with the founder of our order and not take it out on the rest of us."

"You are not going to fool me," Aunia said.

"My dear innocent child. I am here to help."

"Help?" Aunia leaned toward the stack of wooden boxes. Each one probably weighed several pounds. If she could grab one... see if there was something she could throw and knock the painting over. Maybe she could heave an entire box. But if they fell. She could handle bruises but not the noise. The wererats would come back. She hesitated.

"Of course, with help," Gabryella said. "The worlds stand ready to transform into their next incarnation. The Dama star stands poised too."

"You set a spy upon us in Worley. Attacked us and—"

"I set no spy."

A metallic squeal sent a cold chill through Aunia. She leaned to see the door. But she couldn't. A wererat was to come in, attack her, and there was nothing she could do. She held her breath.

There was no other sound until Gabryella spoke. "Please dear girl, let me help you."

Aunia returned her attention to the mirror. She had no way out. What would it mean to take Gabryella's help? "We met Darla. A fireling same as you."

"My housekeeper?"

Gabryella's startled tone jarred Aunia.

"I'm far more than a serving wench," a silky voice said from behind Aunia.

Darla. She stood so close Aunia could feel her breath.

Aunia curled her fists. At least the fireling wasn't wearing Aunia's blue gown anymore. Instead, she wore form-fitting breeches and a poofy red shirt.

Aunia's feet came free and she staggered a step back... but toward the painting. No good. She reached for the boxes.

"You want to call the column of wererats?" Darla said.

Aunia glared but she pulled her hands back to her sides. She remained where she was pinned between Darla and Gabryella in the mirror. "You're working with Bibb."

"Not anymore." Darla laughed. It was a happy, musical sound. "He isn't doing so well since he decided to visit your head."

Aunia squeezed her fists tighter. Bibb. Mathias' enemy. And hers for having the Da Vennen attack her. "He was the aurimite?"

"Aurimite? Oh, I do like that title," Darla said. "Certainly more dignified than mindbinding."

Gabryella's face filled the mirror. "A soul is a flame granted by the Veil itself. To bind another's mind is to spit on the fire that made you."

"Yes, yes," Darla said, "And you believe the spaces between the veil should be left untouched. Even though our great founder has his magnificent Nonderu kingdom."

Aunia wanted to slip away but she was stuck between the two of them. And she needed to find the compass. Between the firelings, Gabryella seemed to be the lesser evil.

"Gabryella is not your friend," Darla snapped. "And no, I'm not listening in on your thoughts but I can guess them. Bibb has no mind to use the compass at the moment. And yes, I know where it is."

Aunia sucked in a breath.

"What are you talking about?" Gabryella's large face shrank back within the mirror, her form visible again.

Darla tilted her head and smiled. "Oh, the First Flamekeeper of the Fireling Order knows nothing about Etos' Trinity. All the magic that can be harnessed with those tools? Bibb got the compass from a certain tree from a certain grove that is watched by a certain Chandarion. He used it to find faebloods. Faebloods that you've been trading salamander lights for."

"Darla," Gabryella's beautiful face twisted. "Fire easily can burn the one wielding it."

Darla rolled her eyes. "I wasn't wielding any of that. Bibb kept faebloods for himself too. Making a wererat army but you both already knew that. Well maybe Gabryella didn't. But I can tell you something neither of you knows. It was me who told him an Eaburrai-made tool is more than its parts. I talked him into harnessing this chunk of Chand ice with pretty flowers inside."

Blood drained into her feet and Aunia lost whatever else Darla said. A chunk of Chand ice with flowers embedded inside? Bibb had the Naoma Stone.

Darla turned her attention to Aunia. "Oh, don't look so pale. You found a way to destroy Bibb's mind."

But it hadn't been her. It had been Q'thonos who had trapped the intruder in his obsidian mirror. And Darla didn't know that. Air froze in Aunia's lungs. She had to...had to...had to pretend to agree. It was the only way to get to the compass and the Naoma Stone. But she had to look calm.

Darla continued, "I commend you for that. He was getting so annoying. And I spoke true when I said I wanted to work with you. Come with me. I'll show you where the compass is."

"You've grown cold, Darla." Gabryella crossed her arms. "And wisdom means not confusing knowledge with understanding."

"Understanding?" Darla set her hands on her hips. "Ironic, considering how much you do not understand."

Darla stretched her hand toward Aunia. "We possess two out of the three items. Wielding them and ruling the worlds is within our power."

Aunia bit her lip. She wished Gabryella's mirror could be a portal away, but even if it was...she couldn't risk moving farther from Mathias.

Darla walked past Aunia to the framed painting and slammed it face-down. When she turned, she held up a circular instrument in her hand. "You with me now?"

CHAPTER THIRTY
ESCAPING THE LOCKS

*Shadows should be asked politely what they're hiding before
you slice them open. It could be a friend meant to warn you,
or perhaps a sheltered truth not ready to be seen.* — A quote
from the Adventures of the Lord Chance of Mimsy

"I heard the word," Mathias said. "What do you mean?"

Jovaryn's voice dropped to a near whisper. "The Boggleman's Nonderu lies in a pocket inside the veil. It's not in Ahnu-Endynia. It's between. There are a few who know how to create these
pockets. And what is on the other side. Is anyone's guess."

"The boys with the pancakes were going to go through," Keston said.

"To torment prisoners." Mathias glowered at the strange symbols
that hung at nose level and glanced back at the sleeping wererats. "We
should be fine."

"Well, fine or not, the way is open." Jovaryn pointed to a spi-
ral-shaped glyph. "And we should hope there isn't a regiment on the
other side."

"Hang on," Keston paused from stripping a sword and sheath from
one of the wererat boys. "Look familiar?"

Mathias walked back to Keston, who pointed at a symbol under the lad's vest. It was a figure eight laying on its side with a vertical line splitting it in two.

"We saw that on Da Vennen in Dalin," Mathias said.

"Bibb has a long reach," Jovaryn said.

Mathias frowned. "Do you know what it means?"

"It's a secret order within the Da Vennen but that's all I know."

"Why not more?" Keston asked.

"I was too much of a troublemaker. I was never told."

Keston nodded and handed Mathias a short sword with its sheath. "A little more than a glorified knife."

"Better than what we had." Mathias wrapped his hand around the stiff leather covering the hilt. Keston buckled one around his belt. As did Jovaryn.

The blade was about twenty inches long. Pommel slightly better than a lump of iron filed to a point. Still, it was longer than his dagger and it gave him a blade for each hand. He undid his belt and slid the leather frog onto it. Keston and Jovaryn, who returned to human form, did the same.

Sword in hand, Mathias sucked in a breath. "Ready."

An electrical current brushed against his skin, raising the hairs on his neck and arms as he stepped through the barrier.

The space was dim and smaller than the guest dorm back at Eddac Tower. Smooth indigo painted walls. Low ceiling. A table with crude instruments along one wall. Mathias shuddered thinking about what they could be used for.

A cell with an open door took up the other half of the space. A scrawny man in his mid-twenties slept in a pile of hay. He might have had blond hair. It was hard to tell under a single burning torch. And manacled to the ceiling, tiptoes barely touching the floor and arms extended too far... On the Harp... that was Jules and he wasn't moving.

His dark red hair was matted to his dirty broad face. Bruises ran along his arms, his bare chest. Wrists cuffed in chains. All his captors had allowed him for clothing was a pair of trousers that were ripped to the knees. Oh, Thuroes please... Jules wasn't moving.

Mathias hurried to his friend's side, teeth braced shut against the storm battering his chest. "Jules," he choked out through a throat full of sand. He reached out, steeling himself for the feel of cold flesh and pressed fingers against Jules' neck. A heartbeat thudded against Mathias' finger pads. His knees trembled. "He's alive!"

Keston raced to the far side of the table where a small desk and stool stood. He grabbed the stool and hurried over, stumbling once. He caught himself, hopped the last two steps to Mathias, and set the stool down in front of Jules.

Mathias set his boot on its seat.

Keston shoved him back and pulled a slim nail and a long tooth from a bone comb from the lining of his boot. "You've ever picked a lock?"

Mathias blinked, he hadn't realized Keston knew how. Then again, it shouldn't surprise. But he could assist. Quickly, he wrapped his arms around Jules' lower thighs and lifted him a few inches, easing the weight on cuffed wrists. Jules felt like a bag of damp feathers. Too light.

The stool rocked as Keston stepped up but he kept his footing. "Matty? The light."

Without thinking, Mathias squeezed his hand, and the egg-shaped light appeared where Keston worked. Scrapes and clicks slid over the cuffs.

Sixteen scrapes. Seventeen. Mathias raised his gaze across the room. Regretted it. It infuriated him to see saws of various lengths, pinchers, awls, hooks, and other metal implements littering the table by the desk.

All the Eaburrai... what were they planning and what had they done to Jules? And had they found Aunia?

Jules gasped, flung his arms as wide as the chains would allow.

"Keep him still," Keston growled. "These are half-rusted."

"There's another here," Jovaryn called. He was stooped over the prisoner in the dirty hay.

The man jerked, pulled himself into a sitting position, back against the wall. His mustache and scruffy beard half-swallowed his fearful expression.

Jovaryn stepped back. "Cody?"

"Don't know a Cody," Keston said as he worked, "but if you can get him on his feet... I'd hate to leave anyone here. Ah, got one."

A chink popped and Jules' left arm slammed against Mathias' shoulder. Jules sank broken fingernails into Mathias' throat.

Mathias released his hold on Jules' legs to grip his hand and force it from his throat. He croaked. "It's me. Mathias and Keston. Jules. It's us."

"Matt?" Jules eased up on the pressure but for only a second. His hand spasmed and tightened. "No. Can't be you. Let go of me."

"It is us." Mathias yanked Jules' hand off. Wedged his friend's arm between their bodies as he tucked in, head behind Jules' midback. He squeezed tight. He hated to restrain... but...

"Almost there," Keston barked. "Keep him talking."

A squeal of metal on metal sent prickles dancing along Mathias' spine and he hunched his back into a curl.

Bone snapped.

"Let go of me," Jules yelled.

Keston cursed. "Jovaryn, find me something long and skinny on that table."

Jovaryn looked over, mouth open like he'd argue...but he nodded. Stood. Walked to the table. The second prisoner, Cody, staggered to his feet. He held up his hands where faeblood metal cuffs covered his wrists. His included metal loops and a lock that kept his wrists together. "Free me. I'll help you however I can."

Faeblood. Who knew if he was a wererat yet.

"Come on. I'm a friend." Cody shook his wrists. "I've done missions for your Dar Elect's apprentice."

That statement set Mathias' teeth on edge. "Our Dar Elect does not have an apprentice."

"She does," Cody said. "Wendalin."

Mathias blinked. "That's Dar Syrick's apprentice."

The man rolled his eyes. "Everyone knows the two share her labors. Who knows the sad day when a Dar must be replaced."

Cold, shame, and heat filled Mathias' chest, his cheeks. The last Dar to be replaced was Zeller.

"Please, flyer," the man croaked. "I'm a friend."

Jovaryn approached, holding out a hair pin. "I'll vouch for him."

"You?" Mathias snapped.

Keston took the hairpin from Jovaryn's fingers. "Looks like a woman's probably been in here. Or a token from one."

"Bibb fell," Jules gasped. "Darla. Darla took over."

"Bibb... fell?" Jovaryn stepped back. "How?"

Jules shook his head, then thrashed.

"Jules," Keston crooned. "Even in the desperate circumstance, Lord Chance remains stoic. Waits for the impromptu moment and—"

"He was up in Bibb's lab. Strapped in and he'll be scrambled for a bit," Cody said. "But he said Bibb dropped to the floor convulsing and the fireling woman rushed in. Grabbed Bibb's compass. Took over everything. It's why he's here, not there."

Mathias risked a glance at Cody. "Why Bibb—"

"No. Why Jules is here." Cody said. "Bibb was trying to break him."

"Got it," Keston said over snick-click sound.

Jules came free. Twisted in Mathias' arms.

"I'm setting you down." Mathias lowered his friend to the straw. Kept his grip steady even with the clipped punch glancing off the back of his head. It hurt, but he shrugged it off. The blow was not one of Jules' usual powerhouses.

Jules scuttled away and halted in a seated position beside Cody. He gave him a once over and looked back to Mathias. "Shadows should be asked politely what they're hiding before you slice them open."

Mathias lowered himself to his haunches, wrinkling his nose at the touch of the dirty straw."Leave it to you to quote philosophy while being rescued."

"A proper escape demands equal parts courage, chaos, and contemplation." Jules blinked several times. Looked at Mathias like he really saw him.

"I've been worried sick about you," Mathias said. He chewed on a litany of imagined words. Questions. Weeks of worry. Jules had disappeared while Mathias had been at Aunia's village. The last communication had been Jules bespeaking that he was cured of a wererat bite, that the healer was getting wine to celebrate...

Mathias turned cold. That wine had probably been Navenra-laced. "Who brought you here?"

"Didn't see faces." Jules erupted into a fit of coughs.

Keston removed his waterskin which was fastened across his back. He knelt near Jules.

"Don't drink no more."

"Fair enough." Keston removed the stopper. Took a swig himself and handed it to Jules. "It's only water."

Jules took it. Guzzled. "How long?"

"You've been gone a few weeks," Mathias said.

"Water too?" Cody reached for the waterskin.

Jules handed it over. "No. I mean here. I had the window before. Could count the days."

"They had him, and me too, at the old temple complex," Cody said. "Bibb was... figuring out how to convert flyers. Had a failed experiment."

Jules stifled a sob. "Patrick. Garret."

Mathias closed his eyes. Those traitors had... been Navenra'd. "Jules," he whispered. "You sent Brinsaber away."

Jules wrapped his arms around his knees and wiped at his dirty face. "They... they were forced to do the unspeakable."

"And you were saving Brin."

Jules nodded. "Where are they? The knight-sons."

Mathias' intestines twisted. They were flyers and they had tried to kidnap Aunia. Who knew what they would have done to her.

"I saw them in Worley's dungeon," Jovaryn said quietly.

"Lyle," Mathias muttered. The lord of Worley was also being influenced by the Da Vennen and Bibb.

"Whatever they've done," Jules said. "Bibb used that witch compass to get into their heads. You have no choice."

Q'thonos had said Bibb was the aurimite. Part of Mathias had suspected Darla. But Bibb? At the Cold Festival he should have run the jack-a-nape through instead of punching Bibb in the face. "We'll take care of the Arch-Vicar."

"I approve but..." Cody shook the iron cuffs on his wrists again. "I can skip us all out one by one if you get me free."

"Like I said, I'll vouch for him." Jovaryn remained standing at Cody's side.

"We don't... I don't know this faeblood," Mathias said. "We're in—"

"They brought him here from Dalin with me," Jules said. "He's the reason Dalin wasn't overrun with those walking mouths."

"How? By summoning a twister?" Mathias asked. It was a story the workmen at the destroyed guild hall had told.

"Saw a woman dump a barrel of water on one of the beasties," Cody said. "It fizzled and dissolved. But it took more than me to call up a storm. I just led it."

"Who else?" Mathias asked.

Cody shrugged.

Mathias rolled his eyes. Find the plans. Find Aunia. Get all of them out safely again. Safely. How could he leave behind someone who had saved lives. "Kest. Get him out of the cuffs. We'll need all the help we can get."

Keston hunkered in front of Cody with the hatpin and thin nail. The lock came away... not easily but quicker than Jules.

Cody rubbed his wrists. "We need to know what's going on around us."

Mathias rose. "You're not in charge."

"I'm a faeblood. If anything, I know how to preserve my skin." Cody turned to face Jules. "You said sometimes you could see back on Bibb when he invaded your mind?"

Jules shuddered and hunched his broad shoulders in. "Don't like that but..."

"Wait, you can see back?" Mathias asked.

Jules' breath turned ragged. "Experiments. Poisons and magic and metal and... Brinsaber."

"Jules. You're safe now," Keston said.

"Jules this is important. Bibb will attack Tamore. Maybe Tatia. He's..." Mathias swallowed hard. "Jules, that compass... It moved the Dama star next to the Harp. We need to get it. And find an innocent who is here as well. If you can see back... Please. Can you try?"

Jules' eyes narrowed with complete lucidity and he snapped. "His mind is worse than the sewers."

Mathias drew back.

"But I'll do it." Jules curled his arms against his chest and rocked. Several long moments spun before Jules' breath caught. "He's abed. Small room. Not asleep. Not moving. He's... not all of him is here."

"Jules said when Bibb fell yesterday, he was screaming about salt," Cody said,

Mathias blinked. After Q'thonos had placed a salt head cover on Aunia, two eerie reflections had appeared inside that obsidian mirror and one had disintegrated. He wished he would have asked Q'thonos what would happen to an aurimite who got stuck in a mirror... or disintegrated in one. And if Bibb was gone or trapped... who was the cobwebby voice in his head?

Jules leaned deeper against himself, chest resting on his knees. "She's there."

"Who?" Mathias knelt in the dirty straw. "Jules. Who?"

"Fireling is with Bibb. There's... there's a blonde girl with her."

Mathias locked eyes with Keston. Fireling? That had to be Darla. And the blond girl had to be Aunia. *Taf?*

Pictures, Taf sent back, his silvery voice sharp in Mathias' head.

Mathias curled his fists. Pictures. Right. He visualized himself flying on Taf's back over the city and realized he needed a location. "Jovaryn, where is Bibb's keep?"

"The temple with the bell spire," Jovaryn said. "We fell almost overtop of it."

"That would be it," Cody said.

"I need to get there." Mathias turned to Keston. "Aunia's there."

"You can't," Jules said. "There's machinery. Dark stuff and—"

"I have to." Mathias rose and turned to Cody. "Can you skip me to that temple?"

Cody scrambled back. "You mad? Whoever was captured, they're lost."

"He's duty-bound," Keston snapped.

Duty bound? Mathias clenched his teeth. No. This wasn't for duty-sake. This was for Aunia. "Skip me to the tower as close as possible. And after, skip Jules and the others somewhere safe."

"We'll go to Lambert," Cody said. "My family's winery."

Jules staggered to his feet and grasped Mathias' hand. "Who are you saving?"

"The world may be chaos," Mathias said tightly, "but when you find the right hand to clasp...it makes better than a kingdom."

"A Lord Chance quote." Keston nodded with a tight-lipped smile. "I'm going with you."

Mathias shook his head. "Get the information to Nyrissa. And if all else fails, find Fallo before anyone else does. He knows about that time-turn spell. That might be our only hope."

CHAPTER THIRTY-ONE

POTENTIALS

Edvaras hated the idea of being a Chandarion and so he sabotaged the augury. This is the story we are told. The question I ask is if the augury is meant to happen, how could it be stopped? — Thalindra Archon, Arcanis Primis of the Mystic Court

D arla walked away from Aunia toward the corner opposite the tables. "Bibb's bedroom is two doors down. But this is a shortcut."

Aunia followed. What choice did she have? Darla had the compass. She had to follow Darla to find it. And after? Aunia needed something to knock Darla out. She did have the knife that Caedmon had given her in her knapsack... unless Darla had removed it when the knapsack was in her possession. She also couldn't rummage without being seen. No, better to watch for a weapon while she walked or...summoned Mygul. It had appeared at the Green Harpy when she was upset. It always did then, if it was going to.

She was certainly upset now. But there was no pinching at her temples. All she could feel was weight in her legs and what felt like a creature gnawing at her belly. And then gagging. Aunia covered her mouth and nose with a hand.

"Yes, I know. I haven't had time to get this cleaned up," Darla said. 'Just walk by the basket please."

The basket in question, half-hidden in shadow, was filled with wet cloth and the stench was overpowering. However, what Darla stood before made Aunia pause. The air looked as if it was dressed in a black curtain and hanging from it were iridescent glyphs. Glyphs like the cloth over her father's cage in Nonderu... except for the spiral designs.

"Come on." Darla pulled a metal stylus from her pants pocket and touched one of the hanging symbols. It chimed, low and soft, and the entire dark panel rippled. "I've the compass and I promise on my life that Chand ice stone is through here. Or do you want to stay here all day?"

Darla stepped into the dark curtain of air and vanished.

Aunia chewed on her lip, her knees shaking. The compass. Darla had the compass and the Naoma Stone. Aunia swallowed hard, pinned her shoulders back, and walked through.

She entered a small room with white walls. A chest of drawers beside her with several burning oil lamps, and a bed across the room along the other wall. A bed with a man lying there. Bibb. His thin face looked gaunter and waxier. His black hair had more white streaks than in Dalin. He still smelled like citrus fruit and patchouli but that crackling presence he exuded at Dalin was gone. If he weren't wearing the same beige robe, she might have confused him with another.

"Congratulations," Darla said from beside the dresser. "You did an amazing job cracking his mind. Timely. He was thinking of pulling darkwraiths into our world. May I ask how you did it?"

"He shouldn't go in other people's minds." From Aunia's periphery, she spotted the door. It bore several locks. Locked in. And darkwraiths? They were... That name sounded familiar.

Darla snorted. "Would that include your pegasi?"

Aunia tensed. Stars, how much did Darla know? She scanned the room again... carefully. There wasn't even a chair she could swing.

"You don't want to answer. Telling. But more important right now... he did underestimate you." Darla stepped between Aunia and the bed-ridden Bibb. "Many do that, don't they? They see a girl. A faeblood. Maybe even a potential. But they don't see the fire already burning through your veins. Maybe they do see your fear when you don't know what to do."

Aunia straightened, focusing her thoughts on only what was important. "You said you had the compass and the Naoma Stone."

Darla blinked, then tipped her head. "Alright. But I need an oath. A binding one where we can cut through any lies and uncertainties. The augury's time is almost spent and you and I can transmute it into whatever we want."

"Transmute?"

"By knotting fate-threads where we want. Yes, I know about them. These instruments read our thoughts. Our desires. We think what we want and they show us how. Shame we don't have the hourglass as well. We'd be able to freeze our desires to get in place but no matter. I've portal tiles. We can skip."

"Because you can't skip on your own," Aunia said.

Darla crossed her arms. "I could say the same of you."

A rap sounded at the door and a low gruff voice barked, "I would see the master."

Darla bumped her forefinger against her lips and pitched her voice to sound cheerful and agreeable. "He's resting peacefully."

"I am his physician. Open the door."

"Woundbinder, I am his second. He's made me, not you, so," Darla called. "Stand down and remain outside the door."

"I will call the others and smash down this door."

"And incur his wrath when he awakens?"

There was a long silence outside the door. "I will return."

"And I will send for you when he wakes," Darla said.

Aunia fidgeted with her fingers. Darla's situation was precarious. The wererats didn't want to follow her. Maybe she could bluff her way through? Get the compass and skip. She'd done it before. Accidentally to Dalin though she had no idea how she did it. But she had skipped deliberately when she left Scorched Earth. Had even transported herself close to Eddac Tower... Granted she materialized high up in the sky... and she had landed hard on her belly. Could she survive another fall like that? What would happen if she skipped higher into the sky? Maybe there'd be no help but to try. Staying here would be worse. "Can I see the compass?"

"Vow to me that you will follow me without question."

Aunia stiffened. "That would be foolishly stupid. Vow to me that you mean no harm. To me, and the people I love."

"How would I know the people you love?"

"How about everyone but firelings?"

Darla stared at her and laughed. "Good I'm probably no longer a fireling."

Aunia stepped forward. "You give your oath first and then—"

Raw power surged forward, grabbed Aunia by all four of her limbs and pinned her to the wall.

"I don't have time for this." Darla pulled the compass out of her pocket—circular with a flat top and encrusted with red gems along the sides—and set it on the dresser. It looked like spiderwebs trailed from it and was hooked on something from the dresser.

"Ah, you see the threads? Good." Darla yanked open a drawer and pulled out a fist-size clear stone with blue, black, and yellow flowers embedded within. The Naoma Stone. Darla had Gaitha's stolen Naoma Stone.

"These devices work very well on their own. Even better tied to an energy source. Dar Zeller's amulet worked for a while but this beauty?" Darla lifted the stone into the lamps' ring of light. "It is sheer perfection. And I can get your oath after we arrive at Ignivar University."

Darla reached into the drawer again.

Aunia struggled against her invisible bonds. "I can't leave Mathias."

Darla barked a laugh as she stuck both compass and Naoma Stone into a gray sack. She knotted the drawstrings around her belt. "For your silly pegasi flyer who can't figure out what to do with his heart? Forget about him. Forget about them all. You're worth far more than—"

"If you force me away, I will disappear," Aunia said.

"Threats are getting tiresome."

"Zevara lay a geis on me to stay with Mathias," Aunia yelled. "We'll be pulled back into Endynia otherwise."

"Voice," Darla hissed. She walked closer to Aunia. "Pulled into the Faery world? Oh now, that's a good deception."

"I'm not lying." Aunia kept thrashing. It wasn't helping.

Darla drew very close. "Do you know why the Boggleman wanted to capture you?"

Aunia clamped her jaw shut.

Darla pinched Aunia's chin. "He did it to juice your power. Take the magic he's been storing up to force the choice to what he wants. And Gabryella and her stupidity...sees oh the worlds will just merge and everything will be unicorn dances. Don't you understand we have two-thirds of the Trinity. We can decide."

"I won't do evil."

"Evil? I'm looking to save lives," Darla said. She leaned forward, eyes wild. Her breath touched Aunia's face. "Thread must be bound to ice before the Dama star rises and anchored to living magic. You are that living magic. You anchor the choice. And I have a nice piece of Chand ice. Works great for giving the compass more power... and it will be better to form the world how we want it."

Aunia squirmed. She needed to get out of here. She needed to rip that pouch off Darla's belt and fling her across the room. Stomp on her face. Get away. The woman was mad. And she was not someone else's belonging.

Darla sprinkled portal tiles on the floor at Aunia's feet. "I can get your vow later."

The fireling's arm rose to grab Aunia's arm. And Mygul blasted in front of her.

Darla sailed back, landing hard on the floor. She hissed, scrambling to her feet and shaking her bracelet. A fireball appeared in her hand.

Mygul expanded. Grew into a bubble and wrapped itself around Aunia like Gaitha's shield had in the Birchwoods.

Aunia pulled at her invisible restraints. Fought. She didn't know how long Mygul would stay.

Darla threw the fireball and it skittered across Mygul, shooting sparks. "Your shield can't last forever."

Mathias, Aunia sent her thoughts crying into the air. Where are you?

"Will you summon flyers now?" Darla snarled. "I've got several of them under my spell. Bibb tried to drown them in Navenra. Foolishness. Just a wee bit, wiles, and suggestions. That's what it takes. Even your precious Mathias. Vanish some of his things, get him to doubt and his mind opens wide."

Darla summoned a handful of fireballs, each the size of a spool of thread. She lobbed them at the door's locks one by one. The locks melted and the door smoked. "Woundbinder! The Master is being attacked!"

A scurry of feet sounded outside and wererats, some men and some ratmen, crashed through the doors.

Darla pointed to Aunia. "I want her alive and that shield down."

The wererats rushed forward. One punched Mygul and it shimmered a deeper blue and thrummed like a drumskin. Another scraped its claws over Mygul's surface as if it could be peeled away like bark. It jerked its paw back, blowing on its knuckles. Aunia swallowed hard and Mygul wavered. Stars. Gaitha had power words she would murmur to feed her spells energy. Words that Aunia had never been taught.

A stout strawberry-blonde ratman swaggered in. Glanced at Aunia and the other wererats, and beelined for Bibb.

Too many wererats struck Mygul. Aunia's heartbeat kept time with the blows.

Darla stood beside the strawberry blond wererat. They were arguing.

Tafiriel, Aunia screamed. She formed pictures in her mind depicting her situation. Threw them out toward wherever Taf and Jennium were. Hoped one of them would get her desperate message. Stars, if Mygul fell... she was done for.

Another wererat lunged. Its teeth at the same level as her face. She shrieked and then dropped. The forces against her limbs released. Free... but with nowhere she could go. Not with a dozen wererats crowding in. Mygul's blue barrier became more transparent.

And then Mathias was running through the door, short sword in his hand. He decapitated the closest wererat. Several others dropped to the ground, asleep.

The strawberry blonde wererat struck Darla across the face and she sailed, hitting the wall. She crumpled onto the floor. He drew his sword and swaggered toward Mathias.

Mathias caught the wererat's downward cut with his dagger, stepped into a lunge to skewer, and the wererat stepped away, pulling his sword from Mathias' dagger and slicing toward Mathias' ribs. Mathias jumped back.

"Aunia," Mathias called. "I need your outrage. Not fear. Get mad."

He dodged back, skewered a different wererat and threw the injured being in the strawberry blonde's path. "How dare they attack you? Attack me? Attack our whole country?"

Aunia blinked. Outrage? She'd show them outrage. She curled her fists and Mygul flared into brilliance. It shrank to the size of a deer's heart and seared the snout off the nearest wererat. The creature screamed and fell to the floor. It struck another one and it folded unmoving onto the floor.

From the floor Darla shifted her limbs. Sat up.

"No!" Mathias cried out. His dagger hand was up, catching another blade, and his egg-shaped light flared into existence. It soared at Aunia and she froze, but it hit a wererat she hadn't seen behind her. Its face dented and it fell. Aunia scrambled back.

Darla laughed. "Well, what do you know. Another potential."

Chapter Thirty-Two

THE BELL TOWER

One day, I'll wear my mother's crown, and they'll call it destiny. But none will notice how it cuts, how it hides me. They'll see a queen. Never me. — Princess Keira of Tamore

Darla shook her wrist and blasted a fireball at the doorframe. "Run and your flyers come after you!"

"What are you doing?" The strawberry-blonde wererat screamed. He scooped Bibb into his thick arms, braced his back against the wall, and kicked the bed at Aunia.

Aunia fell back, braced herself for the impact, and Taf's small light darted before her, hit it and changed the bed's trajectory. It crashed toward Darla. Darla incinerated it with another fireball.

The wererat carrying Bibb ran from the room. Bibb's red hair... Red hair?

"Look out," Aunia screamed.

Taf's light flared in front of Mathias as did Aunia's Mygul. They merged into a brilliant shield and bounced a fireball back over where the bed once was.

The merged light shot at Darla. She dropped low. It hit the oil lamps on the dresser. The glass smashed into a million pieces, and oil splattered. If Darla set another fireball aflame, they'd all torch.

"Come on," Mathias cried.

The three still moving wererats raced for the door even as other wererats tried to crowd their way in.

Mathias raised his hand, willed Taf and Aunia's light forward. To his immense relief, the blue and white swirling light barreled forward. It knocked wererats off their feet, and they flew. Many hit the outer corridor wall. Some groaned after they hit. Some thudded to the floor and remained still.

Mathias and Aunia ran from the room. Dawn's light sliced through narrow panes of multi-colored glass. Reds bleeding into murky greens. Amber spilling across rotted-smelling straw. Dawn led to morning. To greater visibility. To less opportunity of vanishing easily. Snarls and barked orders grew louder from the archway where stairs connected the lower floors.

Wererats exploded from the arch. Filled the corridor. Claws scrabbling over flying hay and timber. Rapid-fire *skrit-skrit-skrit*.

Adrenaline shot through Mathias' legs. Keston and Jovaryn. They were down below. Distracting the hoard. Well...No longer. Obviously. In confirmation, a picture invaded Mathias' head. Of Revellie flying close to the ground with two figures upon her and of Taf flying high toward the spiral. In the distance, flyers came... one pale green, another indigo, and a red-gold.

Hauser Tower. The question was if they would help or only be another adversary. Another worry.

For now, they had to go up. To the bell tower. And leap into Taf's saddle. On the Harp, would Aunia be able to do this? He grabbed her hand and they ran away from the archway with the rotating merged lights following.

Peeling murals of Augurite sacrists, the faithful, lined the passage. Warned them with their blackened and crossed-off heads.

Heads and hair. Red hair. Bibb did not have red hair. Mathias' foot kicked at something under the hay and his ankle twisted. He grimaced. Jules had been wrong about who lay in that room. Not Bibb. But whoever it was, a wererat with an insignia on his jacket picked him up and carried him out.

The hallway corridor turned ninety-degrees... a blind corner...and a painted robed figure on the wall, bell in his hands, pointed ahead. Entrance to the bell tower. It had to be around that corner.

The only person living who had that shade of red was the princess.

Aunia stumbled. Dozens of wererats in the corridor were closing the distance behind them. More flooded in from the archway.

Mathias yanked her hand. Raised his sword. The merged light—twining together and rotating—hovered before him. Flared. And surged forward with blue-white brilliance. It smashed into the lead wererat. Split the pack apart with bodies flying left and right. They fell like ninepins—every last one.

"Come on," Mathias snapped, with a tug.

They melted around the corner, feet racing along the corridor. Near its end, a door. Wooden but iron strapped. Unlike the broader doors from the first corridor. They pelted forward. Reached the handle.

The hinges protested with a sharp squeal. Beyond the door, light coiled down from an inside tower and its wooden spiral stairwell.

"Up." Mathias pressed Aunia forward. Shut the door behind them.

The tight stairs were barely wide for one. Aunia went first, using her hands to climb. Mathias followed. Shoulder scraping against the stone-built tower. He muttered, "go, go, go" under his breath. It wouldn't take the wererats long to regroup. Come after them. Some might run away, sure, but being trained to be an army? They'd be back.

Dust gritted under Mathias's palms from the stone wall...the wood plank steps. The scent of tar and weathered timber thickened. They climbed to a landing with a low hatch under it. Aunia pushed it open and exited into a cramped space. A pit with a short ladder out... to the bell tower cage.

Aunia hiked her skirts and climbed, ankles flashing. She scrambled onto a wooden landing and the belfry. Mathias joined her. A great bronze bell hung nearly over their heads. Its lip gleamed in the pale morning light. Its iron fittings, attached to a thick wooden bar, swayed with the draft. It dinged faintly, echoing in Mathias' ears.

Sprawled out on all sides around them lay Spatelly with its reek of salt and rot. Refuse piles scattered beside roadways and roofless buildings. But off in the distance, where barracks and repaired homes stood, an army of wererat soldiers waited to march on Tatia. Dread filled Mathias' bones. They had no physical proof of the upcoming attack except for what they heard from the sleeping wererat boys and things Jules had overheard. Jules. Zeller's nephew. Maybe Nyrissa would listen to him.

"Mathias, look." Aunia pointed northward toward the Forgotten Way, the road connecting Spatelly to Worley.

The sight of six pairs of pegasi wings contrasting with the pale blue sky came like a punch in the gut. *"Run and your flyers come after you."* Was Darla in control of them?

Below came a muffled thud. And another. Splintering cracks came next.

Taf swept by, wingtips grazing stone. No space to land. And Aunia... she had never trained to jump midair onto a pegasus.

He shifted his grip on his sword. Sank it into its sheath. "We're going to have to jump."

Aunia's face paled.

I won't let you fall, Taf sent.

She'll make a glorious mess if she does, came the cobbwebby voice inside Mathias' head. And then it screamed.

Darla. That had to be Darla.

She has the compass and the Naoma Stone, Aunia sent. *It's how—*

"Later," Mathias said. His boots left the stone ledge for one breathless moment as Taf swept by. His fingers grasped for the saddle lip. Sliding on oiled leather. He clamped two firm handholds. Swung his leg up and over. Landed lightly in the saddle.

Aunia, Mathias sent. *We bank and you jump to me.*

She took a step back from the arch's ledge, her face white.

I'll catch you.

Thuds came from below and a wererat's head emerged from the pit.

"Aunia now," Mathias shouted.

Taf banked, wingtips scraped stone. Aunia leaped.

Clamping hard, thighs around Taf, Mathias leaned out. Caught her with both hands. Steadied her as Taf banked to the other side to counterbalance the weight. She shuffled forward, and he gripped her tight, pulling her skirts aside so she could straddle across him. Undignified. Scandalous in some circles—sitting on his lap and facing him. But far better than risking her sitting behind him with no safety straps to hold her in.

To the north, the other pegasi drew nearer. Flyers, who were certain to arrest them. Run or surrender. That was their choice. And there was an attack coming. Jules wasn't even with them to warn Nyrissa of the danger. Jules and Cody, if that faeblood was honest, were holed up at Lambert's Vineyards.

Mathias, Taf sent, his silvery voice quiet. *Nyrissa bespeaks. Surrender now.*

All air left Mathias' lungs. They couldn't. *Bespeak Keston. Tell him.*

Revellie is already behind us, Taf sent.

Mathias swiveled in the saddle. Revellie was indeed behind them with Keston and Jovaryn perched on her back. *Does he want to surrender?*

He says he's with you whatever you decide.

Aunia butted in. *We can't surrender. The Dama star. But we don't have the compass.*

No help for it, Mathias sent back.

Keston bespeaks, Taf sent. *Lambert's vineyard isn't far from here. He suggests we set down. Figure what we can do.*

How do we get there without them following us, Mathias sent. *There isn't any cloud cover.*

Taf looked back over a shoulder. *Perhaps as a potential you need no cloud cover.*

Chapter Thirty-Three

BRINWRAITHS

When the silvery mist rolls in from the tide, Brinwraiths are near. Be they mercy or malice, only Kai-Marin knows their mood. Best hold your breath, for they ride with the wisps to claim the drowned. — Tamorian faery lore

Aunia wrapped her arms tight around Mathias' middle and gripped the back of his jerkin to keep her hands from shaking. Behind them and past the twirling merged lights... Mygul's deep blue heart and Mathias' white one. They swirled in liquid-light and marbled with thin strands of silver. Mathias had commanded it to attack the wererats, and it had obeyed.

Behind that bit of hope, their combined light, flew six pegasi flyers. Indigo, pale green, dark brown, red-gold, and two paler colors. Four from Hauser tower it looked like. She had thought Breen was a good person. Frehn too... And had what Darla said about influence be true. That the other flyers were bent to Darla's will?

Tamore. Not the magical country that Caedmon had told her about. It was awful. The situation was awful too.

She wanted to curl up into a ball despite her heart trying to pump courage through her veins. But her veins had shrunk to threads, and fear froze her lungs.

Aunia leaned her chin against Mathias's shoulder, and he pressed a palm against her back. It was too much. But to give up... she couldn't be like her dad giving up when he stayed hidden in Naoma Sacella. They had to save the worlds. She had to go back to get the compass. How would Q'thonos know where to tie the fate-threads without it? And the compass would help her find her dad. There was also the Naoma Stone. Darla couldn't be allowed to keep it.

"Thread must be bound to ice before the Dama star rises and anchored to living magic. You are that living magic. You anchor the choice." Darla said that. But, what did that even mean? Living magic... like being a potential? Like Darla had called Mathias a potential.

The pegasi flyers were closing. And underneath them, the last of Spatelly with its crumbling buildings gave way to short wooden roads stretching over land that looked as if it had melted and hardened wrong. Miles of mud lined with reed beds and all stitched together with narrow veins of water. Mud and algae, and shimmery gray from where the sun spilled upon it from their right. It was like shards from a broken mirror. And the taste... A slight sweetness coated her tongue...and salt. A thick metallic salt.

She leaned to see below. *Is this the salt marsh?*

Pockets of it, yes, Mathias sent.

Salt. And the sea marsh. Kai-Marin's home when she was in the mortal world.

"These devices work very well on their own. Even better tied to an energy source."

Aunia went still. Q'thonos had asked for halite. Said it was to power the astrolabe. Like Darla was powering the compass. He said to find it in the...

The wraithmere, Aunia sent. *Do you know where it is?*

"We need to lose the Hausers," Mathias yelled.

"We need to get halite," Aunia yelled against Mathias' ear.

"Not now, we're not. We lose them and we get to Lambert's Vineyard."

"But Q'thonos—"

"We'll do no one any good if we're taken."

"We can use our light to protect us." Aunia pulled back to see Mathias' expression.

Protect us how? Mathias sent.

You're a potential. We can—

"It's Taf's light."

It is not, Tafiriel sent.

Mathias frowned. *Of course it is.*

"It's yours," Aunia said. "Darla called you a potential."

"I am no potential."

Why do you think I chose you? Taf sent softly.

The air thickened as they crossed deeper into the marsh. And then the smooth lift they had been riding faltered. Aunia yelped as they fell several yards.

Tafiriel beat his wings harder.

Mathias shifted his weight, and Tafiriel tilted his body to one side. They angled toward a stretch of pale ground, and the air tugged them upward.

Mathias sent, *Taf, let's use the thermals.*

They rose and dropped several more times, Keston and Jovaryn on Revellie following. Aunia's stomach struggled to return to its spot each time. This wasn't as bad as when they fled wyverns over the Grashbear, but not by much.

"They're closing," Aunia yelled. *Mathias? We could use our merged lights to scare the flyers off.*

"Attack our own?" Mathias' gaze sawed through her. *We can't.*

You only knocked the wererats over.

They could be thrown from their mounts. I'll not be responsible for their deaths. Mathias' legs shifted under her. *We shake them off. Zip low to the ground. Circle back... or hunker down 'til we can get to Lambert's.*

"What's in Lambert's?"

"Jules."

Her breath caught. Mathias had found his friend?

In the not-so-distance, Breen's indigo pegasus bobbled. Lost rhythm with another plunge and struggled to gain lift again.

"What if we use it when they're above a pool?" Aunia curled her fists tighter into Mathias' jerkin. It had to be the merged light. If she tried to extract Mygul... She shuddered with the memory of the Da Vennen soldier at Dalin when Mygul collided with his head. But their merged light... it had only toppled wererats over.

There is no coming back if we do, Mathias sent. *Jules... he knows Bibb's plans.*

But they're gaining.

Tafiriel's wings cleaved the cool morning air as they flew over a stretch of ground with knotted humps rising up like the backs of half-buried beasts. It looked as if dark mist was rising up to meet them.

Taf's wings caught a lift that sent her stomach tipping upward.

Thermals will be better. Marshes make the air dicey.

Behind them, Breen and Frehn reached for her bow.

Frehn bespeaks it is over, Tafiriel sent. *If we continue, they'd be in their right to shoot us down.*

"Shoot us d...down?" Mathias' gaze shifted to their combined globe-fire.

More dark mist boiled up... wrapped around the other flyers.

Darkwraiths, Taf sent, his voice a snarl.

Winter lanced through Aunia's soul. Darla had said Bibb had been trying to pull darkwraiths into their world. And as familiar as the name rang through her, they had to be some sort of Dagel demon that she had read about in Gaitha's reading room.

They quarter-wheeled toward the morning sun. The dark mist faded back but tendrils still reached.

Have your shield spell ready, Mathias sent.

They flew toward another pool of water. Salt-brine filled Aunia's nose. Something pale flickered under the pool... lithe shadows rolling in slow spirals. And scales flashed silver-blue.

Another rise. Another tilt. Another drop. A figure broke the water surface. Green silky hair. Both scaled skin and smooth. Water fae but not like the ones she had seen in her father's fishing pond. No, these were Kai-Marin's people. And Kai-Marin was her grandmother.

More of the water fae emerged, head and shoulders. Some peeked out from behind stands of tall reeds that grew beside slick mats of algae. The water rippled. Aunia sent out her thoughts to them. *Help us!*

Those are brinwraiths, Taf sent. *Do not trust them.*

We haven't a choice. They're faeries. Aunia leaned to better see the pool below and she called out in round, salt-tasting syllables that she didn't remember learning. Didn't have to think about. Had she given a poem? What had she said?

The marsh pools rippled, and the brinwraiths lifted up, waist deep in the water. Slender torsos and long limbs. Eyes too big and reflective in their cat-like faces. Silvery mist coiled up from the water, bringing a sting of brine... but it pushed back the dark mist.

They were enveloped in fog.

We must find the wraithmere, Aunia sent.

After, Mathias sent. *Taf fly to Jules.*

For Yasendra's sake, Aunia sent, copying Mathias' language, *You're dooming a world to death.*

CHAPTER THIRTY-FOUR

THE EMPTY STABLE

From what we know, three full Chandarions walk the worlds. Uriah, the first, who is stationed in the Holy Grove. Illysa, founder of the pegasi force who has vanished to lands unknown. And the rogue Edvaras who mapped the stars and could say when the choice would come. — Cody Lambert, of Lambert's Vineyard

Aunia remained silent for the rest of the flight.

They had been able to swoop below the Hauser flyers, moving west and arcing around Spatelly to Lambert's Vineyard, which stood maybe ten miles away. Keston and Jovaryn kept pace on Revellie.

During the jaunt, the merged lights vanished from view. Mathias sank into the saddle, his mind circling the thought of attacking another flyer. Tightness strangled his ribs even as his racing heart slowed. He had escaped that fate because of Aunia. Because she asked for help from brinwraiths.

He wondered if she knew that brinwraiths often called on will-of-the-wisps after they had summoned mist. Any child growing up near the salt marshes knew those two faery types worked together to lure humans to their demise. But the draw to collect bog iron for coins still brought people with long sticks and baskets.

The land turned lush. Stripes of silver-green and rich brown filled the grounds. Trellises and grapevines. Stone buildings dotted the rise. The air smelled warm and sweet.

Pale, squat houses with arched doors wide enough for carts, sat beside paved terraces. Sheds lined up in neat rows. Warehouses. Barns. A narrow press-house with small windows perched high sat near a cookhouse.

Mathias frowned. No smoke issued forth and that was strange. The workers would need lunch before long. But there were no field hands tending the grapes. No dogs barked at their approach.

Abandoned? Or was everyone crowded in the two-story manor with a red roof. That stood on the highest hill, peeking out over a stand of tall cypress.

You sense Jules? Mathias sent to Taf. He curled his fingers against Aunia's back. He would not bring her to another dangerous place. But... where was Jules?

I think he's nearby. Taf dove toward the press house, and his hooves clattered against the paving stones.

Revellie followed suit, and all four of them dismounted. They stood near a stone stable that sat apart from the press house and sheds. The place was big enough to shelter their pegasi from sight, but the wide doors offered no defense. Worse, the loft would give an archer cover if anyone waited inside.

Mathias kept his hand on his sword hilt. It was possible that Bibb had taken everyone for his army.

I doubt all wererats are faebloods, Taf sent.

Mathias frowned deeper. What Bibb was doing whether these people were faebloods or not was pure evil. Had Cody moved Jules somewhere else? They needed to find Jules quickly. Talk about what their options were.

Aunia moved away from his side, closer to Keston. She was not happy with him. Yes, he had rescued her but they had failed to get compass or halite.

Are we safe to bespeak through Brinsaber? Mathias asked.

The greater the space from a pegasus, the easier for the listener to eavesdrop, Taf sent.

That left out reaching out to Fallo too.

Darla is the eavesdropper. She's using the compass to do it. Aunia crossed her arms and walked back to him. "Bibb invaded my head. And Darla, yours. Whose mind will they invade next?"

"Bibb needs run through," Mathias growled.

"Bibb is incapacitated." Aunia raised her voice. "And a wererat carried him out."

"That wasn't Bibb."

"Yes, it was."

"Bibb doesn't have red hair." Mathias should have punched Bibb the first time the man pulled out the witch compass.

Aunia looked at him like he was addled. "He had black hair mixed with white."

Technically, Taf sent, *it's not a witch compass. Those were—*

"Guys," Keston stepped forward. "Maybe we can save this for later. This place doesn't feel right."

Pigeons scattered from the stable's loft window.

"Let's secure the stable first," Mathias said, "Then the—"

"Comfortable manor?" Keston quirked a half-smile. "Jules would barrel for there."

"Keep your guard and a repel arrow spell at the ready." Mathias drew his sword and padded slowly to the open doors.

Light fell through high slats and sparkled the floating dust. Cobwebs feathered along the beams in the corners. One trough at the back end still held a bit of water...maybe still potable. But it was empty. No animals. Empty harness hooks.

"It smells like they only just left," Aunia murmured. She stood at the opening. Keston had pushed past her but Jovaryn remained at her side.

"Yeah," Jovaryn said, "but the grapevines look too well-attended."

"Looks like they left willingly," Keston said.

"I wouldn't say willingly," a gruff, slow voice said. A man with sun-brown skin and iron gray hair stepped out of the last horse pen. He held a pitchfork out like a weapon. "Didn't think I'd find a flyer nosing through my stalls. You lose your sky, or just your principles?"

Taf, you could have warned me, Mathias sent.

He wasn't there before.

Mathias held his hands, palms out. "We're looking for our man. He came with—"

"Cody," Jovaryn said. "I know your son. We rescued him from Spatelly."

The man spat on the hay-strewn ground. "Don't trust flyers."

Then another voice came. "I'll vouch for them."

Cody stepped beside the man. His blonde hair looked freshly washed and still damp and his facial hair carefully groomed. "The one beside the girl is Jovaryn, an augurite and a loyalist. The two flyers, I'm sorry, I don't remember their names but they came and rescued Jules and me. And the girl? I haven't had the honor."

Augurite? Jovaryn was an augurite. Then he too probably believed the choice was coming... and how could he not? The Dama star was almost inside the Harp. Coldness jolted through Mathias, but he made himself remain still.

Keston stepped forward and identified himself by not only his first name but his last as well, and mentioned his father's name too. Then he pointed to Aunia, gave her name and finally Mathias. "He is, for the moment, the one in charge."

"For the moment?" the man said.

Keston shrugged. "We're only part of our unit."

The man set his pitchfork down. "Roddy. Roddy Lambert. Cody, get them water."

Mathias and Keston both called their pegasi inside while Cody slipped past Roddy to a stack of barrels, popped a lid, and filled a bucket. He repeated the process for both pegasi.

While Taf and Rev took a long drink, Cody stepped back to Roddy, and the two argued in low voices.

Roddy hit the tines of the pitchfork onto the floorboards and his attention turned to Aunia. "You best beware, girlie. We had a pair of flyers come in two weeks ago demanding we line up and... All a ruse to take our folk."

"Dark blonde with a bowl-shaped haircut and a curly-head with dark hair?" Mathias asked.

"Friends of yours?' Roddy drawled.

"Hardly." Mathias shut his eyes. Patrick and Garret. Bibb had gotten to them. Navenra'd them. Probably invaded their minds. Made them do horrific things. It made Mathias sick to think of it.

"If you're thinking of helping us, you must," Aunia said. "The choice is coming. It's coming tonight or tomorrow."

"One world dies," a girl, slightly younger than Aunia, appeared. Her light brown hair was braided and coiled around her head, almost regally. Her dress though was plain and serviceable.

"Pippa, go back," Roddy said.

"Go back?" Keston said. "You've a trapdoor back there?"

Roddy held up his pitchfork.

Keston bespeaks we really don't want to sleep them, Taf sent. *They probably have more hiding.*

"We just want to collect our man," Mathias said. "We can be on our way—"

"Or you can help us," Jovaryn butted in. "The girl speaks true."

Roddy exchanged a look with Cody. "Take 'em up to the manor."

CHAPTER THIRTY-FIVE

ASTROLABE

Some would say when in doubt, a leap of faith. I say consider what squeezes your gut more. The chance you are wrong or the certainty of what will happen should you do nothing. — Jules Mayrell, flyer of Brinsaber

Aunia wanted to trail behind Mathias, but he kept slowing to match her pace. Cody, who walked beside his sister, Pippa, had already turned around twice to ask if they needed assistance, and Keston, who walked behind them with Jovaryn, also asked what was wrong with them. Wrong with them? They didn't have the compass for one. Or the halite. Or the Naoma Stone.

Aunia kept her gaze fixed on the hillside road that led to the manor house. "We could have gotten the halite before going to—"

"Our helper's house," Jovaryn cut her off. He stepped beside her, giving a little head shake, a warning not to say Q'thonos' name. He said in a low voice, "I can't summon a tunnel, Aunia. My portal tile is lost."

Pippa turned around. "You're the reason for the blue storm over the Grashbear?"

"You heard of that?" Keston said.

"A lot of the wererats were whispering on about that," Cody said. "I told Pippa it might not be you."

"And we had those two flyers showing up... on horses." Pippa walked backwards up the paved road. "They were quite abusive about how it was wrong to transport civilians on pegasi. Said they wouldn't be like the flyers who carried a faeblood."

Aunia didn't know what to say to that. She had been warned of what she could say to Tamorians. She definitely didn't trust them. She wasn't sure if she should trust Jovaryn, who walked beside her, but he was honest with his actions. He just hadn't been upfront with it.

But Darla had been upfront. She wanted to do something about the choice coming...to manipulate it. Would a manipulated future—where there was at least a future, not annihilation—be worth it?

"You don't want to admit you are," Pippa continued walking backward and chewed on a knuckle. "A few of the others say it's a sign of the end. We've already been hearing whispers of ghouls and other dark things crawling out of the cracks of the veil. Some even say that the Elderbind is in the world."

Aunia lost her footing, and side-stepped. Mathias reached to steady her, but she recovered on her own. She had seen the Elderbind in the clearing with the creek and willow trees near Q'thonos' house. "How did the Elderghast get put into a tree?"

Pippa gave her an incredulous look. "You don't know?"

"She isn't from here," Keston said.

Aunia glared at him.

"Adar? You cannot be from Uttalo... the passing is too dangerous. And you don't look Mezzapian.

"She's from Edvaras' village," Mathias said.

Pippa froze on the road, as did Cody.

"The place actually exists?" Cody asked.

Aunia sucked in a stuttered breath, teeth clenched. She knew what Tamorians were capable of. She said nothing, but she did nod.

"Then you know if we are at the choice," Pippa said. "We are, aren't we? When will the Dama appear? Do you think she'll pick us or the faery world?"

Aunia pushed past them and continued walking to the manor. Keston was saying something, she couldn't hear it. And she had no idea what she'd do once she got to the house.

Mathias wanted to see his friend. Then they'd decide what to do. How could she convince Mathias what needed to be done? Stars. She wanted to just strike out on her own or go run and hide in the vineyard... she couldn't. First choice, she'd wind up in Pavari. Second choice... well, second choice was not an option. Besides both times she ran, something came looking for her. Darla. The Elderbind.

She stepped up onto the manor's porch. Windows stared out at her with slanted shutters blocking any view of the inside.

Cody, after stepping on the porch, walked to a carved oak door and held it open.

"Aunia," Mathias called. He held out a hand.

She frowned at him and walked through the doorway. It was cooler inside and the sun beating down had been pleasant. She hadn't realized how cold she felt as they flew.

Jovaryn and Keston both passed her into the antechamber and into the next room.

"Aunia?" Mathias again was at her side, eyebrow raised.

She huffed a breath and hurried into the next room where a long table and broad hearth dominated the space. Sideboards, covered with candelabras and unlit candlesticks, lined the plaster walls. Above their heads were dark wooden beams.

Jovaryn, on the other side of the room, tapped at a shuttered win-dowsill. "It was better as a waiting area. It's a bit cramped now."

"Negotiations. Da didn't want the Da Vennen further in the manor. And I think cozy might be the better term," Cody said. "A bit of wine, fire in the hearth, Yasco's fiddle."

Aunia frowned. "The two of you know each other?"

"We met in Dalin a few seasons back." Cody turned to face her. "I was there with a wine wagon."

"And you didn't bring the rest of the team home with you." Roddy walked in from the antechamber.

"Wasn't my fault. Sometimes new help doesn't stick," Cody said in a low voice. He took position beside Aunia, gave her a once over, and brightened with a smile. "You do look tired."

Aunia blinked. Was he telling her she looked awful? She stepped away from him. Yes, she was tired. She'd been awake for over a full day. But how would sleep find her? If she didn't do something fast, a world would die.

Mathias inserted himself between Aunia and Cody. "You said Jules was here."

"Upstairs resting," Cody said. "Come on, I'll take you up. You can visit and I'll find some rooms so you can sleep. We'll hustle some food after."

"Food won't be lavish," Roddy said and crossed his arms. "We're down to basics."

"But you'll be fed," Cody said. "Aunia, do you want some water or something?"

Water. When was the last time she drank anything? Aunia walked to the other end of the room where open double doors led into a hallway. Closed doors lined the space and at its end rose a set of stairs with a wooden banister carved to look like laden grapevines.

She headed down the hallway.

"Wait up," Cody said. "I'll lead."

They were about halfway up the stairs when Aunia staggered. She fell back against Mathias and he caught her. Her knapsack squashed between them and a corner of a book jabbed into her back.

"You okay?" Mathias steadied her. Kept an arm wrapped around her back.

Part of her wanted to wilt into his arms. Part of her wanted to kick him. She straightened. Arched her back and gave a little shake to reposition the starbook and set her hand back on the banister.

She was two steps from the upper landing when memory of Kai-Marin's voice rolled in her head. 'Wisdom unfollowed means nothing. But perhaps you will take the time to read.'

Kai-Marin had told her to read. The only thing Aunia had to read was the starbook. Kai-Marin's book though her father had possession of it. She would get answers from her dad eventually on how he came by it. If she ever found him. But when she got into whatever room they put her in...

"Here we are." Cody opened the first door in the hallway.

The room itself wasn't tiny, but it was cramped with three sets of bunk beds made from light-colored wood. A figure sat up from the closest bottom bunk. Dark red hair. Broad face. And a golden glow.

"Aunia," Mathias said, "Let me introduce you to Jules."

"Stay abed, Jules," Cody said. "Better introductions later. The lady needs to take her rest as well. Mathias, I'm putting her just two doors down from you."

Mathias frowned but he nodded when Cody pointed out the door. He entered the room with Keston. Mathias did not shut his door.

Cody, a wiry man, was a bit older than Mathias, Aunia decided. And she did offer him a grateful smile when he opened her door. "Your royal suite, mi 'lady Doom."

Aunia turned as soon as she entered and frowned. "What do you mean by that?"

Cody raised his hands. "All in fun. I make bad jokes when I'm nervous. And you make me nervous."

"Me?"

"Jovaryn sees a mighty glow about you."

Aunia frowned, looked past Cody but the wererat was gone. Maybe he went down the hall. The room, painted with swirls of sunset colors, was at least the size as the room that Mathias had gone into, but this had an enormous bed at its center and a desk placed below a broad window.

"My mother's personal guest room when she yet lived," Cody said. "The bed is supposedly like sleeping on a cloud. Pippa could vouch for that. I never had the pleasure but I hope it suits. Sleep well."

And with that, Cody left, closing the door behind him.

Aunia shrugged her knapsack off and leaped onto the bed with a muffled whuff. She pulled herself into a cross-legged position and retrieved both astrolabe and starbook from her knapsack. Setting the astrolabe beside her, she settled the starbook onto her lap. Frowning, she flipped through the book. Unfamiliar pages scrawled in a strange language. She could have sworn there had been entries in her father's bold handwriting and near the front of the book. She did finally find an entry in her father's hand.

Chandarions are imbued with almost limitless power. Something Olivia did not have. But if she had my amulet, the one gifted me by the mission from the ocean, she could have honed her power. It would have been like a lens with the sun.

Mission from the ocean. Aunia shifted uncomfortably. Her father had repeated mission from the ocean many times when she was little. Did he mean Kai-Marin? That thought made her stomach coil and made her want to fling her amulet across the room. But... When had he stopped saying that? After Nehla had died. She clenched her teeth. Digging through memory? What good would that do. She kept flipping. She had seen pages about the astrolabe while they'd been at Q'thonos. Part of it could be instructions. If they had no way of getting back to Q'thonos... well... they were going to have to do something on their own.

She got to the back of the book and found nothing. Frustration needled her belly and chest. Mathias told her to get angry. Well, she was angry. And where was the pinching pressure against her temples?

The book's pages ruffled and flipped like a strong wind blew through. Startled, she reached to stop it and a page sliced her. She brought the paper cut to her lips. Troll dung and apple-pated ...

The book was open to the astrolabe pages. She leaned forward. Lines pointed from different pieces of the astrolabe to tiny loopy lettering.

The main body of the astrolabe, what Mathias had called the matar, read 'The Vessel of the Worlds' and the markings along its rim read 'The Circle of Bounds.' Aunia ran a finger along the astrolabe, identifying parts based on the illustration. A thin layer of crusty salt lay along the rim... sort of like the red crystals running along the lip of the compass. It was from those crystals that energy threads connected the compass and the Naoma Stone.

Aunia bared her teeth. She wanted the Naoma Stone back. But what if the halite was like the compass' crystals. Something for energy threads to cling to? Something to draw power from.

Fate-threads, Tafiriel sent. *Jennium says they are fate-threads. They can connect to a power source and they can connect to anything and everything.*

Jennium, Aunia almost scoffed at the name. Her faery friend had been gone for days. Well, she had appeared at Q'thonos but now she'd just talk through Tafiriel? *Jennium can come to see me if she wishes to talk.*

When no reply came, Aunia went back to the illustration. Her uncut finger traced the drawn edge of the astrolabe and she bent lower to the page to read tiny handwriting there. 'Fate is all powerful save for the limits of will and love.'

What was that supposed to mean? She moved to delicate inked circles, drawn overtop the matar, Vessel of the Worlds. They glistened. Aunia touched the page but the ink was dry. Long dry. She drew back her hand and gasped. The illustration had changed.

Instead of seeing something relatively flat, the astrolabe had opened into a globe made of concentric rings. And the piece that looked like metallic lace, the star map, it curved and became a cage of brass lines. At each tip it looked like tiny stars hovered, glinted as if lit from within. A cage made of constellations like a piece of the night sky?

She glanced back at the physical astrolabe. A slender bar lay flat over the astrolabe's body but in the illustration, it stretched upwards like an upturned needle, and light clung to its edges.

Aunia slid the book out of her lap and held up the astrolabe. There had to be a way to open it up into a globe like the illustration. It didn't budge. Frustration flared, and pain pinched at her temples. Breathe, she told herself. Her thumb grazed some of the salt clinging to the astrolabe's edge and the amulet under her gown made a lurch, thumping off her collarbone.

"Ow," she muttered. And then jerked straight.

The astrolabe peeled into engraved circles, curving outward and upward. Unfolding with clockwork grace. Hidden struts slid into place. The whole device swelled into a hollow sphere, a cage of golden glowing lattice. Threads of silver shimmered inside, quivered like spider silk caught in a storm.

The astrolabe seemed to take a deep breath. And what looked like webbing erupted in all directions from the astrolabe. Up, over, down. From her periphery, there were strands by the side of her head. Fate-threads. Shimmered like spun glass.

What had been a tool for measuring the stars had become something far greater: a holdable well of fate itself. Fragile and terrifying and... At first Aunia only stared. Silver threads quivered at every tremble of her hands. She moved the alidade, sighting along its arm. Threads bent toward it, tugging together. Two crossed, sparking where they touched.

Her breath caught. If she could touch them, she could knot them. She could tie destinies with a single turn.

She reached out and the threads swayed wildly, slipping past one another. Staying out of her grasp. She shifted the alidade again—too far. The lines tangled into a snarl, twanged, and sprang apart.

Q'thonos would take this instrument and with it being powered by halite he'd have the ability to touch those threads. They'd be linked firmer to the sides of the astrolabe.

She stood up and walked to the center of the room, eyes wide as some fate-threads fell away and others gathered from the astrolabe. The where. Where they needed to stand. What fate-threads to tie. But she had to do something. Doing something was better than doing nothing.

One fate-thread flowed from the astrolabe and out the window, while others went through the floor and the ceiling. She wouldn't know what it did until she tried... What was the worst that could happen?

She fixed her gaze on one thread, thinner than the others and near the representation of the Harp's lowest star. Remembering her father's entry, she brushed her fingers against her amulet and with the other hand, reached out to catch it.

The thread flared white, seared her fingers with a living pulse, and the manor shuddered.

A shout came through the timbers. A scream. And then the acrid tang of smoke and burning wax.

Heart thundering, Aunia released the thread and the astrolabe folded in on itself becoming what it once was. Something infinitely flatter.

Jovaryn burst into her room and shut the door behind him.

Aunia stiffened.

He looked to the astrolabe, to her face, and then back to the astrolabe. "I am being truthful about your dad. He insisted on it to protect you. And you need to be truthful with me."

She heard the words but they made no sense. "What happened downstairs."

"Well." Jovaryn raised his eyebrows. "All the candles in the house flared. A table cracked. And Roddy choked on a bone he found in a plate of strawberries. What did you do to open the astrolabe?"

Aunia glanced at the closed instrument. "How would you know—"

"I was apprenticed to Hebsolum. He has possession of the hourglass. I was trained to know what the instruments do. To find and return them to him."

Aunia gripped the astrolabe tight in her hands.

"He is not getting that," Jovaryn said. "What did you do?"

"I didn't mean to kill anyone," she wailed. "I just wanted to see if I could do what's needed. We can't get back to Q'thonos' and—"

"If a Chandarion, a potential, or better using the instruments correctly, the Dama star can be pushed away from the Harp," Jovaryn said. "Yes, you are right. You might be able to do this. But Aunia—"

"No." Her shoulders shook and she rose, still holding the astrolabe. Aunia walked to the desk, breathing. From the unshuttered window, the Lambert estate spread out. "I'm nobody."

"Nobody?" Jovaryn crossed the room. "You figure the Boggleman would seek to capture a nobody? That he'd force me through the veil into your village to see if I could capture you. Oh yes, I was there. I saw what you could do. And I deliberately went back empty-handed. Faced the punishment. But it isn't only the Boggleman. Bibb wants to capture you. And Darla... You are far more than you think. Your magic—"

"I don't want it to be. I just want to be..." Aunia froze. Ordinary. She was going to say ordinary. For the first time she understood why Limi didn't wish to become the Eldest Daughter. "I don't know what I am."

"At the least, you are potential," Jovaryn said.

Aunia crossed her arms.

"You cannot hide who you are, Kai-Marin's granddaughter."

"Leave me alone!" Aunia flung herself back onto the bed, pulled herself into a fetal position with a pillow over her head.

CHAPTER THIRTY-SIX

INVADED

Philosophy teaches us that the price of freedom sometimes means not choosing the road we prefer, but walking the road that still exists after choice has burned the rest away. If that is the path you must walk. . . You will not be alone. — Dar Zeller, flyer of Startengo

A loud crash brought Mathias out of sleep and onto his feet. He grabbed his wererat short sword from beside his bed, and he and Keston raced into the hallway. He paused for a second at a sharp scrape behind him. Jules. Staggering forward. Sword in his hands and he had banged into the wall. He was still recovering from his imprisonment and torment.

"Jules." Mathias' voice hitched. "Stay."

Jules shook his head, the motion brittle. "Won't be left behind."

Mathias gritted his teeth. They couldn't wait.

"Protect the girl." Keston pointed at Aunia's door with the tip of his sword.

"She's the one Bibb wants," Mathias yelled.

Jules nodded and staggered down the hallway.

Mathias thundered down the stairs, Keston behind him.

"From here," Cody called from the doorway into the cramped dining room. "Everyone's mostly fine."

Mathias slowed his pace, but only by a little, and marched past various shut doors and into the dining room. If there wasn't clear evidence of a disturbance, he'd be searching these rooms next. Or flying Aunia out of here... With Jules? They'd have to leave Jovaryn behind.

Cody stepped back, allowing them in.

The long table, occupying most of the room, had been cleaved in two with the halves standing up like conical tents. And a haze filled the room. The smell was a blend between caramelized and charred sweetness and acrid grease.

Mathias moved deeper into the room and the back of his head tingled like it had in the betwixting tunnel. "What happened?"

Roddy, sitting on one of the wooden chairs, leaned over his knees, hacking. Pippa, her golden-brown hair darkened by the dim room, kneeled at his feet, scooping mashed up strawberries onto a broken p late.

Roddy laughed himself into another coughing fit.

"You haven't opened the shutters. Why blow out the candles?" Keston asked.

Mathias jerked his attention to the sideboards. All the candles, beeswax and tallow had been lit and snuffed.

"We didn't light them." Pippa, still on her hands and knees, held up a chicken wing bone, then dropped it on the broken plate. "He coughed this up and all he was eating was strawberries."

Keston stepped past Mathias. "There's no bones in—"

"We know." Pippa rose, eyes red, and plate fragments in her hands. "At the day of choice, reality shall fray. One world shall perish, the other stay."

"I saw the Dama star. The choice is coming. We should pray and pray hard that the Dama blends both worlds," Roddy said, his voice hoarse. "I have the verses."

Cody leaned against the door frame, arms crossed. "When did you become enamored with fireling dogma?"

"Firelings hid us when the wererats came," Pippa said.

"Be quiet," Roddy snapped, then leaned forward, hacking in tearing heaves again.

"What fireling?" Mathias asked. There was only one fireling he was aware of in Tamore. Darla. She must have come over when Dar Syrick's border spell weakened.

Roddy thumped the center of his chest with the heel of his fist. "You can't stay here."

Cody dropped his arms. "We spoke about this."

Pippa crossed the room and set the plate pieces on a stand which sat between two of the shuttered windows. "I contacted Mistfen Tower."

"What?" Cody demanded.

"If our world is chosen, or the worlds do blend, we need to be in good standing." Pippa sniffled. "Cody, you haven't seen. Most of us have been taken. Turned. If we live, we don't need the crown taking our lands."

Mathias gripped his sword hilt tight and moved to the center of the room, toward Roddy, despite the pounding on the back of his head. These paupers had presented hospitality and now betrayed them. If this table hadn't cracked. . . They wouldn't have known until the Mistfen came to arrest them. *Taf, we need to get to you.*

Cody interjected his scrawny body between Roddy and Mathias. "Don't hurt them. They're idiots, yes. But they're the only family I have."

Mathias halted. He wouldn't have killed but a fist to the nose... "Flyers don't murder."

Pippa moved to Roddy's side, palms raised. "They might not even reply. The banner over the house—"

"They're looking for us." Mathias forced the heat of his anger down. Yasendra be blessed, his head hurt. Pressure like a wineskin bursting at the seams. He turned to Keston. "We need to leave."

"You might get caught," Cody said.

"No choice." Mathias turned for the steps. Get his belongings. Get to Aunia. Get to the stable. And Jules? Could he stay aback a pegasus? He couldn't even stand solidly on his two feet. Maybe he could stay. Warn Frehn and the others about what was coming. He could hope they wouldn't punish a flyer who had recently escaped Da Vennen imprisonment.

"What if I have an alternative." Cody reached under his loose linen shirt to the waistband of his trousers. He pulled out a playing card.

Keston stepped forward. "Is that what I think it is?"

"A card without a deck?" Mathias snapped.

Keston shook his head. "A communication card. From Adar. My dad traveled. Commissions, remember? I've seen one before."

"Exactly right." Cody raised the card inches from his face, a bit of silver glinting. "Basil? Basil, can you hear me?"

There was a long pause. Mathias turned to hustle back up the stairs and...

"Cody!" Basil's voice issued from the card as if he were talking through a window. "Wendalin has been worried sick."

Mathias turned around. "The Dar's apprentice?"

"No time. The manor dining room at Lambert's. Get here now." Cody ran a hand over the face of the card. He then returned it to his waistband's pocket.

How many communications cards do peasants have? That question rose in Mathias' head but it sounded cobwebby.

Basil appeared at the end of the table closest to the hallway before Mathias could voice the question. The rover clung to a satchel strap that he wore cross-bodied. His gaze lingered on Mathias' face then he hurried to Cody's side.

A jolt of hatred hit Mathias, and he stepped back. He didn't hate Basil. Even if he didn't fully trust him, he was grateful to the rover for rescuing Aunia. Pressure mounted inside Mathias' head and he wobbled on his feet.

"Give Wen my regrets," Cody said. "I've been imprisoned for the last... I don't know how long. Is she okay? The mission?"

"Mission?" Mathias said sharply. "You've been working with wererats all this time?"

"What?" Cody's face creased in confusion and shock. "Of course not. Basil. We need to get these flyers out."

Mathias lifted his sword. "We can't trust you."

"Mathias." Cody lifted his hands. "You saw me rescued."

"What mission?"

"Matty, we don't have time for this," Keston murmured.

"You will tell me." Mathias stepped forward.

"Bibb's wererats left days ago for Heavensfeet," Basil said. "My sources say they plan on attacking before the Warm Festival."

"Aunia can operate the astrolabe," came another voice. Jovaryn stepped into the room and he nodded at the table.

A searing pain rocked Mathias nearly off his feet. He locked his knees to keep from falling.

Basil turned to Mathias. "Did you get the halite?"

"I can't trust you," Mathias repeated.

"Trust?" Basil frowned and pulled open his satchel. From inside he retrieved Mathias' pouch and another that Mathias had taken from Sorrel.

Mathias stepped forward to claim them.

Basil, stepping back, poured the contents of Sorrel's pouch into his hand. Portal tiles. "I'm curious where you got these."

Mathias pointed a chin at the tiles. "Wererats at Eddac Tower had them. We retrieved them after they were defeated."

"And this?" Basil dropped the portal tiles back in the pouch and pulled out a marble finger.

Mathias' his mouth went dry. He stammered, "From the ruins near Aunia's village..."

Aunia and he had climbed a mountain to the first village that Edvaras had built before it was moved to Naoma Sacella. They had found the observatory where Edvaras had stored his starcharts. They'd been destroyed. And they found evidence of marble ones. Moving statues. Like Hebsolum, the marble giant. Mathias had seen a person in Aunia's village—Kron—become a marble one. Mathias had found that piece of marble... assumed it was from a regular statue but what if... "Did you find Fallo?"

"Maybe we worry about Fallo later," Keston said.

"You don't understand," Mathias said. "The time turn spell. That might be what works the spell."

Time-turn. Well, that's interesting, said a silky voice from inside Mathias' mind.

Mathias froze. Lifted a hand to the back of his head.

"Time-turn?" Cody said. "Like reversing time? What good will that do?"

Mathias cried out for Tafiriel but the floor was caving and the colors around him swirled. So much echoing in his head.

It should have been her but you'll do, said the cobwebby voice. *Stop fighting.*

"Matty," Keston called. He sounded as if he were shouting from across a river. "Matty! Are you okay?"

The ground ceased moving but the landscape had changed. Instead of being inside a vineyard manor, he stood on a bony hillock with the smell of salt on the wind. Darla faced him. She wore Aunia's gown and she was twisting the ends of her dark hair.

"I'm not here as an enemy," Darla said, almond eyes crinkling as if she were sharing an important secret. "I'm here to tell you we should work together."

Mathias lifted his sword... but his hand was empty. "How am I here?" And more importantly, where was Aunia.

"Does it matter?" Darla said. "Our worlds aren't meant to merge yet—"

"One will die." Mathias stepped forward, clenching a fist. "Not merge."

"Our dogmas don't matter," Darla snapped. "Aunia has the astrolabe but she needs to be in the right place. I have the compass. I can find the right place. And if your Fallo—"

"We've no idea where he is."

"Well two out of the three should do."

Mathias stalked away from her. Ran a hand through his hair. The Dama star was so close to entering the Harp. "You did this to—"

"I did?" Darla jabbed a finger to the sky. "Bibb did this. And we can undo it. You, me, and Aunia."

Mathias blinked. The night sky hung overhead. But it had been late morning. This couldn't be real.

In the distance, Keston's voice bubbled as if underwater. "Jovaryn, go get Aunia."

"You just want to hurt her," Mathias said. But Q'thonos had said about the importance of the Trinity working together. What if Darla was speaking truth. Or at least part of the truth?

Keston's voice came again and the syllables 'Aunia' made his heart cave.

Warmth gripped Mathias' shoulders and Taf's silvery voice, knife sharp, cut through the cobwebby voice. *Fireling be gone.*

"Oh, for pity's sake," Darla said. "Go tell your heartbeat to meet me. Five leagues west from Spatelly's rise. Walk as the tide pulls until the air thickens and the gnats gather in swarms."

The hillock. The sea marsh. The very sky was vanishing.

"You won't, will you?" Darla snarled. "Fine. I'll deliver the message myself."

Chapter Thirty-Seven

IDENTITY

Beware of those who would slaughter a flyer's good name. Public's trust is hard to regain but not impossible should truth be on your side. — Nyrissa Rieson, Dar Elect and flyer of Lydinairre

"You cannot hide who you are." Those words circled inside Aunia's head until she finally threw the pillow and yelled, "And who do you think I am?"

But Jovaryn was no longer in the room. She hadn't heard him leave. Not that she wanted to talk to him. Yes, he turned her dad into a wererat but she believed Jovaryn when he said her dad insisted. Her dad couldn't have been bitten in that cage if he hadn't wanted it. And, well, Jovaryn had been apprenticed to Hebsolum, and after, perhaps unwillingly, to the Boggleman. It meant he knew stuff. He knew the astrolabe could open.

Stars, the choice was coming... and she had been stupid with the astrolabe. Perhaps Jovaryn could help her use it in a way that would save them all.

Aunia set her jaw and stood. He neither told her if someone died or not, but if someone had, she didn't think he would have left. But she needed to see what had happened. She crossed the room, opened the door, and startled. Mathias' red-headed friend, Jules, stood outside her door.

He straightened from the wall. "Go back inside. There's danger afoot."

Aunia opened her mouth to protest, but Keston's voice rang out, shouting Mathias' name. It sent fingernails across her soul. She bolted past Jules.

"Wait," Jules called.

But she didn't. She leaped down the last three steps and pelted through the hallway into the dining room. Broken table. Keston...and Basil. They knelt on the floor. Pippa frantically waved at her. And someone lay before them.

"Mathias!" Aunia shouldered Pippa aside and landed hard on her knees beside Keston. "What happened? What's wrong with him?"

She took Mathias' hand into her own. It felt so cold.

Heat burned against her eyes. This was her fault. Playing with the astrolabe. Picking the wrong thread.

No, Taf sent. *His mind is being attacked.*

Aunia wiped her forearm against her face. *But he's resistant to magic. He has—*

Not all magic.

Darla?

Yes.

Aunia gripped Mathias' hand tighter. She would rip out Darla's hair strand by strand.

"Aunia." Mathias' voice sounded raw and strained. His usual green glow looked tattered and it was shot with dark gray.

"I'm here." Aunia ran fingers along his cheek. "Fight her."

Keston's knee bumped into hers. "If he's being attacked like you were, we need Q'thonos."

"I need no one." Mathias opened eyes that swirled with dark-gray... Darla's eyes. "Aunia. Darling."

That term from Mathias' letter to Keira... She released Mathias' hand.

"You should have convinced me to get the salt." Mathias' tone washed over her, silk-smooth and sarcastic.

"Get out of him, Darla," Aunia demanded.

"Darla? That's the fireling who's been helping us," Roddy said. He stood near Jules at the back of the room.

"Helped us to escape the Green Harpy, too." Keston's whisper was hoarse. "Now we find out the price tag."

The fireling smiled with Mathias' lips. "I gave your beloved coordinates to find me. The place you need to be to knot the choice from coming."

"Firelings believe the worlds will merge," Keston interrupted.

"This is not the right time," Darla snapped, "Bibb brought the star's movement prematurely. Who knows what will happen."

"How do you know it's premature?" Basil asked.

"I don't speak to Mystics," Darla hissed. She turned Mathias' face back to Aunia. "You've the power to stop this. I have the means to tell you where. The question, lovely, will you meet me there?"

Aunia gritted her teeth. "I'll speak to him. Now leave."

"Don't take too long," Darla said.

Mathias' eyes closed and his body relaxed against the floor. When the deep gray in his glow slunk away, breath returned to Aunia's lungs.

"Mathias?" she called.

He opened eyes that shone spring green. He rolled over onto his side and sat up.

"Matty, how are you feeling?" Keston asked.

Mathias sank his face into his hands.

"Embarrassed," Jules said from the doorframe. His complexion looked gray but he stood taller than before. "No flyer wants to be over-powered. Particularly not with their mind."

Keston nodded.

Mathias didn't move.

"Sounds like Darla only wants to help you," Roddy moved from Jules and sat again in a dining room chair.

"She works with wererats," Aunia snapped. She scanned the room. She didn't see Jovaryn.

"Flyers are coming." Keston slowly rose. "We have to go. Or hide."

Roddy leaned forward. "I'm not letting no pegasus flyer—"

Cody ran to the window and looked through the shutter slats. "They're down at the pressing hall. Da, we must. If we don't—"

"Can't skip you all, but we've these." Basil dumped portal tiles onto the floor. In the light they would've sparkled, but here in the dim they looked splotchy. Basil arranged them in a circle.

"Can you make the circle smaller?" Keston said.

"Smaller?" Roddy protested. "It's barely big enough as it is."

Keston clenched his teeth. "Smaller the safer."

"I've spaced the tiles best I can." Basil stood. "The other factor is how far we travel."

"What are you talking about?" Aunia asked.

Keston shot her a sardonic grin. "Oh, the possibility of going through tiles and never coming back out."

"Keston." Mathias shook his head.

"You can... you can just disappear?" Aunia asked.

"Cody," Basil called. "Where are we going?"

"The Hollow," Cody said. "Pippa, come help."

Mathias rose to his feet. "How do we get Taf and Rev?"

"The hollow is under the stable," Pippa said. "We just need to get there first. Da."

"Fine," Roddy rose from the chair. "But I cross through first."

"You need to take two with you," Basil said.

Roddy cut Basil a glare but Basil shrugged. "They don't know where they're going, do they?"

"Sure, you don't have an entire travel chamber stashed away?" Keston asked, then muttered in a low sing-song voice, "They're safer."

When no one replied, Keston rolled his eyes. He grabbed ahold of the back of Roddy's off-white shirt. "Come on Jules, we'll go first. Oh, and everyone not guiding where we're going... clear your mind before stepping through."

Roddy stepped in with Keston and Jules clinging to him, and they were gone.

Aunia sucked in a breath. Like skipping but with the possibility of being trapped in nothing? Keston had been nervous. Aunia's heart skittered over her sternum. But not going... the other flyers would find them eventually. She squeezed her eyes shut and gathered her courage.

Pippa's face was before her when Aunia opened her eyes.

"Knapsack," Aunia said.

And then Jovaryn was there, pressing it into her arms.

"Ready?" the girl said. Unlike her father, Pippa offered Aunia her hand. Mathias gripped the back of Pippa's dress near the shoulder blade and the three of them stepped through.

The room's dark beams were replaced with weathered gray and the semi-polished wooden floor was strewn with hay. They were inside the stable. Roddy and Jules were rushing for the back of the wide space. Revellie stood outside of her pen. Tafiriel stepped out of his as well. Keston closed the pen door.

"Move," Pippa called, hustling forward.

Cody appeared in the space where they had stood. He was with Jovaryn.

"Where's Basil?" Aunia asked.

"Scooping up portal tiles," Cody said. "He'll skip here. Move. All the way in the back. Behind the hay bales."

Aunia followed along but she slowed as they got to a spot of air that looked as if a translucent blanket hung before her. It was decorated in glyphs like the air sheet in Spately. "What is that?"

"You see it?" Cody said. "Not everyone can. It's open. Just raise your hand and walk right through."

But a person didn't need to raise their hand. She had walked through one of these before from Bibb's workshop to his bedroom. The question was where did this one lead?

Outside the building, footsteps approached.

"Go," Cody hissed.

Their party, with the pegasi, walked through and entered a cave. It was dim except for the light from oil lamps and a cook fire in the center of the space. Large wooden boxes were neatly stacked three deep and a dozen bunkbeds huddled near the cave's back. Several children played on the floor near the boxes while women worked on what must be supper.

Aunia watched the spot where they had entered for several long moments until Cody and Basil walked through. Her breath eased in her chest.

A squeal from what sounded like a door came from above.

Roddy stepped between Aunia and Mathias, his voice low. "The fireling says no one can hear us from this side but—"

"Darla made this place for you." Aunia lifted her chin. It had to have been Darla that made the passage at Spately too.

Pippa shushed her. "We don't like taking chances."

"Place seems deserted," said a tenor voice from somewhere above. Probably a younger flyer.

"Someone put up the banner," a deeper voice said.

They waited in silence until the flyers' conversation died down. While they waited, watery stew was served in wooden bowls. Aunia sat on the cold stone floor with hers. The food was hot and she was hungry. Time spun out. They needed to do something. "Darla said she gave you coordinates?"

Jules eased in beside Mathias and sat between them. "Darla tells just enough truth to make it plausible. Signature of hers. Disbelieve her and you may discover she was telling truth. Believe her and she'll laugh at you for making assumptions."

"I'm glad you were found, Mayrell," Basil said.

Jules frowned. "You know me, sir?"

"Make it point to know all the flyers in towers," Basil said. "And you make a good point. Firelings are slippery things. A rogue one? Best thing we can do is tunnel back to Q'thonos' and—"

"The Mad Wizard?" Cody asked.

Basil waved Cody's concern away.

Aunia leaned forward. "Where did Darla say to go?"

Mathias frowned. "Sea Marsh."

"Where we were?" Aunia balled her fists. The halite was there. They needed to get that, but they might not have time. "We have to go back. I want that compass. She stole the Naoma Stone, and we need—"

"You can't go," Basil said.

Jovaryn stepped forward. "I'm afraid we have to. We need that salt."

"There's a bit of salt on the rim," Mathias said.

"Not nearly enough," Jovaryn stated. "And we need salt crystals. Halite isn't optional. It not only powers, it helps keep focus, and that is imperative. Without it... we don't stand a chance. And we need to do what must be done."

"And we won't stand a chance if we go to the wrong place," Mathias said. "I don't know. Maybe we should follow Darla's directions. Out-numbering her, we might be able to get that compass from her."

Jovaryn leaned against the rock wall. "It's more than that. Each instrument in the Trinity is only as powerful as the hand that wields it. If the compass is tethered to Chand ice... That's what the Noama stone is, isn't it?"

Aunia nodded.

"It's Chand ice fashioned by Edvaras' magic," Basil said. "But we also risk handing the astrolabe to Darla. She won't be there by herself."

"Thread must be bound to ice before the Dama star rises," Mathias whispered.

"What?" Basil said.

"Something I read about the augury," said Mathias.

"Well, the compass is tethered to Chand ice. And the Dama star is almost in the Harp." Aunia jumped to her feet. "We have to go."

Basil's expression turned cloudy. "It's dangerous."

"Basil, she's at least a potential," Jovaryn said, "And she already oper-ated it."

Aunia lifted her chin. "We're two potentials. Darla called Mathias one too."

Chapter Thirty-Eight

TAKING COMMAND

Leadership is not certainty; it is the will to stand so others have something to stand behind. - King Darnell. Long live the king.

"Potential?" Mathias sputtered. "The fireling's a liar."

Basil stepped forward. "What happened that she said that?"

"Mathias has a light like my globefire," Aunia said.

My pega..." Mathias frowned. The Lambertians had stopped talking amongst themselves. "I've...crystals on my belt. Regular ingredient magic. Things a flyer can do."

Keston raised an eyebrow.

Basil repeated himself.

Aunia leaned forward. "His light attacked just like my Mygul and—"

"This is pointless. We need to talk about plans." Mathias stood. He strode to the darker sheet of air. The one that not everyone could see. He did not need or want Aunia telling them that the two lights had merged. And he couldn't be a potential. If he were then Zeller wouldn't be dead. He would've found a way to destroy Bibb on the Bellow sands. He would have flung every wererat across the sky.

He rubbed the sole of his boot along the floor. Smooth for a cave. A created cave. Like the prison where Jules and Cody had been kept. You just walk through and you're somewhere else.

In a hollow between the worlds, Taf sent.

Kind of like stepping through a travel room, isn't it? Mathias sent. *You slid for an instant along the veil to your destination? Skipping is that way too, I imagine.*

This is a pocket inside the veil. More like Nonderu where the Boggleman lives.

"I imagine getting a wild pegasus would be something a potential could do," Keston said softly.

Mathias turned to face them. The flyers, Aunia, Jovaryn, and Basil remained in their small circle. Most sat on cold stone.

"Zeller always thought there was more to you." Jules rubbed at his chin. "Said you've a green glow about you."

Aunia startled. "Your Zeller saw that?"

"Through his amulet? Yes," Jules said.

Cody brought over a blanket and set it over Jules' shoulder.

Jules smiled his thanks at Cody and bundled in. "But Mathias is right. We do need to come up with a plan. Can we see this astrolabe?"

Aunia frowned, but she dug inside her knapsack and pulled it out. "I'm not sure I should be the one using it."

"Because you broke a table?" Jovaryn asked.

"Mathias has operated astrolabes before," she said. "Back when he was at the Silver Tower."

"You remembered that?" A small burst of happiness spread over Mathias' chest.

Aunia looked at him like he'd sprout wings.

Mathias crossed back to her and held out his hand. "How about if we both figure it out? It shouldn't be too complicated."

"It opens," she said and handed it to him.

The instrument felt heavier than it should. Heavier than when he had touched it at Q'thonos' house. He raised it toward the torchlight, frowned at the shadows it cast, and his egg-shaped light popped into existence.

"I wish Mygul showed exactly when I wanted," Aunia murmured.

Mathias shrugged slightly and continued examining. He touched the engravings around the face-fronting lip. Some of the symbols were constellations. Not all. Even some of the symbols etched into the alidade, the sighting bar, sitting across the astrolabe's face looked strange. And the rete? That spidery brass cut-out, usually marked for only the brightest stars... It had hundreds etched finely and interwoven with more strange glyphs. Some of the glyphs similar to those floating on that sheet of air only a few yards away. "Okay. This big round bit is the base."

"Vessel of the Worlds." Aunia tapped the astrolabe's rim. "And the Circle of Bounds."

"Matar and rim."

"That's not what the starbook named them," she said.

"A name is just a name," Mathias muttered. "Consider the mater like the ground everything sits on." He moved his finger from the frame to the rete, the rotating map cut-out, and gingerly rotated it a few degrees. Its thin, curved lines slid over the edge of the astrolabe. "And what you need to do is—"

"It opens up," Aunia repeated.

Mathias frowned for a moment. "Yes, there are probably more plates inside. Discs for different portions of the sky. Take a look here." He tapped the intricate explosion of stars along the rete's metal. "All you do is match up to the ones you see overhead. There are too many stars here. Strange but... But you concentrate on what you recognize. The bar here, the alidade...you point it at the star you want to measure and—"

Aunia clenched her fists. "It opens up."

Footfalls outside the hollow returned and several of the Lambertians shushed them.

"Did you hear something?" Breen's voice filtered down.

Everyone inside the hollow froze, except for Basil, who padded over to stand behind Aunia.

Mathias swallowed hard, fingers clutched around the astrolabe, his heartbeat whooshing in his ears. The Hauser flyers had joined with the Mistfen Tower. Maybe some of the Mistfen had been among those who had chased them in the Salt Marsh. There had been two pegasi that he hadn't recognized.

"Feels like they're nearby," Frehn said. "Drink?"

"I don't drink wine, commander," Breen said.

"Fair enough. Keep looking."

The flyers' voices retreated, and Aunia grabbed the astrolabe from Mathias' hands.

"Look. See?" Aunia slid a thumb along the astrolabe's edge, breaking a bit of salt away. The astrolabe peeled apart. Turned into a globe of interconnecting and concentric bands of metal. It hovered on her palm. Silvery strands thinner than spiderweb floated out of it in all directions.

He reached his finger to touch one.

"Don't," Jovaryn said. "You touch one and who knows what'll happen."

"It's why the table broke," Aunia said softly.

"And my Da choked on strawberry bones?" Pippa strolled over from the cook fire. She held out her hand to take the empty bowls.

"Your Da's always guzzling food," said an older Lambertian woman. She remained near the fire.

Pippa pivoted slightly. "A bone from eating strawberries?"

"If we don't know which thread to touch..." Mathias rubbed at his knuckles. This mission was doomed to fail.

Pippa crouched down in front of the astrolabe. "I don't see any threads."

"You don't see the glyphs to this place either," Cody said.

Pippa rose. "Can't help I'm not faeblood."

Jovaryn pushed off the nearby wall. "The halite attaches to the rim. It will light the right threads. All Aunia will need to do then is think her intent."

Mathias wet his dry lips. "So, we have to get the salt. Fight Darla for the compass, and we'll know where the real 'where' is."

"Getting the halite on the astrolabe and having it in a potential's hand... It will provide the counterbalance to whatever Darla will bring," Jovaryn said.

Mathias ran a hand through his hair. "Aunia, you know how to close that?"

She bit her lip, closed her eyes, and the astrolabe shuddered closed.

Jovaryn nodded approvingly.

Basil puckered his lips in contemplation, then nodded.

"That leaves us with figuring out how to get out of here." Mathias paced.

Footsteps sounded above them again and a thought hit him. Why was Frehn drinking wine while they were searching?

"I don't think our other flyers are budging," Jules said, his voice low.

"If we could make Darla skip here, we'd have the initiative," Cody said. "We could strike that compass right out of her hands."

"She's not so good at skipping," Jules said. "She'd get mad when Bibb would rub that in."

"Not a full fireling?" Cody crossed his arms.

"She was the housekeeper for Gabryella," Aunia said.

"Gabryella, First Flamekeeper of the Fireling Order?" Basil slid closer to her. "That's a story I'll need to hear."

"Hear later," Jovaryn said.

Jules held a fist in front of his chest. "I do know Darla has some formidable toys."

Mathias pivoted toward his friend. "Like what?"

"Like a metal writing rod that lets her make betwixting hollows." Jovaryn pointed at the glimmering wall and the glyphs.

Mathias blinked. He reached into the inside pocket of his jerkin and pulled out the steel stylus wrapped in silver wire. "Something like this?"

Jovaryn's eyes widened. "Where'd you get that?"

"Attic at the Green Harpy," Mathias said. "Think it was Darla's. Could we open this to the coordinates she gave?"

You're trusting the coordinates? Taf sent at the same time that Aunia asked the same.

"If we go anywhere, we should get the salt," Jovaryn said.

"Any salt in the sea marsh will do?" Keston asked.

"No," Jovaryn said. "We need to go to the Wraithmere."

"The brinwraiths would've known that," Aunia said. "We should have asked them—"

"Not helping," Mathias snapped. He closed his eyes against the hurt on her face. "I'm sorry. We should have. There was probably a way. I was just focused on getting us out safe. I should have considered more what you were saying."

"I'm sorry too." Toying with her amulet, Aunia rose to her feet. "I could egg Darla into coming here."

"Woah," Roddy called from the bunkbeds. "Don't be angering our patron."

"Da," Pippa called from the fire. "There's our world on the line."

"With flyers over our head? I'm agreeing with Roddy," Jules said. "I don't think that's smart."

"Maybe they'd help us," Cody said.

"Maybe they'd think we're traitors," Keston retorted. "The Da Vennen have been great about spreading false rumors."

The silver cord wrapped around the steel rod bit into Mathias' grip. He sucked in a long breath, not sure what he needed to do. He wished for a moment that Jules was in better shape to give orders or that Fallo was there... if he could be completely trusted.

The eavesdropper is still out there, Taf sent. *But he wouldn't be at the Grashbear yet.*

We are on our own, Mathias sent. "Basil, can you skip the others...or portal tile them elsewhere. Someplace safer? And take Jules?"

CHAPTER THIRTY-NINE

GLAMOR

Oh, illusion? That's just make-believe magic in a flirtatious mood. Let it twirl with a person's own perception and they won't care what's true. They'll lean in, desperate to be fooled.
— Basil Mensani, of the Mensani caravan

There was nothing to be done except stand there. Aunia rubbed at her knuckles while Jovaryn explained the dangers of what they planned to do.

"So, I have to bleed on this thing." Mathias stood facing the glyph door and holding up the metal wand.

Jovaryn nodded. "Darker magicks usually rely on blood but it's just a fireling we're dealing with. It isn't like this is the Elderbind."

Her head jerked up.

"From the War Between the Worlds," Keston murmured. He stood beside her, along with both pegasi. "It's how Illysa and Uriah contained the beast."

Her heart creaked with slow and awful understanding. "I saw the Elderbind at Q'thonos' when I ran... when I went for a walk."

Keston's eyes widened, then his voice came out tight. "Never thought I'd be walking stories of legend."

Aunia looked away. Most of their stories of legend were tales she had never heard before. Her father had done everything to keep her ignorant. Caedmon, the village's blacksmith and storyteller, had complied with her father's wishes. She could almost remember Caedmon once telling her about the Elderghast when she was very small and her father had barreled into the smithy, all red-faced. He demanded she run on home.

"After you smear your blood on this rod," Jovaryn said, "you'll place your marks over Darla's glyphs."

"Basil," Mathias called. "The people?"

Basil worked near the bunkbeds organizing a ring of portal tiles.

"Mark me. I am protesting," Roddy said.

"You'll want to be elsewhere whether Darla pours in or not," Jovaryn said. "It's possible this place will collapse."

"Collapse?" Roddy growled. "I knew I didn't want flyers finding this place."

Basil put that last tile down and straightened. "Do you have somewhere in mind?"

"Meela's old place." Roddy stepped to the edge of the circle. "Iffin' you haven't been there, hold on to my shirt."

Two preteen boys pushed forward and grabbed a hold of Roddy's shirt. They stepped into the circle and vanished.

Pippa stepped forward. "Anyone with only a vague collection, come take my hand."

A young woman with a child held on her hip walked over to Pippa.

"Safe travels," Cody said.

After that, the rest of the vineyard people filed into the portal circle and vanished one by one.

Mathias handed the metal wand to Jovaryn and pulled out his dagger. He nicked himself under his pinky finger, took back the wand and smeared his blood over the metal. Mathias' eyes met Aunia's. The green in them had darkened as did his glow. "I don't know fireling glyphs."

"I don't know many either." Jovaryn touched one that looked like a curved 'x.' "That one is a lock." He pointed to a spiral. "And that one is open."

"Mathias?" Jules stood before the portal tiles with Cody and Basil. "You're a flyer who has consumed Navenra. Like me. It changes us. Be careful. With both you and Taf."

Anguish passed over Mathias' face. It made Aunia want to run a hand over his cheek and tell him it would be okay.

"I will," Mathias said. "And after we get the compass from Darla, I'll have Taf bespeak Brinsaber. Have him come back to you."

Jules closed his eyes. "I only sent him off to—"

"Protect him," Mathias finished. "I know."

Jules passed through the circle as did Cody. Basil scooped up the portal tiles and put them back in the pouch.

"Those are mine," Mathias said.

"No," Basil said and winked. "I think they're stolen." He then vanished from sight.

Aunia hugged herself. Basil didn't even say goodbye.

"Okay," Mathias said. "I mark the glyphs. Aunia calls for Darla with the amulet, Taf sleeps her, and we get the compass."

Jovaryn sucked in a deep breath. "Yep. That would be the plan."

Mathias lifted the wand and drew a spiral over the curved 'x.' He went on to the next symbol and drew a seven-pointed star. The air shivered with a low hum. He drew another star and tendrils of dark air flapped like canvas.

"Aunia, your turn," Jovaryn said.

Grabbing her amulet into her fist, Aunia visualized Darla in her mind's eye and considered the mean things that Velli and Sigmus had told her over the years. But taunts would not move Darla. Aunia bit her lip. She didn't like lying but... if this worked. "Darla," she called, "I need your help."

They didn't have to wait. Darla sauntered out of the ripped air's seam where Mathias stood and flicked him on the forehead.

Mathias grimaced as he grabbed Darla's arm. He jabbed the point of his dagger into her side. "We'll be taking the compass now."

Darla's eyes went flat.

Mathias went down with an anguished cry and Darla lunged.

Tafiriel clattered forward. Forced Darla back.

The fireling dropped beside Mathias. Grabbed him by his hair and held his own dagger to his throat. How did she get Mathias' dagger?

"Play nice," Darla said. "I know about how pegasi repel magic but the dagger isn't magical at all. Plus, I can call the other flyers around here."

Keston snapped, "You can't—"

"Oh, I certainly can. Doesn't take much to get into a flyer's head after they drink some of Bibb's private stash."

"Let him go," Aunia said. Ice hollowed her insides and anger flared.

"So speaks the liar?" Darla said, eyes glittering.

I can't sleep her, Tafiriel sent. *Neither can Revellie.*

Aunia stepped forward and stiffened. Jennium sat at Darla's shoulder. Stars! Darla had turned Jennium. The faery shook her head and a light bell floated in the air.

Darla turned her head momentarily as if tracking the noise. She then glared at Aunia. "I'll free him if you come with me. No more fighting. You'll walk through first because your word... it's not so good."

Jennium sent a mind picture of Mygul. Aunia blinked. She'd love to call Mygul on demand but it didn't work that way. Not like Mathias could call on his light.

"Aunia. Tick-tock." Darla dug the dagger tip against Mathias' throat and a thin line of red trickled down.

Anger. Mathias said that anger was her trigger to make Mygul appear. Well, she was mad but hovering against it was also fear and uncertainty. Maybe she shouldn't have tried to trick Darla. Maybe she should have just gone with her. Maybe she still should.

Another mind picture hit. The portal circle that Basil had made... There were still tiles on the floor but not all of them. Basil had scooped a few up.

What was Jennium telling her? Try to escape or lure Darla in there? They still needed the compass. Aunia sent a mind picture to Jennium.

The faery shook her head. An image of an unfamiliar room formed inside Aunia's head.

"You don't have the compass," Aunia said. Their plan had been for nothing and the threat to Mathias' life was all too real.

"Do you think me stupid?" Darla asked.

Mathias hissed as another line dotted down.

Darla laughed. "You coming now, Aunia?"

Come on, Mygul, Aunia thought, willing the pinching sensation into her temples.

"Stop whatever face you're making," Darla said.

Tafiriel stomped and Mathias went limp in Darla's grasp.

Something... a stone maybe... thunked against Darla's head, and bounced away. The fireling hissed and lifted the dagger over Mathias' chest. Mygul materialized, raced forward and struck Darla full in the chest. Darla flew back, striking the wall.

Keston and Jovaryn pulled Mathias back. At the same time Pippa... Pippa? She ran to the portal circle with the astrolabe high in her hand.

Darla growled. Sprang up. Gave chase. To the portal circle.

Pippa jumped in.

Aunia cried out.

And Darla jumped in after her. They were gone.

Basil appeared.

"You sent them to the nothing?" Keston blurted. "The girl was... an innocent. And we needed that astrolabe."

"Pippa is fine. Never here. It was a glamor," Basil said. "Courtesy of Jennium."

Aunia clutched the knapsack. Felt the metal object under her grip. "The astrolabe is here." Then she turned to Mathias and fell beside him. Gripped him by his jerkin.

He's safe, Tafiriel sent. *I slept him.*

Aunia blinked. "You..."

Slept him. Yes, Taf sent. *He'll wake soon.*

"I thought Darla might be too much," Basil said. "Jennium and I came up with a Plan B and C."

"And Darla is in the nothing," Keston said.

"She'll be fine. A fireling will twist out and if not, well Etos won't let his tools stay in the void." Basil shot Aunia a wink. "You could call your grandmother for help."

Jovaryn stepped forward. "You may have more abilities than me but I have knowledge you don't. The sea-witch only wants her sister back. She has no care for our world, the faery one, or mortal kin."

Aunia swallowed hard. She'd figured the same thing but to hear it out loud bruised her insides. Family was supposed to care.

"I suppose you can call out for your great-aunt," Basil said with a wink.

"Call Yasendra? Well, that would be... different," Keston said.

Mathias jerked awake and Aunia wrapped her arms around him. She would never forgive Darla for threatening him. He returned her embrace and she trembled, soaking in the warmth returning to his hands.

"Hey," Keston said.

Mathias and Aunia broke apart and Keston handed Mathias his dagger. "You'll want to mop up the nick to your neck but if you're okay Matty, we should go."

"You should." Basil stepped in and gave Aunia a hug. "Please be careful."

"Did you know Jennium was with Darla?" Aunia said, her face muffled in his shoulder.

Basil pulled back, and Mathias tugged her away. She let her fingers slip from Basil's shoulders and allowed herself to lean against Mathias, setting her hand on his chest. He was alive, and they were free of Darla for a little while but... They did not have the compass. But then, neither did Darla.

"I did," Basil said. "But when a person's mind isn't totally their own. . . You have to keep your cards breasted."

CHAPTER FORTY

STORY

Every dangerous story begins as truth told too beautifully. It is how it may slip past your reason and nest in your soul. — Queen Shaleia of Tamore

"The question is where are we going and how," Jovaryn said.

Mathias curled his arm around Aunia but he also touched a forefinger to the prick at his neck. It had stopped bleeding. Why couldn't you sleep the fireling?

Stop touching, Taf sent. *And I don't know. There's a magical barrier around her.*

Mathias clamped his jaw. Before his mind's eye grew a crowd of faces. Faces of servants. Of merchants. The Queen and her court. Towers of flyers. His parents. Mathias swallowed hard. His little brother's face. Zeller's. Nyrissa's with an expression of abject betrayal and anger. People glaring at him with stunned disbelief and pain. His weakness. His betrayal. On the Harp, he couldn't even protect himself from his own dagger.

You are not at fault, Taf sent.

Same difference, Mathias sent back. It was like being on the Bellows sands all over again. Helpless. Unbelieved. Weak.

And as long as you keep trying, you succeed. Doesn't matter if you fall. Keep trying.

Keep trying? Nyrissa didn't believe me. Why should anyone?

If she had… What would have changed? Taf sent.

What change can I make when I'm not in control?

We'd be in a worse situation, Taf sent, *and without the astrolabe to fix it. Sometimes serendipity lends a hand.*

Big word for you. A corner of Mathias' mouth lifted. His arm tightened around Aunia. Aunia, sweet Aunia. He had known her for less than a moon and there could be no one more dear.

Basil stood in front of the glyph door squinting. "You can call betwixting tunnels by touching rock."

"Real rock," Jovaryn said. "But even then, if Mathias hadn't destabilized the last tunnel we were in, we could've been stuck forever. I told you, I'm not so good with it."

"I can't do it at all." Basil pointed at the glyph door. "Though with Jennium's help I can see the markings here."

"We could fly out. Mount up and run," Keston said.

"With Frehn and whatever flyer is out there on our tail?" Mathias said. He brushed a kiss against Aunia's hair and stepped away to the door. They needed to figure this out. He. . . needed to figure this out. "Darla came here how?"

"Probably hollow to hollow," Jovaryn said.

"Could we go through another hollow, one that's closer to Wraithmere?"

Jovaryn frowned. "We don't know exactly where Wraithmere is but… yes. If the hollow isn't locked."

"How do we find another hollow?" Keston asked.

With your heart, Taf sent.

Mathias turned to face his pegasus.

You are a potential, Taf sent. Like Aunia can see, you feel. You feel it in your blood. If you work together...

"Like a compass," Mathias said, then tapped his teeth together. There were times he felt things. Sometimes they were true. And this couldn't hurt. "Jovaryn, do I need to reblood this wand?"

"No. Once will attune it to you," Jovaryn said. "I know there's a hollow in Spatelly but it's sure to be guarded or locked."

"We might be able to find another," Mathias said. "Aunia?"

She stepped by his side.

"You heard Taf?" he asked.

She nodded.

Tafiriel, can you link us closer? Aunia squeezed his hand. *And with Jennium too. She can give me pictures from Darla's thoughts.*

A pale golden shadow flitted over Aunia's head and settled on her shoulder.

"Your Jennium was being a spy?" he asked.

"Spy is such a strong term," Basil said as Tafiriel stamped his front foot with a nod.

I don't know how this works, Mathias sent.

I don't know either. Aunia wrapped her other hand around her amulet. *But I have this.*

Landscape entered Mathias' mind. Bibb and Darla's temple. And Spatelly's rise on the western hill. Landscape blurred after that, running fast and then more clear. Glittering water, patches of algae, and rough humps of land. This was the sea marsh. But how many leagues? Walk as the tide pulls. Until the air thickens and gnats gather in swarms.

The marsh continued to stretch. Pools of brine shimmered between knotted roots and half-sunken reeds. Crabs clustered in the shallows, leaving star-shaped prints. Broken timbers from who knew what rose like ribs from the mud. Grasses and reeds waved and then...

Mathias felt a jolt, a pull. *There.*

The landmass rotated under the vision and a bulge of stubborn earth emerged from soupy mud. Grasses grew taller, coarse and pale. Driftwood bones littered the edges. There was a pull toward Mathias' right but the land before them folded in on itself. Became rosy glass on all sides with plush cushions littering the floor.

We found the hollow, Mathias sent. He scanned the glass walls with its red-hued view of the marsh and found a large curved 'x' glimmering on the eastern wall.

The image disappeared and Mathias jolted, as if jumping back inside his body. He staggered on his feet, blinking.

"You okay, Matty?" Keston asked.

Mathias blinked a few more times. "We found a hollow in the sea marsh but it's locked."

"But you know where it is?" Jovaryn asked.

Mathias nodded.

"Then we, or rather you, unlock it," Jovaryn said. "It can be tricky but just visualize that hollow, find the locked mark and you'll picture yourself drawing a spiral there while you mark the same symbol at the same time on our glyph door."

Mathias nodded. He sucked in a breath and walked up to the glyph door. He willed his arm to stop its tremor. A potential. He was a potential. But on the Harp, he knew the cost. Losing one's life to reforge a heart. Giving life for country. For the world. If he could be a potential... He wouldn't be able to let more people down. He'd be making amends. "Where should I make the mark?"

"On this side, it doesn't matter," Jovaryn said. "Just match it up in your mind where the other hollow's mark is."

Mathias set the tip of the wand onto the shredded glyph door and drew a spiral—

inside to outside.

His arm jolted about three-quarters through the symbol. A loud snick. And a breeze blew in. A hint of salt and stale air.

Jovaryn wrinkled his nose. "A hollow unused for some time."

"It's still Darla's, isn't it?" Aunia asked.

Jovaryn shrugged and looked at Basil. "You coming with us this time?"

Basil tugged at his orange bandana. "The Mystic Court will be wondering where—"

"I think now is more important, don't you?" Jovaryn said.

Basil closed his eyes, then nodded. "Hate other means of transportation. Mathias do lead us through."

"Just push open the door. As big of a door that you think we need," Jovaryn said.

Mathias frowned, took Aunia's hand in his left and pushed the glyph door with his right.

They stepped into a cramped hollow with the rosy glass walls. So little space. Taf and Rev trod on the cushions littering the floor. And Mathias pushed his way past Aunia and Keston to this hollow's glyph door. It was with relief to smack the open symbol and exit. They stood on sturdy ground... sort of. It was an island. A mound of salt-scabbed earth and marsh as far as the eye could see. A drowned country of pale reeds and glinting pools that caught the afternoon light like shards of broken mirror.

"Can you..." Mathias bit his lip. "Call the brinwraiths?"

Basil closed his eyes, shuffled back toward where the hollow had been.

"I can try." Aunia walked to the edge of the water. She stood there for a long moment, tapping her fingers along the side of her leg. She looked over her shoulder, flashed Mathias a smile and a nod. "Brin-born, tide-taken, answer my plea. Uncoil your silence and come to me."

The water lapped forward in slow, deliberate breaths. And then, nothing.

They waited. The sun traveled overhead in a slow but relentless measure. Aunia tried other bits of poems. She tried hissing. And yelling. Splashing the water then wiping her hands on the hem of her gown.

The smell of the marsh grew denser at times, and occasionally a faint sweetness drifted by. Or an occasional bubble rose from the mire with a quiet plop, and a circle of ripples would spread outward, vanishing into mist.

"I don't think they're coming," Keston said.

Mathias looked up from the low rock he sat on. He had been alternating rubbing his thumb over his fingernails and watching Aunia pace along the water's edge.

We need to find the halite, Taf sent.

I know, Mathias sent, *but unless you know where...*

Jovaryn picked up a thin branch of driftwood and snapped it into smaller pieces. "They like stories."

"Bloody ones," Basil said. "And I'd advise it not be a personal one."

"Why?" Keston asked.

"If a story hasn't an ending, they have a default one," Basil said in a low voice.

Keston asked, "What if it isn't personal and it has parts but not known?"

Basil shook his head.

"No seriously. Maybe they'd show up and tell us the parts we don't know."

Mathias shook his head. Leave it to Keston to provide a distraction. "And what story would that be?"

"Oh, I'm glad you asked, Matty." Keston shot him a grin. "A tale that has nothing to do with *us*. Once, over a score and a half ago, a fireling entourage with all the trappings made sail through the channels of the Sea Marsh to the Hagpoint. This, of course, is before Dar Syrick's border spell closed the way."

"Keston," Mathias growled.

"What? No this has nothing to do where they landed." Keston waved a hand. "They moved away from your father's lands like pronto and presented themselves to parliament with a request for an audience with the king."

"We don't need a political tale."

"It's not like I was going to ask questions on why Aeryk married the Queen or anything," Keston said, "though it is higgly how he went from a betrothal from Kylandra to Shaleia."

"Keston," Mathias jumped to his feet, fists balled.

Keston opened his mouth and closed it. "Sorry. I wasn't—"

Mathias forced himself to breathe, and he kept his voice mild. "You shouldn't call royalty by their bare name."

"Hard to marry Kylandra when she died," Jovaryn scratched his forehead. "But don't the stories say she broke the engagement with Aeryk first?"

"Yes, after Wallace Habrett broke his betrothal to Shaleia." Basil gave a slight nod to Mathias. "This is not an appropriate story."

"Habrett?" Jovaryn looked to Mathias. "Oh."

Basil huffed out a breath and pointed past Aunia. "But I think we got their attention."

Chapter Forty-One

RIDDLE

Every riddle is a doorway; it only seems like a wall until you think sideways. — Wendalin Mensani, apprentice to Dar Syrick

The water breathed against the island's edge—slow, sucking pulls that left the reeds shivering and a mist was coming in. Brinwraiths were approaching, silver-blue and green, with skin shimmering between scale and flesh. Aunia swallowed hard. Considered whether to remain crouched at the water's edge or to stand. To stay still and trust or to step back. Could they move onto land?

"Aunia," Mathias hissed.

Jennium, still on her shoulder, ducked under her hair.

Aunia lifted a finger, a signal to wait. Worry already skipped through her veins and scraped her bones. She didn't need his.

More of the creatures surfaced. Some peered partially under slick mats of algae. Eyes mirror-bright and unblinking. Green hair plastered to their feline-shaped heads.

Behind her, Tafiriel or Revellie... maybe both... rustled their wings.

Do not trust them, Tafiriel sent.

"We haven't a choice," Aunia murmured.

More mist floated upward. It smelled like brine and crushed shells and iron. Iron? A faery's bane? The brinwraiths lifted higher, slender torsos gleaming, hair drifting in tendrils.

Mathias moved to her side, and the brinwraiths snapped their attention on him.

Mathias step back, Aunia sent. *They won't hurt me.* She swallowed. She hoped.

He squeezed her shoulder and stepped away. Hopefully to Tafiriel.

"I..." Aunia tried to find saliva in a mouth gone too dry. She tried again. "I am Kai-Marin's kin. And I seek the Wraithmere. I seek it to save both our worlds. Where is it?"

One of the brinwraiths who had been bobbing in the water surged forward. It...she... smiled at her with sharp pointy teeth.

Aunia curled her toes against her sandals. The same pointy teeth as the Jenny Greenteeth at the pond. Were these two faery types related? "We could—"

Poetic and limited. A story for the location and safe passage for all of us, sent a higher silvery voice. Revellie.

Aunia bit her lip and then sucked in a breath:

> "Brinwraiths born of salt and dream,
> keepers of the moonlit seam—
> I offer a story, yours to keep,
> bound in tide and kept in deep.
> In fair return, reveal Wraithmere,
> and grant us passage, safe and clear.
> Take my offer and nothing more..."

Aunia paused. "Be it here or beyond your shore."

The slits in the brinwraith's eyes widened, as did the smile. Its voice was gargled, almost unintelligible. "Tell your tale and if it is worthy, we agree."

Mist wrapped the island, and all that could be heard was breath and the lapping of water.

Aunia tried to think of a worthwhile story while her heart thudded against her sternum.

"You could tell about the summoning of Uriah," Keston called.

The lead brinwraith snarled, surged up onto the shore, its breath in Aunia's face. "*Your* story."

The ring of steel behind her made Aunia cry out for Mathias and the others to wait. "I'll tell you what happened to Edvaras when he crossed the Grashbear Mountains."

"Agreed," the brinwraith said.

It took nearly an hour, if Aunia were to guess, to speak of Edvaras' journey. His love for Naoma and their escape from her home, which led them over the mountains by way of the betwixting spell. His battle with marble ones from Hebsolum to the ones that had stripped his magical Nymer away. She spoke of Naoma's father discovering where they were and killing his grandchildren. Her voice sank into quiet tones when she spoke about Naoma being abducted by the Boggleman and Edvaras going off to find her. And then recently that she had discovered that he had been captured—Aunia did not know how—but he and Naoma both had been trapped inside a Chand ice column in the Boggleman's realm of Nonderu.

You cannot make the tale personal, Taf sent.

Aunia bit her lip. "Kai-Marin came to Nonderu."

"For you?" the brinwraith tilted its head and the slit pupils enlarged to turn both eyes solid black.

Aunia shook her head. "For her son. And on his behalf, she shattered the columns. Whither where Edvaras and Naoma have gone, they walk in one of the worlds."

The brinwraith hissed.

"The end,' Aunia said. "Now. Where is the Wraithmere?"

The brinwraith laughed. A guttural noise. It pointed in the direction where a disc of flattened light glowed against the mist. The sun, closing in toward supper time. "The next island."

It and the others submerged, their figures rippling away, and they disappeared.

They flew, Aunia sitting in Mathias' lap, and Basil clinging to the back of Tafiriel's saddle.

Keston bespeaks we could have found this ourselves, Tafiriel sent.

Maybe, Aunia sent. *But now we know.*

They landed on another island, and Aunia pushed off from Mathias' lap and dropped to her feet. The ground shuddered faintly beneath her sandals. She shifted quickly to keep her balance. The surface did not feel like true ground. More like a crust of salt cracking into jagged plates... like walking through thin glass.

The astrolabe inside the knapsack pulsed, almost like a heartbeat against her back, while her own heart hummed with a strange recognition. Like she was being called. As if this part of the journey would be the easiest. She didn't trust it.

This island was bigger than the last. Did not feel as stable, but it did have a cave with a maw that stared at them from seven paces ahead. A cave in the center of a bone-white, stone hill. At its mouth, an arch of mangrove roots grew. They were rooted in shadow and heaps of sparkling salt crystals that refracted in the late afternoon sun and painted colors along the ground. And the air... it tingled in her nose. It was like all the bad smells had been cleaned away. Aunia breathed in the pure air and hurried forward even as her brain told her to slow.

Mathias followed, as did Keston, Jovaryn, and Basil.

"Beware," Jovaryn said. "Roots don't grow through salt. There's magic afoot."

Mathias rushed in front of Aunia, halting her progress. One arm set in front of her, his other hand gripping his sword hilt. "There are bodies here."

"Bodies?" Keston stepped forward. He let out a thin laugh. "Oh great. Corpse art."

Aunia rose on tiptoes. There couldn't be bodies. Not here... A shiver skittered along her bones. Three bodies—two on Aunia's left and one on her right—lay coated in salt under the mangrove roots. Blended bodies. Half human, half wererat... as if they had died in mid-transformation.

The astrolabe's pulse quickened, and her heart thudded against her sternum.

"Perhaps Bibb or Darla sent some of their... army here," Mathias said.

"Indeed," Jovaryn said. "Not a good sign. But perhaps necessary."

"Perhaps necessary?" Keston's tone conveyed the shock that Aunia felt.

"Necessary as we need Darla to come to us. And those..." Jovaryn pointed to the bodies. "Says she'll know where we are."

"We can't go in there," Mathias said.

"We're with Kai-Marin's granddaughter," Jovaryn said. "We must."

"Couldn't we use what's already out here?" Keston asked.

Jovaryn shook his head. "We need the largest crystals. Those will be inside."

Aunia bit her lip. Set her palm against Mathias' back. "We have to do this. Our world or theirs..."

He turned, his expression grim. He looked past her to Tafiriel. *Keep us guarded.*

Conjure your light, Tafiriel sent.

Mathias curled his left hand into a fist, and reopened it. A light, his egg-shaped white light, appeared.

Aunia closed her eyes, wishing again that she could conjure Mygul as easily.

Fingers curled into her own and Aunia opened her eyes. Mathias gave her hand a little shake. He mouthed, "You ready?"

She nodded. They walked, and he counted low under his breath.

"Into the breach we go," Keston said, tightness thrummed in his words despite his lilting tone.

Mathias raised his sword. "Keep to the center and away from those vines."

Behind her, Keston's sword whistled from its sheath.

The five of them walked through the narrow entrance single-file—Mathias, her, and the other three. She did not look back. Inside, the cave whittled to a narrow tunnel, occasionally forcing them to walk sideways. Their feet crunched on brittle salt. Mathias' white light and even his green glow made the too-near walls shimmer with threads of blue and green—as did the others with their glows of yellows, blues and silver. Shadows fractured as they went. Mathias moved ahead of her slowly. Methodically.

Behind her, Keston muttered, "Lovely sound, isn't it? Like walking on cook's sugar cookies."

"Your humor is at the wrong time," Jovaryn breathed.

"But it is funny," Basil said from the rear.

Minutes spun out forever it seemed and then the space opened into a wide cavern. Wide brine pools polka-dotted the ground. They mirrored themselves on the ceilings with rings and teeth. No, those were stalactites hanging above like glass icicles. The rings were the ripples from the pools after water beads dripped into them.

"Be pretty if it wasn't so eerie," Keston said.

Aunia silently agreed.

She hastened her step to walk beside Mathias. They had enough room to and still skirt the dark water edges while the cave hummed. And the ground crackled under her feet. She grew sleepy. Thought about home. But where was home.

Home is where you are.

Her drooping eyes snapped open. She wasn't sure who said that.

Jennium shot a mind-picture of them walking through the cave tunnels, eyes open and alert.

Sound advice. She resisted closing her eyes again. Thought about what they needed to do. "Jovaryn, do you know how we fasten the salt once we get it?"

"Same as how Q'thonos did. Just put it against the rim," he said.

Mathias set the path, winding them between another pair of pools. They had gotten about halfway when the wider right-handed side pool rippled.

Aunia grabbed Mathias' arm, skittering back as a luminously pale-skinned woman rose waist-deep from the water. Her dark hair shimmered with salt crystals. Her features... They looked carved like Hebsolum in his marble giant persona except more angular. More sensual. Her eyes, nearly white and opalescent, shone hungrily on them. Mathias bumped against Aunia and his light hovered above them.

The woman took in each of them. She lingered on Aunia the longest and then she laughed.

It was the sound of a bubbly brook only with a strange hissing mixed within it. It echoed off the cavern walls and the brine pools answered.

Aunia shifted, stood up straighter. If this faery creature was a predator, it would do no good to show fear.

Jovaryn leaned close, his face inches from Aunia's ear. "Salt drives most faerie things away save the strongest."

"She's a drown-wife or drown-widow." Keston sidled closer. "Depends, I suppose, if she likes her mate."

"Drown-widow?" the faerie said. Her voice sounded musical like the Boggleman's only it ended in a hiss. "I am Morsalka."

"A Jenny Greenteeth of the sea," Jovaryn whispered. "Kin to the brinwraiths."

"I am no Jenny Greenteeth," Morsalka said. "And you shall go no further."

"We...we have to." Aunia pinned her shoulders back and stepped forward.

Morsalka's strange eyes lit with swirls of reds, greens, and blues. "Then a passage fee you must pay."

Basil said, "You're a guardian here."

"A guardian for who?" Mathias asked.

"I'd wager for Kai-Marin," Jovaryn said. "Is it not, Morsalka Brinwraith?"

"I am no brinwraith."

Another mind picture of Jennium's entered Aunia's head. Of her negotiating with the brinwraiths and then her talking to Morsalka. To discuss how to pass? Unlike the brinwraiths that liked stories, Aunia had no idea what this Morsalka would want. And if she were willing to pay. "What is the price for passage?"

Morsalka smiled, her teeth were a bit green and unlike the brinwraiths or Jenny Greenteeth, they were even... humanish...even if the smile itself was too wide. "The answer to my riddle is my price."

"How many hints do we get?" Keston asked.

Morsalka glared at Keston and rose a little higher in her pool. "One for every betwixting in a day."

"So, three," Mathias said. "Morning, afternoon, and night."

"Two," Aunia turned slightly toward Mathias. "Dawn and twilight."

The water rippled from around her waist but Morsalka nodded. "Do you go back?"

Mathias stepped forward. "This is Kai-marin's granddaughter."

Jovaryn lunged, grabbing the fabric to Mathias' sleeve. "Do not tell her what she already knows."

"Indeed," Morsalka lifted up to her knees, and then sank again to her waist. "Do you accept my riddle? Or do you go back."

"Imagine we'll be joining the wererats at the entrance if we get it wrong," Keston muttered. "Won't even get our own pile."

Morsalka's attention snapped to Keston. "Is that important to you, carver-son?"

"She means to save both worlds," Mathias said.

"You seek a choice. One world over the other. How quickly will you sentence Endynia to die? "

"I do not wish the faery world to die," Aunia said. "I want to save both Ahnu and Endynia."

"Humans lie," Morsalka said.

"And faeries deceive," Mathias shot back.

"And three is the magic number. It's three hints, is it not?" Jovaryn said.

Morsalka barred her teeth. "Two she may ask. One I may offer."

Aunia gave Mathias' hand a squeeze, then stepped forward again. "If it's a riddle I must answer—"

"A riddle for each who pass," Morsalka said.

Aunia straightened. "Ask me."

Morsalka bobbed slightly in the water. "A tusk for a wish, a wish for a net, a net for a night with no stars. Name what is paid when the world is caught. Not coin, not bone, but what breaks when the binding holds."

Aunia froze. A tusk for a wish?

Don't think. Become. That unfamiliar voice again. Soft. Lilting. Nothing like Bibb's cobwebby voice.

Tusk for a wish. Three years ago, Nehla, her foster mother, had gone on the yearly boar hunt with Aunia's dad. They were trying for the wish granted by bringing a tusk back. A wish to gain permission to be beaded...married...as second beadings were not allowed. One love like Edvaras and Naoma. Unless. Heat stung Aunia's eyes and the cave and Morsalka turned blurry.

Aunia sucked in a slow breath to steady herself. A wish for a net and a net for a night with no stars. Nehla wanted that wish, to be with her father, and her father... He had wanted to catch something. She blinked. How would she know that. She wasn't there.

"Ah, the confusion is sweet," Morsalka said. "I will give you one clue. We push away that which we do not wish to see, be it of our own device or with the help of another."

The image of flutterbys at the creek entered her head. A Jennium mind-picture? She wasn't sure but as soon as the image of golden multi-winged faeries hit her. So did the overwhelming longing for a wish. Her wish to know her mother.

She loved Nehla yes. Wanted Nehla as part of her family. But there had been an empty spot in her heart. An empty spot that her mother should have filled.

Jennium jingled and shot Aunia snippets of pictures from that night with Limi. Riding doubleback upon their dark-brown mare. Heading for the Sylvanox woods. Sylvanox? She shook her head. She had been in the village the night of the hunt. She had... she had found the starbook and meant to look through it when Sigmus had found her.

'It isn't that,' Aunia heard herself say. She was inside the goat pen. 'There's a darkwraith near the village. Our parents... they mean to face it.'

Dagger-prickles sliced at Aunia's chest. She needed to be calm, to think. She stepped back to Mathias' side. "I ask for a hint when it comes to the word 'net.'"

Morsalka's smile widened, and water slurped over several pool edges. "You stumble on the word, child. Think you nets are merely rope and twine? Nets are anything that binds."

Mathias opened his mouth, and Aunia stepped on his foot.

Morsalka continued. "A tusk paid for a wish. A wish spun into a snare. A net cast wide enough to catch more than he bargained for. Nets do not choose what they hold, and a magical binding... it always comes with a price. With a breaking. Name it, child, that price."

Jennium shot more images at Aunia and a searing memory rose in her throat. A glen in the haunted North Woods abutting Sylvanox. Her father nearly stepping on a rabbit cage. Dark mist... skeletal fingers... much bigger than a whisperer. Aunia's mouth went dry.

Her father had lied to Nehla. Let her believe the tusk wish was for them to have a second beading. The village only allowed one in honor of the great love between Edvaras and Naoma. But he had been after a darkwraith... a darkwraith sent by the Boggleman.

The net... the intended capture. Darkwraith. Something that would capture every good memory and leave a person a broken shell of themselves. Aunia shook. The Boggleman... her uncle wanted her insane. And her father had tried to protect her.

And the night with no stars? She needed to know. She didn't want to know. Aunia shifted on her feet.

Morsalka's pearly white eyes gleamed. "A tusk for a wish, a wish for a net... and yes, a net for a night with no stars. Do you not taste the truth, Kai-Marin's granddaughter?

"Your father wove his snare in darkness, when the heavens hid themselves, and he thought he could catch a shadow in his cage. But it caught more than that, didn't it? You feel your loss? You still feel the emptiness of that starless night, where even your grief was stolen? A choice comes and there will be another night with no stars. No Dama Star to guide you. No prophecy line to lean against. Only nets, tangled and blind, cast into the void. What will they catch then, girl? What will *you* break?"

The words struck like stones against her chest. Nehla's face. Her laugh over pottery, her voice saying *dear one. Wherever love is, you're safe.*

Nehla was warmth torn from her, stolen into silence.

Morsalka's laughter echoed. The shifting of salt hissed through her ears. Aunia wanted to scream away the sound.

Jennium tugged on Aunia's hair. And Aunia...stood before Morsalka, sniffling. Aunia recomposed herself, drove grief down to her knees and pinned it there. 'Name what is paid when the world is caught. Not coin, not bone, but what breaks when the binding holds.'

Aunia tightened her hands into fists, knuckles white. If she spoke now, she'd unravel. That night had netted more than the darkwraith. It had torn Nehla from them. It had stolen her father's love, the village's trust, her own fragile hope.

Then—coolness slid into Aunia's veins. It wasn't comfort, but clarity, and a voice shook against the marrow in her bones. She could see in her mind's eye who had arrived in the glen after Nehla had died with the boar on her spear.

Kai-Marin. Kai-Marin had appeared. Had appeared and stolen her memory.

Aunia's jaw locked. Her pulse steadied. She forced her chin up even as tears stained her cheeks. "This isn't so much a riddle as a mirror."

"Is that your answer?" Morsalka asked.

"No," she whispered, but her voice shook. "The net didn't just catch the darkwraith. It broke *memory*. It broke *trust*. That was the price."

Morsalka pointed at Jennium. "And you cheated your answer with help from another."

Aunia remained standing tall. She did not look away. She had stumbled onto it but she had named it. "The force of the sea may do as she pleases."

"The force of the sea?" Morsalka appraised her and then nodded. She pointed to the stepping ledge at the end of the cavern. "You may go forward."

"You should not go alone," Mathias said.

"Do you face your riddle?" Morsalka asked.

Aunia turned to Mathias and brushed her shoulder. "I'm not. And it's too dangerous to take another riddle. I'll be back."

"You go alone." Morsalka put her fingers together to snap. "That little being on your shoulder may go if she faces and wins the answer to her own riddle."

Mathias, Tafiriel sent, *Flyers are approaching. They have Darla.*

Chapter Forty-Two

EXORCISM

Free will isn't a weapon to wield; it's a light that refuses to be borrowed. — a quote from Lord Chance

Mathias reluctantly released Aunia's hand. He had watched her figuring out Morsalka's riddle. Witnessed the memory of trauma play out across her features. How her body tightened with anguish and pain. Tears had reddened her eyes and streaked down her face, but her expression of defiance barely dipped. The only time it gave was those moments when she turned inwards seeking answers. She was beautiful with her resolved upturned chin and her dark blue eyes snapping with resolve. Color painted across her cheeks, making the sprinkle of freckles stand out. She was the fiery sunset. The brief warning before the storm hit.

He had wanted to protect her. Wanted to shield her from Morsalka's cruelty and Aunia stomped on his foot. A reminder that she was quite capable. In pain, yes, and still capable. She needed not a protector, but an ally. A brother in arms. Though she was far more than a companion to him. He had to understand that she was not made of spun glass. He smiled grimly at her and nodded. "Be careful."

Her face smoothed, and for a moment she looked like a scared little girl. Then, she straightened. "What will you—"

"We need the compass yet. We'll get that," Mathias said. "You get the halite."

"Fate is all powerful save for the limits of will and love. We have the will..." She touched his wrist and a sweet warmth melted his chest.

He blinked. Nodded. "We have..."

She turned, crossed the cavern to the stepping ledge.

"Both," he whispered.

She vanished through an arch. His light followed her.

But he was not in darkness. Another white light danced above Mathias.

"Didn't know you could do more than one," Keston said. "What's the plan?"

Mathias wasn't sure. He nodded to himself and then looked over to the faery woman. "It's stay or meet them. I'd rather keep them from Aunia... and Morsalka."

Morsalka regarded him with glittering eyes.

"I'm sure you don't want others invading your space," Mathias said. "Jovaryn, can you stay here and watch for Aunia's return."

Jovaryn, startled, nodded. "We'll bring out the astrolabe when she returns."

"Good," Mathias said. "Let's go get that compass."

Keston moved to Mathias' side. "Maybe you should bespeak Frehn that Darla is a fireling. Tell him what we're doing. He won't want to risk both worlds."

"Frehn has been compromised," Mathias said. "He offered Breen wine while we were hiding in the hollow."

"Navenra?" Keston's amber eyes flared. "If he hurts her..."

"Basil," Mathias called. "We could use your magic."

"Magic against flyers?" Basil walked beside them toward the entrance. "That never goes well. Do you have a plan?"

"Sleeping any of them is out," Mathias said. He considered his other abilities. He had, after all, shoved wererats aside by his will alone in Spatelly. "You need to know Darla will try to get inside my head again. I've been Navenra-poisoned. It makes a person susceptible."

"Pegasi too?" Keston asked in a high voice.

Mathias glanced back to see Jovaryn still standing at the edge of Morsalka's pool, but the faery was gone. "I don't think so. Taf hasn't been affected. In fact, he thinks he has some immunity now."

Keston's gaze slid from Basil back to Mathias. "Could you anchor your mind to Taf's?"

Mathias frowned. *Is that possible?*

I'll do whatever I can to protect you, Taf sent back.

"Maybe I could get closer to her if she thinks I've succumbed," Mathias mused.

Keston growled. "Maybe we can figure out how the mangrove roots can grab her."

They are almost here, Taf sent.

Mathias, Keston, and Basil reached the edge of the cavern.

Basil rubbed at his knuckles then adjusted his bandana. "Her Majesty isn't going to like me here."

Mathias frowned. "You're a rover. How would she even know you?"

Basil's eyes narrowed, and then he laughed. "I hope you don't miss out on all the clues. I'll stay in the back. I'll do what I can to give you magical cover."

Mathias frowned. Felt like he was missing something. But he didn't have time. "Let's go."

They traveled through the narrow tunnel to the entrance, and a thought hit him. Breen didn't drink.

Taf, bespeak Breen, Mathias sent. *Tell her that Darla is a fireling. Tell her that her unit might be infected with a mind-poison.*

Dusky light filtered through the cavern.

Darla may be eavesdropping, Taf sent.

Mathias curled a fist. *Then tell her as soon as we get out there. At the opportune moment.*

They're here.

Mathias' hand slipped onto the short sword at his side as they neared the entrance. The sun was low on the horizon. Too low, and it made Mathias wonder how long they had been inside the cave. That thought fled as they stepped out of the cavern onto the crinkly salt flat. Near Tafiriel and Revellie and still mounted were Frehn riding double with Darla on his pale green Morganstee, Breen frowned from her indigo Korthalee, Murtagh stared glassy-eyed from his red-gold mare, and the other three flyers from Mistfen, Mathias presumed, also looked glassy-eyed.

"You led us on a merry chase." Frehn sat hawk-like in the saddle, but his eyes looked dull. "You'll come with us, but not on your own mounts."

"Commander, a moment," Darla said. She slid off of Morganstee. "Where is the girl?"

"She really isn't caught up in all of this," Mathias lied.

"I would disagree. And I doubt you would leave her far." Darla looked behind her toward the other island with the hollow.

Mathias refused to look in that direction. He did not want to give her confirmation if she were suspecting that they found that other hollow.

"Step out of the cave," Frehn barked.

Mathias moved forward. So did Keston.

Breen's gaze went to the white light hovering over Mathias' head. He didn't bother to send it away.

Taf gazed at him mournfully from yards away.

"We heard you were in a dark place," Keston said to Darla. "How did you meet up with flyers?"

"You left Lady Darla behind at Moonstepper where wererats were," Frehn snapped. "Only to kidnap her later and leave her behind again. You are beneath contempt."

Darla set her rounded face in a pout and swept her black braid over her shoulder. "Make that Mystic cease the light."

The faces of the other flyers twisted with hate—rigid, unblinking, too synchronized to be real. Several held notched bows. Not Breen. Her eyes fastened squarely on Mathias, and her Korthalee took a step back.

Basil stepped out of the cave, holding his hands up, palms out.

Breen is asking what you mean by a mind-poison. And how you know Darla is a fireling, Taf sent.

Tell her everything about Navenra. As quick as you can. The wine.

Breen stiffened. She moved her hand from drawing her bow and rested it on Korthalee's shoulder. Her gaze darted to Frehn, then to Darla. The change was small but unmistakable. She was taking in the truth. And that put her in danger as well.

Keston bespeaks Breen to fly off, Taf sent.

Bespeak Keston, we need all the allies we can get.

"I won't ask this again," Darla said. "Where is Aunia? Where is the astrolabe?"

"Last time is good," Mathias said. "Then I won't have to tell you the same answer. Where is the compass?"

"You think I can't find her?" Darla unlaced a gray pouch at her belt and pulled out the compass with its red crystals lining its sides.

Unlike when Bibb held the compass in Dalin, there were spider webs clinging to the crystals. They moved from crystal to her pouch. Crystals to flyers. Darla held out the compass, and its needle spun clockwise, then counterclockwise, back to clockwise. More threads sprung from the crystals. They twisted as if seeking a target. Some shot up into the sky where the Harp constellation would show in under an hour.

Darla cursed. Glared at the compass. Glared at the section of sky where threads twirled.

"So, that's how you've been pulling the Dama star toward the Harp," Mathias said.

Breen's face paled and a beat later she cried. "Yasendra preserve us. She's changing the augury."

I showed her what you see, Taf sent.

Frehn's body jolted at Breen's words, and Morganstee's wings flared. The other flyers only blinked.

"Mathias and Keston are enemy," Darla snarled. "Nyrissa has declared it so."

Frehn shook himself again, a weak gesture.

Give in, an acidic voice sounded inside Mathias' head. Definitely not Tafiriel. *Let Aunia and I save our worlds. Accept your fate.*

Pressure welled in the back of Mathias' head. He winced. "You are following a fireling."

Frehn blinked. "Fireling? All firelings are banned from Tamore on pain of death."

"Me? A fireling?" Darla, still standing beside Morganstee, caressed Frehn's knee. "Do I look like a fireling to you?"

The pressure against the back of Mathias' head felt like it would burst. *Say you lie. Say you give up.*

"I am not going anywhere," Mathias growled, fighting to say each word with crisp clarity.

The salt under his feet turned to liquid fire, and the sky turned red.

Illusion, Taf sent. *All illusion. Anchor your thoughts.*

Anchor? Oh, his head hurt. Anchor. Like a core memory. Like manifesting when they had been in Pavari.

He reached out for images of Aunia. He could see Aunia standing before him, her expression vulnerable and strong when she had said, 'Fate is all powerful save for the limits of will and love.'

He should have told her that he loved her. Should have taken her in his arms before she left. Should have kissed her. But she would have thought it was only because he feared for her. All three kisses...sweet on his lips with his knees melting had started with him being afraid. He wanted one—not based on fear for her. In celebration of her. Celebration for their connection. He longed for her like a drowned man wanted air.

Salt returned under his feet. The slurps of sea marsh nearby. The fading of the light.

You've failed Aunia before. You'll fail her again.

Mathias swayed. He might fail her, but he'd try every day to be worthy.

Let them bind you.

Murtagh and two other flyers dismounted. Pulled rope from their saddlebags.

"Breen. Bow," Frehn called. The blankness in his eyes had returned.

Mathias drew his sword. Darla thought she could keep him apart from Aunia. She could not.

Breen shifted her weight forward in the saddle, and Korthalee clattered toward them. The light over Mathias' head flared. It swept out toward the flyers, elongated and rose into a burning white wall. It passed through Breen and Korthalee, leaving them untouched. But it slammed into other flyers. It knocked them back. Knocked some from their mounts. Brought Darla to her knees. Frehn and an unfamiliar flyer rocked against their saddles.

Breen and Korthalee stopped beside Keston. "I'm with you."

She dismounted, drew her sword... and faced the incapacitated flyers.

Darla's voice coiled tighter. Echoed inside his head. *Give in. You'll be caged, but safe. She will be safe too.*

Mathias' light faded away and his legs trembled. He landed hard against the salt. He had given everything, and Darla was still ripping through his mind. His gaze caught the cave mouth. Aunia inside. Fighting for light, for hope. For him. For their world. And Q'thonos had exorcised Bibb from Aunia's mind. Had exorcised. With salt and a mirror.

He lifted his sword. The surface from the wererat short sword was dull. And the light overhead was dim. But he also remembered visualizing what he needed when he worked with the hollows. Could reality be changed from within one's mind? There was only one way to know. He needed a mirror. The sword easily could be visualized to be reflective. He fastened that in his mind and scraped a shallow handful of salt with his fingernails. He pressed the salt against the steel and concentrated on Aunia. On their world. On everything good and right.

The salt caught flame, and the sword blazed.

Darla shrieked inside his skull.

Mathias raised the glowing weapon. He imagined a reflection of himself there and a captured one of Darla devoid of her smirk. Eyes closed and voice raw and steady, he said, "You don't belong."

The sword shook in his grasp.

You are mine. Darla's voice screamed in his head.

Pain bent Mathias over his knees. The steel wand clattered from inside his jerkin. He blinked. He touched the rod to his temple, to the salt, to the sword and drew a curved 'x.'

"Not yours. Not ever."

Darla shrieked. Staggered to her feet and shuffled back.

The flyers on the ground rose.

Frehn straightened. He pulled himself into a proper seated position on Morganstee. "Take her."

Darla gathered a fireball in her hands, and backtracked closer to the water's edge. "I can destroy you."

"Hold," Mathias cried.

Across the water, shadows poured. Dozens. Hundreds spilling over the water. Not Brinwraiths. Wererats. Wererats, some in the shape of giant rats, some as ratmen, some with their bodies half-shifted. All of them moving atop the water.

Keston called, "Commander, perhaps we should pin our dispute."

"There's more." Breen shoved her curly chestnut hair behind an ear. From the west, fire light bloomed like morning first ray. Only it wasn't. Twenty figures wearing red fireling robes bobbed from four flat-bottomed barges. Their presence made the air ripple.

The wererat tide froze at the sight of them. Snarls filled the air. Hackles presumably raised. The Firelings answered with their own hiss. Sparks danced in the air.

Frehn stared at the gathering armies, his sword arm drooping in shock. "This... this is impossible..."

"No." Mathias kept his eyes fixed on Darla. "This is war."

CHAPTER FORTY-THREE

THE SEA WITCH

Blood and tide. One is fleeting and warm, the other endless and cold, and yet both claim me. I have watched empires rot beneath the waves and still the tide comes back. It always wins, because it cannot do otherwise. — Kai-Marin the Sea-Witch

The last step through the arch felt like dropping from a damp throat into a stomach. Aunia stood for a long moment, taking in the endless cavern. Under Mathias' white light, the rounded walls and ceiling, ribbed with salt and veined light, sparkled like the inside of a geode until it faded into blackness. The floor also glittered. It took Aunia a moment to realize that some of the shimmering below were reflecting pools. Here was all the halite she would ever need for the entire scope of humanity.

She sucked in a breath, and the heavy mineral tang stung her tongue with its sharpness. Under the salt, the air tasted of stormwater, lightning and bone. She raised her hands for balance and moved down three rounded steps onto the salty floor. She wouldn't need to go far. Get the salt. Get back. Or try attaching the salt here first. Flyers were on their way with Darla. Mathias was trying to get the compass. If all went well, they'd be on their way to knot fate-threads and prevent the choice from coming. And if things didn't go well... Aunia shook her head. She neither wanted to die nor have the faery world crumble to dust.

"Fate is all powerful save for the limits of will and love. We have the will." That was what Aunia had told Mathias. It was a passage she had read in her father's... in Kai-Marin's starbook. They would tie the fate-threads.

The chill of the steps turned colder the moment Aunia set her sandaled foot onto the salt-laced floor, and it crunched. The limits of will and love. What did that even mean? Her father had had the will to capture a darkwraith. And Nehla had had overwhelming love for her father. But Nehla was dead.

Aunia kneeled, salt digging into her knees like teeth, and pulled her knapsack from her shoulders. Jovaryn said just to set the salt against the astrolabe. That was all that it would take.

What had happened to that darkwraith? She remembered... just a bit that Kai-Marin had taken it. And another question broke to the surface. Had her father known what the price would be? Or was it just an awful accident?

A plink... water dripping from the ceiling jarred her. She had regained a memory... partially... but had no time to reflect on it.

She pulled the astrolabe out of the knapsack. It felt heavy in her hands. Darla had attacked Mathias before. Would she do worse this time?

Aunia ran fingers over the halite crystals, testing their fragility. Rough and dry at first touch. Some of the deeper veins wept a film of moisture. She wrapped her hand around a shard...cold to the touch and tingly... She tried to pry it loose. It held fast. She pressed harder, and the salt bit into her skin. A drop of blood fell. The air around her hummed.

She drew her hand back. It was dusted with tiny sparkles of salt. Too small to use.

She wiped her hand on her dress and whispered, "I'm not here to steal. Only to borrow what's needed for Etos' compass."

"Maybe I disagree with Etos," a terrible voice boomed.

Aunia jumped. The sound came from everywhere at once. The pools. The ground. The air in Aunia's lungs. Its hurricane howl shook her ribs but undertones of lyrical softness brushed against her skin like a lullaby.

A young girl with pale blue skin and large opal-sparkling eyes stood only a few feet away. Her long hair shifted through shades of rich blues and greens, and thick-petaled flowers pinned in her mane—swayed though there was no breeze.

Every time this girl inhaled, the pools in the cavern trembled. Responded to her lungs instead of being a windless chamber.

Aunia had seen the Eaburrai's reflection on the pond surface at Moonstepper but to see Kai-Marin standing so close... Overwhelm surged through every vein. Aunia clenched her fists. She had seen Kai-Marin before. In the North woods when Nehla died.

Aunia rose to her feet. Clutched the astrolabe in one hand. "You took my memory away."

A faint mist gathered around Kai-Marin's bare feet. The Eaburrai's gaze remained unblinking, but her next words came out like a pattering of soft rain. "You asked for a wish, and it was what I could give."

Aunia clutched the astrolabe tighter. "You stole from me."

"You asked me to return the dead."

Droplets of water escaped Kai-Marin's hair and spritzed along the halite crystals even as Aunia blinked back tears.

"I also provided a salt spring nearby," Kai-Marin said. "A reminder for the day."

"For me?" Aunia stepped forward, salt cracking under her feet. "Or for my father?"

The light in Kai-Marin's eyes dimmed. "Humans are so possessive. And they complicate matters."

"Complicate? The villagers told me I had caused Nehla's death. That me leaving the village..." Aunia scrubbed a tear from her cheek. "I swore I was not at the North woods that day."

"You did not cause the woman's death." Kai-Marin's tone edged with the start of a storm. "That fault was the Elderbind. He sent that darkwraith. And your father should have gone by himself. He might have been lost though. Sad as it was, it may have been a merciful necessity."

"Necessity?" Aunia spat.

Aunia, Taf warned. *You speak to an Eaburrai.*

"A child who has seen monsters is timid." Kai-Marin narrowed her eyes. "You have much you need to do."

Several bubbles snapped on the surface of the nearest pool, and the smell of sulfur mingled with the sharp salt tang.

"Because," Aunia sputtered. "You need me to fix something? Or is it to fail? Do you want the augury's choice now or have it wait?"

"I get my sister back either way, but she'd be happier if all her descendants didn't die."

Aunia blinked. "You are my grandmother. Does that mean nothing to you?"

The faint drip of water from the ceiling stopped and the pools flattened into glass.

"Meaning is a mortal luxury. I cannot afford to feel as you do." Kai-Marin's tone, though flat, carried a strain beneath it. "Still. It does not mean nothing."

The moment hung between them. Brittle yet stubborn like the salt crystals.

"You're just like Darla," Aunia growled.

Kai-Marin blinked, then laughed. "The fireling? She is a sad little girl who couldn't rise in society and wished her parents loved her. Do you not see? What she wants is to find someone to cling to. For status sake. Her latest grab is you. She sees you as a means to power and validation. You have every ability to see this yourself, Aunia. All you need do is open your eyes."

The Sea-Witch walked to the nearest pool—only as big as a bathtub—and sank to her heels. Her reflection rippled on the water, and the halite at water's edge unfurled like white blossoms. The crystals rose, and a large salt bloom broke off into Kai-Marin's waiting hand.

"Where is my father?" Aunia asked. "You took him, didn't you?"

Kai-Marin's eyes hardened, opal light flaring into storm brightness. "Do not ask me to choose between blood and tide, Aunia. The sea always wins."

"What harm is there in letting me know where he is?"

"When it's time. Not before. And you have a task before you." Kai-Marin stood up, walked to her, and held halite crystals in her slender blue hand. "Will you be so belligerent and allow a world die?"

Aunia almost asked Kai-Marin about not agreeing with Etos. She bit her lip instead and took in the Eaburrai before her. The sea-witch matched her height. "How... how do I attach halite to the astrolabe?"

Kai-Marin touched a tear line on Aunia's cheek. "Salt calls to salt."

Aunia blinked. Mathias' wand needed blood. This instrument took tears. She wiped the bit of wetness from her face and slid it over the astrolabe's rim. Then, reached for the crystals in the Eaburrai's hand. The halite lifted from Kai-Marin's hands and flew to the astrolabe's sides. Once it touched, it crept like frost over water until the rim of Etos' instrument was coated.

"A word of advice to a granddaughter." Kai-Marin stepped back. "The Elderghast may be bound but his influence has been felt since the time of your birth. Should he appear, he will bring darkwraiths. Do you remember what will keep you safe?"

Aunia's mouth turned dry. "Hope." Darkwraiths, smoky shadows with ember bright eyes. They had the ability to bring forth your worst fears and to suck all vitality from your bones. She sniffled, remembering how she had to think of hope while Nehla died. "And happy thoughts."

"You should hurry." Mist gathered around Kai-Marin, and then, she was gone.

She should hurry? Mathias!

Aunia nearly slipped up the rounded steps. She threw herself through the arch, reminding herself that Mathias' light still twirled over her head. From there, Morsalka's cavern appeared.

Jovaryn stood beside the pool, blinking against the light.

"Come on," she yelled. "We have to hurry."

Chapter Forty-Four
FIRE AND SHADOW

Some wars are won not by the blade, but by the heart that refuses to stand aside. — Dar Zeller Rieson, flyer of Startengo

Darla stepped back from the water's edge as the wererats neared. She partially turned; eyes fixed on Mathias. Distinct fear and uncertainty flickered over her face. It made Mathias nervous. Though she was out of his head, this fireling had found a way for wererats to walk on water. And she presented lies so convincingly. On the Harp, what were they going to do against so many?

Look to her feet, Taf sent.

Mathias tipped his head. At first, it looked like the last reflection of sunset bled across the salt but the small square edges at the side of her boots... Those were portal tiles.

Frehn looked to his men, who were still dismounted. "We fly."

"No," Mathias said. "Aunia is still in the cave."

Growls from the approaching wererats overpowered the marsh waters sluicing over the shore and the whistle of the wind.

Frehn's expression cracked, just for an instant. A flicker. Fear, frustration, disbelief. Then came the calculation. The commander's jaw flexed, and Morganstee's wings extended. "No help for it. We take to the sky."

The other flyers scrambled back onto their mounts. But not Breen.

"Breen," Frehn called.

Breen tossed her curly chestnut hair back and tugged at her blue scarf. "My father stood at Moonstepper. One man against a horde of Da Vennen. I am his daughter. I'm staying."

Morganstee snorted, pawing at the salt ground while Frehn's hands tightened on the reins, knuckles white. "You'll honor him better by surviving."

"Breen," Keston croaked. He cleared his throat. "Good thing I'm staying too, so you and Mathias don't get yourselves eaten."

Snarls trembled through the salt, and Frehn's head snapped toward it.

"Perfect punctuation," Keston said.

The commander's expression turned to granite, but his eyes lingered one heartbeat too long on each of them. "Then make it count."

He kicked Morganstee's flank, and the pale green stallion launched upward. The others followed, their wings kicking up loose salt.

Mathias felt their loss of presence immediately and braced himself for the upcoming ground shake from wererat feet. Basil yet hid in the cave mouth shadow. A rover... and a Mystic. "Basil, you work magic without ingredient. How?"

"I've crystal for the energy," Basil's voice called from the cave.

"Oh, still it, Mystic," Breen said. "Think I don't know about you or your relationship with the Queen?"

"If you are seeking to employ magic," Basil said, "then know that the energy lies everywhere for the taking. All you need is the desire. To give yourself permission to strike the tinder and set it aflame."

The words caught Mathias off guard. *"Energy lies everywhere for the taking."* And he could feel it. The hum in the air. The charge under his skin. He hated how much it wanted to answer Basil's call, but it also gave him hope. "For the taking? That's how Darla speaks."

"Difference is in the purpose. You will be seeking to protect," Basil said. "Desire. Permission."

Movement beyond the shimmer of salt caught Mathias's eye.

Fire flickered between Darla's fingers. And her face...It was positioned in profile. Toward firelings who sat calmly in their boats. Had it been the other firelings who had magicked the wererats to walk... No. They weren't walking on water. They moved and crawled over shadow, which lay over the water.

Darkwraiths, Taf sent, his silvery voice grinding into a hiss. He, Rev, and Korth bounded toward their flyers. *Elderghast soldiers.*

"Woah," Keston cried out and Breen notched an arrow.

Behind them and at the entrance of the cave, mangrove roots rustled.

A low hum followed Basil as he exited the cave mouth and walked between the slithering roots. His hands were lifted. He was humming. Not music. Instead, it matched the creak of the roots. Seconds ticked by and at last the roots stilled.

"We can't afford to wake these," Basil murmured.

Mathias swallowed. "And how did we wake them?"

Basil grimaced and looked out at the approaching menace. "It would appear to be sudden movement."

"Are you kidding?" Keston turned toward Mathias, his expression said he expected a command.

On the Harp, Mathias had no idea what to order.

Breen set a hand over Keston's arm. "We sleep them."

The first wave of wererats reached the shore and crumbled into slumber.

Darla, skittered back from the approaching army, halting when she was physically between the wererats and Mathias. She threw him a glance. It was like the edge of a knife catching light. Did she want him to believe she wasn't in command of this force?

She rotated to face the wererats. Wererats who crawled over their fallen comrades. The compass had appeared in her hand. She held it high. In the other hand she threw a fireball, and it arched overhead. "Obey me."

Silvery spider threads floated out of the compass. Some passed through flames. All of them tangled into the wererat army.

The faces of the wererats—their muzzles and partial human faces—twisted in agony. But still, they trudged forward.

Mathias braced for the scrape of claws on salt. For Darla to take control of her army or for the wererats to gut her on the salty ground. He wasn't sure which would happen.

Salt plates snapped and cracked as they marched.

And then, a thick hiss of shadows poured forth. They enveloped the fireling. Sent her sprawling on the ground. The wererats marched by her. Except one. The strawberry blonde one, Woundbinder, tried to pry the compass from Darla's hand. She grabbed his ankle. He went up in a column of flame. The wererat force veered around her.

Mathias gripped his sword. Tried to pull power in his other hand to shove the wererats back. But they came. Though some fell under Keston and Breen's sleeping spells. They would not be able to sleep all of them. They were in the hundreds.

Mathias glanced to the heavens. Toward where the Harp would soon appear. Tonight. If they didn't tie off the fate-threads tonight, a world, theirs or Tafiriel's, would die.

Frehn bespeaks that it's not too late to fly, Taf sent.

Mathias gritted his teeth. His white light, contrasting the darkening sky, flew at the center of the shadow mass. The shadowy middle drew back, but the dark flanks rose with dozens of pairs of glowing ember eyes.

On the Harp! *"All you need is the desire. To give yourself permission to strike the tinder and set it aflame."* Permission. Not command. Not control. Just permission. But what to do? Without a plan?

Mathias wondered if death would be instantaneous. *Taf fly.*

Not without you, Taf sent.

Rev and Korth stayed near Keston and Breen.

Mathias sucked in a long breath, tightened his grip on the sword, and stepped forward. If death would come, he'd make every wererat rue the moment they stepped into his path.

Keston and Breen followed his move.

The shadows were almost upon them and wererats followed. Teeth flashing slick and yellow. The stink of wet fur and brine. Water dripping from their pelts like rain on glass.

The protective dome, Taf sent.

Protective dome? A memory slammed into Mathias. Heebles, toothy demons with no faces, attacked Aunia and Gaitha within the birchwoods. Gaitha had summoned a protective dome to keep them safe. Aunia had conjured a protective dome in Spatelly.

Protect. He glanced to Keston and Breen... Basil was behind him. All three pegasi. That's what he truly wanted. Not glory. He just wanted all of them to live.

His light hovered between them and the fast-approaching horde. It contracted. Expanded. And snapped toward him. It hit like a breath reversed—air and pressure—folding through his chest and out again. It left a sizzled brush, like he'd been rubdown with burlap but...

Mathias blinked. He and the others stood inside a white light dome. A globe-shaped shield that shone like living glass.

Ember-eyed shadows twirled around them. Whispered horrors that turned Mathias marrow to ice. But the wererats had halted. Some stood on rat legs. And then the ones in partial human form twisted their hands into the air. Conjured fireballs. And flung.

Chapter Forty-Five

THE SUMMONING

If the Elderghast escapes the Sacred Woods, call him. Seven voices, one song. Stand together, face the storm, with Uriah, correct the wrong — 'Summoning of Uriah' song

Auni ran and Mathias' light, darting over her head, made the salt dust on Jovaryn's long dark tunic sparkle. And then, for an instant, she wasn't in the salt cave. She was back in the North Woods—Nehla laying in blood with a dying boar on her spear and a darkwraith hovering. "Let go!"

He darted toward her. "What happened?"

Heart thudding in her ears, she skidded to a halt before him. "Kai-Marin said darkwraiths are coming. Mathias is out there."

"You spoke to Kai-Marin?" Jovaryn said.

"Darkwraiths." She grabbed Jovaryn's sleeve with shaking fingers. "Come on!"

"Aunia." Jovaryn's voice hit her—the sharpest she had ever heard. "Darkwraiths come from the Elderghast."

"I know. Kai-Marin said."

"It means his reach is longer than we knew." Jovaryn pointed at the astrolabe in her hand. "But you got the salt."

"I have." A sob broke through her. It echoed off the cavern walls. "We have to think happy thoughts."

"Listen, listen," Jovaryn said.

His grip on her wrist anchored her. Helped her to breathe.

"You are, at the very least, a potential. And you've the astrolabe powered with halite. You are powerful. You have to believe that. No matter what we find out there. You can save our worlds. Now, repeat that."

Raw, hollow sadness and icy fear unrolled through her body. Was Mathias already dead? How could she summon happy thoughts?

"I am powerful," she forced out. The words tasted like splintered shield. "I can save our worlds. And. . . If anything has happened to Mathias...I will burn Darla down."

"Happy—"

"That will make me happy," Aunia snarled. Holding the astrolabe like a lifeline, she stalked toward the exit. "Come on."

The tunnel suffocated her or would have if Mathias's egg-sized light hadn't floated over her shoulder. It was something mentally to cling to, and it threw a glimmer over the salt veins in the walls. Her fingers slid along its bumpy surface. Slick. Cold. Strangely pulsing beneath her touch. The exit and more light approached. Light too bright and too steady to be lightning.

She edged forward. The air outside reeked of burnt salt and seaweed. Dread pulled at her insides.

Mathias stood a few yards from the cave mouth within a shimmering sphere of spun glass... Like Gaitha's once upon a time. But his was white, not blue. And he wasn't alone. Keston, Breen, and Basil, stood there too. They were the only stillness in the chaos.

Jovaryn bumped into her back.

Aunia hissed. How could she reach them?

Darkwraiths hovered over top the bright protective sphere. Wererats were further back and several of them lobbed fireballs. The reason the wererats kept distance? Mangrove roots writhed like dark snakes. They flailed in wild arcs. Some roots struck the light barrier and recoiled. Others tried to grab at wererats. Even those too far away... And they tried to grab darkwraiths, which they passed right through.

Aunia walked slowly to the entrance. More corpses were under the salt piles where the mangrove roots sprouted from.

Mathias? Aunia sent. No answer. *Tafiriel? Tell Mathias that they must hold onto happy thoughts.*

Mathias turned. Through the glow, his eyes locked onto her. The sphere wavered, flickering for the barest heartbeat, and then steadied again. His muffled shout cut through the roar outside. "The Star's almost in the Harp!"

Those words struck her like a snapping bowstring.

She wanted to run to him. Be at his side.

One of the wererats spotted her. Yelled and moved forward. A mangrove root snapped forward. Grabbed the wererat and flung it toward the cave entrance. It thudded against the outside wall.

Stars, she could not reach Mathias through mangrove roots, wererats, darkwraiths, and the light barrier itself.

"Aunia?" Jovaryn sounded sick. "Look past the wererats."

Clutching the astrolabe, she squinted and willed herself to see what Jovaryn did. Disbelief and terror pummeled her in the face. A great yew tree loomed at the shoreline. Its roots sunk into black water and its thick trunk split into four massive boughs. Limbs bent outwards, ready to grab. Bark pulsing with a sickly gray glow. Dark mist poured out of it.

Dark mist that expanded into darkwraiths. And Darla. The fireling lay on the ground nearby it.

The Elderbind had appeared.

Aunia gawked until a thwack jarred her. Arrows were raining from above. She shuffled forward until only the lip of the cave exit remained above her. A handful of flyers flew above the darkwraiths and shot at any wererats who drew nearer. Stars! How was she going to get to Mathias? And did he have the compass? Her heart collapsed to her knees.

"You are powerful," Jovaryn had said. She sucked in a breath. And darkwraiths fed on despair. She could not... could not let them win. No matter what the obstacles were. She'd die with a smile on her face if she needed.

The astrolabe in her grip started to hum with a low, steady resonance. Began to glow. In her periphery, salt veins in the wall shimmered. She moved forward.

A mangrove root slammed against the rock beside her. Jovaryn's hand shot out, a dagger flashing. A second root, dismembered, hit the cave mouth floor. It hissed, spraying a briny sap.

"Walk slowly," Jovaryn said. "They react to sound and movement."

Blood surged in Aunia's ears. She complied, easing forward despite the astrolabe tugging her toward Mathias and the light barrier.

She spotted new corpses beneath the mangrove roots. It hollowed her. How many of the wererats had been turned against their will? Had been lied to? Manipulated?

Several wererats ran for her and she had to shove her understanding aside.

One of the darkwraiths floated toward her. Turned the world to ash and darkness.

She closed her eyes. Trusting the roots behind her would provide shielding from the wererats. She forced air through her lungs. Pictured

Mathias and his smile when it reached his eyes. Of Keston when he told a bad joke. Of Basil, when he sat with her at the rover fire and told her of her parents. She thought of Breen, who told her she'd been impressed with Aunia's compassion.

The astrolabe glowed brighter. Spidery threads from the instrument's rim spread out. Reached for the sky where the Harp and the Dama star hung. So close. Minutes maybe from it being too late. But she had the astrolabe. And Darla had the compass. She could get the compass. Skip herself to where she needed to go. She was powerful. She could save the worlds.

More spidery threads shot from the closed astrolabe. They passed around and through wererats. Some impaled darkwraiths and forced them to drift away. Others darted to the roots of the Elderbind where Darla lay... To Darla's hand and the compass.

The fate-threads on the compass drew a gasp from Darla. She clumsily pulled herself into a seated position and glared at Aunia from across the yards.

"Come on, Darla," Aunia whispered. She needed the fireling to be away from the Elderbind. "Get yourself over here."

Several balls of fire bloomed in the sky over the water and struck the yew tree.

Darla's face lifted. She shrank. But then she stood up. Woodenly. With the compass in her hands and spidery threads poured out. The fate-threads came tearing forward to Aunia. It looked like an attack. Her fate-threads coiled around Darla's and writhed in the air. But she, not Darla, was a potential.

Aunia was powerful. If she could wrap her fate-threads around that compass, she could yank it straight out of Darla's hand. Aunia was certain of that. After all, touching one fate-thread at the vineyard manor had caused a table to break in half and caused bones to appear in straw-berries.

More fireballs struck the Elderbind. Its limbs thrashed but the people throwing the fire seemed to be safe.

Aunia stepped further out.

Darla's face twisted in pain and defiance. She conjured up more fate-threads to tangle into Aunia's.

Aunia clutched the astrolabe tighter as a tug pulled her several inches forward. She now stood beside the light barrier. Mathias was facing her. Watching. Yelling something. Banging against the barrier. She couldn't hear him.

Aunia pulled against the fate-threads knotted into the compass' fate-threads.

Darla slid toward her nearly a foot.

Above Darla, the yew tree shook and crackled deeply like a hundred funeral pyres. Gaps appeared within its thick limbs. One limb twisted down with a wet, splintering crack. It grabbed the fireling.

Darla screamed, "No! I served Bibb. I served you!"

The compass in the fireling's hands strobed. Its fate-threads with-drew. And wrapped back and cocooned Darla in shadow and light. And then...The tree ate her.

Darla's screams persisted as bark formed over the gap where she'd been swallowed. Darla. The compass. Both were gone.

Aunia staggered back. And the darkwraiths rushed forward.

But not before a flutter of wings landed on Aunia's shoulder. Jen-nium. It wasn't mind pictures that the faery sent but words. *If the Elderghast escapes the Sacred Woods, call him. Seven voices, one song.*

The light beside her... the light barrier protecting the others... fell, and Mathias screamed her name.

CHAPTER FORTY-SIX

URIAH

I dreamed there was still a cure in you, brother. But I see now, some wounds are too deep for time, and even love cannot unmake what hate has forged. — Uriah, beloved of Yasendra

The only thing that had been on Mathias' mind was to reach Aunia. And then, the barrier had fallen. Air ripped from his lungs with an onrush of sound and motion.

Jovaryn, who'd been protecting Aunia, had fallen. And the tree he had seen outside of Q'thonos' not only moved... It had eaten the compass and Darla whole. The compass still glowed under its bark.

Three wererats had slipped past their defensive sphere? But they had fled...after Jovaryn had sacrificed his life.

Mathias felt his heart cave for Aunia. She'd been so close to the barrier before. Close enough that he would have seen the light leave her eyes when she... His voice had cracked when he screamed her name.

She had looked at him, eyes wide. Hair whipping in the salt wind. Astrolabe flaring in her hands and the darkwraiths had pulled away.

"Mathias," she called, her voice was a bare squeak. The salty ground beneath them shuddered. Groaned. And that awful tree pulled up its roots one by one. A black stench rose and the hissing mangrove roots behind them, stilled.

"The Elderbind," she whispered.

Mathias' blood turned to ice-slush. They were going to die. They were going to die and those he could have saved with his barrier would die too. Unless they could flee. He raised his sword.

Basil's voice rose—wild and terrified. "If the Elderghast escapes the Sacred Woods, call him. Seven voices, one song."

Seven voices. For summoning Uriah. His voice. Aunia, Keston, Basil, Breen. But Jovaryn had fallen and—

Telepathic voices work just fine, Taf sent.

"Do you hear that?" Aunia asked.

There was a chant on the wind.

> "Ash to ember,
> ember to sigh,
> Balance holds while stars stand nigh."

"Firelings," Mathias said. "Who knows what magic they're conjuring."

"Get the girl for the Master," screamed an unfamiliar wererat. He was tall and thin, and stayed in the shadows.

The horde, which had been retreating, surged forward.

Breen and Keston, a few yards on Mathias' left vaulted onto their pegasi, wings cutting through the mist.

Keston bespeaks they will cover you, Taf sent. *Sing!*

"Jovaryn," Aunia called. Her expression went cold—grief collapsing inward and fury. The astrolabe's glow sharpened to white fire, searing the air around them.

Jovaryn lay several feet away beside a wererat corpse, his fallen shape coated in salt. Dagger still clutched in his hand.

Sing? "Aunia, let's go!" Mathias yelled.

She wasn't moving. And then fireballs from faeblood wererats flew, cutting Mathias' escape to Tafiriel. Arrows from above rained down. They passed through darkwraith shadows and struck the approaching wererat front and flanking line.

Nearby, Basil's voice rose over the storm. It was low at first. Then it gathered strength.

> "Call Uriah where the stars belong,
> Lest Elderghast's will grow strong."

Breen and Keston's voices joined from above. They flew and dodged under the layer of darkwraiths.

Mathias lifted his sword, stepped in front of Aunia, and braced. *Taf, fly.*

The first wererat lunged. Its mace flashed toward Mathias' left shoulder. Mathias pivoted his back foot toward the right, moving his body out of danger. He drove his blade under the creature's arms and into its ribs.

> "When light is torn and night is long—"

The ratman gasped. Slid off the steel. Mathias wrenched his blade free. Caught another blow mid-swing. The clang rang through his bones. Sparks scattered across salt and shadow.

> "Rise, and right what has gone wrong."

He parried another strike. Sliced across a ratman's wrist.

Aunia stayed close—her elbow brushing his back. Heat radiated from the astrolabe.

But then she screamed. Mathias whirled, raising his sword and barely catching an attack. But did. Aunia's left arm bled where claws had torn through cloth. A wererat had gotten behind them.

Basil skipped beside Aunia. Grabbed her, and the two of them reappeared slightly behind and on Mathias' other side.

Mathias skewered Aunia's attacker.

The rover raised his hands, curving his arms as if he held up two shields. He stamped his foot and jerked his forearms forward. Wind took the wererat force and drove them back. "Bring the barrier back. Anytime is good. And sing! Call Uriah where the stars belong."

Stars belong? The Dama star was going to enter the Harp. There was nothing they could do. The only hope for all was if the mortal world died and took the Elderghast with it.

"Lest Elderghast will grow strong."

Dear Thuroes. That tree was coming closer. It would swallow them up.

The wererat force had been blown back and were just outside the Elderbind's grasp. They were fighting for every step forward when the Elderbind crashed through their rear guard.

"It's just Mystic wind," the wererat commander shrieked over wererat screams. "Put your backs into it. Get the girl. Kill the rest."

Aunia's hair, free of her braid, twirled around her head. It slashed against the white light hovering over her as she curled her fists. A pulse of indigo-blue fire burst from her sternum and coalesced midair into a blazing globe. Mygul. Its surface crackled like living flame.

The orb streaked forward. It zipped through ranks of wererats. It struck the wererat commander square in the chest. The impact exploded in light, searing Mathias' vision with purple spots. And the wererat commander? He toppled, smoking.

Some wererats fled. The Elderbind caught them, branches whipping. It stuffed bodies into woody gaps that groaned shut afterwards. The rest of the wererats marched forward. Mygul hit them like wrath itself. Tore through their lines. Melted metal. Burned flesh. It drove the wererats back. Even darkwraiths shrank away.

"We gotta get out of here!" Mathias looked to the sky. *Taf!*

Another layer of darkwraiths, their shadowy bodies coiling and unfurling hung between where Taf and the others flew and themselves. Their whispers stabbed into Mathias' mind, voices layered and cruel. *Faithless. Loveless. You'll end like your father.*

Another hissed—*Zeller died because of you. Your brother died because of you. Everything you touch rots. Everyone you love will die.*

Mathias staggered back, sword shaking. The words, truth, sliced into his marrow.

Aunia's shout cut through the din. "They exploit your hurts. Anger. Sadness. It's how they get in! Fight them. Fight them with joy. Anything that makes you glad you're alive! Even if it's air in your lungs."

Her voice cracked with urgency. Nearby, Mygul streaked over the field, incinerating wererat by wererat. Their force had been decimated. Those remaining stayed out of sword range. But beyond Mygul's blaze, the Elderbind crawled upon its thick roots ever nearer. They were almost within its limb reach.

"Sing for Uriah. Now!" Basil yelled.

Mathias's throat burned. There was no happiness left to summon. Just exhaustion and defiance. But he could sing. Even if one world burned, they could face the end in glory.

He drew breath and shouted into the wind,

> "Call Uriah where the stars belong,
> Lest Elderghest's will grow strong."

Aunia joined him. The melody cracked, but the song carried. It rose through the fire and smoke toward the darkened sky. Other voices joined in. The flyers above.

The song rose through Mathias until it wasn't only in his throat—it was in his bones, his blood. The rhythm steadied his breath. It lifted something that had been too heavy within. Something too heavy for too long.

Across the marsh, firelings stood on their flat-bottomed boats and flung more fireballs. Fireballs in furious blooms of orange light against the Elderbind. And Aunia's Mygul slammed wererat after wererat. Mathias kept singing. Even if it was only to keep the darkwraiths out of his head.

Line after line. Note after note.

Mygul faltered. Its fire dimmed from indigo blaze to trembling cobalt. And Aunia? Clutching the astrolabe, she was pale and shaking.

The last of the wererats...maybe fifty...saw the globefire's weakness. They puffed out their chests. Snarled emboldened.

Mathias missed a line in the song. They couldn't die from a wererat's hand nor be eaten by a tree. Thuroes be blessed, he was a potential.

The light that circled Aunia's head. His light. It shot outward but instead of attacking wererats, it plowed and fused into Mygul... Like it had in Bibb's lair.

The dark blue flare reignited. Burst with new fury and swirled with white light. Wererats screamed as the light struck. They scattered in panic. Some broke ranks and fled.

The Elderbind's roots grabbed some of the fleeing wererats. It tossed some with force and they splashed into the marsh. Others were gorged into knotholes.

The Elderbind. It filled most of the horizon. So close. The air thickened with heat and shadow. Every breath tasted of resin and ash. And the sound of the tree's heart pulsed through the ground, syncing to Mathias's own until he couldn't tell which belonged to who.

Mathias croaked,

"Call Uriah where the stars belong, lest Elderghast's will grow strong."

The ground lurched under Mathias' boots. Water slapped against the island's edge. And a light burst upward—too bright to look at. It grew to the height of the Elderbind. The light faded and a man with a bear-pelt draped over his broad shoulders, appeared.

The figure's hair, a rich bronze-red, was the same color as Princess Keira's. His face? Stern and timeless. But it was his eyes that held Mathias captive. They were his mother's eyes both in shape and color.

Aunia clapped her hands. "Uriah!"

Uriah faced the yew from Mathias' left side and the sorrow on the Chandarion's face was heavier than rage. "Iriath," he said softly, voice resonating like a bell through fog. "Return to your prison."

The Elderbind answered with a shriek of bending wood. Shadows peeled away from its trunk and darkwraiths—hundreds more, all slick with tar and glowing coal eyes—floated up.

They swarmed through the air, tearing at the light, clawing for Uriah. All happiness in the world extinguished.

Aunia sidled closer to Mathias, slid her hand in his. Basil huddled closer to them as well.

"Be it on you then." Uriah strode forward. Every step made the salt lands tremble.

Darkwraiths dove, but he caught them in his hands and flung them against the tree.

Limbs cracked. The yew groaned. And then, Uriah seized the Elderbind's trunk with corded arms and locked his wrists together.

"I have known love," Uriah thundered. "I have known family. I have known things that are greater than myself. And what of you?"

The tree convulsed, roots thrashing.

"Jealousy. Anger. Hate." His voice deepened, echoing through the marsh. "It has eaten you hollow, Iriath. But even now—your wraiths could be free. Each one could leave you if they remembered the light. Remembered love. You cannot hold them if they remember *that*."

Some of the wraiths hesitated. They turned ember eyes upward to the flyers above. And then—one by one—they sank back into the tree.

Uriah's eyes flared white. He turned his head to look at Aunia and his voice thundered, "Your kin brings help."

The Elderbind thrashed harder, frantic to break free. The entire marsh shivered.

Beside Mathias, Aunia clutched the astrolabe. It unfurled—three concentric clockwork rings. And from the place edged with halite, silvery fate-threads stretched to rat...to tree... to stars.

Aunia placed a finger against one thread, and salt spray from the marsh cascaded upwards like a backwards waterfall. One of the fireling boats capsized.

The fireballs, which had paused, returned. Several struck the ground near them.

Aunia hesitated to touch another thread. "We need the compass! We need to know where."

The Elderbind expanded. Contracted. Its bark cracked.

Uriah's voice rang sharp. "Merge!" He looked to their combined light. "Like them!"

CHAPTER FORTY-SEVEN

THE CHOICE

To be Chandarion is to live as both wound and healer—half divine, half doomed, and never whole until the heart of the worlds beats again. — The Veil Codex, a forbidden text in the library of the Mystic Court

Aunia's knees wobbled, and the taste of salt in the air burned her throat but the despair locking the astrolabe under unfeeling fingers lessened.

The wererats had scattered back well beyond the battle between Uriah and the Elderbind. They huddled by the shoreline. But she, Mathias, and Basil remained... barely out of reach of the yew's branches should Uriah falter.

Uriah and the Elderbind... Uriah, taller than the Green Harpy and bathed in a red-rose glow. His bear-fur cloak had slid from his shoulders and his muscles strained. Yet, he held fast to the Elderbind's flailing limbs. Even while darkwraiths had wriggled back into every knothole the yew tree had.

She chanted, "We can do this. We can take it. We can end this."

The chant had been her protection. Her shield against the darkwraiths' onslaught of horror and sadness. Nehla's death, graphic and immediate. The awful aftermath. Gaitha's coldness. Oskan's icy rage. Velli's pity. And Sigmus, he had turned nastier and insisted she was demonspawn that the Boggleman should take. It was also then that her father became more distant. She was alone, except for faery creatures. She'd be alone again.

Mygul soared back to her, its light twirling around Mathias' white light. It bathed her arms with blue and white. Maybe it bathed Jennium as well who was hiding in her hair with a tiny hand against the back of Aunia's neck.

She could see starlight above her now. The layer of shadows was gone. The terror, however, was more pressing. The Dama star lay so close to the Harp's first string. In moments it would cross that thin void and the choice would be made.

A deep whump-crash shuddered. It rattled Aunia's bones before her ears caught up to the sound. Another massive wave struck the sea marsh. Brine and mud pattered down. And two more of the fireling's boats had flipped over. Most of the wererats who huddled at the shoreline were swept out into the water. The ones that didn't had no choice but to retreat closer to Uriah and the Elderbind's battle.

Aunia shook herself. The compass. She had started yanking it from Darla's hand before. Perhaps she could now. She lifted the astrolabe and its rings spun in her hands. She had already tried a few more fate-threads. The last one had created a sinkhole where Jovaryn's body had been. She couldn't think of that now. Jovaryn. . . He had told her all she needed after the halite was on the astrolabe was concentrate on what she wanted.

Well, she filled every nook in her mind with the desire to get the compass. But which fate-thread? She reached her forefinger on a strand leading to the Elderbind and...

Uriah and the Elderbind vanished before her skin felt the tingle against the thread. She gasped and Mathias kept her from falling. Beyond her, brinwraiths attacked firelings and the wererats who swam or treaded through the murky waters.

Stars, the Dama star was a bare fingernail clipping from the Harp. The choice was coming. Death was coming. And all they could do was witness the Dama star cross into the Harp.

She leaned against Mathias. Spent. Empty. In dread.

"We just need the where," Mathias said, and he cast his eyes skyward where Tafiriel glided down. He brushed his hand against her arm. Against the astrolabe.

Where he touched, energy crackled.

The Where. The place that the compass would have shown. All the stupid things the astrolabe had done was because they were in the wrong place.

Her heart thudded through her closed eyes. She wanted to cry and let the salt bury her. She lifted her head. What if she touched a fate-thread to look for an answer?

She sucked in a long breath and held out her hand, hoping beyond hope she would touch the right one. And her father's heavy handwriting blazed in her mind. "The place is not stone nor star, but heart and hand. Where the bearer stands, the worlds turn."

Aunia's breath caught. Q'thonos had pointed out that passage. And now? The words struck deep, pulling a thousand whispers loose from memory.

Breen's voice after she had told Aunia to shut up, "Who you are doesn't matter. It depends on what you do. And where."

Keston's teasing quip. "You're always in the middle of trouble. It's like trouble isn't a place—it's you."

Nehla's laugh, soft in a sunlit kitchen, when Aunia was a child. "Where is safe? Wherever you are, little star."

Aunia blinked. The astrolabe glowed brighter where she and Mathias touched it. And overhead? Their combined light twirled.

All of it crashed through her like the tide had. She knew. Not from study. Not from guessing. But because the astrolabe itself sang it through her veins.

She looked at Mathias. Sweat-coated. His beautiful face was pointed toward the Harp, his expression forlorn and eyes, haunted "Mathias?" Her heart pounded in her ears." We are the where."

The astrolabe's rings locked with a resonant clang, a sound that felt as if it echoed through the marrow of the world. The air quivered. Lines of light unfurled from the instrument.

Mathias' gasp was sharp. Visceral.

She felt his reluctance and fears—that being a potential meant burning out, that he'd be consumed by destiny before he ever found his place. It was raw, sharp, enough to make her chest ache with it. But mixed within it was hope.

Mathias, believe, she sent.

He dropped his sword. The blade sank into the salt-mud with a dull hiss. Then his hand found hers. His fingers coiled between her fingers and the outer astrolabe's ring.

The instrument seared with light between their hands, threads snapping and reweaving around them. She could feel Mathias' presence burning in her bones, braided into her own.

More silvery threads unfurled from the instrument—fine lines of gold and indigo and green. They streamed outward and wove a luminous web across the sky.

Mathias sucked in a breath as if he'd been struck and his expression of disbelief prickled against her thoughts. The knowledge that he was seeing it too—the tangled weave, the threads running not just around her but around him and braiding together... She shivered and his fingers tightened. His thoughts steadied into something harder, fiercer...and joy bloomed. *If we are the where, then I will stand here with you. If it burns us, we burn together.*

Aunia's breath hitched. Her body, her throat ached with the weight of it. His choice. His courage. His acceptance. For years she had carried the sense that she was a burden, the fragile one, the girl tethered to faeries and loss. But for the first time in her life, she didn't stand at the edge of the worlds alone. All that mattered was Mathias' hand gripping hers and their lights swirling above them as one. They were together. Partners. Equals. *We are the where. Together.*

The threads flared again, weaving tighter, stronger.

In her periphery she saw or maybe felt Keston, Breen, and Basil draw closer. Other presences were there too but it did not matter.

A chord of light, musical and vast, rippled through the air, through her bones, through Mathias. The rings flared, the star-map in their hands twinkled with motion. His power—rooted, grounded, steady—rose to meet hers, bright and volatile. The astrolabe pulled it all inward. Devoured the divide between them. Twined them together in one living space.

One of the fate-threads swelled with raw brilliance. Caught fire—not with flame, but a luminousness purer than a million stars. The marsh vanished in the brilliance.

Above somewhere the Dama star moved untimely toward a choice. A choice not meant for today. A choice that would bow to wherever she and Mathias stood. And together. Today. They refused to choose one world over another.

Aunia could feel Mathias' heartbeat thudding against hers. The rhythm of their magics syncing. They weren't just holding the astrolabe—they had become part of it. The pulse of the stars moving and worlds aligning. One pulse. One power. Souls braided through the astrolabe's burning heart.

She might have blinked if she had eyes. Through spinning rings and etched constellations, a heart of light pulsed. A whirlpool of living color. A galaxy folded inside brass. Twilight indigo coiled around molten green that shimmered like the veins of leaves in sunlight. And at its core, gold burned. All of it pulsed in time with the worlds' heartbeats. This was the pattern of their magic. . . the magical nymers that had chosen them. All their faith and hope and fears...all braided together in a luminous spiral. This living heart...if the astrolabe had one...it was beating with theirs.

If it burns us, we burn together.

But Aunia did not want to burn. She wanted to live. She wanted to be with Mathias. Enjoy the sweetness of life. Feel the wind on her face. The grass beneath her toes. See the fae folk play tag across a water's surface.

In the distance she could hear voices calling. Voices summoning her closer. And further away. And then a thud against a shoulder blade.

The astrolabe spilled out of her. . .their hands. Onto the salty ground.

Chapter Forty-Eight
CASTLE IN THE CLOUDS

Tatia was born from a thought and a longing — Uriah's gift to the sky, so his Eaburrai wife might wake to clouds instead of sorrow. — Basil Mensani of the Mensani caravan

Mathias stared upward, breath caught in his chest. The Dama star, no longer at risk from slipping into the Harp constellation, gleamed in his periphery four fists off the zenith and southward. Yasendra be blessed! They had knotted fate-threads and dragged a star across the heavens. The idea of it brought a wall-weight crushing his mind. Making it stutter. He blinked.

A faint sound. Aunia's breath, shuddering near him. He shuffled to face her, feet unsteady. She was there. Equally disoriented. Eyes wide. Tears and starlight caught on her lashes. For a moment, their souls had intertwined through the astrolabe's heart, and he had felt her not just beside him, but *within him*.

They fell against each other instinctively, seeking balance. His arms found her waist; her fingers curled against the back of his neck.

They stood there like that while time spun out. Two souls trying to remember where the boundaries were. He buried his face in her hair, breathing her in, grounding himself in the sweet summer scent of her. It mingled with smoke, salt, and something softer—hope, maybe.

She was the anchor that kept the world from crashing in. But around him... the weight, the sound. The thick, cool air filling his lungs. The pounding of his heartbeat against ribs that suddenly felt far too solid. He pulled a hand from Aunia's waist. Looked at it, remembering when it hadn't been a hand but light and threads... merging, spiraling, bound together in an eerie song.

He leaned in closer to her. He could *feel* her still—echoes of her courage trembling under her exhaustion.

Aunia, who acted from hope when reason had already surrendered.

Whose heart led even when fear should have stopped her.

Through her, he had tasted what it meant to *believe*—not in orders, not in the chain of command, but in something raw and luminous. Her hope had burned through his restraint. Had shown him that courage wasn't always steel. That it could be soft and trembling and yet, still take a step forward.

But even with seeing their differences, he understood their similarities. They had both been lonely for the same reason. Building walls to keep from being broken again. Both searching for something that made the emptiness make sense.

Standing here in the aftermath, he knew why she needed to find her father. It wasn't just to uncover truth. It was to belong. To close the wound of being unseen, unanchored. And he understood that ache as well. He spent years serving duty over love, hiding behind a veneer of discipline and distance. But maybe...just maybe if she continued trying to grab the courage to reach across her own chasm, he could, too.

He tightened his hold a little, wordless. Together, they could face whatever came.

And then something jingled.

A faint, tinkling sound—metal on air. Jennium. Instead of a gold-colored shadow, he could see the darkness of her hair, her complexion of bronze and sunlit earth, her yellow-petaled clothing. Jennium tugged at Aunia's hair, pointed with a tiny hand to Mathias' left.

Basil lay on the ground a few feet away. His rover coat was scorched, and one of his hands looked burned. Mathias's throat tightened. But the rover's chest... it rose and fell. He lived.

Relief spilled through Mathias but Aunia gasped and dropped to her knees before him, yelling Basil's name.

Jennium landed on the rover's forehead. Fell to her hands and knees and knocked on the man's head with her tiny fist.

No response. Just the faint rise and fall of his chest.

He frowned, wondering what had happened. Knowing, without knowing exactly why, that Basil had ventured near them.

The mystic-rover shuddered, sat up, and leaned his face into his hands. After a breath, Basil shook himself and looked skyward. "You did it!" he croaked, a grin splitting the soot on his face. "And you're *you!*"

"Me?" Aunia rocked back on her haunches. "What did you do? Why are your hand and your clothes burned?"

Basil winced, glancing at the blackened edge of his sleeve, and the blisters on his hand. "Trying to keep..." He faltered and looked at Mathias.

Mathias' heart thundered in his ears. "*And all seven will come together and merge and become the new heart.*" Create a new heart? Would he and Aunia done exactly that if they hadn't come apart? It had only been the two of them. He shook his head. Was this because of Etos and the astrolabe? That thought sobered him.

Overhead, Keston and Breen swooped in on their respective pegasi. Frehn and the others joined them. Their excited voices carried. They chattered about the light show. And about Uriah and the Elderghest. That they bore witness to the mythical and fantastic.

"You think Uriah destroyed the Elderbind?" asked one young male voice.

"No," Keston said. His gaze fixed on the sinkhole. "He took it back to the sacred grove. Remember, that is his brother."

Mathias rubbed the center of his leather jerkin and then pulled out the pages he had discovered in the Green Harpy attic from his inside pocket. In the dark, he couldn't read the spidery script but he knew what it said. "Thread must be bound to ice before the Dama star rises" and "...shatters if the ice isn't anchored by a counterweight of living magic."

Mathias faced Basil and lifted the sheet of paper. "Thread wasn't attached to ice."

"May I see?" Basil asked.

Mathias moved to Basil's side. He wanted the Mystic to see, and his white light appeared, glowing faintly overhead... as if it were mostly spent. He pointed to the paper. "See? And this... the counterweight of living magic."

"I'd say you and Aunia are the counterweight of living magic. And I'd be careful doing what you did. But thread attached to ice?" Basil turned toward Aunia. "You still have your father's amulet, do you not?"

She nodded, gaze sliding to where Uriah and the Elderbind fought. "And Darla had the compass tethered to the Naoma Stone. We've... we've gotta get that back."

Darla. Now locked inside the Elderbind. Dead. Or worse.

"That'll be a tall, tall order." Basil pushed himself to his feet, keeping his burned arm curved against his chest. "And one for another day, perhaps."

Jennium jingled around Basil's head.

Aunia chewed on her lip and whispered, "Fate is all powerful save for the limits of will and love."

Basil swallowed hard. He turned to the sinkhole where Jovaryn's body had fallen. "Jovaryn," Basil said, "he thought himself lost. But his will to see the augury saved…. The worlds saved."

The mystic-rover pulled his orange bandana from his head, blew his nose, and then reached for Aunia, patting her back. "He took a blow meant for you. He had the will to step forward. That was the power of his will. Ours too. To hold the line even when it looked impossible."

Grief tightened Aunia's features. Mathias felt the ragged swell of it pushing against his chest. Lodging in his throat. But with it also came a deep gratitude. Jovaryn had deserved better from him.

Basil's gaze flicked between them. "And the love the two of you bear for each other? How could fate ever stand a chance?"

Footfalls crunched over the salt. The flyers approached. Keston and Breen walked on one side with Murtagh. Mistfen flyers on the other. Frehn anchored the middle.

One of the Mistfens pointed to the nine dazed-looking wererats gathered at the shoreline. "What do we do with those?"

"Kill them," said another Mistfen.

"Because they're wererats?" Aunia turned, fire in her eyes. "Not all wererats are bad."

"No one is completely bad," a silky voice said. Gabryella stepped from the shadows—mahogany curls tumbling, her low-cut green gown swaying like a serpent's skin. She raised her hands out in peace. "I mean no harm. Indeed, even when we were attacked by brinwraiths, we did our part to keep you safe from the Elderbind."

"The fireballs," Mathias said. "Why?"

Gabryella shrugged. "We believe the veil will fall and the worlds will merge, but we do not want that creature loose when it happens. Commander Frehn, should you bind them, my folk and I are happy to skip them to whatever detention center that you desire."

Frehn put a gloved hand on the hilt of his sword. "No fireling has permission to enter Tamore. Not since Queen Julia's order."

Gabryella rolled her eyes. "An offer only."

Frehn gave her a pointed look. "You have broken the treaty already."

"Hardly," Gabryella said. "The Wraithmere is neutral territory. You cannot claim the entire sea marsh."

"You may depart," Frehn said.

The fireling tilted her head, studying him. "You've been tampered with. I can see it. But it looks like you'll be difficult to manipulate in any future endeavors. And I'll go. Peacefully. On everything sacred that we believe in, I swear. I only want a word with Aunia. A closure for Darla's sake."

Frehn frowned. Looked at Aunia who scrunched her face but nodded.

The Hauser commander turned to Basil. "And you were seen freeing prisoners in Worley."

"What?" Aunia interposed her body between Frehn and Basil. "His caravan holds a seven-pointed star from the royal family. He only—"

"Peace, Aunia," Basil said. "I'll travel with you to Tatia. I will happily speak with Her Majesty."

"Aunia, if I may have a word?" Gabryella said.

"I'll go with you," Mathias said to Aunia. He didn't step in front of her... he wasn't sure she even needed his protection, but she craved solidarity. He had felt that when they had joined.

Aunia nodded. Reached for his hand.

Gabryella shrugged.

They walked away from the others with Aunia's raised chin screaming defensive defiance.

"I understand Darla tried to force you to go to Ignivar University," Gabryella said.

Aunia crossed her arms. "She did."

"Would it be of interest for you to know that I forbade anyone from manipulating the veil? But someone did and that nearly happened tonight. There's a faction... I'm not sure what they want or who they are... but they are not my friend. And, they are not yours."

"Darla was one of those?" Mathias drawled.

Gabryella shrugged. "Perhaps. Darla was someone with middling ability and a thirst to be great. She also had little patience for the work. I think she may have gotten in over her head. Her desire to cling to perceived power. She was my housekeeper. Her wish. She thought groveling at my feet would gain her entry there. When that didn't happen fast enough—"

"She only wanted to learn?" Mathias frowned, thinking of all the books inside Tatia's library.

"Learn?" Gabryella laughed. "Learning happens anywhere. Ignivar University is the only way to become a flamekeeper."

"And a flamekeeper is what?" Aunia asked.

Gabryella smiled. "Darla would have seen you as a means to gain entry into Ignivar. It could have been successful too. But I can't help but wonder if her offers to help you didn't come from fear of who she fell in with."

"My help?" Aunia said.

Gabryella nodded. "She warned me through a mirror painting that he wasn't who others thought and that he would destroy us all."

"He who?" Mathias said. "What does that mean?"

Gabryella shrugged. "I do not know. It was all she said before something grabbed her and she was gone. Gone. Presumably, she came here. I don't think her decision was totally hers. Either way, that faction is still in play. I wouldn't tarry here long. Be well."

And with that, Gabryella disappeared.

Aunia turned to Mathias, confusion and doubt warring in her eyes.

He reached for her hand. "No one is all bad, nor all good. It's our actions that count." He exhaled. "And ours have saved the worlds... for now. We still owe an audience with Nyrissa and the Queen."

Jennium darted from Basil back to Aunia. Circled her head.

"We'll have to go with them to Tatia, but Aunia, I swear, I will help you find your father."

Aunia had a faraway look in her eyes. Then she blinked. "Tatia is where we should go. I know where my father is."

"You... do?"

Breen came running up to them. Keston followed, his steps more somber.

"If anyone wants excitement," Breen said, "You two are the landmark. Come on. We need to go."

With Aunia's hand in his own, Mathias followed them back to the flyers and the pegasi. He released her hand and walked to Tafiriel, certain that Frehn would insist that Aunia ride with Breen.

"I will speak on your behalf to the Dar-Elect." Frehn stepped forward and saluted Mathias. "But for you commander, I cannot do the same."

Mathias stiffened. "What happened to Fallo?"

"No idea," Breen said. "He was flying east and he simply vanished."

"Vanished?" Mathias set a hand on Taf's neck.

I cannot reach him, Taf sent.

Mathias closed his eyes. *Like Patrick and Garrett?*

No. I do get a vague sense of him and Paderro. They're just sleeping or...

Mathias glanced back to the sky. "Fallo has less than two weeks. He's been bitten."

"If we find him in time, I pledge he'll get the Don't Turn potion. And then, consequences. As for seating arrangements, Mathias... You choose." Frehn turned to face Breen. "I also need to say, your father would be incredibly proud of you."

Breen's usual rigid posture loosened, and her complexion pinked. "Thank you."

"Yes, he would have been." Keston clapped Breen's shoulder and then pulled himself onto Revellie.

Mathias looked at the wererats down at the shore. "And them?"

"We'll send other flyers," Frehn said. "Basil—"

"I'll take him," Keston said but his face had turned again to the sinkhole. "For Jovaryn. And for all who suffer because their worth is hidden."

Jovaryn's worth. Jovaryn was worth far more than he ever was given. Mathias held out his hand for Aunia to mount. She leaned against him in the saddle and Mathias closed his eyes. Reina. On the Harp that poor little girl. All he'd be able to offer her would be services that honored the man and a memorial stone to remember him by. It was the least he could do. Jovaryn was a comrade in arms and he had fallen saving Mathias' heart.

They took to the sky under the stars... under the Dama star. Who knew which constellation it would drift to next, but they had time. Mathias, Aunia, and the others glided forward toward a castle in the clouds.

AHNU-ENDYNIA GLOSSARY

Adar – (Ah-dar) – A country immediately south of Tamore and east of the island country of Bellatine.

Aeryk de Wyvert (king-consort) – (Air-ick dee WHY-vert) – minor nobleman who gained title of king-consort when he married Princess Shaleia when she became Queen. He was responsible for a rebellion to overthrow the Queen and was executed for his treason. He is the father of Princess Keira. He was born and raised in New Berlyn, in the northern part of Tamore.

Aetherwind – The island seat of the Pavari Court where Zevara rules. This island, along with all islands in the land hangs in the sky and is connected with silver chain bridges. Aetherwind is made of black basalt mountains and near its tallest peak stands Zevara's bright-white stone castle. This island also is home to a Veil Door.

Ahnu-Endynia – (AH-new EN-di-nya) – Conjoined worlds of both mortal and faery worlds. Ahnu is the mortal world and Endynia is the faery world. These twin worlds occupy the same space yet are separated by a thin veil made of ethereal material. Very little can pass through the veil without a specific entrance/exit, such as a Veil Door, as an example.

Ag-Haggy – A mountain on the Grashbear that looked like the wide tooth in a giant's mouth; however, it exploded at the climax of Faeries Don't Lie when the marble giant ripped through it.

Aiket – (Ah-KET) – One of the wererats from the blade-cave den who works with Basil.

Arensvald, Grand Duke of Uttalo - (AR-ens-val, Grand Duke of uh-TAY-low) – Naoma's father and historical figure. It is said he killed his own grandchildren.

Augury, the – The belief that if all seven Chandarions recreate the Heart Between the Worlds, then the lifeblood will beat through both worlds, saving both. But if the Chandarions do not succeed by a certain time, then the Dama Ximarae will have to choose which world will live and which one will die.

Aunia – (AH-nee-a) – Sixteen-year-old protagonist. Wheat-blond hair, dark blue eyes, heart-shaped face. This impulsive faery-friend is Rune's daughter.

Augurites – A para-religious order who believe in the augury (another word for prophecy) that one of the worlds, either mortal or faery, will die if the Chandarions don't all arrive to fix the Dama's shattered heart.

Aurimite – (ARE-ee-mite) – A psychic listening spell which infected both Aunia and Mathias. It is created by using magic through Etos' compass which was in Arch Vicar Bibb's possession.

Axe-Pickle – A mockman troll leader.

Bacrae Noir – A type of red wine from Lambert's Vinyards. It is greatly sought after for its full-bodied wine and smooth, lingering finish. It has notes of blackberry jam and dark chocolate.

Barnabas Gearhart – Traveling blade merchant who is a family friend of Keston and his father, Jayden Pendar. He is a bear of a man with fluffy blonde hair and a short, curled beard.

Baron Chazelle – (bear-on SHAY-zell) – A visiting noble at the Green Harpy who gained audience with Lord Lyle of Worley. He is a stout man who often wears clothing that are too tight.

Basil Mensani – (BAH-sill Men-SAW-knee) – Rover Mystic from Tamore.

Baxter's Way – Major Tamorian highway connecting Tamore to Adar and Bellatine.

Bearpaws – A landmark pair of tall hills near the ghost town of Idenweigh which is located near the Grashbear mountains.

Beggarfauns – (Beggar-fawns) – A gourd-like plant which grows near blade-caves. Sought after as an ingredient in spells. They can move on their own.

Bellatine – (Bell-ah-tine) – An island country south of Tamore. Home of the Mystic Court. It is also known for its naval shipping.

Berrydell (village of) – A village that is situated a few miles from the bottom of the hill where Eddac Tower stands. It has thin roads crisscrossing between fifty-some houses.

Besmarion – (Bes-MAR-ee-on) – A spring festival consisting of feasting, dancing and flirting.

Besnik – (BES-nick) – A short rover lad who is 14 years of age. He is a mischievous who has possession of a far-viewer.

Betrothal stone – A magical item that is sometimes sent from the gnomes of Terralium, the faery court of earth and snow to help determine who the heir of Tamore should wed.

Betwixt – The space between the worlds—a combination of both and yet neither. It is the undefined space between the worlds. Normally encompasses the veil. It can also mean an in-between place or time, such as dawn and dusk.

Betwixting Spell – A spell Edvaras cast which called all tunnels and caverns throughout the world to appear and create a passageway through the Grashbear Mountains. This tunnel allowed Edvaras and his followers to escape Tamore. It also created a spill-over side effect which remains in effect. For example, there are the sometimes-there and sometimes-not-there Blade-caves.

Bibb (Arch Vicar) – Leader of the Da Vennen cult, a soldier religion. The order's background dates to the time of Rhugante before the kingdom of Tamore came into existence. Bibb is a tall man with a thin hooked-nose face. He has black hair streaked in white.

Birchwoods – (Birch Woods) – A magical Betwixt place that is in between the worlds of Ahnu-Endynia. Magic runs unimpeded there and the unexpected—good or bad—can happen.

Blade-cave – A cave that is sometimes there and sometimes not. The villagers in Naoma Sacella call this the Betwixting tunnels. Some believe if the cave disappears while a person is inside then they are absorbed for all time. The sheep cave near Naoma Sacella is one of the blade-caves.

Bloodball – A past event which many of the royal family were slain.

Boggleman – (Bah-gil-man) – Antagonist. A slim white-haired man with a creepy musical voice and of indeterminate age. He has a scar running from an empty eye socket to his jaw. His fingers on his right hand are jutted out oddly as if they had been broken and left to heal badly. He intends to see the human world die.

Border Spell – A spell created by Dar Syrick which prevents firelings and dark fae from crossing into the kingdom of Tamore. Wyverns have been eating at the spell and have greatly weakened it.

Brainhedge – One of two hedges made of living brainhedge trees (looks similar to an osage orange hedge) which runs along much of Baxter's Way.

Brainhedge Tree – The largest tree in the Brainhedge. It is significantly taller than the others and at its foot stands a gate made of metal and living wood. It allows passage for those who possess a key to be able to partake of the water.

Brainmere – The grassy section between the two hedges of brain-hedge trees which runs along the highway of Baxter's Way and separates the Marchlands of Froidelune and Dalin. A creek with waters with magical properties flows here.

Branimir the Hunter – (BRAN-a-mere the hun-ter) – an Eaburrai from the Eaburrai Court. A companion of the Dama and minor deity.

Breanne – (BREE-ann) – Eighteen-year-old villager who is getting "beaded" (married) to Tinner. Limi's friend. Xissa's daughter.

Breezlings – A type of faery. They appear to be hand-sized with large purple eyes and translucent silver wings. They predominately live in the realm of Pavari.

Breen Haldrayne – (BREEN HALL-drain) – A pegasus flyer stationed at Hauser Tower. She has curly chestnut brown hair and freckles and typically wears a blue scarf around her neck which belonged to her deceased hero father. Her pegasus stallion is Korthalee.

Briar – The cook at Eddac Tower.

Brinsaber – (brin-SA-ber) – Pegasus to Jules Mayrell. Brinsaber has been hiding somewhere in the Grashbear.

Brinwraiths – (BRIN-rayth) – Type of water fairy that lives primarily in sea marshes. They are known to work with will-of-the-wisps and will create silvery mist to help drown intruders. They are silver-blue and green with skin that shimmers between scale and flesh. They have green hair and feline-shaped heads. Their eyes are mirror-bright and unblinking.

Britchway – A small town in the Dalin province and located north of both Dalin and Eddac Tower. This town was damaged severely by fire caused by fire salamanders and wererats during a Besmarion festival.

Caedmon – (KAYD-mon) – Chief, blacksmith and story teller of the isolated village of Naoma Sacella. He was like a second father to Aunia. Short cropped hair and corded muscles. He is of medium height.

Camlo – (Cam-lo) – A fifteen-year-old year old rover lad. Cousin to Besnik. He had dark eyes.

Canthelark singers – (CAN-the-lark singers) – A type of singer, who perform together with almost otherworldly beautiful and high-pitched voices.

Casmia – Rover woman from the Mensani caravan who dances.

Cassian Worley – (CASS-ee-un) – A young nobleborn who is a scribe for his father, Lord Lyle of Worley. He has longish-hair that he usually wears pulled back and he favors tall boots. A former foster-brother to Mathias Habrett, he and Mathias were once close but Cassian's desire to to be an artist threatened Mathias' reputation with his own father

Catiryna Pemble – (CA-tear-eena PEM-ball) – Commander of Stanz Tower. She is an outspoken woman who is maybe five feet tall with fire-colored hair. She rides a steel gray pegasus stallion named Yantexio.

Chand Crystal – This byproduct from Chandarion magic is greatly valued. Its uses include boosting the intensity of magic spells. Pegasi riders carry a tiny crumb of Chand crystal, usually in the form of a necklace or a ring, which helps their telepathic connection to their individual pegasi.

Chand Ice – Sometimes called Frostheart. This physical by-product of the shattered Heart of the Worlds can be used to store Nymers and can help boost the intensity of a magic spell.

Chandarions – Foretold in the augury that there will be seven individuals who will be imbued with magic in the form of Nymers and they will recreate the Heart of the Worlds.

Clavis Peak – (Cla-vis Peak) – A sole mountain where Edvaras and his followers lived until the settlement was attacked, and then abandoned.

The community was moved to Naoma Sacella. The villagers of Naoma Sacella believe this area to be taboo. It has also been glamored magically so it is invisible.

Clurichauns – (clear-ree CON) – A type of faery. They are typically depicted as small, wizened beings resembling older men, often with rosy cheeks and a mischievous twinkle in their eyes. They typically are drunkards or are prone to it. Some of the clurichauns living in Dalin include Mara, Sharpish and Gargle.

Cody Lambert – (KOH-dee lam-BERT) – A faeblood who has been imprisoned in Dalin's prison. He is originally from Lambert's Vineyards. He has a working relationship with Basil, Jovaryn, and Wendalin. He has blonde hair.

Cold Festival – Annual festival with a variety of activities from balls to markets. This event takes place during the last five days of the Tamorian year.

Craymore – An innkeeper in Worley who runs the Green Harpy. He is a a short furry man who sometimes engages in unethical activities for profit.

Cyndrix – A fire salamander who was consumed by the Boggleman's cape.

Cyril – Footsoldier at Eddac Tower. Deceased.

Da Caladorian Vennen soldier order – (da CAL-a-door-ee-an VEN-ann) – Often known simply as the Da Vennen. They worship the Rhugante Bear and are loosely based on Mithraism from first century AD in Italy. They do not believe that humans should use magic. The sword and the plow is their motto. They also enjoy the privilege of Uriah's edict which allows them to be outside of Tamore jurisdiction, except for the most egregious crimes. Unfortunately, it appears that their order has been infiltrated and certain higher ups are not only using magic, but are utilizing them for their own nefarious desires.

Dagel demons – Types of dark fae who have crossed into category of great evil.

Dalin – (Dah-lin) – The capital city of one of the marchlands in the kingdom of Tamore. It is known for its sword manufacturing. It has a bustling market due to its close location to the trade route between Tamore and Bellatine.

Dama star – (DA-ma star) – A star that can only be seen through a person's periphery. It waffles back and forth between the Harp and Hammer constellations. It is the indicator that the Choice from the augury (prophecy) has come when it enters either constellation.

Dama Ximarae – (Dah-ma ZI-mah-ray) – The main deity and creator of the worlds of Ahnu-Endynia.

Danalissa Habrett – (Dan-na-LEE-sah Ha-brett) – Mathias' mother and Lord Wallace Habrett's wife. Originally from Adar. She was the queen's lady-in-waiting before her marriage. She and Mathias' father were known for their epic love story when they first married. They have moved apart since.

Darkwraiths – Shadowy figures that pull all positive emotions and memories away from their victims. They are able to suck the life force out of people. They are believed to come from the Boggleman; however, they actually come from a darker evil.

Darla Valesco – (DAR-la VAL-eh-sco) – Darla is introduced to Aunia as a servant at the Green Harpy. She had dark hair and a curvy figure. She is good at disguises. There is more to her than meets the eye at first.

Darra Chamber – A chamber that was said to once occupy the castle of Tatia where Chand ice and Nymers from Chandarions were stored. Inside the chamber is a window which looks into the Faery world and also the Eaburrai Court. It was created by Uriah to placate his wife, Yasendra.

Davis – A blacksmith from Dalin who fashions many of the iron bracelets that faebloods are required to wear.

Dead Lands – The land between the Grashbear Mountains and Naoma Sacella. A spell during Edvaras' escape from Tamore consumed all the leyline energy in this area causing most vegetation to die.

Diadem, the – The best inn within Worley.

Didianne (Queen) – (DIE-dee-ann) – A queen from centuries past who is known to have gone mad and she made the Darra Chamber disappear.

Domesday – (Dohms-day) – A written record which gives the names of all high-born families, along with their titles and lands. Updated every decade.

Dominus Titus Valerian – Adarian high ruler. Jayden Pendar, Keston's father, has been employed with commissions for him several times. The Dominus is know to be verbose and tiresome.

Drake Vrael (Lord) – Lord of Vraelfork and Fallo Vrael's brother.

Dryad – (DRY-ad) A tree faery. Aunia encountered one outside of Moonstepper hostel. It had rich polished wood skin and dark hair, tangled with acorn caps.

Eaburrai – (Eh-BURR-ray) – Companions of the Dama. Minor deities.

Eaburrai Court – (Eh-BURR-ray court) – Where the Eaburrai typically dwell. This place is in-between the worlds.

Eddac Tower – (EH-deck Tower) – One of the tower forts which pegasi-flyers reside. Flyers watch over designated territory and towers are found throughout the kingdom of Tamore. Eddac is located in the Dalin province between the town of Britchway and the city of Dalin. Its complement include Fallo Vrael, Mathias Habrett, Keston Pendar, Jules Mayrell, and Patrick and Garrett. Patrick and Garrett are kin to Fallo and they are also known as the knightsons.

Edvaras – (ED-var-as) – Chandarion. Known as the rogue Chandarion who disrupted the augury. Edvaras ran off with his love, Naoma, along with their followers through the Grashbear Mountains and past the Dead Lands.

Edvaras stone – One of the two frostheart stones that Edvaras summoned. Both house the trio of flowers he made for his wife, Naoma. Gaitha avoids using the Edvaras stone for her spellwork as the outcomes are often unpredictable for her.

Elderghast – (Elder-gast) – Uriah's elder brother who caused the Heart of the Worlds to shatter. This shattering caused him to be transformed into a monster and his birth name has been lost to antiquity. He is responsible for the children of Yasendra and Uriah to be dispersed across many lands, an event which caused the War Between the Worlds. His mortal name was Iriath.

Elderbind – This is the place, a yew tree, where the Elderghast was imprisoned. The Chandarion Uriah is its custodian and he watches over it in the Sacred Grove. However, during more evil times, the Elderghast has learned how to make the tree roots move.

Ella – Taya's mother and the rover's lead fortune-teller. She and her husband, Karr, were killed when Taya was ten.

Elowen – The head stable keeper at Eddac Tower.

Elris (Prince) – A past Tamorian prince who married a rover. His descendant was Olivia.

Emmet Dalin (Marquis) – Lord of Dalin. This twenty year old lord holds the title of being sixteenth in the line of Ice-steel, and Protector of the free people dwelling within the Grashbear's shadow. He is the son of the deceased Marquis Charl Dalin, descendant of Grand Marquis de Idenweigh. He has a boy-slight frame, russet-gold skin, and dark eyes. He often wears a circlet fashioned like a bent sword adorning his curly-haired head.

Etos – (EE-toes) – An Eaburrai from the Eaburrai Court. A companion of the Dama and minor deity. Etos is the second youngest of the Eaburrai and he was jealous of his youngest sister, Yasendra, he hated her punishment for breaking the world heart. To help her, he created the Trinity. He is also known as the Wanderwright and the Tinker.

Faery Courts – The four elemental faery courts include: Terralium, the court of earth and snow; Pavari, the court of spring and air; Cascadia, the court of water and summer; and Emberfall, the court of fire and autumn. There are three other faery courts.

Fallo Vrael – (FAH-low Vr-RAIL) – Commander of Eddac Tower and Mathias' superior. He is the brother of Lord Vrael from the Duchy of Vraelsfork. Fallo desperately wants to find the marble giant. He is a broad-shouldered man with a balding head. Paderro is his pegasus.

Fate-threads – Invisible threads that wind through everything and controls destiny unless they are manipulated.

Frehn Bracae – (FREN bra-KAY) – Commander of Hauser Tower and Flyer of Morganstee.

Ferris Runoldi – (fair-riss RUNE-oll-dee) – The Mystic believed to have committed the royal family murders during the Blood Ball.

Fire salamanders – This type of faery can change its size, ranging from thumb-sized to that of a small horse. Generally, it has short limbs and cat-like eyes no matter what size it takes. Most of them have red skin.

Firelings – A magical order from in the southern country of Adar by the Boggleman. They used to be part of the Cragborns, people living in the terraced Tatian mountains. The order and its beliefs are generally in opposition to the Augurite order. They are known to dabble in many different types of magic. This order has attacked Tamore in the past and they are the primary reason why Dar Syrick erected a border spell around Tamore.

Forged Tankard – A tavern in Dalin between the warehouse and blacksmithy sections. The tavern owner is a woman named Brana.

Froidelune (Marchlands of) – (FROY-day-lune) – One of the Marchlands near the Grashbear. It has been separated from Dalin as the two marchlands fought over dominion of the Brainmere.

Gabin – (GAH-bin) – A baby from the Mensani caravan of rovers.

Gabryella ni Brier Reach – (GAB-ree-ella knee briar reach) – A fireling woman with mahogany-brown hair and a fondness of low-cut gowns. She has been working on imprisoning fire salamanders into glass tubes to make salamander lights. She is the First Flamekeeper of the Fireling Order

Gaitha – (GAY-the) – Eldest Daughter of Naoma Sacella. She is Edvaras' true Dar and descendant of Edvaras. Petite woman with a bit of a limp. Dark skinned and graying hair.

Galeena – A faery attendant in Zevara's castle. She appears as a willowy figure the color of twilight.

Ganger – Foreman at the ruined merchant guild at Dalin.

Garrett – A cousin of Fallo and one of the sons to Lord Vrael's knights. He has dark curly hair.

Gavryn – (GAV-rin) - Loremaster of Loravi caravan. He had a dream that Etos the Wanderwright instructed him to gather halite salt so he had his caravan turn down the Forgotten Way where they were accosted by Da Vennen soldiers and imprisoned at Worley.

Geis – (GEESH) – An unbreakable magical obligation or taboo placed on a person. Zevara from the faery court of Pavari has placed one on Aunia and Mathias when they wanted to return to the human world. If they break it, they will be transported back to the faery court.

Ghille dhu (GILL-ee DOO) – A solitary forest faery usually bound to birch groves. Usually shy and gentle. Some believe he is a tooth fairy.

Glevis – (GLEH-vis) – A small mining community close to the Grashbear Mountains. It provides iron and also rare materials to the city of Dalin for manufacturing swords.

Glows – An aura that surrounds a person or a faery. One of Aunia's abilities is to be able to see and read the glows of others.

Grashbear Mountains – A mountain range on the western side of Tamore which separates Tamore from the Dead Lands. This range is home to Mockmen trolls, wyverns, and other faery creatures. It is also riddled with blade-caves from the fallout from Edvaras' Betwixting spell.

Green Harpy, the – Second best inn in Worley. It is run by an innkeeper by the name of Craymore.

Gregwin – Healer who was tending Jules after his wererat bite. Gregwin is a portly man.

Halite salt – Pure, naturally crystallized rock salt. Etos' astrolabe is set up to use halite as a magical conductor for the right person to pluck certain fate-threads in order to prevent the augury from every happening.

Harris – Twelve year-old villager from Naoma Sacella who Aunia's faery friends tease quite frequently. Velli's younger brother and Sigmus' nephew.

Hauser Tower – (HA-sir tower) – A pegasi tower located near Worley.

Hattie – Xissa's younger sister who resides most of the time out at the sheep cottage in the northern hills.

Heart of the Worlds – The Dama's exterior heart which beats lifeblood and magic through both worlds of Ahnu-Endynia until an accident shattered it.

Heavensfeet – A major city near the foothills of the Tatian Mountain range along Tamore's western border.

Hebsolum – The marble giant who lives under the Grashbear Mountains. This being, previous to Edvaras marbelizing him, was the guardian for the Eaburrai Court. He followed Yasendra into the mortal world after she married Uriah. There are rumors that he does not exist after centuries of searching for his marble hand and finding none. Fallo is obsessed with collecting some of this marble.

Heebles – This Dagel demon/faery looks like a moldy gourd with a wide mouth and sharp teeth. It has no other facial features. It has no differential between its head and body. It has two skeletal limbs which work as both arms and legs. Heebles attack in hordes and can strip the flesh off a cow in a matter of minutes. They communicate to each other in ratlike snarls and squeaks.

Heyden, (Dar) – (Dar Hay-den) – One of Tamore's royal magic-users who allegedly uses the stored and borrowed magic of Chandarions, particularly Edvaras'. He used to be a former Adarian dance master.

Hollow – A space hollowed out in the veil, the substance that separates the Faery and the Mortal worlds. Usually the size of a small room or several small rooms. It is created with magical glyphs written by steel and silver styluses.

House of Nobles – A building complex above Heavensfeet where the nobility gather several times a year to help co-create laws with her majesty.

Idenweigh – One of the southern most towns along the Grashbear Mountains in Tamore. A pivotal battle was waged here in the year 996 (70 years earlier than the start of Faeries Don't Lie). The defense was led by Olivia. Currently, the town is mostly abandoned with rumors of it being overrun with ghosts.

Ignivar University – (IG-nee-var yoo·nuh·VUR·suh·tee) – Fireling institution. The university's purpose is to educate firelings, along with providing the necessary information and clout to become a Flamekeeper, or in other words, to be in leadership. **Illysa** – (Ill-Lys-SAH) – Second

Chandarion. Her legacy includes creating the pegasi flyer troops after negotiating a truce with Zevara of the Pavari Court. Also known as the Fire Keep.

Iriath – (EAR-ee-ath) – The human name of the Elderghast before he was stripped of his humanity.

Jaia – (Jay-ah) – One of the flowers Edvaras created. This black, lily-like flower has a stench similar to skunk wrapped in honeysuckle. It is used as the main ingredient in making faery repellant.

Jarl – Rover man from the Mensani caravan. He is father to Besnik and a friend of Niall's.

Jayden Pendar – Keston's father. He is a sculptor.

Jennium – (Jen-nee-um) – Garden faery. Hand-sized and slender with dark curly hair, dark eyes, olive complexion, and iridescent wings. She has unusual abilities which includes a strong tolerance to iron.

Jenny Greenteeth – A water faery, generally with long green hair, and is known for lurking under the surface of ponds and marshes. She snares the unwary, especially children, so she can drown them under the water.

Jovaryn – (Joe-VAR-n) – Wererat boy with disheveled hair and a red ribbon tied around his neck. A follower of Hebsolum. He has been taken by the Boggleman. His quarter faeblood comes from his grandfather Sylvan from Varandu.

Jules Mayrell – One of the pegasi-flyers from Eddac Tower. Mathias' friend and nephew of Dar Zeller, Mathias' late mentor. Jules has a broad face and tousled auburn hair. Before the start of FAERIES DON'T LIE, Jules has been bitten by a wererat.

Kai-Marin – (KI-mare-in) – One of the Eaburrai. Often known as the Sea Witch. She often appears as a young woman with blue hair and slight of build. Her skin is radiant pale blues and greens and she has unnaturally large silver eyes.

Kankari – A new moon festival celebrated each month in the mortal world as a way to entice the moon to return from the faery world into the human world.

Kazik bird – (Kaa-zick bird) – An enormous bird who appears to be a cross between a flame-red peacock and a phoenix. He resides in the court of Pavari and his feathers, particularly the tail feathers, contain concentrated magic thanks to the Chandarion, Illysa. It significantly boosts the telepathic magic of pegasi and flyers. These tail feathers are in great demand. He does not shed feathers often.

Keston – One of the pegasi-flyers from Eddac Tower. Mathias' friend and sidekick. He is flirtatious and charming. He is tall with sandy brown hair and amber eyes.

King Darnell – (king DAR-nell) – Queen Shaleia's father and Princess Keira's grandfather. He was killed along with his wife, Julia, and his daughter Kylandra during the blood ball.

Knight-sons (see Patrick and/or Garrett) – Cousins of Fallo and sons to Lord Vrael's highest knight. They are part of the Eddac Tower unit.

Kobolds – A type of faery. They are chest-high with knobby-shouldered, elongated faces, and sharp teeth.

Krissa – Eleven-year-old villager who helps out with healing duties after the heeble invasion.

Kron – One of the villagers. Limi's mate. Oskan's son.

Ladonia – (LA-dohn-knee-a) – Fish widow who adopted the Bogleman when he was a small child.

Lady Ysabel Ferente – (ee-sah-BEL fer-EN-tay) – A visiting noble at the Green Harpy who gained an audience with Lord Lyle. She is an older woman with gray hair who often wears tiny bells in her head and carries a dragon's head cane.

Leia – Tamorian woman and Aunia's mother.

Leiaphae – (Lie-ah-FAY) – One of the three flowers Edvaras created. This yellow broccoli-stalked flower is used to cast the shrouding spell which will hide Naoma Sacella from all eyes.

Lena – Tharon's sister-in-law who helps to look after Taya and Reina. She is a woman with cinnamon-colored hair and high cheek bones.

Limi – Aunia's foster sister. Gaitha's granddaughter and heir to the title of Eldest Daughter. Limi does not want this position nor the magic that comes with it. Medium dark skin. Brown eyes. Wears her hair in many braids. 19-year-old and pregnant in the FAERIES DON'T LIE. Kron's mate.

Lord Chance (of Mimsy) – Hero in a book that Jules Mayrell reads and quotes from.

Lord Lyle Worley – (lord LYLE WERE-lee) – Lord of the Worley. He is a tall man with high cheekbones and an aquiline nose. His hair is mostly silver, but it used to be black. He comes across very authoritarian. His eyes are cool gray rimmed in amber.

Lord Phrast – (Lord FRAST) – One of the commanders in Arch Vicar Bibb's army.

Lord Ranth Tell – Spatelly's missing lord and one of the commanders in Arch Vicar Bibb's army.

Lord Wallace Habrett – (WALL-is Ha-brett) – Mathias' father. Lord of Wulf's Eye. He and Mathias' mother were known for their epic love story when they first married. They have moved apart since.

Lovari caravan – (Lah-VAR-ee) – One of the family caravan of rovers.

Lumentago Valley – River valley where the island city of Worley stands in the center of the Whisp River. It is also called Wythrindle River.

Lydinairre – (LE-din-air-ree) – Pegasus to Dar-Elect Nyrissa Rieson.

Mathias Habrett – (MAH-thigh-as Hah-bret) – Secondary protagonist and Aunia's love interest. He is a pegasus flyer stationed at Eddac

Tower after being exiled for six months for his unclear role in the death of Dar Zeller, his mentor. His pegasus is Tafiriel. Mathias has dark wavy hair, green eyes, and chiseled features. He is the surviving son of Lord and Lady Habrett. His friend, Keston, loves to call him Matty.

McNarish – A merchant guildsman in Dalin. He is a skinny man who dresses in foppish attire.

Mensani caravan – (Men-SAW-knee caravan) – One of the family caravan of rovers. This one is home to Basil Mensani, his father, Tharon, and more.

Mezzapian – (MEZZ-ah-pee-un) - A person from Mezzapi which is located west of the Tatian Mountains.

Micoh – (MY-koi) – Wererat boy at Spatelly

Miriel – A pretty young woman from Worley who is a friend of Keston's.

Mistfen Tower – (MIST-fen) – Pegasi tower near Spatelly and Lambert Vineyard.

Mistress Madriel – Healer to Queen Didianne

Mockmen Trolls – (mock-men trolls) – Furry troll-like creatures. Most sport tusks. They consider themselves superior to humans, particularly when it comes to mining. While they are not intellectually superior, they are good at finding alternative solutions.

Mockmen Wars – During Olivia's time, there was several large scale battles between Tamore and Mockmen trolls. Olivia was integral to defeating them but she was taken by the Boggleman at the end of the war.

Mollie Mae – A wererat woman from the blade-cave den who works with Basil. Mollie Mae is Basil and Wendalin's mother and Tharon's estranged wife.

Moonstepper Hostel – One of the hostels along the Pardonway. Unlike the others, this one is surrounded by the Pardonway Forest. It is rumored that this is where Thalric Haldrayne kept the rebels from Aeryk's rebellion at bay.

Morsalka – (MOR-sal-kaa) – A drown-wife/widow faery and guardian of the Wraithmere

Moss-gnomes – Calf-high humanoid faeries who like to cavort under shady places and take naps on moss pads. They can dig through any ground as if it were "made of soft butter."

Mudcloaks – A derogatory name for Da Vennen soldiers.

Murtagh – (Mur-tah) – One of the flyers stationed at Hauser Tower. He wears his dark hair in a long braid and flies a red-gold pegasus mare.

Mygul – (MY-gull) – The dark blue indigo globefire that follows Aunia around. It has been known to knock things over to create havoc.

Myles – (Miles) – Stanz Tower's second officer. He has auburn-colored hair and rides a black pegasus mare.

Mystic Court – An order located predominately in Bellatine, which monitors the augury. Its spell-casters tend to use musical spells and faery magic borrowed from their faery familiars.

Mystics – An order of magic-users who use faery familiars. Tamorians tend to distrust them as they believe the order is responsible for the Blood Ball.

Naoma – (NAY-oh-ma) – Edvaras' wife. She was born and raised in the northern country of Uttalo.

Naoma Sacella – (NAY-oh-ma SAW-cell-lah) – Edvaras' isolated village located past the Dead Lands. It is circled by a blue Chand crystal wall.

Naoma stone – One of the two frostheart stones that Edvaras summoned to house the trio of flowers he made for his wife, Naoma. Gaitha uses this stone to help her with more complicated spells as she has more affinity to this one than its brother, the Edvaras stone.

Narvis – A fire salamander in the Boggleman's court whose loyalties are conflicted. See fire salamander for physical description.

Navenra – (NAH-ven-rah) – One of the flowers Edvaras created. This lacy, blue flower was created to increase Naoma's lifespan but instead it restrains free will.

Ned – A faeblood in Dalin who was arrested after the walking mouth (heeble) attack.

Nehla – (NAY-la) – Limi's deceased mother. Aunia's mother figure.

Niall – (Neal) – Taya's grandfather.

Nonderu – (NON-day-roo) – The underground kingdom of the Boggleman. It is located in the Betwixt.

Nymers – Pure energy heart shards which attach themselves to Chandarions and Chandarion potentials. Mygul would be an example of one.

Nyrissa Rieson – (Dar-Elect) – (NAH-riss-ah REE-son) – One of Tamore's royal magic-users who should be able to use the borrowed magic of Chandarions, particularly Illysa. Acting general of Tamore's aerial troops since the death of her father, Dar Zeller.

Olivia – A Chandarion potential. Since Edvaras boxed his own Nymer (Chandarion magic) away, no full Chandarions have been born. Olivia is known in Tamore as the Maid of Idenweigh. She was integral to the victory against the Mockman Trolls in the year 996 (70 years earlier than Faeries Don't Lie). Rumors have it that she was abducted by the Boggleman.

Oomas – Dark faery creatures who are squat, calf-high, and have their eyes on top of their heads. They make good scouts.

Oskan – (AHS-can) – Large bear of a man with salt and pepper braids. Father-in-law to Gaitha's granddaughter, Limi. Father to Kron.

Oswald – Footsoldier at Eddac Tower. Deceased.

Q'thonos – (KA-THOUGH-knows) – An earth-mage who lives within a glade inside the Pardonway Forest. His house looks like three different houses merged together. When in his usual form (he will masquerade as an old man), he has angular features, unruly dark hair, and odd glasses with a hagstone for one of the lenses. Aunia sees him with a moon-silver glow.

Paderro – (Pah-DARE-oh) – Fallo's pegasus. Jet black stallion.

Pardonway – A major thoroughfare that runs through the Pardonway Forest and links the river island of Worley with Heavensfeet, a city at the base of the Tatian Mountains. This highway provide protection from the forest which has been spelled to rend apart anyone disloyal to the Queen.

Pippa Lambert – (PIP-uh lam-BERT) – Daughter of Roddy Lambert of Lambert's Vineyard and sister of Cody Lambert. She is about fifteen years of age with light brown hair.

Patrick – A cousin of Fallo and one of the sons to Lord Vrael's knights. He has a wispy beard and his dark blonde hair is cut bowl-shaped.

Pavari, aka the Court of Spring and Air – One of the seven faery courts in Endynia. This court is ruled by Zevara and is populated with sylphs, windknots, the Kazik birk, and other air-type faeries.

Portal tiles – Magical knuckle-sized tiles that gleam iridescently with reds, greens, and blues. These give the ability of transportation across many miles.

Princess Keira of Tamore – (KEER-uh of TAY-more) – Royal heir. Daughter of Queen Shaleia and the former King-consort Aeryk de Wyvert. She has crimson red hair, heart-shaped face, and is very pretty. She is also overly flirtatious.

Princess Kylandra – Former Tatian heir princess. Daughter of King Darnell and Queen Julia. She died during the blood ball.

Q'thonos the Mad Wizard – (KAY-tho-nos) – He lives within a glade inside the Pardonway Forest and his house looks like three different houses merged together. When in his usual form, and not masquerading as an old man, he has angular features, unruly dark hair, and odd glasses with a hagstone for one of the lenses. Aunia sees him with a moon-silver glow.

Queen Didianne – (Queen Die-dee-ann) – A queen from over 500 years earlier, who ruled Tamore and was known to have gone mad.

Queen Shaleia of Tamore – (Queen SHA-lee-ah of TAY-more) – The current Queen of Tamore. Princess Keira's mother.

Queen Silvani – (Queen Sill-VON-ee) – The mother of Prince Elris. She gave him a royal star as a wedding gift. She was a contemporary of Olivia.

Reina – (RAY-na) – Six-year-old faeblood child with dirty blonde hair who the Mensani caravan rovers took in. She is a fugitive because of her magical abilities and is hiding with Q'thonos, the Mad Wizard who has nicknamed her "Sunray," has given her an amulet that looks like a tiny fork with curved tines that conjures pie. She is the younger sister to Jovaryn and it appears she has foretelling abilities.

Revellie – (REV-ah-lee) – Keston's pegasus. She is a golden mare who has a great sense of where she is at all times. Her telepathic voice is high and silvery.

Rhugante – (Rue-GONE-teh) – Previous to Tamore's existence, the land used to be called Rhugante. Uriah, the first Chandarion and husband to the Eaburria, Yasendra, originated from Rhugante and had been the second-born prince.

Roddy Lambert – (rod-dee lam-BERT) – The Owner of Lambert Vineyards. Father of Cody and Pippa. He has sun-brown skin and iron gray hair.

Rovers (Music People) – Traveling folk who live in horse-drawn wagons. They trade in hard-to-find items and usually have outstanding healing folk, along with fortune-tellers, and musicians. Ordinary folk usually consider them undesirable unless they need a healer or an item that they might have.

Rowan – One of the flyers stationed at Hauser Tower. He has copper-red hair.

Royal Star – A seven-pointed star made of silver or other precious metals. The kingdom keeps track of who is in possession of one of these limitedly available items.

Rune – Aunia's father. Originally from Bellatine. He has medium brown hair and eyes, medium height and a muscular build. He's very graceful on his feet. He also is incredibly secretive, particularly of his and Aunia's origins before they arrived at Naoma Sacella. He is able to use power words, faery magic, and is able to 'skip.'

Ruork – Faery type. Refers to the buglike humanoid and the wasp it rides.

Ryver – A wererat from the Lord Chance band who has Mollie-Mae as its leader. Ryver is a 16 years of age, slender built, and has a wispy short cropped beard.

Salamander lights – A magical device that looks like an incandescent glass tube. It is powered by an imprisoned fire salamander.

Serel – (SER-rel) – One of the Commanders on Pardonway. He has angular features and armor etched in decorative lines. He rides a gray gelding.

Sheavine – (SHAY-vine) – She is a zephyr, a type of wind faery, who lives at Hebsolum's tower in the Pavari Court lands on the tiny island of Aeryth.

Sigmus – (Sig-muss) – Minor antagonist to Aunia, mainly due to jealousy as Sigmus considers Rune to be a father figure. Rune's friend. He is 29 years old, overweight with lanky dark hair.

Sir Nicolas Mims – Poet from the third century.

Skip (or skipping) – The magical ability to teleport from one place to another.

Sophia – One of the Eaburrai. Usually depicted as a scribe working on a scroll with twin cherubs tugging on her robes.

Sorrel – The steward at Eddac Tower.

Spatelly – A city on the outskirts of the Worley province and near the sea marshes. It has several districts including the Quayhold and the Stay.

Stanz Tower – Pegasi rider tower south of the city of Dalin. There is a rivalry between Stanz and Eddac towers. The troops within are commanded by Catryina Pemble.

Sylph – An air faery type. Human-sized with wings. Ethereal, beautiful, and resides mainly on the winds.

Sylvanox Woods – (SILL-va-nox woods) – A portion of woods that abutts the North woods.

Syrick (Dar) – (Dar Sigh-rick) – One of Tamore's royal magic-users who uses stored and borrowed magic from Chandarions, particularly that of Uriah Galarue.

Tamore – (TAY-more) – The kingdom between the Grashbear and Tatian Mountains to the east and west; the Uttaloian Promise Bay to the north; and Adar and Bellatine to the south. Its capital city of Tatia is said to be in the doorway of the faery world and perched on clouds.

Tafiriel – Originally from Endynia, he is a wild-born pegasus, meaning he has crossed over through a blade-cave. He has imprinted with Mathias. His hide is the color of the noon sky and his mane and tail are pale blue.

Tatia – (TA-tee-ah) – Tamore's capital which is located in the clouds above the city of Heavensfeet and near the western Tatian Mountains. This is one of the places in the world which is located in the Betwixt, or poetically said "on the threshold between the worlds." The city was created through magic by Uriah, the first Chandarion.

Tatia's Grove – A magical grove inside the lands of the Eaburrai Court.

Tatian Mountains – Western mountain range that marks the western boundary of the kingdom of Tamore.

Tavish – A foot soldier at Eddac Tower who was killed during a Da Vennen and wererat attack.

Taya – Twelve-year-old rover girl from the Mensani caravan. She has thick dark hair that she tends to wear in two braids and dark blue eyes. After her mother's death, she became the caravan's healer and fortune teller.

Teezo Popkin – One of the mushroom sprites. He is stout with a short cropped beard and hay-color hair. Small enough to use a mushroom cap as a chair. He is a faery friend of Aunia's.

Thalindra Archon (Arcanis Primis of the Mystic Court) – (THE-lynn-dra AR-con) – Leader of the Mystic Court in the island country of Bellatine.

Thalric Haldrayne – (THAL-drick HAL-drain) – Breen's father and hero. He is know to have held back a battalion of rebels and Da Vennen soldiers at Moonstepper Hostel (though some believe it was on the Pardonway) during Aeryk's rebellion.

Tharon Mensani – (THERE-on Men-SAW-knee) – Leader of the Mensani rover caravan.

Thessalie – (This-ah-lee) – Adarian community which follows the more Mystic-centric holidays.

Thuroes – One of the Eaburrai. Depicted as a handsome man with a harp on his lap and with an ale mug toppled over. A river of beer flows from his ale mug with the stream transforming into the sea. Mathias believes he was born under this Eaburrai's watchful eye.

Tinner – Nineteen-year-old villager and Caedmon's blacksmith apprentice. He is to be beaded (wedded) to Breanne.

Trinity, the – Three magical instruments created by the Eaburraian Etos. They consist of the astrolabe, the compass, the hourglass. Their purpose is prevent the augury from being fulfilled.

Tys – A mysterious type of faery who do not like to be forced into one shape. Their untampered shape is unknown.

Uriah Galarue – (YOU-rye-ah Gal-a-roo) – First Chandarion and beloved of Yasendra. Their love affair led to the breaking of the Heart between the Worlds, and created the need for a new Heart. The Dama Ximarae sentenced Uriah, along with his descendants to become Chandarions, destined to watch over and protect both worlds until a new heart is fashioned.

Varren, Colonel – (VAR-ren) – One of the Commanders on Pardonway. He is a tall man with a dark steel breastplate pocked with tiny dings. He typically rides a dark thick-necked bay.

Veil Door – A magical entrance/exit that can cross between the worlds. The one in the Pavari Court looks like a black shadowed s stood a long rectangle that rippled as if it were made of water.

Velli – (VELL-ee) – Seventeen-year-old villager who is often antagonistic toward Aunia, mainly due to jealousy. She is an attractive and slender teen who is on the promiscuous side. Limi and Breanne's friend. Harris' older sister. Sigmus' neice.

Virelin's Third Reflection – (VIR-el-lin) – An exorcism spell to remove anyone who forcefully takes up residence in someone else's consciousness. There is danger of it damaging a person's soul if not performed correctly.

Vraelsfork – (Ver-rails-forks) – A duchy in Tamore which stands near the kingdom's center. Fallo originates from here.

Wendalin Mensani – (WHEN-da-lenn Men-SAW-knee) – Apprentice dar to Dar Syrick. Sister to Basil. Daughter to Tharon and Mollie Mae.

Wererats – Cursed humans who can assume the shape of common rats, human-sized rats, or rat men. A form of lycanthropy.

Whistling Teapot – A tavern in Dalin.

Willard – One of the guards at Dalin.

Wind-knots – A type of storm faery. Finger-sized. Generally they appear as thumb-sized grey-clad lads.

Witch compass – A magical device that points out magic-users with a needle arrow. They typically look like a compass. Bibb's is decorated with little red crystals dotting its outer ridge. Some witch compasses can also suppress other magic within its location. The witch compass that Bibb has is actually the compass of the Trinity and witch compasses have been made to replicate it; however, all copies are a pale comparison.

Woundbinder – One of the wererat army leaders. He has strawberry-blonde fur and he is fiercely loyal to Arch Vicar Bibb.

Wraithmere – (Rayth-mere) – An island inside the Sea (or Salt) Marsh. It has a cave located there with a rich source of Halite salt. Kai-Marin makes this place her home when she is visiting the human world.

Wylie – Rover man from the Mensani caravan. Father to the baby Gabin.

Wythrindle River – (WITH-rin-dell river) – One of the names for the river that flows by Worley.

Wyvern – Dragon-like creature with two legs instead of four. It can exhale fireballs and sometimes toxic gas.

Xissa – One of the council leaders of Naoma Sacella. A no-nonsense woman who wears her greying hair in a bun. Breanne's mother. Head cook.

Yanna – A blacksmith in Dalin. His smithy is close to the Forged Tankard.

Yantexio – (Yan-TEX-ee-oh) – Catiryna Pemble's steel gray pegasus stallion.

Yasendra (Galarue) – (YA-sen-dra) – Youngest of the Eaburrai. Fell in love and married Uriah, the first Chandarion. Their love affair was directly involved in the breaking of the Heart of the Worlds. Her depiction as a blond girl running has not been seen on any recent murals.

Yasko Coates – (YAS-ko Coats) – Lena's younger brother. He's quite good with the violin.

Zeller Rieson (Dar) – (Zel-lar Ray-son) – One of Tamore's royal magic-users who uses stored and borrowed magic of Chandarions, particularly Illysa's. General of the Tamore's aerial troops until his death.

Zevara – (zee-VAR-ah) – The Great Sylph, leader of the Court of Air and Spring, also known as the Pavari Court. She is a tall fairy woman, with translucent skin that is paler than milk. She has long flowing silver hair and large delicate-appearing wings though sometimes her wings appear to be large, gray, and falcon-like. Her voice is a rich silvery voice similar to Revellie's.□

ACKNOWLEDGEMENTS

Sometimes life happens. It reaches out and throws you on your ear. I'll be quite honest—this book was difficult. Needing to find a new living situation without warning turned life juggling into something beyond a challenge. It ate up all the wriggle-time I usually factor in, and there were certainly quite a few times I was sure I'd have to delay this book. I'm still amazed I pulled it off!

Perhaps in a way, it made having this book go out in time all the sweeter. I suppose I did not "Hide" from the challenge though sometimes (winky-face), I thought about it!

In my day-to-day, I'm setting up for a new chapter. I have friends and family I've been able to lean on, who also remind me how resilient and strong I am. For everyone who made life just a little bit easier—thank you!

I do have some special shout-outs:

First, to my mom, sister, and brother-in-law (M. Christine Runkle, Rachel & John Cawley)—thank you for welcoming me and the kid into your home. Your support means the world.

To Lou Schlesinger and Elizabeth Burton: your insights and enthusiasm are beyond invaluable! The fact that you stepped up to be alpha readers, particularly since I had to write fast and furious, is beyond amazing—especially how dedicated and quick your turnarounds were, despite your own projects. You ask amazing questions and give me clear insight.

To my Saturday Epic group: Brenda Carre, Bruce Paulik, Tyson Dutton, Valérie Leroyer, and Pat Hauldrin—your friendship as we meet to talk about not only our writing accomplishments (and struggles) but also what's happening in our lives is balm to my heart and motivation. I can't wait to see how far each of us travels along our authoring paths. I'll be there cheering you on, just as you have for me.

Lusine Torossian, I so enjoy our Thursday sprint sessions. Not only do I get so much done, but it's great to have someone to brainstorm with.

To M. Colin Alston and Leann Burke: your continued presence in my life and friendship is a huge gift. Thank you for continuing to step up for every virtual launch party I hold. I've said this before and mean it—when you're ready for your launch parties, I'll be there.

To Cristina Tanase: I can't imagine having a different cover designer. You always seem to know what I want before I do.

To my street team, the Fae Furies: thank you for your continued support. I'm hoping to bring more magic into our group, and I look forward to seeing yours bloom as well!

To my ARC readers and book-tour hosts: you provide life-blood by letting other readers know this series exists. It's so important to me to share the message that, no matter what, each person is whole unto themselves—that they are enough. Your enthusiasm, dedication, and support mean the world to me!

A special thanks to Apex-Writers: working alongside David Farland's legacy writing group is an adventure every day! The friendships I've formed, along with the resources available, make me feel like it's Christmas every day!

To my Superstars tribe: I can't wait to return to see you all. It makes my heart glad that I've found friendships here. So much learning and inspiration come from this group. Anytime I think I can't, I think of you—and I know I can.

To Wulf Moon and the Wulf Pack: "How to stretch yourself and thrive" is a motto I carry from this amazing group of movers and shakers. I've said it before and I'll say it again: if you want to learn how to get your short stories into respected markets, this is where you want to be.

A special shout-out to the Greater Lehigh Valley Writers Group (GLVWG): without you, I would not be where I am. Thank you!

To my Canadian critique partners: Wonnita Andrus, Merilyn Liddell, and Monica Sagle Zwikstra—your thoughtful feedback and encouragement continue to help shape this story. Book 3 done, and Book 4 soon to start—I can't wait to see what you think!

Additionally, to my family and friends: thank you for your patience during those periods I hid away in my worlds of faeries and prophecy, particularly when I tried to play catch-up. A special thanks to Kelly for being the kid's person for Pennsic this year—it made a difference and significantly reduced disappointment.

A special thanks to my readers: this book exists because of you. Your excitement for faeries, magic, and adventure fuels my inspiration every day. Thank you for diving into the **Heart of the Worlds** universe.

And last—to all the flickering lights in the world who are probably having a tough time of it. To those who try, despite being knocked down. To those who look out for others and bring light and love into the gray and the horrific—please know that you are amazing and deserve to be celebrated. I wish all bright and positive things for each and every one of you!

With love, gratitude, and faerie dust,

TF Burke

ABOUT THE AUTHOR

TF Burke is a seasoned writer, storyteller, and passionate advocate for the authoring community. A former officer of the Greater Lehigh Valley Writers Group (GLVWG), she served from 2009 to 2013 as both president and chair of the record-breaking Write Stuff Conference—an event celebrated for its sold-out workshops, industry speakers, and vibrant book fair.

Today, Burke works with New York Times bestselling author David Farland's Apex-Writers as an administrator, coordinating an impressive lineup of weekly Zoom sessions featuring industry leaders, bestselling authors, and rising voices. She also crafts content for blogs, newsletters, and social media, presents on writing and publishing topics for various author groups, and regularly hosts Apex's writer-focused calls—including Strategy, Mindcraft & Wings, and Midweekers.

Her published works span hundreds of newspaper articles, blog posts, and works of fiction. She is the author of the Heart of the Worlds YA fantasy series, bestselling Faeries Don't Lie and Faeries Don't Forgive, along with this current book, Faeries Don't Hide; and short story collection, Whirl of the Fae: Myths, Legends & Secrets. Her award-winning origin tale False-Gold Wishes & the Darkwraith, and her short story A Firefly's Conscience and the Psychopath (featured in the MurderBugs anthology), showcase her flair for blending myth, mystery, and the unexpected. Her fourth book, Faeries Don't Love, is scheduled to be released in September 2026.

When she isn't writing or championing fellow authors, Burke can often be found crossing blades in medieval-style fencing tournaments and melees—a pursuit she's enjoyed since 2010. She also loves exploring museums, libraries, and ancient ruins, forever chasing the spark where history meets imagination.

If you've enjoyed her stories, please consider leaving a review on Amazon, Goodreads, and/or your social media platforms—your words help others discover these adventures that blend an epic quest with wonder and heart-felt discovery, both within one's self and how we connect with others.

Also by TF Burke

Heart of the Worlds

Book 1 – Faeries Don't Lie
Book 2 – Faeries Don't Forgive
Book 3 – Faeries Don't Hide

Whirl of the Fae: Myths, Legends & Secrets
False-Gold Wishes & the Darkwraith
A Firefly's Conscience and the Psychopath

Aunia's adventure continues!

Available on preorder & releases 9/29/26

Going to Tatia should have been simple—clear their names, find the missing magical room, and open the way to the sea-witch's realm.

But nothing about fate is ever simple. Aunia is certain her Eaburrian grandmother holds her father captive, yet the closer they get, the more the past refuses to stay buried.

Forces thought vanquished rise again, and one shattering revelation turns their world upside-down.

www.ingramcontent.com/pod-product-compliance
Lightning Source LLC
Chambersburg PA
CBHW070802030726
47504CB00003B/660